KINGDOM
OF
TOMORROW

KINGDOM

OF

TOMORROW

BOOK OF ARDEN

GENA SHOWALTER

 Montlake

Text copyright © 2025 by Gena Showalter
All rights reserved.

No part of this book may be reproduced, or stored in a retrieval system, or transmitted in any form or by any means, electronic, mechanical, photocopying, recording, or otherwise, without express written permission of the publisher.

Published by Montlake, Seattle

www.apub.com

Amazon, the Amazon logo, and Montlake are trademarks of Amazon.com, Inc., or its affiliates.

EU product safety contact:
Amazon Media EU S. à r.l.
38, avenue John F. Kennedy, L-1855 Luxembourg
amazonpublishing-gpsr@amazon.com

ISBN-13: 9781662530524 (paperback)
ISBN-13: 9781662530517 (digital)

Cover design by Faceout Studio, Molly von Borstel
Cover image: © eastern archive, © Black moon, © Suwannakitja_Chomraj, © Lamai Prasitsuwan, © alias612 / Shutterstock

Printed in the United States of America

*To those who helped me through one of the harshest,
hardest seasons of my life: Mike and Vikki Tolbert,
Shane Tolbert, Shonna Hurt, Michelle Quine, and
Jill Monroe.
To the great lights of my heart: Victoria, Riley,
Mariana, and Maple Showalter.
To my brilliant editors, Maria Gomez and Melissa
Frain, for taking a chance on me and offering such
keen insights.*

A multitude of people, and yet a solitude.
—Charles Dickens, *A Tale of Two Cities*

Prologue

To: Tagin Dolion
From: Baracas Heta
Subject: A potential problem

Your Highness,

The following is an encrypted exchange between the Soalian known as Sparrow and an unknown associate referred to as "Unicorn." How would you like me to proceed?

BEGIN EXCHANGE

Sparrow: You're ready for your first mission. Agreed?

Unicorn: Considering I submitted a formal request eight months ago, yes. Agreed.

Sparrow: You weren't ready then. You're barely ready now.

Unicorn: Have you even read my file? I'm the best of the best.

Sparrow: We'll find out soon enough. You will recruit Arden Roosa.

Unicorn: Seriously, read my file. The best of the best—in battle. Recruiting isn't my thing.

Sparrow: Recruiting is every Soalian's thing. But don't worry, I'll take care of introductions.

Unicorn: Why do you want her? Who is she?

Sparrow: She's the one you will recruit, as previously stated.

Unicorn: Stop being stubborn. Why should I risk my life for hers?

Sparrow: The Book of Soal. Why else?

Unicorn: The Book is your answer for everything. But why seek Arden Roosa specifically? (See? I can be stubborn too.)

Sparrow: Perhaps you need a reminder of law 2.1.5.44. Book of Soal, volume 2, section 1, paragraph 5, verse 44: Whenever it is within your power, aid the maddened.

Sparrow: You were once maddened, yet I risked my life to recruit YOU, a snot-nosed kid whose issues had issues.

Unicorn: Fine. I'll do it. But you may not like my methods.

Sparrow: What, are you going to use your "signature charm?"

Unicorn: . . .

Unicorn: . . .

Unicorn: Maybe.

Sparrow: Soal help us all.

END OF EXCHANGE

~∞~

To: Baracas Heta
From: Tagin Dolion
Subject: re: A potential problem
This is a job for the High Prince. My son lacks charm, but he never fails.

CHAPTER ONE

Fear isn't an emotion but a force; it starts with a
spark and grows until it torches your entire life.

—*The Book of Soal* 1.18.3.25

249 AR (After Rebuild)

The waiting room smelled of clashing perfumes, nervous sweat, and
old sandwiches. Too many people crammed inside the circular space,
turning the midlevel of the high-rise silo into a pressure cooker.

Conversations crested and crashed with varying degrees of irritation
as men, women, and children arrived and departed through a central
bank of elevators. I shifted in the world's most uncomfortable chair
and studied my surroundings for the thousandth time. Green-and-gold
posters decorated the drab, windowless walls.

BE OUR EYES AND EARS.
ALL BEFORE ONE.
WE ARE CURED.

The same images hung in most buildings throughout the province.
Comforting reminders that we weren't alone. We had help against
the Madness.

I stiffened with familiar tension as the most feared word in existence echoed inside my head. *Madness, Madness, Madness.* Perspiration dampened my skin, and I darted my gaze, searching for any signs of infection in the people around me. No one was exhibiting telltale symptoms. Still. The air seemed to thicken, making breathing more difficult for me. *Stop!* The others were fine; I was fine. There was no need to panic. *Please don't panic.* Not today.

Inhale. Exhale. I lifted my hair, welcoming a fresh draft to my nape. But the hem of my dress inched up my thighs, and I hurried to smooth the soft but worn buttercup yellow material into place. *Call my name. Please.*

A baby cried, launching a new cycle of grumbles from the old woman at my left. I'd heard the nerve-shredding chorus for three hours straight and wasn't sure how much more I could take.

I brushed my gaze over a guy across the room—someone who hadn't been there minutes before. My attention zoomed back to him. He was peering at me thoughtfully. Didn't hurt that he was super cute, with deep-set eyes, chiseled cheekbones, and a clean-shaven jaw.

He offered me a stunning grin, and my brain blipped, deleting my newest litany of complaints. I waved. What? I was single, and outside of panic attacks, I tended to fixate on random things.

He made a funny face, inspiring an unexpected smile. I couldn't help but make a funny face right back.

Barking a charming laugh, he drew the attention of half the room's occupants. Even as he ducked in his seat, his cheeks flushing, he presented me with another stunner.

"Arden Roosa," a harried voice announced over the intercom.

Heart leaping, I jumped to my feet. "Present!" Embarrassment scorched me as soon as I comprehended what I'd done. I'd been waiting long enough to learn the drill. Hear your name, take the elevator up, and discover if your dreams were forever crushed.

My legs quaked as I trudged to the bank and stepped into an open stall. Mr. Smiles rose and started forward, erasing the distance between us. Anticipation sparked. Maybe, just maybe, I was about to score a date *and* celebrate a lifelong goal today. Fitting rewards for controlling my anxiety the past four hours.

"I'm—" he began, but the doors closed, cutting him off.

Or not.

My shoulders rolled in. Forget the boy. The entire fabric of my life hinged on the coming verdict. Inhale. Exhale. In, out.

The elevator came to a wobbly stop. *Ding.* The double doors slid apart.

Head high, I stepped into a hallway. Huh. The twenty-second floor wasn't exactly the peaceful, professional oasis described in pamphlets. Small cubicles abounded, multiple phones rang at once, and two armed knights in body armor stood at the ready with their backs to a wall. Soldiers in CURED's army. Our royalty.

Their presence was a much-appreciated precaution, even though they watched me with cold, unwavering stares as I followed the instructions I'd received. Eighth block of cubicles down, third compartment on the right. It smelled better in here, at least, with hints of stale coffee and oversweet perfume.

Stopping at the correct entrance, I pasted a smile on my face. The only occupant was a fiftysomething woman with messy salt-and-pepper hair, wrinkled clothing, and strain etched into every line of her face.

Here she was, my level-two life adviser. The woman whose recommendation would decide the direction of my entire life. Currently, she read an air screen while clacking her blunt-tipped fingernails against her desk, striking a keyboard made of light. A green-and-gold CURED mug and various stacks of biodegradable flyers cluttered her workspace.

In a matter of minutes, mere seconds, she would tell me if all the special classes, holiday camps, and expensive tutors my mom had worked night and day to afford had been enough to earn a spot at CURED's most prestigious agricultural school.

I squared my shoulders and cleared my throat to let her know I'd arrived. "Ms. Butler? Hi. I'm Arden Roosa."

"Have a seat," she said without glancing my way. "I'm still processing your records."

My carefully practiced cheerfulness slipped, preshredded nerves fraying further. I'd been assured the upgrade from a level-one to a level-two adviser exponentially increased the odds of my success. The only reason I'd paid double the tax to meet with someone of her prominence. And yet, she'd done zero homework on my situation.

Pressing my tongue to the roof of my mouth, I eased into the chair beside her desk. Minutes bled together as she read aloud.

"Exemplary student. Extreme anxiety disorder, blah, blah. Standard stuff. No known association with Soalians."

"Of course not!" Even the thought brought shudders.

"Tested high in the sciences, creativity, and language. Why is there a two-year gap in your schooling—ah. Okay." Clack, clack, clack. "You worked odd jobs to pay your mother's bills while she underwent treatment for the Madness."

Yes, and the memories of Mom's wellness journey still haunted me. The medications and therapies had so depleted her, she'd needed another year to facilitate a full recovery. Although she *wasn't* fully recovered. Mom might never be herself again. "I've never tested positive."

"That's good, but the delay is a major hurdle." The clacking resumed, and I started perspiring again. "The paper you submitted to the Center for Agriculture was a nice touch. Very well received."

"Thank you." Pleasure bloomed, and I sat up straighter. I'd poured my heart and soul into that paper, doing my best to depict my driving passion for the Great Soil and Seed Anomaly.

"Hmm." Ms. Butler frowned. Typing, typing. "This is interesting. You qualified for—hmm," she repeated.

I tried not to scream. "Please tell me there's no problem."

Heartbeat. Heartbeat, heartbeat.

Her chair whined as she swiveled to face me. The slightest hint of sympathy emanated from her. "Look. I have a quota to meet, so I'll jump right in. Despite those ill-advised gap years, you were selected to attend the Center. Congrats. They only accept the best and brightest. You report to class on Monday."

Joy like I'd never known exploded inside me, and I laughed. I'd done it! Soon I would be experimenting with soil and seeds, doing my best to grow food as abundantly as the people who'd lived before the Fall of Nations.

"Unless," Ms. Butler added with a pointed look, breaking into my thoughts and happiness.

My breath hitched. How quickly I tumbled from the highest of highs to the lowest of lows. "Unless," I squeaked, and shook my head. "No *unless.*"

"Your mother owes a significant amount in back taxes, and someone has to pay."

"But that can't be right," I replied, confused. I'd paid everything off. "You must have misread the file. There's no debt. We filed for medical clemency both years."

"And she received it—for the first year. Her last filing for disability relief was denied. She no longer tested positive; therefore she should've been at work, doing her part, paying her fair share."

No. No! I shook my head with more force. "She was nothing but a skeleton with hair, barely able to crawl out of bed. I handled her bills, and I never received a rejection for our request. Whatever was due, I submitted."

Ms. Butler lowered her chin, any trace of sympathy evaporating. "I can help you lodge an official complaint with CURED, Miss Roosa. In fact, I can summon the knights on duty and get the process started right now."

Acid filled my churning stomach. "No, no complaints," I rasped. Like any rational person, I valued CURED. Also, making waves never ended well.

"Your mother will be moved into Gradon next week," the adviser said, hurrying us along. "The good news is, she'll pay less in taxes, allowing her yearly allotment to slowly but surely reduce her debt."

"No!" Not Gradon, the province with the most outbreaks. What's more, Mom would be too far away for me to visit. There was no way I could afford a pass to leave Lucrea, much less a round-trip bus ride.

"However," Ms. Butler announced, and I went still, even my heart seeming to stop. "If you agree to attend Fort Bala Royal Academy, become a lady-in-training, and serve for three years, your mother will be allowed to stay where she is, without incurring further penalties, and her past due balance will be paid in full. This is a onetime offer, void the moment you leave this office."

A protest brewed at the edge of my tongue, stayed only by my clenched jaw. "I know little about Theirland, nothing about military service, and less than nothing about interrealm travel and combat."

"That's why you'll be taught and trained."

Unlike the more daring kids in my class, I'd never entertained a desire to visit the realm fused to ours. Couldn't imagine being outside in the dark in either world, going head to head with hordes of maddened too far gone for treatment.

I tried again to make her understand. "I'm not—"

"Look. Judging by your transcript, I'm guessing your mom spent multiple paychecks on furthering your education rather than saving in case of an emergency."

Blood drained from my head, igniting a dull ring in my ears. Ms. Butler wasn't wrong. I'd attended expensive lectures and purchased the necessary tools to grow my own indoor minigarden. A pricey endeavor.

"Think of it this way," she added. "Three years is a blip. When your term ends, we can revisit your desire to attend the Center."

"But you just said the two-year gap is a major hurdle." Think of the trouble a five-year gap would cause!

Again, she continued. "If you rack up enough honors, you'll probably earn special privileges within your desired field. This is a win-win situation for you, Miss Roosa. I suggest you take it."

The idea of me, Panic Girl, becoming a hardened soldier who traversed between two realms to protect civilians from an otherworldly sickness was nothing but laughable.

"So what's it gonna be? Agriculture or family?" Ms. Butler demanded. "I need an answer. Not that there's really anything to think about. This is a no-brainer to me."

No, this was a nightmare. I mean, I'd heard of this happening to others. Kids who'd been drafted to pay a loved one's debt. But I'd never thought it could happen to me.

"I'll do it," I croaked. "I'll sign up." Mom was my person; I'd do anything for her, even put my life on hold again.

"Excellent." Satisfaction danced in the adviser's eyes, as if my decision affected her future as much as my mother's. "You'll report to 1984 Minitrue Street at ten tomorrow morning. Don't be late. The bus waits for no one, and it's your sole transport to Fort Bala. You're allowed to bring a single bag. No weapons, food, or mementos. They'll only slow your progress."

I struggled to catch my breath. Fort Bala, where a doorway between worlds was said to exist.

"Due to the intricacies of your training, you'll be forbidden from seeing or contacting family and friends. Be sure to say your goodbyes tonight." Ms. Butler swiveled in her chair, refocusing on the screen and typing. "I'm sending instructions to your data bank. You can access it at home. Have a nice day, Miss Roosa, and be CURED." A certain dismissal.

"Be CURED," I echoed out of habit.

Numb, I stood and stumbled from the cubicle. The knights hadn't moved from their posts. Again, they watched me unflinchingly, almost as if they hoped I'd do something. Anything.

Tears stung my eyes. I wouldn't see my mother, my best friend, for three years. If I even survived the academy.

Chapter Two

I tell you now: consider your ways.

—*The Book of Soal* 1.37.1.5

I burst outside, entering the bustling cityscape. People from every spectrum of society rushed about. Across the street, a man invited pedestrians to try his "asylum experience." Near an enormous sculpture of a winged woman with crab claws, three knights and two lords in full protective gear arrested a group of people who were shouting, "Soal is life, CURED is death! The Kingdom of Yesterday comes!"

Soalians. Those on the cusp of infection. I shuddered. They believed a god named Soal lived in a magical library and he instructed them to destroy CURED, the only entity capable of protecting the rest of us. Anyone sane recognized how ridiculous it all sounded . . . but Soalians weren't sane.

Citizens for Unified Reform, Education, and Defense made mistakes, but who didn't? CURED ensured we survived in a world gone mad.

Tomorrow, I would join its ranks.

Say your goodbyes tonight.

My next breath emerged as a short, rasping pant. No matter how fast I traveled along the sidewalk, maneuvering through the crowd, I couldn't escape a growing sense of doom. I'd only ever fought one maddened, and only to defend myself after she broke. I'd never come closer to dying.

Sizzling sunlight failed to warm my chilled skin. I tried to focus on my surroundings. Buildings of varying sizes and shapes lined the busy streets. A blend of sleek new constructions, old barns, and lavish crystal palaces that bisected different apartments, shops, and offices. Oddly shaped structures made from a shiny golden alloy fused with those made from ordinary brick.

As I turned a corner, an intoxicating floral fragrance hit my nose. Familiar. Despised. Icy fingers of dread crept down my spine, and my racing thoughts fragmented until a lone mantra remained. *Ignore the Rock, ignore the Rock, ignore the Rock.*

But I couldn't. A section of it stretched along my right, and as always, I felt as if a thousand eyes were upon me, observing me with x-ray vision. Maybe they were. Small metal dogs patrolled the top of the stone, their eyes recording everything that happened, allowing operators to monitor the feed twenty-four seven.

Slinging my arms around my middle, I attempted to make myself smaller. Pieces of the Rock occupied every province in every nation. Truly, there was nowhere you could go without bumping into a seven-foot-long, seven-foot-high section. They were impossible to miss, move, or destroy. Not even explosives affected them. And yet, with their translucent, mirror-esque stone and intricate web of internal veins filled with a bloodlike liquid, every inch appeared fragile. On the outside, strange round symbols contained disjointed lines. No matter the weather or season, the most exquisite foliage bloomed along the upper edges. A cruel development, considering the Rock was also the source of the Madness.

Ahead of me, a woman knelt before the structure, reverently tracing her fingertips around a circle. Another Soalian. I huffed with disgust. She wasn't the least bit worried about infection or her coming arrest. And she would be arrested, then placed in a treatment facility with the others.

When I passed her and cleared the last of the stone, I expelled a sigh of relief. I would go home and—

"Arden Roosa!"

The unfamiliar voice halted me in my tracks. Hoping against hope someone from the Department of Edification and Labor had come to tell me there'd been a mistake, my mother owed nothing, and I should report to the Center ASAP, I pivoted. Surprise jolted me when I spotted the speaker. Mr. Smiles, the guy from the waiting room.

"Yes?" I said when he stopped in front of me. Oh, wow. Sunlight adored the symmetrical perfection of his features, turning him into a work of art come to life. He was far more handsome than I'd realized. And tall. Around six two, with broad shoulders and lean strength packed inside a blue shirt and a pair of dark slacks.

"Hi." He peered down at me with sparkling eyes. A grin teased the corners of his mouth. "I'm Shiloh Cruz. I thought you should know my name since I learned yours. Gotta keep the scale between us balanced."

As people passed by, I remained rooted in place, my brain train veering onto a fresh track. He'd chased me down to . . . flirt?

I responded with blunt honesty. "You shouldn't miss an appointment with your life adviser to speak with me." I wasn't worth it. No one was.

"I met with him earlier. I was—okay, please don't be creeped out, but I was leaving when I spotted you. I decided to hang around." His grin developed a bashful tinge. "I seized my chance to introduce myself."

Heat seared my cheeks. "Let's back up a minute. There's a scale between us?"

"I really hope so." He punctuated the words with an earnest nod.

A big, toothy smile threatened to bud. "You're the first person I've ever met who considers a scale a good thing."

"Because it is. I'll reveal a fact about myself to you, then you'll reveal a fact of equal value about yourself to me."

Ah. "A tit-for-tat situation."

"Exactly." He winked, and it was the cutest thing. "Walk with me?"

Tomorrow, my life would slip off its axis; I should enjoy my freedom while I could. Also, he smelled like sandalwood, a man musk that should be classified as a mind-altering drug. "Yes. I'd like that."

We moved along the sidewalk at a leisurely pace. "I'll start," he said. "I have an older half sister and brother. They're twins. As children, we were as obnoxious as you might imagine. Not that I'll ever complain. They taught me physical combat, psychological warfare, and how to sense suspicious activity."

I snorted. "They sound fun."

"They are. Mostly." He nudged me with his shoulder. "Now it's your turn. Enlighten me, please. Tell me all about Arden Roosa."

"It's just my mom and me." Once, though, there'd been four of us. My chest squeezed. Soon after the death of my sister, Amelia, my dad took off. "Mom is my best friend."

"I love that." Shiloh beamed, as if I'd given him a long-awaited gift. "I'm twenty-three years old, and I'm working as a medic."

Oh, how interesting. "What field?"

"Nope." He shook his head, a lock of hair falling over his brow. "Give me my tat. Age and vocation or subject of study."

Silly, charming man. "I'm twenty. I've worked a ton of odd jobs the past two years." Everything from calling citizens to inform them of delinquent tax payments to manning an assembly line of meal bars. The world's most tasteless but affordable staple. I'd even monitored the robot-dog camera feed for a time. "My passion is agriculture." I offered no more, merely arched a brow, demanding a response to my previous query.

He braced, as if expecting a blow. "I specialize in . . . the Madness."

Clearly, he expected me to freak out. Maybe run from him. Many medical professionals avoided anything related to the Rock, too afraid of becoming infected themselves. "That's an interesting choice."

At my lack of dismay, he sighed with relief. "My grandparents were killed during the Great Regret. I've made it my mission to find out why and how to prevent such a tragedy from ever occurring again."

"That's awful. Not your mission," I clarified, "but your loss." The Great Regret was a terrible stain in our history. A time when a myriad of infected broke at once, murdering thousands of innocents in a very short period.

"It really is. I have so many questions. Why does the infection incubate faster in certain hosts? What causes people to ultimately break? Is there a way to make treatment more humane?"

His enthusiasm warmed my heart. And, since he'd clarified for me, I did the same for him. Leaning closer as we walked, I said, "I'm determined to solve the Soil and Seed Anomaly. For me, there's nothing more satisfying than watching tiny seeds mature into a big crop. When my hands are in the dirt, I'm single minded." Unwavering. "There's no world outside of what I'm doing." Little frightened me. I tasted a measure of genuine peace, and oh, it was divine.

"I know I only just met you," he said, his words heartfelt, "but I have a feeling you'll succeed."

Pleasure gave my steps a little extra pep. "Agriculture fascinates me. Have you ever seen an apple? A tiny seed contains everything needed to produce an entire orchard. And nature isn't the only one to experience such a miracle. Honestly, I see seedtime and harvest in everything now. A thought ripens into words, then actions, then character. Even human beings start with—" Oh, no, no, no. I did not just go there. "I'll stop babbling now."

"Please don't." He looked at me as if I'd threatened to trash his new favorite toy. "Have a food with me and tell me more. Tell me everything."

"*A* food?" I laughed outright.

"Any food. Breakfast, lunch, dinner, or dessert. Or a drink. Coffee. Water. All of it at the same time."

I snuck a glance at him through my lashes, a wee bit befuddled by his enthusiasm but also soaring. The few guys I'd dated had played it cool from start to finish or propositioned me outright. There'd been nothing in between. "Like, an official date with you? Today?"

"Very much an official date," he confirmed with an emphatic nod. "Now. Please."

I mean, I'd probably never see him again. But it wouldn't hurt to—

A guttural scream pierced the air. Everyone paused, including us. I didn't dare to breathe as my insides twisted into sickening knots and the scope of my world constricted.

Someone had just broken with Madness.

Another scream preceded a series of grunts and groans. The crowd surged into action. Bicyclists sped away. Citizens with enough extra trills to rent a motorized vehicle burned rubber, some swerving to avoid pedestrians, others crashing into people and parked cars. People on foot hurried to the nearest light stand—a steel pole stationed at select street corners, topped by a cluster of pritis stones, the only thing capable of repelling a maddened.

Right now, the golden light projected by the pritis offered the only safe haven, but available spots were filling up fast. I tried and failed to force my legs into motion. Gurgling sounds left me.

Thankfully, Shiloh understood my dilemma, swept me off my feet, and sprinted to a luminous sphere. He scored us a spot in front of the crowd, standing me up to ensure both our bodies fit within the glow of illumination.

I clutched his hand, my gaze darting. Air hitched in my lungs when I spotted the infected. A teenager with wild eyes, a manic expression, and torn, blood-soaked clothing. He scaled the Rock with ease, displaying unnatural strength, incredible speed, and a strange, otherworldly mix of fluid grace and human awkwardness. Every few seconds, he paused to lick the stone and shout "Look at Soal. Love Soal!"

A lord and lady lay unmoving on the ground beneath him, crimson rivers pouring from beneath each piece of armor. A pool of death formed at the base of the Rock, and I cringed. The Madness turned even the most docile of citizens into gleeful killers.

The boy stilled, sniffed the air, and swung his eyes to me. His lids narrowed while his lips curved up, and I had to fight back a tide of vomit. Fear was their favorite meal, and I'd just become his next appetizer.

He zoomed my way at a pace I could barely track. My lungs ossified, and I lost the ability to breathe. To move.

Shiloh yanked me against his side, pressing us both against the people who huddled behind us.

The maddened paused where the light of day met the unnatural pritis glow, a mere inch from my face. Shaking, I pressed deeper into Shiloh's chest.

"Love Soal, destroy CURED," the boy hissed at me. "You are CURED."

A hot tear rolled down my cheek.

"Hey, hey. Concentrate on me, Arden." Shiloh cupped my jaw and lifted my head without breaching the dividing line, seizing my gaze. His tender, unafraid expression made the situation slightly less terrifying. "I'm here, and I won't let anything happen to you. Okay? Since we're not budging from this spot, there's nothing the maddened can do to hurt us, which means there's nothing to worry about."

"Y-yeah. Okay," I rasped. His words made sense. And yet the infected was *right there*.

"My turn to balance the scale and share something about myself." Shiloh brushed the pads of his thumbs over my cheekbones, so gentle. "Anytime I was scared as a little boy, my mom told me to hold on to her and together we would squeeze lemonade out of lemons."

"Did you?" I'd longed to taste a lemon for years. And a strawberry. A peach. An apple. Most of all a fig. Fruit only the incredibly wealthy could afford, and then only in limited quantities. "Make lemonade, I mean." Whatever that was.

A bemused light flickered in his eyes. "I'm not actually sure. But it always helped me feel better. So you just hold on to me, and together we'll make lemonade."

The maddened continued to prowl before us, agitated and desperate to get his hands on me but unwilling to penetrate the light.

"Yeah, okay," I repeated, a bit calmer. My breathing slowed until Shiloh's sandalwood scent registered. I inhaled slowly, rational thought returning. I'd come across many of the infected throughout my life. Witnessed horrific deeds and savage attacks. But I'd survived every encounter. I would survive again.

The maddened spotted a woman and her child at the other end of the street, the pair trying to sneak to a light stand. With an inhuman growl, he flew over, tackling both. Laughing, he pummeled the mother with his fists.

"Look at Soal. Look! You are CURED." He dragged her by the hair and lifted her face to the Rock. The most sickening sounds spewed from his mouth before he licked her face and purred, "*Love* Soal."

Shiloh didn't hesitate. He released me and bounded over. A new flood of fear engulfed my being as he ripped the mom free from her crazed captor and tossed the teen onto the road.

A moving vehicle slammed into the infected. He rolled over the ground but quickly jumped to his feet. Despite a plethora of broken bones, he walked, jogged, then sprinted toward the unconscious, bleeding woman the medic now guarded with his life. The two males crashed together, and a ferocious battle ensued.

Though I quaked, I couldn't tear my gaze away. Shiloh held his own, but he was no match for someone unfazed by any wound. Soon, my new friend would be overpowered. He was already slowing, his strength dwindling. He needed help or a weapon, but for the good of all, only those in the military were allowed to carry guns and blades.

Realization slapped me harder than before. I, the girl who didn't like handling a knife in the kitchen, was to be one of those soldiers.

I whimpered for a thousand different reasons.

An echoing whimper came from the woman's daughter. Oh, dear goodness. The little girl struggled to her feet while moving forward, intending to reach her loved one, no matter the consequences. No, no, no. I couldn't let her succeed. She would put herself and Shiloh in worse danger.

Before my brain comprehended what I intended, I followed Shiloh's path, grabbed the girl, and hustled her toward the light. She fought me, and I stumbled, almost losing my hold on her.

The infected noticed us and forgot the medic. "Love Soal, destroy CURED."

A surge of adrenaline quickened my pace. Almost there . . .

The maddened raced over and swiped out his arm. His fingers snagged in my hair, pulling me back. I began to fall but—

Shiloh tackled him, allowing me to dive into the light with the girl. We huddled with the others, her struggles over. I attempted to slow my breathing as I'd been taught. In, out. In, out.

I'd done it. I'd helped the child. A sense of accomplishment straightened my spine.

Three heavily armed lords and a knight rounded a corner and rushed to take charge. I watched, transfixed, as the knight slammed into the combatants, who were grappling each other for dominance. Shiloh stopped fighting, allowing a lord to press the end of a weapon to the back of his head while the knight immobilized the maddened with a metal net. I imagined myself among their ranks, capable and confident in my ability . . . and okay, yes, I kinda liked it. Hardly seemed possible, though.

A voice rang out over a speaker. "You have been exposed to the Madness. As mandated by Ourland law, you are remanded into custody to undergo immediate testing for the safety and well-being of the public. Until you are cleared, you have no rights. Say you understand your lack of choice as I have explained it."

"I understand," Shiloh responded, calm.

I closed my eyes for a moment. Poor guy. I'd been there, done that.

The little girl vaulted from my arms and raced toward her fallen mama, only to be snatched by a lord. I didn't move, my gaze on Shiloh, who peered in my direction. His calm never wavered, his eyes seeming to say *I'm good. There's nothing to worry about. I wish our date had a better ending.*

I wished the same. For a little while, I'd enjoyed the peace I usually only found in gardening. All because of a sweet, brave medic who might spend the next year of his life withering away as he combated a disease he'd acquired while aiding a helpless woman.

Life wasn't fair.

"If you had no physical contact with the infected, leave," the cold, commanding voice declared. "If you had contact, stay where you are and wait for a lord to speak with you. Be advised, security footage is being reviewed now, and we will hunt you down if you lie."

I hung around to inform a soldier the maddened had touched my hair, but I was quickly dismissed. With no other choice, I walked away. I kept my gaze on Shiloh until the last possible second. He no longer had a weapon pointed at his head, but he was kept seated on the ground, with his arms cuffed behind his back.

If only I could tell him I wished our date had ended better too. That I prayed he was right and we bumped into each other again someday.

When I turned a corner, he vanished from sight. Saddened, I set a course for home.

Chapter Three

Be bold enough to let go of your past so you can
grab hold of your future.

—*The Book of Soal* 2.11.3.13

"For the love of—open, just open!"

The irritated voice penetrated my haze of shock, and I blinked, realizing I stood at my front door. Home already? I must've gotten lost in my head and slipped into autopilot.

Four doors down the dingy hallway, Mr. Garfield beat at his door, attempting to enter the apartment without success.

We lived in a more-than-slightly run-down storm shelter from Theirland. The concrete-like walls kept us safe from the maddened who ruled the night, amid a darkness so thick it could be felt. Each floor contained eighteen dwellings as well as designated common areas, where families and building friends could shop, eat together, play games, or just hang out after curfew. The edifice, like most other apartments, acted as its own town.

Mr. Garfield glanced my way and feigned nonchalance. "Hi, Arden. It's good to see you."

I nodded a stiff greeting at him. He didn't ask for my help, and I didn't offer. I'd heard he was spotted staring at the Rock, and his current predicament seemed to prove it.

I pressed my palm against my dented keypad. The chip in the heel of my thumb registered, and the door bolt released. As swiftly as possible, I soared inside. Mom wouldn't be home from work until closer to curfew—just before sunset. I could use the time to figure out how best to present my new career path.

"Surprise!" Mom jumped in front of me, pretended to blow a horn, and tossed a handful of confetti into the air. As the sprinkles rained to our cracked floor, she noticed my mental state and paled. Her grin faded. "You didn't get in."

The exit shut behind me, and air deflated from my entire being. "Someone broke."

"But you survived." She rushed over to hug me. "That's what matters."

I hugged her back, as surprised as ever by her frailty.

"Did you get into the Center at least?" she asked.

"I did," I replied, unwilling to disrespect her with a lie.

A bright smile spread as she pulled back. "Oh, baby. You did it! I'm thrilled for you!"

"But I decided to join Fort Bala Royal Academy instead and become a lady for the next three years," I added. "Who knows, maybe I'll get a promotion and become a knight."

Her features fell. "Why would you—my taxes." Her shoulders rolled in. "But. They can't do that."

Wait. "You knew about the debt and didn't tell me."

"Of course I didn't tell you." Her lip quivered. "I'm working now, and you're supposed to start your life at long last. You were never supposed to be burdened with this."

"You are not a burden to me," I said, my words rushing out.

"But I am," she cried, throwing her hands up. "I'm helpless. There's nothing I can do to stop this . . . this travesty of justice. Life shouldn't be this way! CURED has no right to—"

"Shh, shh." I pressed my palm over her mouth. If a neighbor had heard those words, they might report us as suspected Soalians. A circumstance to avoid at all costs. "I'm not upset, I promise."

"I already agreed to work more hours and all holidays." Sniffling, she wiped away the fat tear rolling down her cheek. "I'll lodge a formal complaint. I'll visit my adviser and—"

"No." Absolutely not. "You'll let me do this for us." Complaints against CURED never ended well because they were never private. Since all suspected Soalians must be checked out, officials came to your home to conduct an interview and administer a Madness test. People noticed, and gossip abounded. Suddenly friends started avoiding you in the halls. Look at what I'd done to Mr. Garfield!

Besides, Mom didn't need to be working longer hours. Not in her condition. The excitement had exhausted her. Already she panted, glinting with sweat.

"This is a good thing." I pasted on a bright smile and forced myself to believe my words. "An amazing opportunity to obliterate my worst nightmares before I focus on my studies." The hope of becoming a strong, powerful woman able to take care of herself flared anew. To no longer feel helpless when someone broke. Yeah, the very idea thrilled me. I just wished I could attempt it in my own time and my own way.

So why haven't you?

"But. The Madness. You could get infected," she rasped. "I never want you to have to undergo treatment." A shudder rocked her, memories of her experience still fresh. "I hate this, baby. I should have planned better."

"You are not to blame."

She wiped her cheeks and straightened with a snap. "Let's run." Eyes wide, she whispered, "Mr. Garfield has been inside *the* library. It's real, Arden. I'm certain of it. He read me a portion of a book written about him, and it included me. My future. I promised him I wouldn't tell you until you were ready, so please tell me you're ready. We can—"

"Stop!" I burst out, dread choking me. Just before Mom's positive test two years ago, she'd developed an intense interest in the Rock. She'd begun taking long walks just to sneak peeks at the structure. Eventually, she'd tried to beat her way inside it, determined to meet Soal. I'd turned her in the next day.

"The library *isn't* real, nor are there books written about the future. Yours or anyone else's. Mr. Garfield is either infected or well on his way." I gripped her upper arms. "We aren't running. I'm golden, I promise. Nothing gets in the way of my dream, not even death, so we have nothing to fear." Shiloh's logic had worked with me. Surely it would do the same for Mom. "Tell me you believe me." *Convince me you aren't sick again.*

A moment passed as she considered my words. "You're right. Of course you're right." She offered me a wobbly smile. Even still, exhaustion and worry dominated her features. But then, exhaustion and worry always dominated her features, aging the former schoolteacher-turned-nanny far beyond her years. "I let stress get the better of me and reverted to old ways of thinking. My apologies. I won't let it happen again."

I released her and returned the smile as best as I was able. "Come on. Let's make dinner. I really, really want normal right now." I *needed* normal.

"Okay, baby. Normal it is. But there's no need to cook. I've arranged a feast."

I helped her to the table, where she'd hung two signs. The first read **Congrats!** The second: **You'll get 'em next time!** She'd assembled a celebration/sympathy meal featuring bigger portions of the usual grub and a sweetened cube cake.

While Mom and I ate, I told her about the medic with the charming smile.

"You like him, huh?" She spooned a bite with more energy than usual, nearly bursting with delight.

"In my defense, he's super likable."

"A trait that is the downfall of many determined girls." She winked before sharing details of her day, all centered on Bates, a boy she watched. The son of a baron.

I laughed at Bates's antics until my lungs shouted *No more!* But like any special party, this one came to an end. We prepared for the night, barricading the front door. Pritis illuminated the building's entrance but nothing inside.

She walked me to my bedroom, leaning on me more than usual. Leaving her was going to hurt.

We stopped in the doorway, both peering into my sanctuary. A small but cozy room with a twin bed, a built-in dresser, and a retractable desk. Worn but clean. Well loved. A single fist-size window supplied light to my hanging minigarden, where plants (mostly) flourished in various stages of development.

"I'll miss you," Mom said and sniffled. "So much."

Don't you dare cry. "I'll miss you too."

"Promise me you'll give the academy your best."

"I have a best?" I teased.

Unamused, she cupped my cheeks. "Listen to me, young lady. There will always be someone who can't see your worth. That's a fact of life. Don't let that someone be you. Got it?"

"Mom," I croaked, blinking to stop a flow of tears. I clasped her wrists, getting serious. "Listen. As you know, I put in an application for a single-bedroom apartment. I don't know when it will become available, but take it for yourself as soon as it does. Rent will be cheaper. Make friends. You are a treasure others deserve to experience. But stay away from Mr. Garfield." If he was even allowed to remain in the building. "And don't put yourself in danger for anyone. Feel free to throw out my stuff. Everything but my babies. Instructions for their care are stored in my desk drawer. Treat those plants well, and they'll do the same for you."

She twined our fingers, clinging to me. "I'll accept the apartment, but you come back to me."

"I will." Time to end this before I broke down. "I should pack and rest." Not that I had *ever* rested. Not really.

"Yes, of course." She wrapped her arms around me. "I'm glad you're mine, baby."

Eyes stinging, I hugged her feeble form gently. "I'm glad you're mine too. Good night, Mom." I would miss her more than I could ever say.

As my lungs constricted, I bolted myself in the bedroom. An alarm blasted in the distance, sounding across the entire city, and I tensed. Curfew. The descent of darkness had begun.

I didn't let my tremors stop me from double- and triple-checking my bolts, ensuring no one, not even my mother, could enter. This was the way of the world. Share a space at your peril.

How well I comprehended this. I'd been trapped in a locked room with Amelia, forced to watch as the Madness took hold and she—

Nope. Not going there. I hyperfocused on my few struggling plants, watering the pot filled with dark-brown, sweet-smelling, once-native soil from Ourland. The grains had been robotically sifted to remove everything from Theirland. Then I sprinkled ash on the plants with glittery-yellow-but-not-so-great-smelling soil from Theirland, the home world of the Rock and Madness. It, too, was sifted, undiluted and natural.

"I'm listening. Tell me your secrets," I begged the grains. Nothing I'd done had increased my yield by more than 3 percent.

I traced my fingertips over a drying leaf and sighed. "What am I missing?"

Two hundred years ago, people sprayed some mixture of chemicals in the skies for reasons unknown, burning through an invisible veil that separated Ourland, my world, and a previously unknown, unseen realm. The two didn't crash together but merged in an instant. Kind of. They blended, creating two mismatched puzzles that were half Ourland, half Theirland. They were both together and separate. Many of our landmarks had vanished, replaced by theirs. The soils combined in both worlds, which proved detrimental to many plants and trees. Weeds thrived in the mixture, but we struggled to grow enough food for the masses.

One day, after my stint at the academy, I would figure out a worldwide solution. I welcomed the challenge.

Needing a pick-me-up, I pinched the dark-brown dirt between my fingers and inhaled the pleasant aroma. Ah, now that was the good stuff. Highly expensive and sold on the streets at exorbitant rates. How Mom had snagged my supply, small though it was, I still didn't comprehend.

She couldn't afford it, and she'd had nothing with which to bargain. Anytime I asked about it, she shut down.

"I'm going to miss you guys." After returning the precious soil to its pot, I eased onto the edge of my bed. Minutes passed as I waited, tenser by the heartbeat. Eventually, the final siren blared.

Night had arrived.

"One," I whispered. "Two. Three. Four. Fiv—" A distant scream pierced the air. Then another and another. Soon, the sounds of anguish blended, creating a discordant symphony of pain, rage, and terror. I'd heard this chorus every night of my life. A serenade from both new and older maddened as they spilled from their hiding places, ready to play with anyone trapped out in the open.

I shuddered. Usually I cranked up my music or plugged my ears. Tonight I preferred to hear what I was to face. Tomorrow, everything changed. My address. My purpose. Probably my lifespan.

The awful part was, in the morning, I'd still be the same. Arden Roosa, Panic Girl.

Sunlight bathed the busy city as I raced toward the designated bus stop. I'd begun running as a form of stress relief two years ago, and today my dedication paid off. I picked up the pace, my muscles and limbs submitting to my determination. A bag filled with my necessities banged into my side. I'd left the apartment with plenty of time to walk, but I'd also gotten lost in thought and ended up in the wrong location.

The current time flashed from the side of a building, mocking me: 9:58. In two minutes, the bus would drive off with or without me. I pumped my arms faster. Almost . . .

Just as the side door was closing, I soared into the vehicle.

The driver motioned to the scanner. I flattened my palm against the small square surface, letting the machine read my chip. A green light flashed, a sign I had an acceptable social credit rating, with no restrictions and no infection.

No doubt I'd be charged half a trill, the same fee required for any other bus ride. Nothing came free in Ourland, especially in the province of Lucrea, but none of the signs stated a fare amount. It didn't matter what I owed, I supposed. I had already paid the ultimate price—my life.

Heart thumping, I searched for a seat. *Oh, wow.* Full house. Lots of strangers, mostly my age. Half the occupants were sitting, the other half standing. I noticed a girl from my building and a couple of kids from my school, plus a guy named Jericho I'd foolishly dated for a short period last year.

Many in the group looked frightened, while some appeared excited and others oozed confidence. But all were wearing green or blue fatigues, except me. I wore a pink tank and matching running shorts.

I must have missed a mention of fatigues in Ms. Butler's note. Or she'd forgotten to send it. Which sucked! I did own a pair of fatigues; I'd just been so happy to graduate from high school, I'd stuffed the hated uniform in a corner of my closet, and that's where it had stayed.

The bus juddered, rocking me on my feet. I caught myself, rescanning the space, on the hunt for a place to sit. The gal from my school studied me, as if she recognized me but wasn't sure where we'd met. I thought her name was Lark. Jericho, who sat next to her, leered and waved me over.

I pretended not to see him. He absolutely had not changed.

"Arden?"

My heart fluttered as a familiar voice rose above the cacophony of chatter, drawing my attention to the back. Shock kicked me. "Shiloh." He'd passed his health exam. Otherwise, he'd be in quarantine receiving treatment right now.

He arrowed from his spot, bumping into his seatmate before shouldering his way to me. "How did you know I'd be here?"

"I didn't. I'm a soldier at Fort Bala Royal Academy. A lady-in-training."

"A lady-in-training," he parroted. His brow wrinkled. "I don't understand."

"I'm paying bills before I attend college," I admitted, too dazed to filter my words.

"But. You'll be fighting the maddened. Those in Ourland as well as those in Theirland, which are a different breed entirely. Some glow in the dark, and others grow worms instead of hair."

I gulped. It was too late to scare me off. "Yeah, I've heard the rumors." I hurried on. "I'm so glad to see you're alive and unharmed." I ran my gaze over him. He looked strong and healthy, completely unaffected by yesterday's ordeal.

"I went home with a few bruises, but otherwise I'm fine. I passed a full exam. No trace of—" His lips compressed. "You know."

"I'm so glad." My brain finally caught up with the situation. "But why are you on my bus?"

"I do my clinicals at the academy."

Oooh. Yes. That tracked.

He searched my face until the bus took a corner a little too swiftly and we lurched to the side. I accidentally dropped my bag onto his feet.

"May I?" he asked, lifting what remained in my life.

"Will this act of chivalry unbalance our scale?" I teased.

"Very much so." He anchored the bag over his shoulder. With a wink, he extended his fingers in my direction. "But you'll hold my hand, and it will level again."

I smiled and did it. I clasped his hand and held on tight.

"Come on." He gave me a comforting squeeze. "We can finish our date on the drive."

Our fellow passengers shifted, watching as Shiloh led me to the end of the bus. My heart thudded with renewed life, different emotions surging and crashing. Fear of the unknown. More relief. A twinge of happiness. A ray of hope. Buckets of dread and uncertainty. More fear. So, so, so much fear.

He stopped at the spot he'd vacated. "Get up," he told his seatmate, his firm tone permitting no argument.

"Oh, he doesn't have to—" I began.

"Yes, he does." He kept his focus on his friend. "Get up, Roman."

With a snort, the guy complied, standing. "Fine. But only because I love you. Maybe also because I'm insanely curious." He was a few inches shorter than Shiloh, with double the muscle mass. I'd bet he was a couple of years younger. His jovial manner suggested he wasn't upset with his friend or the situation. Beneath the joviality, however, was the kind of sharpness I'd only ever seen in soldiers.

Shiloh released my hand and shifted, allowing me to slip into the vacated seat. He plopped beside me and settled my bag onto his lap. For the first time in forever, I kind of wanted to drape myself over another person. Anything to absorb a smidge of his strength.

"I planned to find you during my next leave," he admitted. "I owe you a food and/or a drink and/or both, and I always pay my debts. And I'm beyond thrilled to see you. I am. But you shouldn't be here. What occurred yesterday is child's play compared to what soldiers encounter daily."

I took no offense. Truth was truth. "My mother was destined for Gradon. I did what was necessary to keep her safe."

"Ah. I understand." He scrubbed his palm over his face. "She's your best friend. I remember."

Exactly.

"I'm Roman, in case you missed my name," the friend piped up, giving me a mock half bow. Well, as much of a bow as he could manage, squeezed into a crowd. "Not *Rome*. Not *Romey*. *Roman*. I'm Little Boy's neighbor."

I snorted. "I'm Arden."

"Yeah. I figured. You're the gardener who looks like a doll and gives good conversation." Roman snickered as Shiloh pinched the bridge of his nose. "Trust me, I heard all about you last night."

My attention whipped to Shiloh, the corners of my mouth twitching. "A doll, huh."

"That's not—well, yeah, it's what I said, but in my defense, you do." He skipped to the next topic with a nod to the beautiful girl at Roman's side.

"This is Mykal Ellison. She's from mine and Roman's building, here for a similar reason as you. She is, quote, unquote, 'screaming on the inside.'"

"Hi," she said with an upbeat wave. "I'm sure you and I will be great friends. Unless you hurt him." She hiked her thumb at Shiloh. "Then we'll become mortal enemies, and I'll be forced to ruin you."

"Noted." I liked her. She was loyal and protective, and I commiserated with her greatly. "Are you two . . ." I pointed between her and Roman.

Both of them recoiled. "Ew. No!" Mykal wrinkled her nose. "He's like an annoying brother to me."

Roman nodded in total agreement. "Don't worry, she seems as mean as a rattlesnake, but she's all hiss and no fangs." He rubbed his fist into the crown of Mykal's head. As she sputtered and batted at him, he easily subdued her.

"See!" she huffed. "Annoying."

"That one is pure panther," he said, motioning to Shiloh and wiggling his brows.

"Please. I'm a domesticated cat, and you know it," Shiloh corrected without heat.

Roman groaned. "Dude. Don't compare yourself to a house kitty. Help me help you win the girl."

Shiloh half stood and drove his knuckles into his friend's bicep. "Better?"

As Roman acted as if he'd been smacked with a tank, I chuckled.

Their camaraderie surprised me. In a day and age when anyone could turn on you at any time, such ease was rare. I don't think I'd ever truly relaxed, not even with my mother. Maybe once with my dad, after he'd defended me from a maddened, but he walked out on Mom and me when we'd needed him most.

I gripped my knees and gazed out the window, forcing the hated memory to retreat. Huge statues of human-animal hybrids peppered the land, each from Theirland. The structures complemented the colossal crystal palaces, also from Theirland, but clashed with everything else.

Every so often, I spotted a tree, and the sightings thrilled me. I'd never been this far south before.

When the bus stopped at a security checkpoint, I blinked, only then plugging in to the present. A sea of glistening crimson sand stretched beyond the windowpane, framed by a tall wire fence. Armed guards marched here and there.

An invisible knife twisted in my chest. Fort Bala.

We had arrived.

"There you are," Shiloh said, relieved. The bus eased up a glittery yellow path.

I bet he'd tried to converse with me the entire ride. "I can't apologize enough," I told him. "I didn't mean to tune you out. It's a habit, and I—"

"I'm not upset. Listen," he interjected. "Don't fight the pain. That just makes it worse."

I sat up straighter. "Pain?"

"Medics," the driver called. Command infused his voice. Conversations ceased. "Report to your posts."

Shiloh reached over to pat my hand before standing. Then he and seven others made their way to the exit and disembarked, leaving me semipanicked. Don't fight the pain of what?

"Lords- and ladies-in-training," the driver called next. "Exit."

With dread curdling in my belly, I did exactly that, following Mykal, who trailed Roman. We filed out, entering a whole new world . . .

Chapter Four

Their throats are an open grave, with the sweetest
venom dripping from their tongues.

—The Book of Soal 2.6.3.13

I lined up in front of the bus with the other gentry, gawking. Never had the mishmash of realms been more evident. Fort Bala was a wonderland and a hellscape, forced to coincide.

In the sky, sharp, opaque beams of sunlight glinted off the jagged seams between worlds, curling in the shape of roses. Thin white cloud wisps dusted the ethereal petals, giving an illusion of snow. The aerial bouquet bloomed across a baby blue sky and served as a backdrop for an imposing military compound. Half crystal palace, half concrete prison, all fascinating.

The yellow sand extended as far as the eye could see, broken only by a smattering of gnarled bladetrees that bloomed with strange orange flowers. The most flowers I'd seen anywhere other than the Rock, and my jaw slackened.

Hello, my beauties. What are you? Tiny ribbons of smoke wafted from an intricate web of spiraling, upraised roots, and I longed for a closer look.

Platoons navigated obstacle courses, sprinted along tracks, practiced with odd weapons, and trained in hand-to-hand combat. Directly before us was a metal dais. A group of armed soldiers surrounded it, guarding the four individuals who stood shoulder to shoulder on its center. I recognized the oldest. Tagin Dolion, king of CURED's military forces and the only son of Emperor Piven Dolion, leader of CURED and the United Provinces of Ourland.

Up close, the clean-cut king was everything he seemed to be in televised interviews. Distinguished. Regal. Handsome and in command of his entire being. A little person around forty years old flanked him on his right while a midthirties female with a perma-scowl claimed the spot at his left. The fourth individual, the youngest male, looked to be in his late twenties. Apart from the five o'clock shadow gracing his strong jaw and a handprint branded into one side of his face, causing the skin to pucker and his eye to slightly droop, he greatly resembled the king. They bore the same heavily lashed eyes, aquiline noses, and plump bottom lips.

Despite their similarities, the younger guy was too rough and intense to be labeled *handsome*, but it didn't matter. He was something far better: Interesting. A warrior forged in the heat of battle, any hint of weakness hammered out of him.

He was a little taller than Shiloh, and more muscular. Controlled brute force to the medic's lean strength. He examined the world around him with an air of detachment.

Everything about him ignited a nervous reaction inside me. I didn't like it. Not one bit.

Didn't help that he was the king's youngest son, High Prince Cyrus Dolion. I would stake my life on it. Like the rest of the world, I'd glimpsed photos and videos of the royal family throughout the years. Images depicting holidays with the family.

The high prince swept his icy gaze over the crowd, but swiftly slid his attention back to me. His lids narrowed to slits. My breath hitched, and my skin warmed. Caught staring. I looked away. My pulse continued to race. I really, really hated this.

"I'm in paradise," Roman breathed, his expression awed. "This is my happy place."

"I want to be anywhere else." When a pallid Mykal realized what she'd said, she slapped a hand over her mouth. "That's not what I meant to say. Let me rephrase. I'm so happy to be here, beyond grateful to help my family, but I'm nervous about the unknown. Not that I don't trust CURED to look out for me." She groaned. "I'll stop talking now."

I flashed her a sympathetic smile. "Trust me, I one hundred percent understand."

Gratitude bathed her delicate features.

"Attention, lords- and ladies-in-training," a harsh voice called.

Roman and Mykal dropped their bags, lifted their heads, and straightened their shoulders, so I followed suit. I made sure *not* to glance at High Prince Dolion again. No, thank you.

"I'm Archduke Baracas Heta," announced the little person. "With me is King Tagin Dolion, High Prince Cyrus Dolion, and Duchess Echo Mimidae."

Don't look, don't look, don't look. The mantra always helped me with the Rock, but not with the emperor's grandson. I failed to prevent my focus from darting his way. Oh, thank goodness! He stared straight ahead, no longer glaring at me.

"Our laws are simple," Archduke Heta continued. "Obey the rules. Respect others. Combat the Madness. If anyone exhibits symptoms of the disease, even a commanding officer, you will inform a superior immediately. Always tell. Failure to do so could cost you and countless others their lives."

He paused, scanning us. "After the Fall of Nations, when the Madness spread through civilization like wildfire, our forebears had to rebuild our great provinces from the ground up. Today, we're better and stronger than ever, and I will happily die defending Ourland."

Cheers resounded from the gentry. The second the archduke raised his hand, they quieted.

"I have no idea who any of you are, but I'm certain you've never ventured into the night. You think you comprehend what's waiting for you out there. Let me assure you, you don't." Grim confidence emanated from him. "Most of you have never encountered glowers, the most insidious of the maddened. Worse than the newly broken, who rampage. Seemingly calm and rational. Stronger. Faster. Impervious to pritis stones. For decades, CURED has kept them from infiltrating public spaces, ensuring your safety. Now, it's your honor and duty to protect CURED in return."

No one uttered a word. Roman was too busy grinning. But me? I was spinning.

The archduke wasn't done. "I didn't pursue leadership, but the Madness called, and I answered. Now, you have done the same. For that, I commend you. But are you worthy to bear our name? We will find out."

To ward off sickness, I pressed my palm against my midsection.

"At the end of your training, we'll award the top lord or lady with a rare prize." He stepped to the edge of the dais. "No taxes for the rest of your life."

I blinked. In an instant, every fiber of my being craved that prize. I could supplement my mother's income, ensuring she didn't need to work from sunup to sundown, babysitting a monster child she no longer had the strength to corral. I would never again have to worry she'd end up in Gradon, prey for predators. But I wasn't the only one bubbling over with sudden excitement. Everyone else wanted the prize too.

Didn't matter. "I will be the top lady," I whispered to myself. Though I had no idea what constituted such a title. The most captures or kills, probably. And loyalty. Strategy too. But it still didn't matter. I would stop at nothing.

Roman heard my personal pep talk. "Shoot for most improved," he advised me softly. "Top lord is the reason I'm here."

I recognized a warning when I heard it and gulped. So competition was fierce? So what?

"Today," Archduke Heta continued, "you'll undergo a full medical examination. For the good of us all, you will consent to whatever tests and medications we feel you require."

"Sir, yes, sir," Roman boomed, and the rest of us echoed him.

Two soldiers motioned us to follow, and I picked up my bag. The pair led us up the hill, toward the palace/prison. I didn't mean to, but I cast a final glance at the high prince as I neared his platform.

Our gazes collided, and my eyes widened. He was glaring so forcefully, his brand pulled taut. I must have done something to offend. Or maybe I resembled someone he despised. Ugh. No. It was my outfit. I'd probably violated sixteen different regulations.

"I didn't get the what-to-wear memo, all right?" I muttered.

Perhaps he read my lips. Perhaps not. Either way, he blinked with surprise.

I was so flustered by the interaction, I tripped on my own foot. Cheeks on fire, I gripped my bag closer. Finally, I passed the leaders, putting the foursome in my rearview.

"So, this might not be the time and place, but I used to date Shiloh," Mykal said from in front of me. "Thought you should know."

I recognized a distraction when I heard it. "Go on." Please.

"As you probably guessed, it didn't last long and it didn't work out, but I want him happy. You returned a smile I've missed seeing ever since his sister—never mind," she mumbled, and said no more.

Oh, no. I could guess what had happened to his sister. The Madness. But she must have survived, since he'd mentioned having fun with her. Still. I knew the horrors of treatment, and my chest constricted with sympathy.

Grains of sand flung in every direction as I climbed the hill. "Why didn't it work between you guys? You both seem pretty wonderful."

"She fell in *lurve* with someone else. Mr. Mystery." Roman tossed a toothy grin over his shoulder and wiggled his brows. "If you can get her to name names, please share with the rest of us. She's so secretive."

"Do you try to be the most annoying person on the planet, Roman, or does it come naturally?" Mykal grumbled.

Another toothy grin made an appearance. "It comes naturally, thank you for asking."

Their easy banter helped ground me, keeping my usual panic at bay. I mean, I was in a strange place, with strange people, expected to fight an enemy I'd feared my entire life and, and, and—*Breathe, just breathe.*

A commotion up ahead yanked my attention outward. I forgot my problems as the trainee at the head of the line collapsed. Wait, the second and third collapsed too. Down went several others, one after the other. What the—Roman's knees buckled. Mykal went down. My blood flashed cold. Did I detect a sickeningly sweet odor in the air?

Run!

I braced for launch, planning to go anywhere else as fast as my feet could carry me. But a thick fog blanketed my mind, and strength abandoned me in a rush. I wobbled, fighting to remain aware, internally screaming. *Sleep. Vulnerable. No!*

The more I battled, the more my nerve endings sizzled.

Don't fight the pain. Shiloh's voice boomed through my head. *Don't fight.*

So badly I wanted to heed him. How easy it would be to let go and drift off. But experience had taught me better. Trust no one. Sleep alone. Always alone. I was currently in public. But the pain! The heat.

Sweat poured over me, and muscles jerked. My lungs flattened, the ability to breathe gone. At last I tumbled into an endless abyss . . .

⁂

"—dead within a month, tops."

"She might surprise us. I hear she fought the toxin longer than the beefed-up brute whose dad served with honors."

"A by-product of fear, exactly what will get her killed. I've been here eight years and examined countless lords and ladies. Those with panic disorders never last long."

The casualness of the conversation lured me from a deep sleep. I tried to make sense of the words, but my brain wasn't fully online yet.

"She wakes," the man muttered.

Finally I managed to hold my eyes open for several seconds. I groaned. The world was spinning. *Inhale. Exhale.* As the momentum slowed, memories invaded. The bus ride. Fort Bala Royal Academy. The competition and prize. Pain.

Stiffening, I took stock of my surroundings. I reclined on a medical gurney, inside a small sterile room cordoned off by a curtain. I still wore my running clothes. On the counter, my bag gaped open, the contents spilling out. Clearly someone had rooted through my stuff.

Tension snatched me in its jaws and held on with a vise grip. An unfamiliar young man and a thirtysomething woman in medical scrubs stood beside the gurney, a wheeled tray between them. The man plunged a needle into a vial, filled the belly of a syringe with gray liquid, and turned to stick me in the arm.

The sharp prick startled me from my malaise, and I yelped.

He didn't react in the slightest.

"Who are you?" I demanded, gathering what remained of my strength. Yes! I collected enough to pull myself into an upright position. "What did you inject in me?"

"I'm Dr. Korey." The woman extended her hand to the medic. He placed a second syringe in her palm. "You're receiving vitamins, vaccinations, and anything else I think you need to survive interrealm travel and keep you and your teammates safe."

Translation: *Shut up and acquiesce.*

A tide of frustration rushed through my veins. All my life, others had dictated what I could and could not do. From what building I lived in to where I worked to what I deserved to be paid. I rarely had a say in even the smallest details. If I'd dared to ask questions, I'd been rebuked without receiving a straight answer. But always I'd rolled with the punches. All before one.

With so much new being tossed at me, I was tempted to do something foolish and protest. A mistake I couldn't afford. Just like I'd done every time before, I gathered and dumped the frustration into an ever-growing cauldron, letting it simmer in the shadows of my mind.

My fate rested in the hands of CURED. Considering I now contended for the title of top lady, I should do nothing to jeopardize my chances of victory. I *must* win that prize.

Saying nothing else, the doctor jabbed me with the second needle. I cringed as icy cold spread through my arm. I, too, held my silence.

From outside the room, a knight gripped the curtain and shoved the material aside. I looked beyond him, seeing a hallway loaded with other exam rooms, some open. Mykal sprawled on a gurney across from me, appearing as traumatized as I felt. Shiloh stood beside her. The sight of him served as an anchor to calm.

Our gazes met, and his beautiful features twisted with concern. I offered him a tentative smile, trying to tell him I was fine. Then High Prince Cyrus Dolion marched into my field of vision and hijacked my thoughts.

He stalked into my room, and my heart attempted to pound through my ribs. Stopping near my gurney, he claimed a file from the table. As he read, never speaking a word, he and his intensity dominated the space. Controlled power formed an almost tangible shield around him. But that was expected. What wasn't? The incredible scent wafting from him, infiltrating every molecule of oxygen.

Mmm. What was *that*? Fairy dust and ambrosia? The sweet cologne so did not fit the skull and crossbones bottle.

"Nice to see you, Cyrus," Dr. Korey greeted, her voice suddenly higher than it had been a few minutes ago.

Oh la la. They were on a first-name basis.

"Leave us," he said, his deep baritone inviting no arguments. He didn't glance up from the file.

The doctor's colleague strode out without hesitation. She lingered, seeming to gear up to spew facts about me. The high prince remained preoccupied, reading the screen.

"My apologies if I wasn't clear," he said, amicable. "Go. Get out. Be gone."

She worked her jaw, cast me a glare as if I were at fault, and exited the room, the curtain swishing behind her. Suddenly, I was alone with royalty.

His nearness put me on edge. I missed Shiloh and his measure of peace. Though I longed to call for the medic, I made the best move for my situation, kicking my legs over the side of the bed and standing. A wave of dizziness struck. I teetered but didn't collapse.

Maybe standing without permission in the company of a decorated officer was a crime, maybe not. Either way, instinct insisted I prepare to run. Only stubbornness held me in place. *Eye on the prize!*

He didn't protest my actions. "Twenty years old. Overachiever. A dedicated rule follower."

The invasion of privacy nettled me more than ever. Teachers, doctors, advisers, and now military personnel had access to every physical, mental, and emotional test I'd ever taken, yet I did not. But just as before, I dumped my frustration and contained my protests, allowing not a sound to escape. *Must win!*

Then he said, "Willing to turn in a beloved family member you suspected of being infected."

Guilt and shame I'd never shed flared with renewed fervor. "I did what was necessary to save my mother and others."

"Oh, I know your reasons for doing it. Assume I've perused every report ever written about you, memorized each detail, and now comprehend more about you than you do. But even I'm not sure what you're doing here."

"Paying a debt. Sir," I tacked on as an afterthought.

"You may call me *High Prince*. I'll even answer to *HP*." He scrolled to another page. "I'm aware of the reason listed in your file. I was asking if your death will make Mama glad she stayed in her nice, cozy Lucrea apartment and let you ship out to certain death, or if she'll regret it for the rest of her life."

A muscle jumped in my jaw. "I won't die." I couldn't. The quality of my mother's life rested on my shoulders. Because he was right. If I died, she would forever blame herself.

"Bubble Gum," he said, finally glancing up from the screen. Our gazes locked. "I'm willing to bet you're killed before our first excursion into Theirland."

Lead dropped into my stomach. "Are you trying to scare me?" And did he really call me *Bubble Gum*?

He shrugged his broad shoulders, not the least bit abashed. "It's too late for your withdrawal. I'm here to offer you a onetime opportunity. Serve as my assistant, and you'll choose your roommate, meet high-ranking officials able to aid your chosen career, and never see combat. Instead, you'll fetch and carry for me. When I have no more use for you, you'll graduate to a safe office job to serve out the rest of your term."

Okay, that sounded amazingly wonderful and checked all my boxes. No fighting glowers and other maddened. Right contacts. Safe office job. Yes, please and thank you.

And yet, I hesitated. "Are you offering me a choice or explaining what you expect me to accept?"

"With me, you will always have a choice," he said, scrolling again. "But you alone are responsible for the consequences."

A surprising turn. He was the grandson of CURED's emperor, son of the military's king, and a high prince on his own merit rather than lineage (supposedly). He could issue a command and compel me to obey or face imprisonment.

Whatever the reason for his show of mercy, I took advantage of my freedom and sought more information. "Will I remain a contender for top lady if I agree?"

A humorless laugh barked from him. He flipped up his gaze a second time, meeting mine. I ignored the little blip of my heart. "Entertain aspirations of being the best, do you, Bubble Gum?" When I pursed my lips in distaste, he laughed again. "You do. How novel. No, as my assistant, you are ineligible for the competition because you won't be attending class, drills, or practice missions. So? What's it to be?"

Good question. Did I stay safe or go for gold? Let fear paralyze me, preventing me from supplying my mother with the life she deserved, or keep my word and face my nightmares?

Plant seeds that could produce a long-term harvest for my well-being, or stick with the status quo?

Take the job, self-preservation shrieked.

But. A small voice in the back of my mind persisted. *What about the prize?* And not just the taxes, but the training. Learning how to protect myself.

"Well?" he prompted.

"I'll do patrol," I croaked. Maybe, if I put my all into this, I would experience true, lasting peace. The holy grail. A prize greater than the one CURED offered.

The barest hint of shock flickered over the HP's expression. "You're sure? The offer expires as soon as I leave."

I wrinkled my nose, reminded of Ms. Butler's offer to join Fort Bala. *Hurry! Act now or lose out!* "Is introducing an invisible ticking clock an intimidation tool I'll be learning here?"

He ran his tongue over his teeth. "Perhaps you didn't understand my proposal. As a lady, you'll be forced to train alongside the others. You'll be injured. That's a guarantee. There's a good chance you'll break bones, get shot, be stabbed."

My small measure of confidence cracked. By some miracle, I maintained a firm clasp on a sliver of hope. What he offered sounded good on the surface, but it also struck me as a trap. I wouldn't face the maddened, but I would face him on a daily basis.

"I'm sure I don't want to be your assistant." If the worst happened and I did, in fact, get killed, I'd rather have a quick end. A trap was just a slow way to die.

"Very well. A foolish choice, but a choice all the same." He gave me another of those negligent shrugs, as if he hadn't cared one way or the other, and returned the file to the cart. "The night will chew you up and spit out your bones. I would've kept you around." With a cool smile, he headed for the exit, adding, "At least until you lost your flavor."

CHAPTER FIVE

Every lie you believe is a blade at your throat, soon
to strike.

—*The Book of Soal* 1.28.4.6

I was still reeling an hour later when Dr. Korey and her assistant
returned to finish my exam and administer another injection. The high
prince might be long gone, but his words stayed with me.

Killed before your first excursion.

Bubble Gum.

Chew you up and spit out your bones.

My hands curled into fists.

"Did we give her aidem?" the doctor asked, looking over the vials
on the medical cart and frowning.

"What's aidem?" The question slipped out before I could run it
through an Is This Smart to Say filter.

"It's a serum that prevents glowers from—"

"Quiet," Dr. Korey snapped, and the assistant went silent. "I told
you to check something, so check it."

Shamefaced, he swiped up the file and poked at the screen. "We
did. Right before the HP entered."

"Then we're done here." She removed and trashed her gloves, then headed for the curtain, only to pause and glance my way. "Did you truly decline the HP's offer?"

Her tone said what she didn't: Are you a fool? I licked my lips. "I did, yes."

"Not even a month," she muttered before striding off, her disgust clear.

"I would've said yes in six languages." The assistant pulled a stack of folded clothes from a cabinet. He tossed the garments my way. "Put these on and wait in the hall. Your bag and schedule are on the counter." With that, he too was gone.

Alone at last. My arms throbbed from the shots, and my brain had yet to recover from the encounter with High Prince Dolion. Trying to control my breathing, I studied the clothes. Green fatigues with gold stitching, similar to my old school uniform.

I dressed in the world's scratchiest clothing and glanced over my schedule.

LADY A.R.

Monday–Wednesday

0500–0530: Wake up / Breakfast

0530–0730: Warm up / Work out (Gym C)

0800–1000: Realms and Travel (Room 2)

1010–1230: Weapons (Room 6)

1230–1300: Lunch

1300–1500: Self-Defense (Gym C)

1500–1550: Battlefield First Aid (Room 1)

1600–1930: Drills (the Dome)

1930–2000: Dinner

2000–2200: Free time

2200–0500: Lights out

Thursday

Free day

Friday

0500–0530: Wake up / Breakfast

0530–0600: Travel to Theirland

0610–1600: Patrol*

1600–0500: Free time

Saturday

TBD by instructor

Sunday

0500–0530: Wake up / Breakfast

0530–0550: Travel to Ourland

0600–0730: Warm up / Work out (Gym C)

0800–1000: Evaluation (Room 2)

1010–1230: Testing (Room 6)

1230–1300: Lunch

1300–1400: Madness Basics (Room 3)

1410–1550: Driving (TBA)

1600–1930: Drills (The Dome)

1930–2000: Dinner

2000–2200: Free time

2200–0500: Lights out

* Breaks scheduled by superior

Both better and worse than I'd feared. Sighing, I left the relative safety of my cubby and entered the hall as ordered. Medical personnel had cleared out. Around twenty other soldiers had exited their rooms, Roman and Mykal among them. The two stood together, whispering. He radiated excitement. Honestly, she did too. The stress had drained from her.

What had changed?

Two guards rounded the corner, dragging a hysterical soldier in uniform past us.

"The old gods will rise and bring the end with them. You know that, right?" His laughter echoed from the walls. "The Kingdom of Today is here!"

I grimaced. A Rock-worshipping Soalian dedicated to the destruction of CURED had infiltrated the military.

The medic who'd worked on me hurried over to inject him with what had to be a sedative. The traitor sagged into unconsciousness.

Fellow soldiers muttered among themselves, and I caught the words *Tome Society*.

Oh, please no! The Tome Society was a small faction of Soalians responsible for the deadliest attacks against CURED. Supposedly the god Soal's finest warriors and those he trained to fight an army of sleeping immortals.

Only when the foursome disappeared inside a room with a real door did I breathe again. As murmurs rose from my peers, Jericho looked me over from top to bottom, wiggled his brows, and snickered. "I liked the other outfit better. But this one will look amazing on my floor."

Nope, he absolutely hadn't changed.

The former ruckus forgotten, everyone focused on me, curious to see how I would react to the implication. To my consternation, I blanked.

"You know what will look amazing on *my* floor?" Roman asked with a calmness I didn't buy for a second. "You. Talk to her like that again, and I'll mop it with your face."

The other soldier went red and puffed up with indignation. "You can try."

Aggression radiated from Roman. More than I had suspected his powerful body contained. Jericho braced, as if ready to launch the first blow.

This could *not* be happening.

"Arden!" Completely oblivious to the brewing cage match, or just uncaring, Mykal smiled and waved me over. "Did you hear my news? I'm—"

"Attention," an unfamiliar voice called. "Nobility on deck."

"Line up." This hard baritone I recognized. High Prince Dolion had returned.

Everyone leaped to obey, rushing into the semblance of a formation as he strode down the hall.

"You're Cyrus Dolion, and you're here, within touching distance," the girl from my school breathed.

"And you're speaking out of turn." He didn't snap the words as he passed her, but somehow his measured delivery seemed far worse. "Don't do it again."

Mykal zoomed forward to take a post behind him. Oooh. He'd made his offer to her, and she'd accepted. That must be her news. And it was fantastic. Genuinely wonderful. And yet, regret overtook me. Had I made the wrong decision?

No. No, of course not. *Eyes on the prize.*

I forgot how to breathe as the HP stopped, faced us, and traced his gaze over every soldier. Hmm. Did his attention linger on me a split second longer than everyone else?

No, of course not. The strange blip of my heartbeat made it feel that way, that was all.

"You are here to learn how to protect your world and those in it," he stated. "But you cannot help others if you cannot overcome the danger to yourself. That is why you will first learn self-reliance." He locked his hands behind his back. "For the next six weeks, your highest priority is you. Only after each of you can hold your own will you train as a team. As your leader, I expect your best always, without exception or excuse. If I don't get it, you'll experience my disapproval." His gaze landed on me and stayed put. "Trust me when I say you do not wish to experience my disapproval."

I jutted my chin, because my only other option was to wither.

"Come," he said with a slight grumbling tinge.

He marched us through the prison side of the compound, snaking around corners, climbing concrete stairs. Along the way, signs offered directions to different locations. The commissary. Locker rooms. Medical. There were no plants, and the lack proved more disappointing than my new leader. Why couldn't I have gotten the archduke or the duchess?

Full-fledged lords and ladies, rather than those in training, strode about with knights, and most ignored us. Several cast us sympathetic glances, as if they recalled their own first days. No conversations took place, the regimented environment reminding me of my years at school. Numerous windows shattered the illusion, however. There were more panes here than I'd ever seen in one building, an occurrence I didn't understand. The maddened loved to break glass. They thrived on destruction of any kind, really.

On the walls without windows hung portraits of former leaders, intermixed with detailed murals. Scenes painted to encapsulate the golden age before the Fall of Nations, a time when there'd been no Rock or Madness. No guarded cities filled with a hodgepodge of mismatched buildings. Flora and fauna had encompassed the whole world, rather than the top of a stone wall broken into small segments and placed throughout civilization. I drank in a wide expanse of lush green grass, flowering trees, and soaring flocks of birds. Clearly, I'd been born in the wrong era.

Though I longed to study the painted images in detail, the HP never slowed his gait.

"This is the Dome, where we'll run simulations and tests," he explained as we ascended to the next level. "Mostly independently, occasionally jointly."

I admit, I gawked. Frosted crystals glittered from the ceilings and grew down walls that had a plethora of cutouts. Each cutout was big enough to fit a single individual. Crimson sand trapped in resin covered the floor. There were no windows or murals here.

We took another hallway and entered a spacious enclosure divided into an entertainment area with games and a dining room with four round tables, each seating five. Lining the perimeter, machines offered different types of food and educational resources.

"This commons is exclusive to your team," High Prince Dolion said and kept walking.

Your team, he'd said. Not *our.*

We entered a hallway. A space filled with gurneys, medical equipment, curtained-off rooms, and Shiloh. We shared a quick smile, and my pulse quickened. He stood with six other medics.

"Learn the route to this medical wing." Still the HP refused to slow. "You'll need patching regularly."

Shiloh made a funny face at me, there and gone, and I would've laughed out loud if I hadn't pressed a hand over my mouth.

My group exited into another hallway, then strode through a set of thick double doors. Finally, High Prince Dolion stopped. He spread his arms and announced, "Behold, your rooms. You'll bunk in assigned pairs."

I tried not to cringe. Actual prison cells, complete with barred doors.

"Lady Pink, you're with my assistant." The line ahead of me parted until I had a direct view of our illustrious superior.

I gnashed my teeth. He did *not* call me Lady Pink in public, after calling me Bubble Gum in private. Wait. Roommate? I hadn't shared a space with anyone since Amelia, and I couldn't do it now. I just couldn't. If Mykal were to break . . .

Heart thudding, blood chilling, I shot my gaze to the HP. He watched me, his expression colder and harder than before.

"Are you done panicking over nothing?" he asked, merciless.

For the second time today, everyone focused on me in unison. Irritation spiced my ever-simmering pot of frustration, billowing smoke hiding my anxiety. For the moment anyway.

Once again I jutted my chin. This time I added a stiff nod to the action.

He swept his gaze over everyone else, dismissing me. "If you do what I say, when I say, victory is yours." Pointing to a digital board on a far wall, he issued his final commands. "Find your assigned room, put up your stuff, and meet me in the commons in thirty. You'll be picking a representative to serve as my second-in-command. Do not be late. And never forget everything is a graded test."

He left, taking his force field of control with him. To my relief, he didn't glance my way again. I didn't think I liked that man even the slightest bit.

Soldiers rushed over to discover the identity of their partner and where they'd be staying. I went straight to Mykal.

"What a great day!" Grinning, she hugged me. "I expected the worst, and in a single moment, all my fears were wiped away."

I hugged her back, desperate for a friend.

Her grin widened as she tugged me to a cell on the far right. "This is ours. The good news is it's the biggest and the best, and our locker room is around the corner. The bad news is Jericho is our next-door neighbor."

"I'll learn to ignore him." As I checked out our space, my shoulders rolled in. We had a sink, a pair of small collapsible desks, and uncomfortable-looking beds that folded from the back wall on both the left and right side. A bowl of meal bars rested atop each thin, plasticky mattress alongside a coil of chain.

Relief warred with ever-increasing trepidation. No doubt we were to lock ourselves in place each night. A common enough practice, though not one I'd ever risked. Though we'd be trapped, neither of us able to attack the other, I was far from comforted. Too many things could go wrong. If she verged on breaking and only pretended to lock up, she'd be free, and I'd be a helpless buffet ready for plunder.

I dragged my focus to the walls. Carved images and messages from previous trainees covered them. I traced a fingertip over the most uplifting of the bunch and cringed. **DON'T DIE.** Maybe I'd paint trees and flowers over the depressing words. I wasn't the best artist, but anything was better than this. If I managed to acquire pots and soil, I could grow my own plants.

"I haven't eaten in days, and I'm starving." Mykal ripped open a bar, sank her teeth into the pale-gray "meal," and grimaced. "These never get better, but we should gobble up. Before I got here, Roman's dad outlined what to expect. The second-in-command is chosen through an endurance competition, and tomorrow you guys will be evaluated for your performance. From strength to smarts to fear response."

Heeding her advice, I gobbled up a bar. The familiar bitter taste barely registered. "Why did you pick me as a roomie?" Why not Roman, a known friend? "Did Shiloh request it?"

"He did, but he's not the reason." She tossed her bag on a bed and gave me a wry smile. "Honestly, I'd really like a friend. Someone I can trust, who relates to me. You strike me as a prime candidate."

Okay. That was a little bit wonderful. I hugged her again. "Thank you. I would really like a friend too. In the name of full disclosure, former classmates called me Panic Girl. Also, I geek out over plants." I dropped my bag on my bed and dug through the contents, hunting for my precious seeds. "If it's allowed, and if I can get my hands on the proper supplies, I'll grow an indoor garden for us." Except. "My seeds. They're gone." Dismay flooded me. Where were they?

"Probably got confiscated." Sympathy etched her delicate features. "I saw a guy rummage through my stuff. He took my music. I *need* my music."

My cauldron of frustration threatened to boil over. "Do you think we'll ever get our stuff back?" Those seeds cost every cent I'd saved since junior high. To have something I'd worked and paid for taken away for no good reason was an injustice I resented with every fiber of my being.

I bit my tongue until I tasted blood. I would get those seeds back. Somehow.

"I really hope so. Oh!" Brightening, Mykal clapped. "Want to know what else Shiloh asked me to do for you?" She didn't give me a chance to reply. "Teach you how to do hand-on-hand signals so you can communicate silently with him whenever you're sent to medical."

My brow furrowed. "Why do we need to communicate silently?"

Nibbling on her bottom lip, she held up one finger, asking for a moment. With quick steps, she went to the door and leaned out to look both ways. After returning to me, she whispered, "We're not supposed to know this, but in exam rooms all conversations are recorded."

I stiffened. The thought of being recorded put a foul taste in my mouth. Worse than the meal bar!

"Roman's dad is an earl, and he demanded the people living in his building, on his floor, learn certain protocols. Nonverbal, in-contact communication is one of them and something CURED won't teach until we reach second tier."

Well, score one for Team Arden! I'd never turn down such a precious seed of knowledge. The more we practiced, a.k.a. watered the skill, the stronger it would grow. "I'd love to learn those signals." Top lady, here I come!

A smirking Roman stuck his head inside our room. "I came to collect my thanks."

"Your thanks?" Mykal snorted. "Not happening, bud."

"Even though I made sure we were both placed on Dolion's team?"

"Your dad made sure, not you."

Roman's expression said *You are making my point for me.* "He did it only because I asked him. So. Where's my thanks?"

"Fine. Thanks, I guess," she grumbled.

"You have my thanks too," I piped up. "I'm glad Mykal is on my team."

Roman grinned at me. "You're gonna be fine, Ardie. When the HP says he'll make winners out of us, believe him. He's the youngest elite officer in CURED history. To this day, he holds the record for the most captures in a day, week, month, and year."

No wonder the guy had such little respect for me. But, um, I kinda hoped the nickname *Ardie* caught on. Anything was better than *Lady Pink.*

"I heard he got the handprint brand while fighting John Victors," Mykal said, digging into another bar. "The Soalian caught flame and marked him."

I scowled. John Victors was the most well-known Soalian, as well as the leader of the Tome Society. He and his minions stole pritis poles, defaced buildings, and burned CURED facilities year round.

"I wouldn't mention the brand. Word is, the HP is super sensitive about it." Roman glanced over his shoulder. "The team is heading to the commons. We intend to set the record for swiftest arrival. And yes, I expect both of you to vote for me. I'll be an amazing second-in-command. We'll celebrate my win after." He was gone a moment later.

Mind tumbling with the tidbits about my instructor, I looked to Mykal. "You ready?"

"Yeah. And just so you know, I'll be cheering for Roman, but only on the outside," she whispered. "Beat him. *Please.* If he wins, he'll never stop crowing. A crowing Roman is annoying."

There was no way I could beat Roman in a contest of strength, but endurance was another story. As a long-distance runner, I possessed stamina in spades. But . . . "I'm not sure I want to be team leader. I have enough stress on my plate with the top-soldier competition."

"Well, keep in mind, the top lady—or lord—is usually chosen from among the team leaders," she offered, batting her eyes.

My back went ramrod straight. "On the other hand, Roman has enough of an advantage already. Plus, High Prince Dolion called me *Bubble Gum* and *Lady Pink*, and he expects me to die quick. I've got a lot to prove. So. I will destroy him," I announced, and I wasn't sure if I was referencing Roman, the HP, or both.

Mykal bounced while clapping. "I knew you were made of determination, drive, and the smarts to thrive!"

I really hoped so, because I was tired of being made of failure, fear, and many tears.

CHAPTER SIX

Some solutions cannot be worked out in your mind:
they must come from an enlightened heart.

—*The Book of Soal* 1.20.3.5

I entered the commons with Mykal at my side. No longer rushed by the HP, I cataloged the finer details. A smaller room than the Dome, but just as spectacular. Crimson crystals layered the walls and sparkled in the light. The lounge area offered soft couches and comfy chairs. In the kitchen, four tables offered intricately carved seats. An island displayed plates, utensils, and an assortment of snacks. From fresh fruits to creamy cheeses to savory pastries.

Everything else forgotten, I floated over for a closer look. Sugar-glazed tartlets topped with strawberries. Double-stacked sandwiches. Seasoned crackers. Vegetable dips. Why was no one digging in? My mouth watered as I reached for a mix of apples and figs baked inside a buttery crust. Delicacies I'd only ever seen in photos and films. Treats I'd yearned to sample for years.

"I didn't give you permission to eat, Lady Pink."

The HP's rebuke hit my ears, and I froze. My mind blanked and restarted, revealing frayed nerve endings. Our illustrious leader had arrived. Empty handed, I straightened and dropped my arm to my sides. "No. Sir. You did not."

"No one touches the food until they're disqualified from the game," he called to one and all. "If anyone wishes to forfeit, do it now."

No one spoke up. I'm sure they remembered his earlier warning. Everything was a graded test.

"Good." The HP stalked past me, and I caught a whiff of fairy dust and ambrosia. Or maybe rose and citrus. Whatever it was, it fogged my head with thoughts I had no business entertaining.

Mykal rushed to take up a post directly behind him. A group of medics entered the chamber, and I swallowed a groan. Great! We required medical personnel for this contest.

Only when I spotted Shiloh did I breathe easier. He and the others settled in at the tables, near a section of the room cleared of all furniture. On the floor was a large painted circle comprising eighteen smaller circles, each with a handgun in the center.

My widening attention whipped to the high prince. He stood in profile, his brand stark against his skin and a beautiful testament to his strength and courage. For a moment, the sight of him distracted me from what was to come. I hated that the mark bothered him. Then I remembered the handguns and tamped down a mewl for help.

He stiffened and commanded, "Pick a ring and claim your weapon."

I dragged my feet to one of the cir—nope, a girl shouldered past me and snagged it. I angled left to—nope. Right. Nope. Sighing, I snagged a ring next to Roman. A spot everyone else avoided. Made sense, I supposed. If we had to fight the people next to us, he was the man to avoid.

I peered down at the gun, uneasy. I'd never handled a firearm and didn't want to start now. To become top lady, however . . . I claimed the weapon, doing my best to hide my apprehension. The firearm was lighter than expected but not quite as firm. Not squishy, but not exactly solid either. Weird.

Everyone peered at everyone else, clearly wondering what to do next. Well, excluding Roman and a few others. They stared straight ahead, ready for anything.

In this position, I had a direct view of the HP and Shiloh. Avoiding the first, I concentrated on the medic. He offered me an encouraging nod. I nodded back. I would've taken comfort in the exchange, but once again, I read his eyes. *It's going to be okay . . . eventually.*

My limbs petrified.

"Let's begin." High Prince Dolion selected the apple-and-fig dessert from a tray Mykal held out for him. Oh, that burned. "I suggest you listen carefully to my instructions. Your weapon holds three pain darts that simulate the sensation of interrealm travel. You will talk and get to know each other, using those darts to eliminate anyone you don't wish to be your representative. If you miss, you miss. If you hit your target and they don't go down, too bad. Exit your boundary in any capacity, and you're disqualified. Fall, disqualified. You'll vote between the final two left standing." After biting into the treat and dabbing a drop of juice from the corner of his mouth, he casually commanded, "Go."

Acid invaded my veins, my thoughts whirling. This must be a trick. Yes, we were to look after ourselves right now. But. Part of looking after myself was ensuring I had a team able to trust me, no matter what. By hurting someone now, I only hurt myself later. That meant, what? The true winner wouldn't discharge a single dart?

"If we're gonna do this, let's do it. I'm Jericho, and I—" A broken grunt garbled his next words. Perhaps because a dart now protruded from his jugular. He jerked as if he'd been hit with a lightning bolt, the tendons in his neck stretching taut. By some miracle, he didn't fall or step from his boundary.

Roman lowered his gun. "I'm Lord Roman Alexander. Here's how this will go. One by one, you will sell yourself to us with two facts and an explanation about why you believe you should be our representative. We'll start with"—he pointed to Lark, the gorgeous girl from my school, who'd been a grade under me—"you. By the way, if anyone shoots her, they'll have to deal with me."

Jericho began to breathe heavily. Beads of sweat trickled over his face.

As confident as Roman, Lark put her nose in the air. "I'm Lady Lark Foster, future archduchess. First fact, I don't need you or anyone to protect me. Second, I'm not interested in dating you. I should be our representative because I'm good at keeping egotistical soldiers in check."

"Consider my protection a bonus, since you're preobsessed with me and all." Roman spread his arms, unaffected by her rejection. Playful and yet still so, well, soldiery. "And I hate to point this out, honey, but you didn't keep me in check." He winced for her. "You followed my instructions."

Lark blinked as she realized the truth of his words. Scowling, she shot him.

Laughing, he plucked out the dart as if it were nothing. "So you need a little more time to come to terms with our powerful connection. Noted."

The object of his fascination huffed and puffed, but she didn't shoot him again.

Whoosh. The guy on my right took his shot, a dart flying.

With a slight twist, Roman avoided a second hit. He didn't turn away from Lark but raised his weapon and fired, nailing his would-be assailant in the throat. While I marveled at his skill, he winked.

Trigger Happy muttered something just before he wobbled and stumbled out of bounds. Disqualified. One down, seventeen to go.

"Please, go on." Roman waved in Lark's direction. "You were saying you don't need a big, tough rescuer in your corner, but maybe suddenly you've realized you want one?"

"Nah," she said, blowing him a kiss with her middle finger. "I'm good."

"Very good," he agreed.

I almost couldn't process what was happening, my anxiety a wildfire and an ice storm at once, yet those two were flirting.

Amid my haze of shock, I missed the ensuing flood of names and information. At least until a guy barked a laugh and said, "Parents, man. They can be the worst. Do you think pre-Fall kids had such ridiculous names?"

Four people shot him without hesitation. Two of the projectiles landed. Screaming, he pitched backward, out of bounds. He lay sprawled on the floor, with white foam dripping from his mouth.

Three teammates eliminated themselves—none of whom were his shooters.

If I could have moved, I would've joined them. My feet had morphed into boulders, keeping me captive as the victim gasped for breath he couldn't catch. Two medics rushed to treat him. It wasn't long before he sat up with a groan and a glaze of pain in his eyes. Cheers resounded as the medics helped him rise and lumber to a table.

"I didn't say stop," the HP said, merciless, and my bones quaked. "Continue."

A new round of names and facts kicked off, blurring together. In the chaos, I retained only Juniper, Miller, and Titus.

Titus was tall and unassuming, but he glared at Roman, ready for battle. "I have no need to sell myself to you or anyone."

Expecting an immediate shoot-out, I froze. When Roman continued making eyes at Lark, ignoring Titus, I sighed with relief and tried to listen to the next onslaught of information. Did I retain anything new? No. Soon I would be forced to speak and—

Every eye landed on me. My stomach churned. My turn had arrived.

"H-hi. I'm Arden. Lady Arden Roosa." The gun nearly slipped from my dampening grip. *I can do this.* "I don't think we should harm each other. We're a team, or at least we're going to be. Plus, we're being graded." Warming up to my stance, I gave a firm nod. "If we put down our weapons, we can—" A sharp sting pierced just below my collarbone.

I sucked air between my teeth. Searing agony consumed me in an instant, penetrating to my very marrow. Tears welled, screams barreling up my throat only to die on my tongue, unheard as my mind caught fire. Beads of sweat trickled down my temples.

Do not fall! Both the HP and Shiloh were witnessing my reaction. If I lost this early, I'd be forever humiliated.

Trembling, I yanked out the projectile. And yet the excruciating pain only magnified. I nearly whimpered. Needing an anchor, I focused on—no! But it was too late. The HP didn't notice me, thank goodness. He was completely at ease, busy selecting a new dessert. I turned my attention to Shiloh. He gripped the edge of his table, ready to leap out of his chair to come get me. His eyes chanted, *Tap out, tap out, tap out.*

Forget the humiliation aspect. I'd finally get to taste figs and apples. But . . .

Drawn by a magnetic force, I returned my attention to the high prince. He settled back in his chair and met my gaze, as if he'd never lost focus of my plight. The intensity of his expression somehow cooled and heated the blood in my veins simultaneously. *His* eyes said, *Are you a top lady or not?*

I stiffened my knees, staying put, and aimed my gun at Lark, my shooter. But I didn't fire yet.

"No offense," she stated with a shrug, "but I don't want someone like you representing me. We require strength and immunity to pressure— my best attributes. You will fold faster than yesterday's laundry."

Her words hurt almost as much as the dart. How easy it would be to fire in retaliation. But I didn't. I couldn't exactly refute her accusation or logic either.

A good leader didn't simply deny accusations. She disproved them.

Using the rejection as fuel, I lowered my weapon without tapping the trigger, demonstrating restraint and resilience. "Thank you for your honesty." I did my best to mask my labored inhalations. "As your representative, I will ensure my actions match my words. I won't harm a fellow teammate even when they deserve it."

She rolled her eyes. "Harming you aided everyone, even you; you're just too stubborn to admit it. But that's okay—you can thank me later." She batted her lashes at Roman with exaggerated innocence. "Unless I'm busy schooling another teammate."

There was a sole weapon I could use to beat someone like her without breaking my campaign promise: wits. "You're obviously too smart to waste a dart on someone you consider a nonthreat. Admit it, you're afraid of me and jealous of my friendship with Roman." Not that we were officially friends. "I might not be the strongest among us, but I've already proven I'm more than qualified. I only met the big brute today, but I've already convinced him to serve as my personal guard."

"Now hold up—" Roman began with a frown.

"I'm jealous of no one," Lark snarled.

Playing right into my hand. "Sure. You're not jealous of me." I winked at her. "But you can't deny you're scared of me. Afraid to go hand to hand with me." I smirked with all the smirk I had. "Me and my team refuse to be led by a fearmonger." An insult I'd only ever heard directed at me.

"I fear nothing!" Baring her teeth, she stalked my way, abandoning her territory to prove it.

"Whoop! She got you, girl," someone said, cackling. "You're disqualified."

Lark halted abruptly, shock replacing her fury. Of course, the fury resurged with a vengeance, fully directed at me. When she stormed off, triumph and relief nearly drilled me to the floor. I'd done it! I'd beat her without firing a shot, proving myself capable.

Roman comprehended my strategy and nodded at me, as if impressed.

Jericho used the distraction to his advantage, shooting Roman, who scowled and brushed the missile from his skin.

"My turn to share a personal fact," Roman stated, and no one, not even Jericho, naysaid him. "I'm from a military family, and I've trained for this my entire life. I'm loyal to those who are loyal to me, and I'll do whatever proves necessary to save my people, even mow down an enemy or a friend. Those who stand with me, prove it. Shoot Jericho and join the HP at the tables. Those who aren't with me, prepare for my wrath."

The color drained from my former date's face when four people aimed. *Pft, pft, pft, pft.* Each dart landed, and down the soldier fell. As he foamed at the mouth, Shiloh and the other medics rushed to offer assistance. The shooters disqualified themselves.

"The rest of you better want to represent us enough to suffer," Roman said, his confidence unwavering.

Though I fought residual pain, I didn't back down. Even as four other soldiers walked away, joining the others at the tables. My heart drummed against my ribs. Only three of us remained in the circle. Roman had a single dart left. Our fellow challenger, Titus, might have all his ammunition or none; I suddenly couldn't recall who had shot whom.

With all three of my darts locked and loaded, I debated my lone option. Join Titus to take out Roman. Because there was no way I could secure a vote against him.

The two guys faced off, acting as if I wasn't there.

"You sure you want to go head to head?" Roman demanded.

"Beyond." With a cold smile, Titus aimed and unloaded two darts into the other boy. The missiles sank into Roman's chest, bracketing his heart. "You aren't the only lord from a military family."

Countenance darkening the slightest bit, Roman yanked the projectiles free. He used his final dart, hitting Titus in the throat. But Titus, too, pulled the projectile free without a reaction.

How were they still standing?

"Finish him, Ardie." Veins bulged as Roman fought an onslaught of pain. "Now."

Hey. I liked Roman. I did. But this was a competition for a rare prize. I needed to do what was best for me and the team, which included keeping my word. Integrity meant something. A treasure more valuable than gold.

"Arden," he snapped.

"No," I rasped, then I repeated it with more force. "No. I won't do it. Titus is my teammate. And so are you. I meant what I said. I won't harm any of you. But I will outlast you." I wouldn't budge from my circle until both of my opponents passed out.

With a grunt of irritation, Roman swiped my weapon and took aim at Titus. "Final words?"

"Hey," I gasped out. He'd stolen my gun. How dare he! "That's mine."

Titus narrowed his eyes, his attention never leaving Roman. "You can't use someone else's weapon. You'll be disqualified."

"First lesson at the Roman Alexander School of Winning. Always take note of the smallest details." Roman arched a brow at his challenger. "You heard the rules same as me. The HP never mentioned theft."

Oooh. He wasn't wrong. But it was still a terrible move, proving Roman lacked a moral compass when it came to the acquisition of power.

Titus paled. "Don't—"

Too late. *Click, click, click.* Roman unloaded my darts.

An animalistic roar left Titus as his body lurched. He teetered and tried to lock his knees, but the dose was too high. Like Jericho and that other guy, he went down foaming at the mouth. For the third time, medics raced to administer some kind of antidote.

"Behold." The HP dabbed the corners of his mouth with a napkin and stood. "Your champions."

"We won!" A grinning Roman dropped the weapon and leaned over to wrap me in his arms. He swung me around. "Don't be mad, Ardie. I did what was best for us all. And don't worry. You're exempt from my wrath." After setting me on my feet, he clasped my shoulder. "Everything's gonna be good now. You'll see."

"Ow, ow, ow!" I cringed from the contact as receptors lit up with remnants of the pain toxin, or whatever it was. "I'm not a supersoldier like you."

"Right." He winced an apology and released me. "My bad."

"The rest of you, vote," the HP commanded. "Out loud. We'll start with you." He pointed to the first lord to be eliminated.

The lord darted his gaze between us, a strawberry halfway to his mouth. "Roman?"

"Are you asking or telling?" the HP queried with an easy tone that sent chills down my spine.

"Telling?" came the squeaked reply.

Okay. No big deal. I'd lost one. So what. I would snag the rest. The others must realize integrity mattered more than brute force. Except, one by one, our teammates cast their vote for Roman. Even Jericho and Titus. I withered more with every dismissal but tried not to show it.

"Congratulations, Roman." High Prince Dolion tossed his napkin onto the tabletop. To the rest of us, he said, "You have your representative."

I balled my hands into fists. Part of me suspected he'd required a public vote simply to embarrass me. "Congrats," I told Roman. Though I wished to cry, I harbored no ill will toward him. Not much, anyway.

He ruffled my hair like he'd done to Mykal, then flexed his muscles. The other soldiers cheered.

"If you're hurt, let a medic tend to you. If not, return to your room for an early lock-in. Tomorrow is going to be a rude awakening for many of you." The HP stalked off, never looking back.

Mykal attempted to give chase, but he waved her off. She met my gaze and grimaced. I tried to smile with reassurance, but my knees finally gave out. Down I went at last.

I never hit the floor. Shiloh jetted over, catching me.

"I'm here, I've got you," he muttered, easing me down. He dug inside a bag and withdrew a needle that he uncapped and shoved into my arm. "Better?"

The pain fled in a heartbeat. I sagged over the tiles, every muscle relaxing. "Much."

"Good." He took my hand and danced his fingers over my palm, signing six different shapes before moving on to his next patient. My lids slid closed as the corners of my lips lifted. He'd just spoken to me in his secret language. But what had he said?

The next thing I knew, Mykal was pulling me to my feet. "Come on, runner-up. Let's grab some snacks before they disappear."

The apples and figs! Needing no further encouragement, I tripped over to the counter, a little stronger with every step. Except. "The desserts are gone." Along with everything else.

Suddenly I hated the HP, my teammates, and even the day. Mykal and I begrudgingly gathered the crumbs and trudged to our cell. We settled on her mattress and split the bounty.

"I need you to decipher a hand message for me," I said, then drew the shapes on her palm.

She furrowed her brow in confusion. "That's what Shiloh signed to you? You're sure of it?"

I bit my bottom lip and nodded. "Is it bad?"

"No? Maybe? I have no idea why he would tell you this, but—"

A buzz sounded over a PA system, and our cell door closed automatically. "Engage chains," an automated voice announced.

I forgot everything else. Dread unfurling, I stood and trudged to my bed. The cold shackle weighed heavy in my palm as my gaze followed the links to a hook in the wall.

"Count down from three?" Mykal asked, sounding just as nervous as I felt.

I nodded because what else could I do? This was the only way to protect each other in case we broke. "Three. Two."

"One," we said in unison, snapping the metal around our wrists. Goose bumps popped up along my arm.

With a heavy sigh, I settled into the uncomfortable mattress. Honestly, this hadn't been the best day, but it hadn't been a clunker either.

"Arden," she whispered from her side of the room.

"Yes?"

"*Lemons.* That's what Shiloh said to you."

CHAPTER SEVEN

When trouble comes, your victory is found
within the book.

—*The Book of Soal* 1.14.15.4

A shrill alarm startled me from a light doze. Not quite asleep, but not quite awake, I blinked open burning eyes and sat up, expecting to see my plants. A buzz sounded, surprising me, and the shackle on my wrist opened. The barred door opened, too, and memories flashed like neon signs. The Royal Academy. The HP. My first loss. I rubbed my eyes and groaned.

Mykal kicked off her blanket, grumbling, "Five o'clock wake-up is a punishment, isn't it?"

A surge of adrenaline drove me from exhausted to wired. My first class began in thirty minutes, and I would learn the HP's opinion of yesterday's test.

"It's evaluation day." I bounded from bed and straightened the covers. "Did Roman's dad give you pointers for surviving judgment?"

"He did, indeed. Whether we agree or not, we're to say *yes, sir; thank you, sir;* and nothing else."

Figured. "Any other advice I should know?"

"Only that we're to inform a superior immediately if we see a red circle with seven broken lines inside it. It means we've been tapped by the Tome Society."

I inwardly recoiled, repulsed by the very idea. "I will absolutely tell," I swore, gathering my toiletries.

She leaned closer to murmur, "Do you think there's any truth to the claims? About Soal, the library, books about our futures, and the sleeping gods, I mean."

How could she even ask that? "Not even a little." Wait. "Do *you* think there's any truth to the claims?"

"Absolutely not." She wrinkled her nose. "Though I admit it would be kinda nice to read a book about my future."

"Not if it means being infected."

"Good point."

We trudged into the hall, other teammates heading in the same direction.

Roman bounded past us with a whoop. "This is a new day. A fresh start. Let's make it count." He pumped his fist into the air. "I expect your best, understand? No slackers."

Rolling her eyes, Mykal linked her arm through mine. "See? He's insufferable."

"I heard that," Roman said, performing a full spin to point at her.

"Because she wanted you to hear it," I quipped, and she nodded.

At the corner, boys veered left, and girls right. We entered a sterile gray locker room, with toilet stalls on one side and shower stalls on the other. A bay of lockers bore our names and contained changes of clothing.

After washing up, I brushed my teeth and dressed in clean fatigues. Eleven minutes until class. Just enough time to grab a quick breakfast.

A rumpled Lark breezed past me as I tied my boots. I opened my mouth to speak, but the words died. There wasn't anything I could say that wouldn't cause problems. I didn't trust her, wasn't sure I liked her, and had no doubts she felt the same way about me.

She offered me a too-sweet smile. "No hard feelings."

Uh, hard feelings. Definitely. However, for the good of the team— *top lady, top lady, top lady*—I forgave her. And because, despite my not-so-high opinion of her, I did understand her reasoning. Panic Girl wasn't strong and courageous. She froze when terrified and crumpled often.

"I'm good," I said. "As our team leader pointed out, today is a clean slate." On my end, at least. With Lark *and* Roman. He'd done what he'd thought was right to win, just as I had. It wasn't his fault my choice had ended in failure.

Lark didn't look as if she believed me, but she moved along. Mykal and I shared a relieved look before heading to the commons, where we wolfed down meal bars, the only food available. Unsatisfied but full, we made our way to gym C. The spacious arena had concrete walls and a dizzying mosaic across 90 percent of the floor. My heartbeat accelerated, my hasty breakfast settling with the finesse of a rock as soon as I noticed the HP.

He stood off to the side, in front of a small office with glass walls, a small table, and a chair on each side. His powerful presence sucked all the oxygen from the room. With his features set in inflexible lines, he revealed none of his emotions, and it sent my buzzing nerves into a tailspin.

Two armed soldiers flanked the door, with a third standing at the HP's side.

He hadn't noticed me yet. Not that I was anything special to him, other than the girl who'd turned him down. I didn't mean to, but I deepened my study of him. He exhibited complete control, keeping his chin up and his brand on full display. His shoulders remained squared, his arms anchored behind his back, and his legs braced apart. A plain white T-shirt, camouflage pants, and combat boots hugged his muscular frame. How was he so scary *and* so attractive?

As if he sensed my scrutiny—or had clocked it from moment one—he slid his gaze to mine. *Zing.* A frisson of awareness pierced me, and my breath hitched. My pulse sped into an erratic dance.

Nerves. Only nerves.

We stared at each other for an eternity, wild thoughts tumbling through my mind. *What's happening? Why won't he look away? Why won't I?*

Ultimately, he narrowed his lids and snapped, "Assistant." An obvious summons. But still he didn't look away from me.

Mykal puffed with irritation and muttered, "He's already forgotten my name, guaranteed." Off she raced, momentarily blocking the HP from my view and ending the staring contest.

Oh, thank goodness!

He thrust a digital reader in my friend's direction. "I expect everything on this list to be delivered on time to each specified location."

The color leached from her face as she scanned the screen. "I don't know what an RVM corrector is."

He showed no mercy. "Don't say 'I don't know.' Say 'I'll find out.'"

"I'll find out," she squeaked.

He wasn't satisfied. "If you are unable to do the job assigned to you, I'll give the opportunity to someone else."

She jumped to attention and saluted him. "I can do it, sir. Thank you, sir." Wide eyed, she mouthed "Help me" in my direction and darted from the gym, a girl on a mission.

For a moment—only a moment!—I longed to give chase. To escape. Instead, I lined up with the other soldiers.

A bell rang, signaling the start of class. The guard next to the HP stepped forward and placed his hand over his heart. A stance we mimicked. I knew what came next.

"I pledge allegiance to CURED," he called, leading us into the same oath I'd recited every day of school, "and the life for which it gives. One world, unified, with protection and respect for all."

The HP marched in front of us. "Yesterday, you were given an opportunity to learn about each other. Before I begin your evaluations, I will gift you with two facts about me and a statement as to why I feel I am qualified to command you." He gave us a moment to absorb his words. "One, I value truth more than I value your lives, and if you dare to lie to me, I will find out, I will punish you, and I'll make it public. Two, I believe excuses are merely lipstick on fear. Finally, I'm the only thing standing between you and certain death."

He did *not* cast a pointed glance at me when he said that. Because he stared. Hard.

"I'll meet with you one on one throughout class." He motioned to someone in back. "I'll start with you. Join me in the office and explain your actions at the vote. The rest of you, run laps."

"Sir, yes, sir," we proclaimed, not quite in sync.

The HP took a seat inside the small glass chamber, facing us, and the officer who'd led us in the pledge stomped a booted foot.

"You heard High Prince Dolion. Go!"

We jolted into action. Meanwhile, the targeted soldier trudged inside the office. Oh. I recognized him as the first lord to be eliminated in the game. Named Cash, maybe. He sank into the chair on the other side of the desk, his back to us.

The meeting lasted eleven minutes, and from what I was able to observe, it didn't go well for Cash. Every time I rounded the mat, I gained a perfect view of the HP's face. He reclined, almost at ease, his expression unchanging as his student talked. And talked. But his grip on a digipen continued to tighten until his knuckles bleached of color. He was big mad and only getting madder the more the lord spoke.

"Faster," our temporary instructor commanded.

I picked up the pace, beads of sweat wetting my skin. Though others tired quickly, I never lagged. Jogging was my thing. I could go for hours.

Finally, Cash exited the office, radiating anger. "Miller, you're up. Leave your pride at the door, or it'll be too brutal to bear."

We were going in order of elimination. Good to know. I should be good and soaked by the time my turn arrived.

As lords and ladies entered and emerged from the enclosure, a pattern evolved, and nervousness almost got the best of me. No matter the actions taken the day before, whether the soldier had used their pain darts, opted out of the competition, or given it their all, they shuffled away, head bowed in shame. Some even cried.

Soon, only the two finalists remained. My pulse picked up speed, as if I'd just run an extra ten miles at a record pace.

"Did the HP tell you to walk or run?" the officer demanded of the girl I thought might be Juniper.

"Run, sir," she wheezed, her ragged, panting breaths making her sound as if she were dying.

"Then why are you speed walking?"

On and on and on we jogged. Titus, the last of the nonfinalists, remained in the office longer than anyone else. Either he'd done something right or very, very wrong. When Mykal returned with a tray of food, the HP finally dismissed him. I ground my molars. The fact that he planned to snack irritated me greatly.

A scowling Titus approached me, keeping pace at my side. "You're next, Arden. Be prepared. The HP made me repeat my explanation over and over, and you can't win with him, so don't even try."

So the high prince wasn't taking a snack break? I plodded toward the office, passing a trayless Mykal along the way. We said nothing—this wasn't the time or place—but our gazes slipped over each other. Her stress mirrored mine.

In the open doorway, I paused, inhaling with purpose. Oops. Terrible idea. I couldn't see the morsels Mykal had delivered, but I smelled something sweet, and my mouth watered.

"You've already received permission to enter, Roosa." Irritation laced the HP's tone.

Ugh. Not a great start. "Yes, sir." I entered the enclosure, legs shaking. The closer I came to him, the more of *his* scent I detected. All that fairy dust and ambrosia, a very soft fragrance for a very rigid man. I couldn't inhale deep enough.

"Sit," he commanded. His facial brand appeared paler and tauter than usual.

I obeyed, trying not to ogle the array of fruits and vegetables plated on his desk. Oranges, strawberries, and some kind of green berry, but also more pastries with apples and figs. My nails sank into my knees. If he ate those culinary delights while I watched, I might scream.

He reclined in his seat, getting comfortable, exuding his usual confidence. "You aren't winded like the others, but you've exercised longer."

Stop staring at the food. "I enjoy running. A fact you would know if you'd read my file as you claimed." Eek. Not something I should have said aloud.

"Oh, I've read your file. It did indeed mention your propensity for logging five miles in the morning and five miles in the afternoon, sprinting to and from work."

I hated that he knew so much about me while I knew so little about him. "Did you read everyone's file with such attention to detail, or am I special?"

To my surprise, he pushed the tray my way and said, "Pick something."

Enjoy a treat, after snapping an inappropriate response at a commanding officer? This must be another test. But to submit or reject, that was the question. No one else had gotten fruit, and I might be resented if I gave in. Or deemed foolish for turning down sustenance.

What would Roman do?

Ugh! Awful question. Terrible. He wasn't a role model. Unless he should be?

Make a decision! "No, thank you." Probably the most difficult refusal uttered by anyone in history, and I wasn't being dramatic.

The HP canted his head, as if confused. "Tell me why."

"You're testing me." An honest answer for someone who claimed to revere the truth.

For a split second, a mix of disappointment and irritation glittered in his irises, and I thought, wondered . . . no. Impossible. No way he'd ordered the food just for me. Or waited for it to arrive before calling me into his office, all to give me a taste of what I'd sought yesterday. What a silly notion. Not just impossible, but beyond unlikely.

Revealing nothing else, he tsk-tsked. "You are failing left and right, Miss Roosa."

Miss, not *lady*. "How am I failing?" I demanded, then remembered my place and withered. "Please explain, sir."

"Absolutes are unbecoming on the lips of novices."

"I don't understand."

"Then you have more to learn than I realized." He tapped his fingers against the desktop, the muscles in his forearm flexing, and oh, I didn't like that I noticed. "Why didn't you use your darts, the sole weapon at your disposal? It would've helped you win a title you clearly craved."

We were jumping into the fire now. I pled my case. "A dishonorable victory isn't a victory. I gave my word, and I kept it, winning everyone's trust." Maybe. Hopefully.

"So you disregarded my command to fight for yourself first in order to curry the favor of your teammates."

"Not even a little. As you've informed us, they will one day become true teammates. Their lives might end up in my hands. If they cannot trust me, I cannot help them and they cannot help me." I huffed. "Did you accuse the others of endangering people they will eventually protect?"

"I did, yes."

Damned if we had and damned if we hadn't. "Both choices can't be wrong. Sir. High Prince." I pushed the title through clenched teeth.

"Motive is the beating heart of every action," he said, and I wasn't sure if it was an explanation or a rebuke. Probably both. "Do you think you made the correct decision?"

I struggled to put together a cohesive thought. Maybe I should have fought for the title and crossed lines. "I'm not sure," I admitted, bowing my head. When I boiled my own motive down to the dregs, I discovered a clear winner, and it had nothing to do with the other soldiers. "My eyes were on the prize."

"You're not sure," he echoed, his flat baritone somehow sharper than a blade. "You don't even know yourself, Miss Rocsa. How then are you able to recognize a true prize?"

He'd called me *miss* again, as if he didn't see me as a soldier. Of course, I *wasn't* a soldier. But he was wrong about everything else; I did know myself. I just lacked confidence in myself. There was a difference.

Always in the back of my mind I wondered if I was making a terrible mistake. Even now, I wasn't certain I'd done anything right. In fact, I was more confused than ever.

Rather than defend my declaration, which could be a huge mistake—see!—I shifted in my seat and said, "You are my instructor. So, instruct me. Tell me what you would have done in my place?"

He didn't hesitate. "I *have* been in your place. Ten years ago, I stood in that same ring. Like you, I opted not to shoot. For me, it wasn't necessary. I invited every candidate to unload their darts into me. Having trained for such a time, I knew I could handle the toxin's effects, no matter how high the dose. With a single act, I proved my strength and protected my team."

That was kind of, well, wow. Awe inspiring and wise, but also insane and kind of hot. But only kind of! He wasn't my type. Not that he was interested in me romantically. Unless he was. But he wasn't. "The difference is, you spent your life training for the military. I've only ever wanted to grow food and flowers."

"Perhaps, but you *are* in the military now." His features hardened. "Shall I tell you where you went wrong, or do you prefer to continue making excuses?"

His previous description clanged between my ears. Lipstick on fear. "Please do," I said, leaning toward him, eager to learn. I'd only been begging for an explanation since minute one, my craving for correction far surpassing my annoyance with him. Correction equaled progress.

"A strong leader takes command of a situation, but a smart one recognizes an opportunity." He paused, considered his next words. "Why do you think CURED offers the top soldier such a staggering prize?"

I hadn't considered it before, but I considered it now. "So everyone will work harder and do their best?"

"Yes. We've already established one of your greatest weaknesses is your indecision. If a team trusts your character but not your commands, will you be an effective leader?"

"No," I whispered.

"If you are not an effective leader, are you a candidate for top lady?"

"No," I repeated, hanging my head.

"But as a lady at the bottom of the barrel, you now have a chance to rise in the ranks rather than crumble under a weight you aren't yet strong enough to carry. You have room to defeat your fear, grow to understand your strengths, and gain the experience you lack. Do you acknowledge this?"

Suddenly, I didn't have to wonder if I'd made mistakes. I had. "Yes," I croaked. He'd pegged me with fiery dart after fiery dart of honesty.

"Fear doesn't forge good leaders, Miss Roosa. It destroys them." Drumming his fingers over the arm of his chair, he watched me, silent. Though he was in his late twenties, his harsh features contained a century's worth of tenacity. Caged aggression glittered in his eyes. "If you'll let me teach you, you will survive longer than originally anticipated. That's my guarantee."

"Sir, yes, sir. High Prince." I stared down at my wringing fingers. "Thank you, High Prince."

He sighed. "You are dismissed."

Feeling as if I'd gotten spanked but maybe, possibly, a little grateful for it, I stood. Clarity was a gift, and his severe but fair critique had scraped off several layers of confusion. Considering how behind the curve I was, I had a lot of work to do in the coming weeks.

"Be CURED, High Prince Dolion."

"Be CURED," he muttered, shifting his attention to the tray of snacks.

For a moment, I thought I sensed raw loneliness and soul-shattering fatigue in him. But that couldn't be right. He wasn't lonely or tired. He was . . . him.

"Is there something else?" he asked without glancing my way.

"No, sir." I hurried from the office and rejoined my teammates. Hopefully my day improved. I was due for an upgrade.

Chapter Eight

Be strong, courageous, and assured; your weapons
are mightier than your enemy's.

—The Book of Soal 1.5.31.6

Head high, I slipped into classroom 2, a sterile enclosure with gray
walls, a digital board, and twenty student desks. Roman, Lark, Jericho,
and Titus had arrived first and chosen their spots.

Roman waved me over as if we were the best of friends. Lark
watched me with an arched brow. Jericho blew me a kiss. Those
three were neighbors. On the other side of the room, Titus stared at
his desktop.

I shook my head at Roman and aimed for Titus. Having taken
the HP's critique to heart, I planned to learn more about each of my
teammates. Especially those I already admired. In the ring of pain, Titus
had stood his ground until the very end, never wavering in his resolve.

"Hi," I said, and he closed his eyes, pretending to sleep. "I know
you're awake."

"I just want to rest," he muttered, ending any hope for further
conversation.

I tried not to take the rejection to heart. Yes, I tried.

Other soldiers arrived, moaning as they sank into seats, sore and
exhausted thanks to two hours of nonstop exercise. From jogging in

place to jumping jacks, sit-ups, and squats to catching and throwing different objects. I admit, I wasn't without aches of my own. High Prince Dolion had made sure we utilized muscles I hadn't even known human beings possessed.

A bell sounded as Archduke Heta strode through the door. A lord in a blue uniform kept pace behind him, an overstuffed bag hanging from his shoulder.

"Welcome to Realms and Travel 101." The archduke stopped in front of the desk, and Titus cracked open his eyes. "Or, as formers students have called it, 'Fears and Tears.' I suggest you pay close attention. When you know the world around you and its rules, you don't have to be the biggest and the strongest to thrive during a mission."

Like many others, I sat up straighter and gave the man my full attention.

"Let's jump right into the deep end, shall we? Theirland is a realm of perpetual darkness. A dimension within a dimension, just as Ourland is. When the invisible veil between the two disintegrated, the worlds fused and blended. At the time, Theirland was abandoned, its people extinct. What lived on was EOS, or what you know as 'the Madness.'"

EOS, the technical name I'd heard in passing on occasion. I had no idea what the letters stood for.

With a wave of the archduke's hand, the wall behind him turned into a full-size screen, lighting up. A long stretch of terrain appeared, showcasing an uninhabited nightscape similar to our own. From the looks of the buildings, many were an amalgamation of Ourland and Theirland construction, with carnival rides sprinkled throughout. Everything from roller coasters to poles with swinging carts.

Huge statues made of gold, marble, and crystals loomed in every direction, far more opulent than the ones in Ourland. They topped structures and lined streets, depicting a mishmash of humans and animals. I spotted no section of the Rock, however.

"As you can see," the archduke said, "the other world mimics our own. The problem is, many of our maddened found their way into

Theirland, making them more difficult to catch. They go without treatment, allowing the infection to reach a point of no return." He waved again, and a new image filled the screen, wringing a chorus of horrified gasps from the students. Me included. "They become mindless killers far more dangerous than those you've encountered here."

A massive number of infected congregated in the streets, each exemplifying the most advanced case of Madness I'd ever seen. They no longer appeared human. Their eyes had no irises or pupils, only lines of crimson branching through the whites. As rumors suggested, worms grew from their scalps and eyelids, with thinner strands wiggling from their ears and noses. A foamy white substance coated their mouths.

Revulsion and panic gripped me. Soon I would be forced to fight these . . . these . . . *creatures.*

Three of the maddened stepped from the screen to stand next to the archduke. A lady yelped. That lady was me. Several of us leaped to our feet, prepared to bolt.

"They are merely holograms," Archduke Heta admonished, fluttering his hand through a creature. "Sit."

Bile scorched my throat as the trio moved forward, prowling along the aisles, hissing at us. I eased back into my seat, knees quaking, and made myself as small as possible. Keeping my gaze on the instructor, I did my best to tune out the unwanted visitors.

"Once a host dies, the worms slough off and poison the soil and plants. Even burning the bodies causes problems, though it's our only option once a kill is made."

No wonder we struggled to grow enough food here and in Theirland.

Juniper raised her hand.

"There might be a time for questions later." The archduke continued on as Juniper slunk back into her seat. "There are two strains of the Madness, and they are at war. The holograms you see here are the Chrysaor, street name *feeders.* Believe it or not, they aid us in our fight against the worse strain, the Pegi, also known as *glowers*. Chrysaor eat Pegi."

A hologram swiped at me, and I screamed, jumping in my seat.

The archduke didn't miss a beat. "Glowers appear as human as we are. Mostly. In the dark, they radiate light." A video of everyday, average humans appeared on the screen. They smiled and chatted. "Don't allow their outer shell to fool you." He showed a series of images, showcasing symbols that blazed in each person's skin as sunlight faded. Circles with swirling lines inside. The same marks found on the Rock. "Glowers can hide among us. They exhibit supernatural strength derived from the Rock and prefer to massacre crowds rather than focus on a single victim, like the feeders." More slides. "Speaking of the Rock, we know it is otherworldly, just as the Madness is, and that it's more dangerous than we can fathom, but we don't know much else."

A hysteria-tinged laugh attempted to explode from me. Through some miracle, I strangled it.

"Prepare yourself. You will face both feeders and glowers in Theirland."

I couldn't breathe, and I really needed to breathe. But I also needed to not have a panic attack in this classroom.

The archduke continued to talk, but his voice grew muffled. Even the muffles proved too much, each comment launching a fresh wave of fright. I smashed my hands against my ears, but it didn't help. My blood heated, but my skin chilled.

As my vision constricted, I soared to my feet. I had to leave. Yes, yes. Leave. Just for a minute. Maybe forever.

Without asking for permission, I sprinted out the door. No one called for me or followed. I careened around a corner. I'd go somewhere. Anywhere else.

"Arden," a familiar voice bellowed in the empty hallway. Footsteps sounded, drawing closer and closer. A warm hand clasped my shoulder, stopping me.

Shiloh! The second his identity registered, I spun and threw my arms around him.

He hugged me tight, his presence a desperately needed soothing balm. "It's okay, it's okay," he said, petting my hair. "I've got you."

I clung to him. He was such an amazing guy. Protective. Fun. Strong. The more time I spent with him, the more I liked him. "How did you find me so fast?"

"I thought this might happen, so I hung close to help."

Panting, I pulled back. "Get me out of here. I can't stay. Can't do this."

"You withstood a pain dart." He clasped my biceps and gave me a light squeeze. "You can do anything."

No! Keep running. But the HP's warning drifted through my mind. *Fear destroys.* He wasn't wrong. And I'd lost enough. Besides, fear was now enemy one. There was nothing more foolish than doing what my enemy suggested.

"I can do anything," I echoed to Shiloh. What did learning more about the maddened hurt? If anything, it would help me. Truth equaled power, according to the ME.

As my breaths evened out, Shiloh smiled. "Don't worry. You aren't the first to bolt. We'll get you a glass of water, and you'll be as good as new."

Grateful, I nodded. We motored down the hall side by side, passing few others before we entered a small cell reminiscent of my own, with a single bed and a private kitchenette.

Upon his invitation, I sat at the foot of the mattress. "Is this your room?" Medical charts and graphs littered the walls.

"It is." He extended a cup of water and sat beside me. Expression serious, he grabbed a reader and typed.

I read the screen.

I overheard the HP and his father discussing you.

My brow furrowed. I could think of no reason good enough for the king, head of CURED's armed forces, to mention me by name. Heart thudding, I typed a message of my own.

What did they say?

His turn.

The king demanded to hear reasons the HP didn't force you to accept the assistant job. The HP claimed it was more important to learn how you responded to the consequences. I lost track of the conversation after that.

I didn't understand. My refusal shouldn't matter to someone of the king's exalted rank. I was a mere lady. The lowest of the low. Practically a civilian!

Before Shiloh responded, a medic poked his head into the room, saying, "Hey. Can I borrow—" He went quiet when he spotted me, arched a brow, and glanced between us. "Freak out over feeders?"

"And glowers," I muttered.

"Just getting her hydrated," Shiloh explained, only slightly guilty.

The guy smiled, all *sure, okay*. As soon as we were alone, my companion typed, Being recorded. Look for a message taped to the gurney in E2.

I nodded, dazed, and he urged me to drink. As I drained the glass, he cleared the screen. He set the reader and the empty cup aside and helped me to my feet. A thousand questions and comments brewed at the end of my tongue, but I pressed my lips together.

His gaze searched mine. He offered me the sweetest smile, as if to say *Everything will be all right.*

I nodded again, and smiled in turn, because I couldn't not. He made everything better.

With his hand on the small of my back, he shepherded me into the hall. I trembled the entire walk to class, but I didn't flee. That was progress.

At the door, I groaned. "This is going to suck."

"Just hold your head high and walk in as if nothing happened," Shiloh advised.

His words rang in my ears as I strode inside and glided straight to my desk. Archduke Heta didn't pause his lesson. Even though multiple classmates glanced my way, no one spoke out against me.

"—unsure of the chemicals used to disintegrate the veil between dimensions," he was saying. "Most of our history was lost when much of the population became infected with the Madness. Only after the birth of CURED did peace and sanity return."

His instruction faded to the recesses of my mind, thoughts of the Dolions' conversation overtaking me. Why did they care if I acted as the HP's assistant? It made no sense.

I'm not sure how much time passed before an automated voice announced the end of class. Soldiers jumped to their feet, relieved.

"Tomorrow, you won't stand until you're dismissed," the archduke commanded. Everyone stilled, no one daring to move. Tension thickened the air, but he offered no other rebuke. "Grab a reader on your way out. They're preloaded with the textbooks you'll need for each class. Dismissed."

Relief resurged, spurring a flurry of action.

"You okay?" Juniper approached me with a concerned expression.

"I let terror beat me for a bit," I replied, popping up. "Happy to say I won in the final round."

"Yeah, but did your opponent die or crawl away to return another day?" she teased.

I winced, and she laughed.

"If only we could do a murder pact. I kill your fears, and you kill mine." She winked and hurried on to catch up with someone else.

I snatched a reader from the desk and tried to follow the girls out, but the archduke called, "Miss Roosa. A word."

Swallowing a groan, I backtracked.

He looked me over before turning away, busy with a reader of his own. "If you ever leave my class without permission again, you'll be kicked from the entire program. Do you understand?"

"Yes," I croaked.

"Then you may go."

I hurried off, aware I had less than ten minutes to reach next period. To my amazement, Roman waited for me in the hall. He slung his arm around my shoulders, a surprisingly affectionate gesture, and led me forward.

"Feeders and glowers are terrifying at first," he said, "but you'll learn to see past your fear, I promise. If anyone can ready you for combat, it's a Dolion. And me! Trust the process, Ardie. You'll get through this and be better for it."

I nodded, appreciating his concern. He was turning out to be a good leader already. Strong and courageous, sometimes playful, but tough when needed. Complicated but also straightforward. "Thank you."

"Anytime. By the way, good thinking, buddying up with Titus. He needs a handler, I can tell."

"That's not—" Oh, never mind.

Roman gave me an encouraging squeeze before hustling to Lark, who had slowed for him.

Imagine. Me, ready for combat. An idea seemingly as impossible as King Tagin Dolion caring what I did or didn't do.

Pensive, I followed a group to room 6, where Duchess Echo Mimidae was dismantling a metal whip thing. No desk for her. She stood behind a counter scattered with weapons. Guns big and small, blades smooth and rigid, and fancy gadgets I'd prefer to never touch.

Clutching the reader to my chest, I picked a seat in back. Perfect timing. The now-familiar bell spilled from the PA, announcing the start of class.

Time to discover what other horrors the day had in store.

"Hello, class," the duchess said, offering us a genuine smile, with no hint of her scowl. "I hope you're ready to learn. If you want to keep all your fingers, pay attention when I speak. And take notes. I'll be throwing a lot at you." She laughed as if she'd told a joke. "Not literally. Not yet anyway."

Most of the soldiers laughed with her. I tried not to choke on my tongue as I readied the digital reader I'd gotten from the archduke.

She continued. "The weapons you carry can mean the difference between life and death. While some work well in Ourland, others work better in Theirland."

Another reason to pay attention to Archduke Heta's lessons.

"We'll be practicing with pyre-guns, netters, semiautomatics, daggers, swords, triwhips, pritis cannons, throwing stars, and spears." She held up an example whenever she listed a new weapon. "If you ever get the chance, observe Archduke Heta with a spear. He's a master."

Each apparatus looked more dangerous and deadly than the last, and my stomach twisted.

"Your weapons are your best offense and first line of defense. And there will be many times you need to defend." She paused to scan us, dead serious. "First principal of warfare with the maddened. They attack on only two occasions. When you're ready, and when you're not."

CHAPTER NINE

Words spoken are planted in the garden of your
heart to feed your life; choose wisely.

—*The Book of Soal* 1.20.18.21

Can't process . . .

Too many weapons, facts, safety features, and warnings jumbled together in my brain. Oh, the warnings. Do this, and you'll fry your internal organs. Do that, and you'll only have the strength to curl into the fetal position and sob. Forget this or that, and you'll ravage such and such.

On the walk to lunch, I felt as if I were drowning in a sea of information. Most of my classmates were already in the commons, congregated in the cozy, oversize living room with clusters of couches, matching recliners, and a pair of coffee tables. The small section designated for dining showcased a wall of vending machines, offering snacks far better than the meal bars. There was no sign of yesterday's circle of pain.

"Did you guys read this?" Juniper stood near the "sandwich" machine, pointing to a sign above the ID pad. "We're charged three trills or a two-hour shift of labor."

Whoa. Three trills was an exorbitant amount for a seven-course dinner, much less a small sandwich. And. Hmm. The amount of labor wasn't even close to being worth three trills. Why—oooh. A test. Everything was. I bet the moral of this one was, don't choose today's stomach over tomorrow's future.

Smart. With my eye on the prize and only four trills in my account, with no new allotment due, the sandwiches weren't even a temptation for me.

"Two hours of extra work is nothing when you'll pay anything. I'm starved." Jericho shoved his way over, pressed his palm against the pad, then pushed a few buttons. The machine spit out the promised sandwich.

"You'll regret that," Titus muttered.

"I have money. I regret nothing." The second Jericho possessed the package, he tore into it, freeing the food and chomping a bite. His eyes closed as he chewed. After he swallowed, he released a moan, as if he'd never tasted anything sweeter, and held out the food to Titus. "You want a bite? Too bad." He shoved what remained into his mouth and chewed too much at once, uncaring as crumbs tumbled out.

A few others rushed over to purchase a sandwich of their own. I admit, envy pricked me. Maybe I experienced a little temptation. But my determination didn't waver. I had a competition to win. Pleased with my restraint, I nabbed a free meal bar and a cup of hy-water. The slightly bitter liquid provided the minerals and electrolytes the bar lacked.

Around me, conversations and laughter rose and ebbed. Roman sat at the center of it all, holding court. Lark perched at his side. A group of six stood off to the side, appearing as shell shocked as I felt. Like me, these soldiers hadn't forgotten our day was only half over. Although, granted, I looked forward to our next class. Learning self-defense aided my mission.

In a corner alone, Titus finished off a meal bar. Out of everyone, he was the one I wished to get to know most. But as I approached him, he stiffened and stalked off.

Okay then. I tried not to let the obvious denunciation sting. Had I done something to offend him?

As I ate, I talked myself into and out of trying to converse with someone else. A desire to do as the HP suggested and get to know my teammates prevailed. Before I could select a second soldier, a sweating Mykal rushed into the commons. My relief at seeing her was short lived.

Spotting me, she hurried over, clasped my wrist and tugged me toward the door. "You've been summoned by His Lord High and Mighty. Don't know why. Run to gym C as if your feet are on fire. Okay, bye!" She let go and shot off with the speed of a bullet.

Dread curdled in my stomach. I didn't have to wonder what had sparked this. The HP had learned of my faux pas in Realms and Travel. I trudged to the gym, hoping against hope I'd bump into Shiloh, my sole source of comfort. Alas, he never appeared.

Worked into a lather but fighting to hide it, I entered the gym. My heart stuttered as soon as I spotted the high prince. He sat on a bench, facing a bank of lockers, his back to me. He'd changed into a tight T-shirt that hugged his broad shoulders and huge biceps. A pair of shorts revealed well-defined legs with a light dusting of hair.

He didn't glance my way but called, "Lady Pink. Come here."

The fact that he'd known of my arrival without turning . . . Trying not to wilt, I marched over and stopped behind him. At least he hadn't referred to me as "miss."

He pointed to the space in front of him. I swallowed a groan and dragged my feet to the commanded spot, suddenly hemmed in by the cold metal lockers and the hot, frightening instructor.

He was in the process of wrapping tape around his knuckles. Beads of sweat dripped from his temples. "You ran out of the archduke's class." My great leader didn't bother to meet my gaze, just continued to prepare for battle. "Convince me you had a good reason to do something so ill advised."

Knew it! "I verged on having a panic attack, si—High Prince."

He worked his jaw. "*Sir* is fine. Continue with your explanation. Because I know you're not foolish enough to think a panic attack makes what you did okay."

Why was *sir* fine now but not before? "No. Yes. I—"

My speech faltered when he stood, suddenly towering over me. He reached over my shoulder for a towel. For a moment, his breath fanned my face. His chest nearly brushed mine. I refused to back up, thereby giving in to a surge of intimidation. Yes, yes, intimidation and *nothing else*. The fact that his incredible scent sent my pulse into overdrive meant nothing.

"Let's be clear. You're telling me meeting the medic in the hallway had nothing to do with it," he said, dabbing his face with the cloth.

I narrowed my eyes. Was I being surveilled? "He was in the area, saw me, and helped. Nothing more."

The HP met my gaze at last, and I almost wished he hadn't. Cold fury stared back at me. "When you exited the classroom without permission, you disrespected Archduke Heta and disrupted his lecture. Both are punishable offenses. As your superior, I'm responsible for teaching you the error of your ways."

"I've learned, I promise. Sir. But if I'd sought permission, I would've disrupted his lecture far more. By leaving, I allowed him to continue without interference."

"Clearly, you've learned nothing. What are excuses, Miss Roosa?"

My lips pursed. Back to *miss*. "Lipstick on fear, High Prince Dolion."

He crossed his arms over his pecs. "Stake your life on your defense of your actions, and I'll inform Archduke Heta no further punishment is required. But I'll also insist you prove your case."

Dang him. He'd backed me into a corner. "What's my punishment?" I grumbled.

"I'll put it in terms you're sure to understand. To produce good fruit, you must be pruned. Consider me the wielder of the gardening shears. Report to my office after drills."

He didn't elaborate, and I didn't push for more details, which would possibly earn a second punishment. But, um, how did he plan on pruning me? Wondering for the rest of the day was going to suck on every level.

"Sir, if I may—"

"You may not. I'll hear my thanks now."

He couldn't be serious. But his hard stare said he was. "Thank you, sir," I gritted out.

"The lighter your sentence, the less honor I pay a man I admire. I'm furious with myself for not locking you in solitary with a hologram. Don't make it worse for either of us."

Put like that . . . "Thank you, sir. Truly."

He held my gaze, silent, and something strange arced through me. Something I couldn't name. Because I didn't want to.

"I should probably, um . . ." I backed up.

"Go." He motioned with his head. "Join the others."

Eager to leave his vicinity, I shuffled over to the mat. The rest of the team had arrived during our consultation. Most gazed at me with curiosity, but only Roman approached.

"You get reamed for what happened in Heta's class?" he asked, ruffling my hair.

"Thoroughly." My nose crinkled as I batted his hand away.

He laughed. "Next time stay put, even if you're screaming. Trust that your instructor will help you."

Yeah, okay, that made sense. "Thank you for the tip. It does help."

"Everything I say does."

I rolled my eyes at him and got another laugh. Two medics strode into the room. Shiloh! Without thought, I waved and smiled at him. His companion snickered and elbowed him in the stomach. Oops. Maybe I shouldn't publicly broadcast our acquaintance. There might be a rule against medics and gentry mixing. But Shiloh waved and smiled in return, unabashed.

"Take your places," the HP commanded, stalking to the mat's center. The bell rang.

Only Roman knew what *take your places* meant, and we followed his lead, branching out to surround our instructor from the edges.

The high prince lifted his face, projecting all kinds of annoyance. "First things first. Cash lied during his evaluation. Now everyone else is being rewarded for telling the truth with a valuable lesson. I never make empty threats."

Our collective attention zoomed to Cash, who hung his head in shame.

"He will remain silent for two weeks," the HP added, not quite scowling but close. "If he speaks, even once, he'll wear a muzzle. One way or another, he will comprehend the importance of having a voice and using it well, or he will suffer."

My dread returned, doubled. Seriously, what did the high prince have in store for my pruning?

"Moving on." His expression remained unchanged. "This is self-defense. You may have taken lessons before, but I'd advise you to forget everything you think you know. The maddened of Theirland aren't like those you've encountered in Ourland."

Thanks to Archduke Heta, I knew that quite well.

"You'll have weapons, yes. And we'll train with them. The problem is, there will be times your weapons fail, or you run out of ammo and the enemy keeps coming. That is why we'll start with the basics. Strengths and weaknesses."

Wonderful. A new nightmare unlocked.

"Feeders are more powerful in the dark. The lack of daylight in Theirland makes an already complicated situation worse, especially while you're dealing with reversal of vision metamorphopsia. RVM is a one-hundred-and-eighty-degree vertical inversion of your visual field. In other words, everything is upside down." His gaze cut to me. "There's no need to panic. The problem is rectified with special lenses."

Miracle of miracles, he'd just uttered a reassurance without bursting into flames.

He waved at someone behind us. "These lenses correct RVM and allow you to see feeders in the dark whenever they enter a five-foot radius."

I looked over my shoulder and spotted Mykal lugging a large box through the door. Strain etched every inch of her. The urge to rush over and help barraged me, but I didn't dare "disrespect" my instructor or disrupt his class. Lesson learned.

She stopped near the HP, dropped her burden, and dug inside it, withdrawing a curved inch-thick metal band she then handed over. He secured the band around his forehead, just over his brows, and danced his fingers over one side. A green light flashed, and a clear screen unfolded over his eyes and molded itself into a type of half mask.

Still trying to catch her breath, Mykal passed a band to everyone else.

"Thank you," I whispered, and she whimpered.

"To activate your lens, tap the button on your right with four swift strikes," the high prince said. "Today, you'll simply wear it while learning basic techniques for avoiding and causing injury to yourself during a battle with feeders."

I donned the device and tapped the sides as told, and the screen lowered and reshaped. Very cool.

For the next hour, the HP demonstrated positions, gestures, tips, and tricks. I admit, I struggled to concentrate. His muscles. They rippled. Worse, he watched us as we copied his motions, offering critiques whenever necessary. With Juniper and me, it was often necessary.

"Do you enjoy harming yourself?" he asked as I beat at the air.

I'm not annoyed, I'm not annoyed. "I do not."

He stalked over and righted the angle of my thumb, then guided my fist to his chest, mimicking a punch. After returning my thumb to its original position, he guided my fist to his chest a second time. "Feel the difference."

"Oh! I really do." But only after my brain switched back on. The warmth of his touch . . . the roughness of his calluses . . . *help me.* "My error puts too much pressure on my thumb."

"Correct. Now let's address the bigger problem. Fear is talking to you, and you're coddling it rather than treating it like the enemy it is. Talk back. Tell it to leave, then hit me."

What? "No!" This was a test. How did one talk to fear, anyway? "Even I know better than to strike a military officer."

"But you haven't yet learned to obey one, I see," he quipped. "Hit me."

"No," I snapped.

He slitted his eyes. "I suggest you rethink your stance, Lady Pink."

Fine! If he insisted on insisting, he left me with no choice. "I'll do it. I'll smack you."

"In the face."

That was even worse! I licked my lips and shifted from boot to boot. "I'll do it. I'll smack you. In the face. With my fist."

"Now," he barked.

Yelping, I squeaked, "Leave, fear?" Then I did it. I punched him. Kind of. Maybe *tapped his cheek* was a better description. Or I would've tapped his cheek if he hadn't blocked me.

He swiped his tongue over straight white teeth. "Don't ask a ridiculous question. Make a bold statement. Fear doesn't listen if you don't mean it. So mean it and hit me. Hard."

"You're acting as if fear is alive." I tossed up my arms. "A living thing."

"Isn't it? It speaks to you, and you listen. It leads, and you follow. It commands, and you obey."

Dang him. "Why would it be afraid of me and obey *my* command?"

"Because it's fear. It can only give of itself, and it always backs down in the face of a stronger opponent. Hit me," he repeated.

I didn't want to, but I also did want to, but I didn't, but I did. "Leave, fear." Punch. I missed the HP completely.

"Lady Pink," he growled.

"Leave, fear." Swing.

Block. "Again."

"Leave, fear." Okay, yeah, I'd used a firmer tone and produced a surer swing that time. Not terrible. I swung with more force.

He blocked. "Maybe I wasn't clear. Hit me hard enough to break through the mental barrier that's telling you how weak and incapable you are."

Anger stirred my pot of frustration. "Leave, fear." I swung, putting a little thrust behind the blow.

He blocked once more but said, "Better. Again."

"Leave, fear." Swing.

Block. "Harder. Again."

A kernel of strength dropped into my heart, swiftly taking root and choking out trepidation. I could do this. "Leave, fear." Punch.

He blocked, but not quite as easily. "Don't be afraid to hurt me."

Too far! "Of course I'm afraid of hurting you!" I tossed my arms up.

He rolled his eyes. "Your fright insults me. Do you think I'm capable of protecting myself from a novice, Lady Pink?"

"That's not . . . I don't think . . ." Gah! I hated that he always made such good points. "I could hurt you accidentally."

"Another insult." He bristled, as if gearing for a real fight. "You will punch me in the face as hard as you can. I won't block. If you draw blood, I'll reward you with apples and figs."

Excuse me? I must've misunderstood him. "You cannot be bribing me to injure you."

"I am. Until you accept the power you posses—"

Punch. As his head whipped to the side, pain exploded through my knuckles. "Ow!" I shook my throbbing hand. As the discomfort faded, horror took its place, deluging me.

I forgot everything but my foolishness. I'd punched him. Me. Even though he'd commanded me to do it, he was going to punish me. He had to. I'd failed the test. Surely. Lowly lords and ladies did not physically abuse their leaders for any reason, ever.

He straightened, wiping a drop of blood from the corner of his mouth. A smile curved his lips, there and gone. "Good job, Lady Roosa."

"Sir, I wish to apol—you're kidding me." A ball of light cast golden beams into the shadowy corners of my heart. He'd called me *lady* without *Pink*! Because I'd done something correctly and aced a test. Bonus: The strike itself hadn't been nearly as awful as I'd imagined.

Grinning, I pumped my fist high in the air. "That's right I did a good job. Chew on that, Sir Grumpus!"

When he tilted his head and blinked at me, I realized what I'd just said and sank into myself. Something must be wrong with me.

"My apologies, High Prince Dolion. I didn't mean to refer to you as—I shouldn't have—"

"Out in the field, feeders will surround you." His voice was low, almost affectionate. "That's an unavoidable fact. At some point, you'll need to deliver a quick pop to an opponent's face to buy yourself precious seconds and escape an untenable situation. When feeders are jolted, they become confused. Confused, they turn on each other." He lifted my hand and brushed his thumb over my knuckles. I'd already noticed his warmth and calluses, but there was something different about this touch. Something infinitely sweeter. "You landed your blow, and you didn't break a bone. Now you know you can do it when it counts."

Goose bumps spread over me. Okay, I needed to stop reacting to contact with him. It wasn't appropriate or welcome. I should stop noticing the sexiness of his appearance too.

"Thank you, sir." Determined, I pulled from his grip.

He lifted his lashes, his gaze holding mine. Caged aggression radiated from him. "Do you have the confidence to strike me again?"

I didn't let myself think, just threw another punch. No holding back. "Leave, fear."

This time, he captured my wrist, and he flashed another quick grin. "That was your best yet."

A megawatt smile bloomed, and there was no erasing it. "Thank you, sir."

"I may make a soldier out of you yet, Roosa." He walked off to help another lady, calling, "Medic, check her out."

I turned my grin to Shiloh, who hurried to my side. "Did you see me?"

"I did. You did good." Appearing amused, he cleaned and bandaged small cuts I hadn't realized I'd sustained. From the HP's teeth, no doubt. As quietly as possible, Shiloh said, "We both have Thursday off."

"Only two days from now," I replied just as quietly. Thank goodness! This was my first full day of academy life, and already I required a break to recharge.

He wrapped my knuckles with tape. "Will you go on another date with me?"

Ribbons of pleasure unfurled. No need to consider my response. "Yes." I liked this boy and the comfort he provided. He didn't make me nervous, as the HP did. "I would love to."

"Good. Meet me at transport at six. In the morning," he clarified.

Transport? Whatever that was, I'd find out. We shared a soft look before he returned to his post. At the end of class, I saluted the HP. He traced his fingertip over the scab forming on his bottom lip, rousing another smile in me which roused an answering smile from him. Just a flash, there and gone, but enough to thrill me.

Spirits high, I waved to Shiloh on my way out, then removed, folded, and pocketed my RVM band as I followed my teammates to first aid, where we endured a fifty-minute lecture from Dr. Korey about possible injuries amid combat. I admit, my good mood fizzled fast.

Afterward, I attended drills. The HP sent a knight to teach in his place. That soldier taught us proper battle formations and had us perform countless trust exercises while we wore our lenses. For a brief period, I experienced the awfulness of RVM and the horror of seeing a feeder spotlighted in the dark, when the creatures became the center of your world.

"The more you practice, the faster your eyes will adjust," the soldier called at the end of class.

Everyone else headed to dinner, but I set off to search for High Prince Dolion's office. Dread settled on my shoulders. The time had come to receive my punishment.

CHAPTER TEN

If you heed correction, you will always return to the
right path.

—*The Book of Soal* 2.19.12.7

"There you are!" Mykal flew down the hall, an arrow aimed straight at me. Since I'd last seen her, her strain had only increased.

"I want to hear all about your first day," I said, giving her a hug.

"For starters, I think I made a terrible mistake. All I do is fetch, fetch, fetch. Though I did get to set up a date between our illustrious HP and Countess Soti's oldest daughter." She exaggerated a pinched expression, making me laugh, even as my brain performed a series of somersaults.

High Prince Dolion was seeing the daughter of the woman responsible for administrating CURED's finances. Interesting. Not the least bit disappointing. Not that his romantic life was any of my business.

"I'm supposed to escort you to His Royal Highness as quickly as possible," she told me. "My orders were explicit. Every minute you're not there, we're late."

Ugh. "He's eager to shear."

"I don't know what that means. But for whatever it's worth, I don't think you'll be flogged, imprisoned or kicked out." Guided by a map provided by a new wristband, she rushed me through hallways, up staircases and elevators, and through common areas filled with knights who'd graduated to different levels within the academy. She used the chip in her palm to key us past locked doors and bypass checkpoints.

After we cleared a heavily armed door, the building's interior changed from prison chic to total fantasyland. Elaborately carved tables and chairs occupied a lobby, set up strategically to allow easy viewing of an array of statues covered in gemstones. Unlike the statues in my province, these had no human parts, only creatures of myth. Dragons, winged horses and monsters of mysterious origins.

Countless pritis beamed from the ceiling, illuminating crystals that shimmered from within. Wow. I'd never seen the stones up close or so many in one place. Pretty!

"Spectacular, isn't it?" she asked.

We entered a large chamber, the thick, heavy door closing behind us, and—I gasped. A piece of the Rock. It divided the otherwise empty room. I lurched back to press against the wall.

"No, no." Mykal clasped my hand and yanked me onward. "It's only a replica used for study. There's no danger."

"But—"

"There's no faster way to reach the HP."

Okay. All right. Boiling tension downgraded to a low simmer, allowing movement from my limbs. Still. I kept my eyes averted until we exited into a wide hallway.

Mykal released me as soon as we reached a red door. She knocked twice before entering without awaiting a response. I hadn't yet screwed my head on tight enough when I noticed the HP. He stood in front of his desk, leaning against the edge, speaking with his father.

I skidded to an abrupt halt. King Tagin Dolion, leader of the armed forces. The be-all and end-all, whose word was law. Here. In person. His presence added weight to the air, as if the force of gravity had intensified.

Breath sawed between my lips. "Leave, fear," I whispered for my ears alone.

Maybe they heard. The pair looked my way, but neither displayed a reaction. Was that good? Bad?

Mykal saluted, and I followed suit.

"Wait in the hall, Miss Ellison," the HP said, pushing the command through his scabbed lips. A scab I'd given him. I gulped.

Off she trucked. Should I leave too?

The king nodded a greeting at me. "It's an honor to meet you, Lady Roosa."

My eyes widened. "It is? I mean, thank you. Sir."

He chuckled. "It is indeed. My wife read your paper on the Soil and Seed Anomaly. It impressed her so much, we asked Cyrus to watch over you." He patted the high prince's shoulder. "I hope you don't mind."

Excitement burned my trepidation to ash. The HP's mother had read my paper. And liked it! There was no reason for Shiloh to investigate what he'd overheard. This explained so many things. Why the HP and the king had focused on me upon my arrival. Why the HP first offered me the job as his assistant. Even why he might, hopefully, spare me from a punishment he felt I deserved.

Wait. I hadn't responded out loud. I should speak. "I don't mind at all," I burst out. My cheeks heated as my exuberance registered. "I'm the one who's honored, sir." This man's dedicated guidance had prevented many other Great Regrets from occurring.

The high prince was right. A leader could make or break a team.

"I didn't know your mother is a grower," I told him. The fact that his parents were married blew my mind. With an astronomical marriage tax, few couples took the plunge. My parents certainly hadn't. Plus, most people were afraid of creating permanent ties in case either party broke with the Madness.

"Ah. You assume his wife is my mother," was his response as he straightened, his posture as rigid as the rest of him.

Oops. I had. The heat in my cheeks reached the blistering point. At least he'd sounded amused by my blunder.

Before I could stumble out an apology, the king moved the conversation along, saying, "I'll leave you to your meeting. Be CURED, Lady Roosa."

"Be CURED, King Dolion."

He gave his son's shoulder another pat before striding from the room. The door shut behind him, but gravity didn't right itself.

Rather than refocus on the sole other occupant, I occupied myself with a study of his spacious office. It was as luxurious as the rest of the palace portion of the building. The walls, though, were gold, not crystal. A conference table with legs carved to resemble those of a lion complemented four chairs reminiscent of the animal's head. But there were no personal items anywhere. No doodads on the desk. No portraits, photos, or holograms providing a peek into the HP's favorite people, places, or things. No plants.

"You need flowers," I stated before I could think better of it. "And plants. Lots of plants."

"Agreed."

"If you have access to soil and seed, I'm happy to grow them for you." I made the offer and experienced instant speaker's remorse. I did not need to be shut inside his office with him on the daily.

"I called you here for a reason, Bubble Gum." He acted as if I hadn't spoken, a specialty of all higher-ups, and I didn't know whether I should be relieved or offended. "Let's get to it."

Right. I inwardly cringed. "Go ahead. I'm ready to do my penance."

The corners of his mouth twitched, and the sight confused me. "Your prize is there." He pointed to a platter of desserts on the table, near a large jug with the word *Lemonade* scripted on a label.

So lemonade was a drink! And oh, my mouth watered. But, um, did the HP know about the code word I shared with Shiloh?

"Why give me a prize and not—oooh!" Because I'd smacked him in the face. Giddy, I bobbed up and down on my heels. "What about my punishment? Aren't I supposed to shed fear?"

"The loss of free time is the punishment, not the shedding of fear. That is a mercy on my part and something you should value." He strode past me to lift the plate of desserts, each seeming to feature apples and figs. "Which one will you sample first?"

Nibbling on my bottom lip, I examined the offerings with a sharper eye. "This one, please." Yes, I slurred my words. No, I didn't care.

I plucked the creation from obscurity. Anticipation spiked into enthusiasm as I popped the little morsel into my mouth. Oh, my goodness. The sweetness! Juice ran over my taste buds, and I moaned. "I knew I'd love these." Live without them? Never again.

"They have become a favorite of mine as well," the HP said, his voice low and thick. "A prize worthy of a throbbing lip."

Tingles slipped over my spine, and I jerked my gaze to him. Surely he hadn't meant to sound so *carnal*. Or maybe he had. Daaaang. He looked carnal, too, his eyes hooded.

I swallowed and dabbed my tongue to the corners of my mouth.

He pulled his gaze from me, set the plate on the table, and busied himself with a stack of papers. I hurried to refocus as well, choosing a second pastry. My eyelids slid shut as new flavors exploded on my tongue. I could do nothing but savor the honey-dipped heaven.

When I remembered where I was, why I was there, and who I was with, I inwardly cringed. Oops. Should I, perhaps, attempt to converse while I stuffed my face?

No need. He took over. "Use the supplies to list your fears. All of them," he commanded. "I don't care if the list is a thousand pages long, leave nothing out." He was back to using his firmest tone. "Do not leave this office until you finish." He strode off without another word.

Oookay. He definitely hadn't flirted with me earlier, even for a millisecond. Anyway. The urge to snoop around proved strong, but I didn't give in. For my "punishment," I must only list my fears? What, did he think the length would humiliate me?

Joke's on you, HP.

Whistling under my breath, I poured myself some lemonade and got comfortable at the table. The first sip of the yellow liquid proved as world changing as the sweet treats. Tart yet sugary and my new favorite beverage. I drained the rest and nearly overflowed my cup with my next pour. In between guzzling, I finished off the remaining treats, loving every bite but the last. I admit, I pouted.

I heaved a sigh, snatched up a pen and a piece of paper and scribbled a single word. There. Done with my assignment.

After securing the page to the high prince's desk, I strode into the hall, surprised to find Mykal just outside the door, barring Dr. Korey's entrance.

"—did he go?" the doctor was saying, irritation dripping from every syllable.

"He didn't tell me. Nor did he mention when he planned to return," Mykal responded, unafraid to go toe to toe with the other woman. Good for her!

Dr. Korey noticed me and slitted her eyes. "Why are you in High Prince Dolion's office without supervision? That isn't allowed."

"I was only doing what I was told," I said, high on apples, figs, and lemonade.

Mykal nodded her support. "The next time I see the HP, I can let him know you disapproved of his orders to Lady Roosa and that you'd like to speak with him."

"No, I'll find him on my own." The doctor gave me a final glare before stomping away.

"You realize she has a crush on the high prince and now hates you for getting special treatment, yes?" Mykal deadpanned.

"She hates everyone, I think."

"Yeah. Accurate." My friend clutched my hand. "Tell me you're done. I'm cleared for rest and relaxation as soon as you are."

Oh, thank goodness. "Start relaxing, baby, because my assignment is completed."

"Life is worth living again!" Cheering, she threw her arms around me. As we hustled down the hall, she told me, "I have had *a day*. All I want to do is go to our room and teach you hand signals." She lowered her volume and leaned into me. "There's so much I wanna tell you but can't. Not out loud. Just know you won't believe half the things I've overheard and seen."

Oooh, I must find out! We made the journey to our room without incident. The only teammate we encountered was Jericho, who lounged inside the cell beside ours, tossing a ball at the ceiling. He was too absorbed in his task to notice us. The other soldiers must be in the commons, socializing. How they found the energy I might never know.

As Mykal regaled me with stories she wasn't afraid to voice, tales of fetching and carrying, and the snobbiness of the boss's maybe, maybe-not girlfriend, Nova Soti, she taught me signs for each letter in the alphabet, as well as two key signals I "must know." *Help me* and *kiss me*.

I snorted. "I'm not asking Shiloh to kiss me while he's on duty." But I was excited to tell him about the lemonade.

"Are you sure? Because I heard about your upcoming date. And I couldn't be happier for you." She hooked a lock of hair behind her ear. "He's an amazing guy."

Agreed. "So, tell me about *your* guy," I said, shining the spotlight on her. "Mr. Mystery."

Her expression turned dreamy. "He's absolutely, utterly perfect." She threw herself flat upon the mattress, giggling like a schoolgirl. "He's in the military too. A knight. Like you and Shiloh, we have Thursday off. I'll get to see him."

"How did you meet?"

"He lives in my building. But don't tell Shiloh. Or Roman. Or anyone!"

"Your secrets are safe with me." I meant that. I was a vault.

The automated voice sounded over the PA system, announcing the approach of curfew. Our conversation ended as teammates returned, filing into their rooms. Mykal yawned, spurring me to yawn as I trudged to my bed. We secured our shackles as the cell door closed, and she was snoring softly only seconds later.

The trials of the day caught up with me. From the magnitude of what I'd learned about the Madness to the enormity of the expectations assigned to me. Plus, my knuckles throbbed, thanks to my incredible bravery with the high prince. Hey, a girl had to take her victories where she could. But I couldn't sleep. I merely tossed and turned.

Again and again, my thoughts veered to the HP, three descriptions coming to mind: *enigmatic, unwavering,* and *smart.* Okay, so, a fourth word attempted to assert itself. *Sexy.* I disregarded it, considering it had no bearing on the situation.

How would he react to my "list" of fears? Predicting his responses wasn't in my wheelhouse. What if he regretted his leniency with me?

By the time the morning alarm went off, I'd worked myself into a lather. I lumbered to my feet with a series of groans. My eyes burned, and my muscles screamed in protest. But with Mykal as my cheerleader, I made it to the locker room, where I showered and dressed in clean fatigues.

In the gym, Shiloh waited at the side with another medic. He glared at the floor, angry. Oh, no. Had he gotten in trouble for aiding me yesterday?

Determined to find out, I moved toward him, only to halt when High Prince Dolion marched in. My nervous system kicked into hyperdrive at the sight of him. He hadn't shaved, and his clothes were torn and wrinkled.

"Line up," he snapped. Uh-oh. He was in a mood too.

Everyone rushed to obey. He stopped in front of the clear office, uncapped a marker, and wrote on the wall in big black letters, **TODAY WE ARE WORKING ON:**

I swiped my tongue over my lips. Beneath those words, he hung my note. *Everything.*

CHAPTER ELEVEN

There is only one battle, and it is between
good and evil.

—The Book of Soal 2.10.6.12

"Apparently *everything* includes death by exhaustion," Roman muttered as the entire team hobbled to our rooms. Others groaned in agreement, me among them.

Warm-up involved being stalked by hordes of feeder holograms. In self-defense class, we were pitted against machines that projected holograms of ourselves and left battered. Drills included practicing what we'd learned yesterday in bouts of hand-to-hand combat. Afterward, the HP appropriated everyone's free time, not just mine, and forced us to run obstacle courses outside while knights acted as feeders, working to stop us. His version of immersion therapy, I guess.

I slogged into my cell and fell onto my mattress. Mykal was already asleep and chained.

Man, I missed my plants and the scent of earth. But I missed Mom and her encouragement more. She gave the world's best hugs and had the most infectious laughter. No doubt she was locked inside her apartment, in desperate need of rest but too busy worrying for me to get it. How I hated that. I wanted only to make life better for her, never worse.

The barred door shut, and I clasped my shackle shut around my wrist. All night, I drifted in and out of sleep, but I never managed to doze for more than an hour. When the morning alarm sounded, I wasn't ready.

"Guess what?" Mykal exclaimed, bounding over. She looked as bright as the sun. "It's Shiden Day! Or do you prefer *Ariloh*?"

"You're making this weird," I grumbled, shucking off my open chain and rising from bed.

"That's my specialty."

Hopefully, Shiloh was in a better mood today. I hadn't seen him after warm-up, when he'd seemed so upset.

I trudged to the locker room while Mykal skipped, pausing here and there to beckon me onward. "Hurry up, Ardie! We can't be late, or we'll get bumped from the train. No Bala City. No date. Did I tell you I'm meeting my boyfriend?"

Looked like the nickname was sticking.

Maybe it was the exhaustion. Or the stress of being at the academy. Either way, I didn't understand half of what she said. "Bala City?" I'd never even heard of it.

"A playland for soldiers. I've been once with Roman and his family."

A myriad of other questions bubbled to the surface, but I was too drained to engage in conversation. I zipped through a shower, then riffled through my locker and the few clothes I'd brought from home. Disappointment set in. I should've added a pretty dress to my travel bag. Just one! Even a pair of cute jeans. Because I'd packed so sparingly, my best option for the most anticipated date of my life was a blue tank top with matching running shorts. Basically a replica of the pink set I'd worn on day one, eliciting scorn from the HP.

"—second-in-command."

My ears twitched, catching Lark's voice.

"He doesn't get a day off," she told Juniper, who entered the locker room with her. "He's attending a meeting with all our instructors."

Poor Roman. Attending such meetings equaled torture. But also fortunate Roman. He had the greatest chance of becoming top lord. Not that I'd given up. I'd just shifted my focus. Improve first, then go for gold.

"Come on, come on." A bouncing Mykal dragged me through the building. She wore a frilly red dress, and she looked beautiful. "Have you ever been underground?"

"Never. And I never will." The infected most often broke in the dark, and those with full-blown Madness loved to congregate in underground tunnels.

"Okay, so, that's not true. Or it won't be true in roughly three seconds." She led me through a set of double doors and to the ledge of a staircase leading down. Far down. Into a pool of darkness.

Foreboding skittered over my spine. Nope. Not happening. I dug in my heels, then endeavored to retreat.

She grasped both my wrists to stop me. "It's perfectly safe, I promise. Armed guards are posted all around. I've made the trip multiple times to fetch stuff for His Majesty. Besides, if you refuse, you gotta stay here. No date."

Fine. Deep breath in, out. I refused to give in to fear, missing a day of fun I craved with every ounce of my being. "I-I'll do it. Because I'm brave," I said, forcing my feet to shuffle forward. One, two, three. "I mean it. I'm brave," I repeated, quickening my pace.

"So, so brave," Mykal praised, matching my stride.

Down we went, a musty odor saturating too-warm air. At the bottom was a platform illuminated with pritis light and overflowing with soldiers both in and out of uniform. Different conversations mingled together, echoing from rocky walls. Not bad. But how was I supposed to find Shiloh?

"What is this place?" I asked.

"A way station. Bala City is just outside the base. The trains go back and forth throughout the day."

Brakes squealed, a grate against my ears as a series of massive metal carts stopped beyond the platform. I came to a halt when the crowd parted before one cart in particular, revealing the opening of its doors. The HP stood alone in the center of the compartment. The sight of him sent my nerves into hyperdrive. Did he commute to work?

Mykal pulled me toward his section. "Let's take his place!"

As he strode forward, he noticed us. Easy to do, considering we were the only people willing to approach him. Oh, did he look good, his sharp edges softened. He still hadn't shaved; a thick shadow covered his stalwart jaw. A black shirt hugged his broad shoulders and strong chest while fatigues displayed muscular thighs. His smolder momentarily erased my ability to think.

A monotone voice announced, "Departing to Bala City in five minutes," and a throng rushed over, eager to board. I lost sight of him. Good, that was good.

"Oh! I spotted my guy. Bye!" Mykal darted off, disappearing in the crowd.

I took off too. Strangely enough, the crowd parted for me. No. Wrong. Not for me but the high prince. We stopped in front of each other, people giving us a wide berth.

"Too bad you're on leave," he said, humor glinting in his eyes. "I'm impatient to continue combating your fear of everything."

I couldn't stifle my groan. Or a jolt of surprise. He might be teasing me. "What do you have planned for us?"

"I won't ruin your day off with the answer."

"It's that bad?" I groaned again.

"Actually, Bubble Gum, it's worse." He looked me over and almost smiled. "I prefer the pink." With that, he strode past me, leaving me reeling.

I watched him, eyes wide. Had he maybe, possibly issued a compliment? In, like, a flirty manner?

No. Absolutely not. I'd mistaken the sexy tone in his office, and I was mistaken about his flirtiness now. He was only being nice because of his father.

Relieved—only relieved—I called, "Guess you're gonna call me Lady Blue now." Two could play this game.

"Don't be silly." He performed a slow spin as he walked. "Pink and blue make purple."

Why, why, why did that strike me as the peak of awful?

"Don't have too much fun today," he added. "Tomorrow is a pruning day."

Great. Wonderful. A crush of people enveloped me before I could respond, forcing me to motor in the opposite direction.

The closer I got to the train, the tighter the crowd became, the more I struggled to make progress, and the harder I longed to return to my room. No wonder Mykal had rushed us. If you didn't arrive early, you didn't fit in the windowless carts. But make it inside I did, passing my infection scan just as the doors closed behind me. The cart wobbled, then shot into action, zipping along a dark, narrow tunnel at a faster and faster rate.

How was I supposed to find—"There you are," a familiar voice called.

Shiloh! The handsome medic shouldered through the throng. My relief was so great, I threw my arms around him the moment he was within reach. "I'm so happy to see you."

He hugged me back, almost clinging.

Remembering yesterday's scowl, I asked, "How are you?"

"I'm with you." He pulled away with a smile that didn't quite reach the rest of his expression. His usual sparkle had dulled. "Everything is good."

Anxiety screwed with my heart. What was going on? Unfortunately, now wasn't the time for a conversation. But I did take his hand and sign "lemons."

A tiny flicker of relief flared in his irises, and he linked our fingers. We stayed like that until the train stopped. He guided me from the cart, through a tunnel, up a flight of stairs, and into a sunlit city. We cleared the crowd, and a fantasyland opened around us.

"This can't be real," I breathed. Massive statues topped marble daises, where costumed people danced. Other monuments crowned oddly shaped buildings made of a shimmery silver material that seemed to ripple with the wind. Lights flashed from signs advertising reducing or increasing the age listed on your birth certificate as well as walk-in surgeries to change anything you disliked about your body. Holograms beckoned pedestrians inside stores. Superfast music played in the background. I almost couldn't process the splendor.

"There's more," Shiloh said.

As we slipped down the street, I gaped at this and that, relying on my companion to guide me. I only snapped into protect-myself mode when we came to a section of the Rock. Utilizing a skill I'd perfected over the years, I kept my focus anywhere else. Or tried to . . .

The surface. It seemed to thin, becoming translucent and revealing a handsome bearded man wearing a red robe. He stood *inside* the stone. For once I didn't feel as though I was being watched by a thousand eyes, but two. Even with the metal dogs and their cameras, I felt seen by the man and no other as he tracked me with a narrowed gaze.

I gulped. No way I was seeing him. Just no way. Thankfully, the stone returned to its normal color and he vanished amid the maze of crimson veins.

Some kind of hologram, no doubt. Yes, yes. Only a hologram. But why had I seen it? I didn't dare ask Shiloh. Curiosity about the Rock only ever led to suspicion of infection.

I forced myself to forget him and concentrate on the cornucopia of scents drifting from every direction, crashing together to create a slightly amazing, mostly unpleasant perfume. Various kinds of vehicles zoomed on roads made of multicolor bricks, while pedestrians walked and skated over—I gasped. The sidewalk was transparent, allowing us to peer into a long stretch of the underground railway.

"Tons of uniformed officers live here," Shiloh explained. "CURED owns everything and ensures the families of officers are rewarded with the bulk of jobs and homes."

Hmm. Maybe I could snag a better job and residence for my mother. "How often do the infected break here?"

"Rarely. There's maybe one every three months."

Whoa. A break happened every week in Lucrea. At least! So, yes. I had a new mission: Get my mother moved to Bala City. Technically, I wasn't allowed to have contact with her for three years. But. If I avoided the place, there shouldn't be a problem. And, really, exceptions might be made if I succeeded in getting the right people involved. Like, say, High Prince Dolion. Would he help me?

Shiloh led me around a corner, saying, "I hope you like doughnuts."

A breakfast staple pre-Fall, or so I'd been told. "I had one when I was a little girl and I remember loving it." Wait. Clutching his arm, I jumped up and down. "We're eating a doughnut?" Already my mouth watered. Except. "How much are they?"

"Free." He flashed a smile, and a little more of his sparkle returned. "I won a coupon."

I thrilled with every step closer to our destination. Oh! I hadn't told him my news about the Dolions or lemonade. "Guess what? I met King Dolion. Turns out he asked his son to look out for me because—"

Shiloh whipped to face me, anger radiating from him. "Did he threaten you too?"

"The king threatened you?" My brow wrinkled. "How? Why?"

He looked about, tightened his grip on my fingers, and ushered me into an alley, where fewer people collected. As we crossed to the other end, he quietly said, "The king pulled me aside to ask about a correlation I found between eating pieces of the Rock and drinking the liquid inside it, with recovery from the Madness." He pursed his lips. "I can't be the first to notice. The pattern is so obvious, there's no getting around it."

"There are no pieces of the Rock. No way to tap into its interior." To my knowledge, no section of the otherworldly structure had ever even cracked, no matter the methods employed against it. It never even acquired a layer of dust!

"There are ways. At least, that's what glowers demonstrated. I've watched videos. They fed multiple maddened both the stone that isn't stone and the liquid, whatever it is. No matter the severity of the illness, the sick recovered instantaneously. Worms died and sloughed off."

Anxiety pricked my nape. Like Shiloh, I looked about. "I'm sure they manipulated the camera feed somehow. But I don't think we should discuss this." I decided to save the description of lemonade for another day and let the subject of the Dolions drop completely.

"That's the problem. No one wants to talk about the Rock. Not what it is or how it works. We're told it's the source of the Madness, but how can we be sure when we can't study it? What if the Rock is truly the cure and that's the reason feeders react to it the way they do? What if, deep down, they sense their only source of hope?"

Dread slithered over me. This was Soalian talk, and if anyone overheard it, we'd both end up in a treatment facility. "Shiloh."

"The only way to find out is to run tests," he continued, his frustration amplifying. "But how can we run tests when CURED forbids it?"

"Shiloh," I repeated. "You need to stop."

"I'm not infected," he rushed to inform me. "The king ordered a daily test. When I came up negative this morning, he told me that my so-called evidence verged on extreme Soalian-speak, on par with John Victors, and recommended I switch my field of study. He also threatened to boot me from the program if I discussed the reason for the change with anyone."

I opened and closed my mouth, no sound escaping. What should I say? What should I *think*? On one hand, I hated that someone as wonderful as Shiloh was going through this. I hadn't forgotten his passion for curing the Madness, or why. On the other hand, I understood the king's reasoning. Messing with the Rock could unleash consequences the world wasn't prepared to combat. The results of Shiloh's research must be a mistake. He'd messed up somewhere. Or, as I'd said, the glowers had tricked him.

"What's happening to you is terrible," I rasped, deciding to empathize with what I understood. The delay of a dream. I wrapped my arm around his waist as we snaked around a corner. "What are you going to do?"

"Figure it out or pick a new field of study." His posture stiffened with determination. "There's nothing else I *can* do."

He must be gutted. "I wish I could wave a magic wand and, poof, fix this for you."

"Come play with me." A woman dressed as a lizard beckoned from the shadows of a statue of a half man, half lizard. "The things I can do to you. . ." She unrolled a forked tongue and flicked it in our direction.

We ignored her. "While I'm without a wand," I told Shiloh, "I *can* balance the scale between us."

His brows winged up. "Okay, I'm intrigued. How is the scale unbalanced?"

"Well, just before we met, I learned I'd achieved my lifelong dream of being accepted into the Center for Agriculture and Life Sciences. But. To free my mom from the shackles of debt, I agreed to spend three years at Fort Bala Royal Academy. I was a mess. Then this charming guy showed up and made me forget my troubles. Suddenly I had a reason to smile. Now I owe him a day of fun and adventure."

We stopped at the end of a long line. He gazed down at me, the full megawatt sparkle reignited in his eyes. There was no mistaking it. His irises were a festival of lights.

"Balanced scales *are* important," he said.

"I concur." I straightened the already-straight neckline of his shirt. "Have I told you how handsome you look today?" He wore jeans and a comfortable tee with the words TRUST ME I'M ALMOST A DOCTOR scripted across the chest.

"So I'm charming *and* handsome." He teasingly puffed out his chest. "Good to know."

I chuckled as we moved up the line. "The most charmingest and handsomest in all the land."

He chuckled, too, but quickly got serious. "I think you are the most beautiful woman I've ever seen."

Dazed, I peered up at him. "Thank you."

He peered down at me, and a thread of longing uncoiled between us. The air thickened.

He wanted to kiss me; I knew it. Honestly, I wanted him to kiss me too. And I could ask him to do it without saying a word. Mykal had taught me the hand sign. But I didn't do it. For some reason, the HP's face flashed across my mind. That caged aggression in his eyes. That hint of amusement and that almost smile. His intensity. My stomach flipped inside out.

"Hey! Move up," someone called, and I jolted.

The moment with Shiloh ended as quickly as it started. We stepped forward, both nervously laughing off whatever had happened. Or hadn't happened. I didn't let myself consider why I'd hesitated or how I'd inadvertently planted an unwanted seed of desire for Cyrus Dolion.

I balled my hands into fists. Seeds could be dug up. That unconscious flash didn't have to mean anything. Crush on my instructor? The son of the king. Grandson of the emperor, the most powerful man in both worlds. No. We weren't even friends.

Shiloh was an amazing guy. I wanted him and only him. End of story. No need for further thought.

Arden Dawn Roosa.

"Yes?" I twisted my head this way and that and spun, searching for the woman who'd spoken my full name.

"Is something wrong?" Shiloh asked, confused as he looked around.

"No, I—" Across the street, a beautiful young lady draped in a red robe crooked her finger at me. Recalling the bearded man who'd worn something similar, I frowned.

Her mouth moved, as if she were speaking. Somehow, I heard her as if she stood directly beside me. *Shiloh's execution is set. If you'd like to save him, say nothing and follow me.*

My jaw slackened. Her voice. I hadn't heard her with my ears. I'd heard her in my mind. I opened and closed my mouth, questions and statements dying one after the other before one emerged. "How are you doing that?" I demanded.

"Doing what?" Shiloh asked, his confusion escalating.

She said nothing else. Just pivoted and disappeared around a corner.

"Arden?" my companion prompted.

I should forget her. Pretend what happened didn't happen. No doubt she meant me harm. But a need to speak with her stirred within me, strengthening into a tug before becoming a full-blown obsession. Resisting became impossible. I had to know how she'd done what she'd done and what she knew about Shiloh.

"I'll be back," I muttered, rushing off before my date could respond. At the intersection, I paused for traffic. No one else traversed this area, so I had no trouble finding my target.

I lurched, halting as if I'd hit a brick wall. She had positioned herself in front of the Rock. The very Rock I had (not) seen the bearded man standing in.

What was I doing, letting a strange woman lure me into the unknown? Archduke Heta had taught me the importance of my surroundings. I didn't know this space, but she did. She might be infected. A Soalian hoping to brainwash me. To use me as a key into the base.

Still. I couldn't leave without answers. "How did you speak inside my head? Who are you? What did you mean, *execution*?"

"I'm Ember Cruz, Shiloh's sister." Small circles with inner lines began to radiate a low-watt golden glow from her skin. "This is your first official invitation to the Tome Society. Join us and help me save my brother."

I reared back. Glower! My knees knocked, her connection to Shiloh doing nothing to diminish my fright.

Tone wry, she said, "I'll take your horrified expression as a no. But understand this. I'll ask you only thrice and no more. The sooner you accept, the better off we'll all be."

I would rather die than join Soalians bent on destroying CURED. "If you actually had access to books detailing the future, you would've known not to waste your time targeting me." The words frayed as I pushed them past clenched teeth.

"Eventually, you'll say yes and we'll become friends. I've seen it." Her unwavering confidence shook mine. "I'd like to save you the regret your delay causes, but I can't force you. You are the god of your own world, after all." With a sad smile, she backed up and disappeared inside the stone.

Inside it. Exactly like the bearded man.

But that couldn't be right.

There was no way I'd seen what I thought I'd seen. This was my hologram theory in action. Yes, yes. Another hologram. The real problem went deeper. A glower had invited me to join the Tome Society. Had threatened me with Shiloh's death.

By some miracle, I returned to him without slipping into hysteria.

"Everything okay?" he asked, his brow wrinkled.

Better to dive right in. "Is your sister's name Ember?"

He closed his eyes and groaned. "Please tell me she didn't ask you to join the—" Lips pressed tightly together, he went quiet.

I gave a clipped nod. "She did. She called my name, and I foolishly followed her. She told me you've been marked for death."

Another groan left him. "I should have warned you. I can't apologize enough for failing to do so." He pinched the bridge of his nose. "Don't believe her. She hates CURED, and she'll do anything to convince me to join her cult, even pressure my friends."

Well, no wonder she'd sought me out and given me the hard sell. But the realization didn't ease the pressure in my chest or stall the questions rolling through my brain.

"Let's forget it happened," I suggested. For now, anyway. Later, I planned to dissect every detail. "I owe you a day of fun, remember?"

"I do like a girl who keeps her word," he said, but his smile wasn't quite as bright.

Determined, I pasted a happy smile on my face and amped up my efforts. For half an hour, I regaled him with tales of my first attempts at plant propagation. He was still chuckling when we reached the head of the line and placed our order.

After devouring a doughnut more delicious than I remembered, we visited a garden maze, played like children at a park, sampled different foods he had other coupons for, and exchanged life stories. I cheered him up—I know I did—and he helped me feel safer. I didn't think of Ember or the bearded man until I lay in bed that night, chained to the wall, with Mykal sleeping soundly on the other side of the room.

Knowing glowers, my enemy, wielded such an incredible ability to walk into solid structures opened a mental door to a boatload of fear.

Door. Door. The word echoed. If the Rock was a doorway to an actual library, as the Soalians professed . . . did that mean Soal existed?

Stop this! Of course Soal and his library weren't real. Besides, even if something the Soalians claimed was actually true, it didn't change the devastation they caused the world. They were evil, and they deserved to be imprisoned.

I rolled to my side and pressed my palms to my churning belly. The chain rattled, abrading my wrist, but it couldn't drown out my riotous thoughts. I needed to tell the HP about the invitation. But should I? He'd want to know why I'd been chosen. The truth could jeopardize Shiloh's career at the worst possible interval. But if I failed to tell the high prince the truth and he later found out, I'd look guilty. And there was always the chance this was some kind of test.

No need to make a decision right now. Tomorrow marked my first trip to Theirland.

Ugh. The reminder threw fuel on the fire of my fear.

Sleep beckoned anyway. The last thoughts to drift through my mind before sleep pulled me into the dark brought a small measure of comfort. *The HP isn't a bad guy. He'll help me with all of this. I can trust him. Maybe.*

CHAPTER TWELVE

Be cautious; be vigilant; be wise; the enemy's greatest
weapon is his lies.

—*The Book of Soal* 2.21.5.8

"We're not traveling to Theirland today."

Roman's loud call filled the women's locker room. Frowning, we
flooded into the hall, joining him and our other teammates.

The second-in-command stood in the center before the two rooms.
"I don't know why, so don't ask. We'll proceed with our regular schedule
today and go tomorrow."

A reprieve. Nice. I returned to my locker and finished preparing for
class. When I finished, I raced to gym C. The coming warm-up meant
I was seconds away from seeing Shiloh and High Prince Dolion.

Anticipation warred with nervousness and determination. There,
in that moment, I made a decision. I would tell the HP about the
invitation. Letting him find out another way would do no one any
good. But I'd take a risk and leave out Ember's name. Although, I did
need to mention the execution threat, bluff or not. However, I would
confess my intentions to Shiloh first.

Argh! He wasn't here. The HP didn't show up either. Both absences
bothered me, agitating my stress response.

As the day progressed, my agitation magnified. There had been no sign of either man. Maybe someone had overheard Shiloh's talk of the Rock and tattled. He might be locked in a room with the high prince, undergoing an intense interrogation.

"Roosa," Duchess Mimidae snapped.

I blinked into focus, realizing my turn to fire a netter had arrived and every member of class was fixated on me. Cheeks heating, I stepped up to the designated line and aimed the heavy gun at a dummy set up on the other side of the classroom. My grip trembled as I squeezed the trigger. A metal net unfurled as it whipped toward my target. Dang. I'd missed, the net adhering to the wall beside the dummy. So far, I'd done my best with the throwing stars.

"You're too stiff," she said. "Next time exhale a deep breath before you fire."

Disappointed in my performance, I hustled to the end of the line to await my redo.

Titus stepped up to bat and executed a perfect shot.

"Excellent," the duchess praised. "A netter is your best choice when you come upon a glower or any feeder in need of treatment rather than death."

The bell rang, and we hurried to lunch. Then came self-defense, then first aid. Again, there was no sign of the HP or Shiloh. My worry for them sprouted thorns. By the time drills arrived, I felt as if I'd been tied to a rack and stretched beyond my limits.

I entered the Dome and drew up short. At last! Both males were present. But. Hmm. Neither appeared happy. Shiloh glared at the floor again, his hands fisted. The HP maintained a blank expression, but the usual force field around him crackled with tension. My stomach sank. Something had definitely happened between them.

Maybe today wasn't the best day to share my intentions.

"Line up," the HP bellowed, never glancing my way. "Hustle."

The entire class rushed to obey, and I could do no less. We put ourselves shoulder to shoulder in the center of the room.

He walked in front of us, his arms behind his back. "Tomorrow you will step into Theirland for the first time, officially becoming realm walkers."

I cringed inside. Many soldiers cheered.

Our leader barked, "This isn't a time for celebration but dedication. You won't be doing patrol because you aren't ready for it. But you will be paired with an established knight and watch a patrol from the safety of a POD. Afterward, I expect you to write a paper explaining everything the soldier did right and wrong, citing information you've acquired in your classes."

Okay, that didn't sound so terrible. From my studies, I knew a *POD* was a private observation deck, protected by a clear unbreakable shield.

The HP stopped and scanned the line. When he came to me, his gaze lingered for a heartbeat longer, and I thought he maybe, possibly, searched for something. But what?

"Today, we'll play a game that mimics what you'll witness with the knights. See the cubbies carved into the wall?" He pointed. "Each opening acts as a shelter for a lone soldier. Currently seventeen are available. There are eighteen of you." He motioned to Mykal, who dragged in a box of practice armor in the shade of bronze. The color for lords- and ladies-in-training.

"Suit up," the HP commanded, and we rushed to obey. "Like your assigned soldier, you'll compete in the dark. Though those in the field will encounter real feeders, you will be hunted by a hologram designed to detect fear and noise. You'll only see it when it comes within a five-foot range. Stay aware. Remember, you can't help others if you can't help yourself. If a feeder grazes you, you won't be disqualified, but you'll hurt. Once you're tagged, you become a permanent target. The game doesn't stop until every cubby is filled. The one stuck out in the open is eliminated. We'll run the drill again and again with minor differences until we crown a winner, who will receive three meal vouchers to be used at their discretion."

I fought for calm as the weight of the armor settled into place. He'd listed everything I despised, all rolled into a single activity. The dark. Being stalked by a maddened. Battling others for safety. Pain. But. Those vouchers. How wonderful to share "a food" with Shiloh, my treat.

I cast a peek the medic's way, hoping to engage him and rouse a smile, if only for a moment.

He stalked from the room.

If the HP noticed, he didn't show it. He scanned the line of soldiers, impassive. "Any questions? Good. Engage your lenses."

Trembling, I obeyed. A small screen lowered over my eyes and molded into a half mask. Just as the shield darkened, I caught the HP's gaze. In a moment of camaraderie, he offered a brusque nod, surprising me. Then the world around me vanished, and my thoughts centered around the only problem that mattered. I—saw—nothing.

Inhale. Exhale. If I'd been smart, I would've practiced with the lens outside of class while I'd had the chance, exactly as suggested. Bad decision to ignore good advice. Today I'd probably choke on the fruit of my choice.

"Go," the HP stated simply.

Someone bumped into me. Yelping, I tripped forward and collided with another soldier. Murmurs, grunts, and screeches created a frightening chorus. A piercing scream added to the chaos.

My heart galloped. *Leave, fear. I'm brave.* I extended my arms and threw my feet forward, panting breaths clogging my ears. My nose wrinkled. What was that atrocious smell?

A feeder flashed before my vision, eyes wild, teeth bared, the worms on its head sticking straight out, giving the illusion of spikes. No! I tried to dive out of the way. Too late. Sharp pains exploded inside my brain, and I shrieked, my knees buckling. I dropped like a stone in water, crashing into the floor. Someone tripped over me, kicking me in the gut, setting off a fresh chain reaction of pain.

Coughing, I crawled away as fast as I could. The cubbies, where were the cubbies?

Sweat beaded on different parts of me. When had the room become wall-less? I must be going in circles. Which way, which way? The north and south had cubbies, the east and west did not.

"Over here," Roman called from across the room, as if he sensed my desperation.

"Where?" Lark demanded.

"Follow my voice," he responded.

I didn't know about her, but I took Roman's advice. If he was safe in a cubby, he was where I needed to be. I could help myself to safety, then turn my efforts to aiding others, like Roman had.

Lark grunted and cursed. Had she gotten tagged? I quickened my pace. Other trainees issued warnings and pleas for aid. Shrieks and thumps ebbed and flowed.

"Learn to detect the slightest hint of a feeder's approach," the HP instructed.

The death stench hit me again. This time, I acted faster, diving and rolling. My brain rattled against my skull, but I didn't scent the maddened anymore. Invigorated, I crawled with swift determination.

Boom! My forehead greeted the wall at long last. More discomfort. More dizziness. Rising to my knees, I paused to orient. The decision cost me. The same wild-eyed feeder flashed over my vision, too close to avoid. Tag!

Searing agony flared anew. Despite it, I shoved myself along the wall. Panting, grunting, wheezing. Finally! An open cubby. Noooo! I bumped someone.

"Taken," Titus announced, no doubt ready to defend his hideaway despite sounding sympathetic.

Adrenaline surged, and I crawled faster, panted harder, feeling my way. More cubbies, more occupants. Open! I threw myself inside the tight space and stood, pressing my back against the wall, making my body as small as possible. Raspy breaths pumped my chest up and down. I'd done it!

"Round over," the HP announced. "Lenses up."

I pressed the button and blinked rapidly against the onslaught of light. No sign of the holograms. Six soldiers toppled from their cubbies to writhe on the floor in various stages of torment.

With a groan, I eased down and stretched out. "I'm dying," I muttered. "Or dead. Yeah. Definitely dead."

"Walk it off, Roosa," the HP commanded.

Walk off being *dead*?

"Cash, you're out."

The fallen lord-in-training raised his thumb in a show of acceptance.

Our merciless leader announced, "Line up."

I left the security of the cubby with a groan. Behind me, a door slid shut. One less competitor, one less cubby.

The HP motioned to the medics, who rushed over to examine anyone with an injury. Someone I'd never met had taken Shiloh's place.

I glanced at the HP, seeking answers. He watched me. When he arched a brow in question, I knew what he was asking. Could I handle more?

"I'm brave," I mouthed. I'd find Shiloh later and find out what was going on.

The corner of the HP's mouth twitched. "Recall what I told you about RVM in Theirland. Outside of CURED's buildings, the world appears upside down unless you're wearing a lens. On the off chance your lens ever fails, you must learn how to operate accordingly. I'm programming your goggles to invert your vision. Engage."

I pressed the button, causing the lens to lower again. In an instant, my world went topsy turvy, the ceiling swapping places with the floor. Nausea instantly struck. Around me, several soldiers toppled, unable to stand. How I remained upright, I wasn't sure.

"During round two, there will be two holograms rather than one." The monsters appeared at the HP's side, and I flinched. "Activate dark mode."

I swallowed a ball of apprehension as I adjusted my lens, but it didn't help. Especially when the cloak of darkness returned, erasing my surroundings. Fewer people, double the holograms.

"You've probably noticed the sensation of being upside down stays with you, even without visual aid," our leader said. "Learn to deal with it. Go."

Ack! With a huff, I charged for the wall with more confidence than before. Pandemonium ruled when other trainees did the same. I crashed into someone and ricocheted backward, slamming into someone else, who shoved me. "Sorry, sorry," I blurted before I could stop myself.

A hologram flashed into my line of sight. I didn't hesitate, diving to the right. Someone—Juniper—grunted. Oh, no! My actions caused her harm. But I didn't apologize. Not this time. Noise would only draw a hologram our way. Instead, I scrambled up and charged for the wall with renewed energy, ducking and dodging any trace of action while my entire world remained inverted.

Come on, come on. I must, must, must almost probably be close to the cubbies.

Fingers snagged in my hair, yanking me backward. I landed on a fallen lord-in-training. Someone stomped on my hand. I yelped at the pain but surged to my feet, determined to win this. Not for the meal vouchers—not anymore—but to feed a stubbornness I hadn't known I possessed. I could do this.

Another hologram flashed into my path, reaching for me. I twisted to avoid—boom! Another soldier knocked into me, and we crashed to the floor. Others rushed over me as I grappled for purchase.

An elbow slammed into my face. More pain flared, and my world spun. Stars winked inside my head. Blood poured from my nose, a loud roar in my ears.

I swiped at my mouth, mopping up the blood, then stood, burning through every ounce of adrenaline swamping my veins.

"Round over," the HP said as I took my first step.

"No!" The denial burst from my tongue. I couldn't have lost in round two.

My world righted as I lifted my lens. Oh, I'd lost all right. The cubbies were filled, several teammates eyeing me with sympathy.

Jericho winked. "No meal vouchers for you and your new bump buddy, eh, Ardie. Bet you lost your shot at top soldier too. Not that you ever had one."

I ground my teeth, angry, disappointed and embarrassed.

"Roosa, you're out," High Prince Dolion announced, devoid of emotion. His arctic expression proved worse than my injuries. "Get her to an exam room."

A medic rushed over to press a piece of cloth beneath my stinging nose and help me to my feet. I stumbled out the door as the HP began his explanation of round three. For some reason, leaving him was the last straw, and I teared up. It wasn't that the HP was a comforting presence. I just—I missed my mom more than ever. And my plants. And Shiloh and Mykal. The HP was the next best thing. Someone I had begun to kind of, sort of trust.

The medic ushered me to the medical sector. He tried to whisk me into exam room one, but I recalled Shiloh's promise the day I'd run out of Archduke Heta's class and entered the second instead.

"Is Shiloh around?" I asked as my companion collected a vial of blood.

He walked out of the room, silent, no doubt afraid of being recorded. Alone, I checked the gurney for a message from Shiloh. Dang. Nothing.

I sat again, acting totally normal as the tech wheeled in a large machine. He x-rayed my hands and face, then gently palpated my nose. Sharp stings flared and subsided.

"Well?" A second try wouldn't hurt. "Is Shiloh around or not?"

"Do not leave this room," he said, exiting with the machine, then closing the curtain.

I lay back. Sat up. Walked around. Sat down. Hours passed before High Prince Dolion entered as if he owned the place, easing a tight knot of tension between my shoulders. Except, hmm. A fresh cut marred his branded cheek, a bead of blood leaking from the edge.

"Anything broken?" he demanded. He hadn't changed since I'd last seen him, yet he looked completely different. Frayed to the point of exhaustion, maybe.

"No, sir." The medic rushed up behind him. "She's cleared for transport."

I gripped my knees. Shouldn't I be the first to hear news about the condition of my body?

The medic motioned to the HP's wound. "Should I bandage your—"

"You are dismissed."

The medic beat feet.

The HP pulled the curtain, excluding our third wheel, and collected my reader. "How do you feel?" he asked, looking over the information. No emotion infused his voice.

"Isn't that a question you should ask my doctor?" I batted my lashes at him.

"Probably. But I asked you."

Honestly? "I'm fine." Mostly. "How about you? What happened?" I motioned to his wound. "You're bleeding."

He hiked his shoulders, unconcerned. "I hit a door on my way here."

"No, really. What happened?" I asked. His lips pursed, and I barked out a laugh. How unlike the always-observant HP. I wonder what had distracted him. "Who won the competition?"

"Who do you think?" His dry tone told me all I needed to know.

"Roman." Of course.

"It came down to him and Titus. Roman reached the cubby first but offered it to Titus in exchange for a truce. Titus refused." Satisfaction flashed over the HP's features as he admitted, "Jericho is the one who hit you, and he lost the round after yours."

I didn't like Jericho, but I couldn't blame him for the hit. Who knew how many soldiers I'd injured during the game.

Dr. Korey entered, smiling when she spotted the HP. She opened her mouth to speak.

"I require time alone with the patient," he announced before she uttered a word, never glancing up.

She paused, clearly startled by the statement. "I'm your doctor, not some random medic." Determined, she crossed to him and placed a hand on his shoulder. When he stiffened but continued reading, she reached for his face. "Let me tend to—"

He jerked from her touch and scowled, giving her the briefest glare. "Go."

Hmm. Rumors about his disdain for the brand were true. A tidbit for the mental file I was compiling on him. But the real headliner was the certain romantic relationship between the HP and the doctor. They might not be a couple right now, but at some point they had been.

With a stiff nod and an embarrassed glance at me, she too left us alone. I had a sinking feeling Mykal was right. Dr. Korey was the type to blame others for her problems, and I'd just climbed to the top of her hit list.

"Why are you here?" I asked and sighed. "Sir."

"Several reasons, but I'll only discuss one." At ease again, he settled on the stool beside my bed, his attention riveted on me. "I have questions, and you have answers."

"You're not the only one with questions," I muttered.

"Very well. We'll do an exchange, and I'll be as forthcoming as you. So tell me. Have you noticed any strange behavior from your boyfriend, the medic, lately?"

Oh no, no, no. He must suspect Shiloh of being a Soalian, like Ember. Or he'd learned of my encounter with the woman. I floundered for a response. "Um. We haven't put a label on our relationship."

The HP offered a humorless smile, all *lady, please*. "Allow me to rephrase. Have you noticed any strange behavior from Shiloh Cruz?"

When I hesitated, he added, "I'll make it easy on you. Do you think it's possible Shiloh is a Soalian? More specifically, do you believe he's working with a group led by his sister, Ember Cruz, who serves as one of John Victors's seconds? Yes or no?"

And there it was. Confirmation of my fears. I shifted, uncomfortable. If I said no, which was what I honestly believed, and the medic ever tested positive or consorted with his sister, I'd be castigated for my poor judgment or suspected of aiding him. But saying yes would only doom both Shiloh and me to endless testing and suspicion. I might be kicked out of the academy.

"I'm dealing with a possible head injury, High Prince Dolion. We should probably save this topic for another time."

The HP remained undeterred. He stood and moved directly in front of me, a tower of strength and determination. His heady scent enveloped me, and I shivered. Without thought, I began to reach for his wounded cheek, intending to wipe away a new bead of blood. Thankfully I caught myself before making contact. At least he didn't cringe from the thought of contact.

"Give me an answer," he demanded.

I licked my lips. Very well. "Anything is possible, but that doesn't mean it's happened." There. A nonanswer. "My turn to ask a question. Do *you* think Shiloh is a Soalian working for his sister?"

"Since I'm being as forthcoming as you, I just say maybe I do, maybe I don't." He leaned in to lightly pinch my chin and shift the angle of my face. The (almost) affectionate action, his incredible warmth, and those wonderfully abrasive calluses rattled me more than ever. A muscle jumped beneath his wound. "Jericho left you with a bruise."

"I've had worse, and so have you." Look away from this man? Impossible. His intensity held me captive with a stronger force than his gentle grip. He was just so beautiful.

Beautiful. Yes. The perfect word to describe a man whose usually harsh features were softened like this. And his lashes! So long they curled at the ends.

He released me to lift my hand into the light, examining for any bruising. "You did well today," he said, and he sounded 100 percent serious.

I double blinked. "I lost in the second round. To my knowledge, I'm the only bleeder in the group. I did anything but well."

"You kept moving and utilized the skills you've gained. Fear didn't stop you. You did well," he repeated, tracing the pad of his thumb over my knuckles.

I didn't mean to, and couldn't explain why, but I turned my hand, offering my palm. He gave a soft stroke across the center that I felt in my bones. A gesture born of concern, nothing more. Only concern.

Noticing the discoloration on my wrist, he glowered. His gaze snapped up to mine, and his stance hardened. "The bed chain?"

"Yeah, no big deal."

He tightened his grip before releasing me. "Tell me about Shiloh, Arden."

Persistent HP! He must mean business. He'd used my first name. "I met Shiloh the day before I came to Fort Bala, which means I've known him one day longer than I've known you. In what way do I qualify as an expert witness for either of you? Cyrus," I added, because why not? Fair was fair.

I expected a rebuke. He merely stuffed his fingers into his pocket. "Very well. We'll try this another way." When he withdrew his hand, he held a plastic baggie containing a dozen—

"My seeds!" I exclaimed, clapping.

He passed the baggie to me. "I'm not your enemy. But I'd like to be your friend."

I clutched the treasure close to my chest and disregarded the wild pounding of my heart. "You are my instructor. Ourland royalty. We can't be friends?" A question that should have been a statement. Maybe. Probably. I *had* let him stroke my palm.

"Usually," he said, his tone drier than sand, "*thank you* is the correct response to such a kind gesture." He reached into his other pocket and withdrew . . . something.

"What are those?" Two flat, pupil-size disks a little darker than my flesh waited in a small ivory container.

A moment passed, as if he carefully considered his next words. "You're going to wear these."

"And *these* are?" I insisted. If you couldn't get to a finish line one way, try another.

"You'll learn the answer if your heart rate reaches a certain threshold."

Hold up. I clasped his wrist when he reached for my face, stopping him before he made contact. "I'm almost certain I've reached the threshold, whatever it is, nine hundred times today alone."

His expression gentled. "Your imagination can be an asset if you use it properly. Until then, trust me not to hurt you."

I ran my bottom lip between my teeth and pried my fingers loose. "All right. Yes."

With a slow, gentle stroke, he smoothed my hair to one side, raising a new tide of goose bumps. He tilted my head the direction he wanted it and adhered the first disk behind my ear. He repeated the action with my other ear, so steady. So strong and capable. I loved the rich hues in his skin as light bathed him.

Uh-oh. *Look away!*

But I didn't.

My heart thudded against my ribs as he straightened. "We were discussing the medic," he prompted.

Inner shake. "Shiloh isn't maddened, if that's what worries you. As you've probably been informed, he is now tested every morning."

Cyrus—whoa. I couldn't afford to accidentally refer to him by his given name in public. So, rephrase. The *HP* gave me another humorless smile. "Did he speak with a Soalian while you were in town together?"

Heat drained from my entire being. "No." I cleared my throat. "He didn't." Did the high prince suspect that I had?

"Very well," he repeated and turned to go.

Thank goodness, a reprieve. "What's going to happen to him?" I croaked.

Cyrus—argh! *The HP* paused to glance over his shoulder. "You don't know him well enough to receive an update about his well-being. Correct?"

Busted. "He's a good guy. I'm certain of *that*."

"Then neither of you have anything to worry about." The HP took a step forward, only to pause again. "The next two days will be tough. Though we're leaving a day late, we're remaining in Theirland forty-eight hours. But you'll be pleased to know these interrealm trips carry more weight for top lady than anything else, even the title of team leader."

Something about his demeanor . . . as if he knew something about my upcoming assignments I didn't. "Are you saying I still have a shot?"

He ignored the question. "You will be discharged within the hour. Spend the evening in your room, recovering. That's an order you will obey. And whatever you do, stay calm." Voice going low and husky, he added, "Or not. As always, that part is up to you."

I thought I detected . . . anticipation? But that couldn't be right. There was no reason he would welcome a freak-out.

He walked away before I could question him further. Oh, yeah. He clearly knew several somethings I didn't, and I didn't think I was gonna like what I learned.

CHAPTER THIRTEEN

When you are teachable, you gain understanding,
but those who despise instruction lose what
understanding they have.

—*The Book of Soal* 2.2.4.25

I didn't rest and recover, but I did stay in my room. The HP gave Mykal the evening off, too, and we holed up, practicing hand signals and discussing Shiloh. Neither of us had any idea what was going on with him, so we could only concoct theories and suppositions. I didn't let myself think about my odd interaction with my enigmatic instructor. Didn't let myself miss my mother or my plants. A true feat!

When curfew arrived, Mykal secured her shackle as usual and gasped. "Okay, this is new."

"What?" I asked, fastening my cuff. Oooh. "Mine's padded."

"Yeah. Mine too."

Other soldiers cheered from their rooms. They must have received pads too.

I recalled the HP's reaction to my bruises and knew. A warm sensation spread through my chest, loaded with admiration and even affection. He was responsible for this. Underneath the gruff, he was a good guy.

Things quieted down quickly throughout the ward, and Mykal drifted to sleep. I dug out my reader and dove into a study guide featuring Theirland, enlarging photos to better examine the finer details. I did my best to memorize street layouts and monuments. Not that I'd be going on patrol. Not really. But. Knowing whether or not my assigned knight took a proper route would elevate my evaluation. Plus, I'd be in a new, strange world, and I should be prepared for anything. Something could go wrong during transport. And what if the building collapsed? We'd lose our shelter. What if I got locked out inadvertently or a thousand other horrific, life-altering things?

Irrational imaginings. Yes, I comprehended that. But my understanding didn't stop those scenarios from playing inside my mind. Trying to focus, I flipped to the next page. Whoa! The text blurred as a red circle with seven broken lines overtook the screen. I went still.

The Tome Society.

Foreboding prickled the base of my spine. Words appeared on the screen, as though someone was typing a message directly to me. Do you hunger and thirst for truth, Arden?

Ember. I had no doubts.

My grip on the device tightened. I cast a quick glance at Mykal. She slept on, undisturbed. Deep breath in. Out. I didn't know how the Soalian had hacked into my reader, but if CURED learned of this, I could be blamed. Labeled a traitor.

My tremors intensified as I read the remainder of her message. Rather than trust the custodian who steals your money, imprisons you and your loved ones, and profits from your sickness, consider the supposed enemy he discredits. If your decisions don't start lining up with your destiny, your books will be shelved with other tragedies.

Anger surged. The fact that my first reaction wasn't a desire to toss the reader across the room but intrigue at the possibility of reading books written about my life disturbed me greatly.

I typed a response, wanting a record of my refusal in case the powers that be discovered the interaction before I confessed. You're good at this. But sowing dissent won't reap your desired harvest with me. CURED protects us.

A response appeared. Denial doesn't disprove my words.

I worked my jaw and jabbed my fingers at the keyboard. My lack of knowledge doesn't prove you're right either.

Another response arrived within seconds. Don't believe me. Start digging. The enormity of CURED's gains will shock you. Find out the true purpose of Theirland. Figure out why the Rock blooms with such sweet-smelling flowers. Learn the origin of pritis stones. Or are you too afraid to ponder simple questions because they are conveniently considered the obsession of an enemy?

I didn't have a ready answer for her. In this, she wasn't wrong. All my life, I'd shut down any thoughts involving the Rock or Soal as quickly as possible for the very reason she'd stated. But CURED didn't encourage us to fear the Rock for profit, as she'd implied. We feared the Rock because we should.

Shiloh's voice wafted through my mind. *The king pulled me aside to ask about a correlation I found between eating pieces of the Rock and drinking the liquid inside it, with recovery from the Madness. I can't be the first to notice. The pattern is so obvious, there's no getting around it.*

The moisture in my mouth dried. Maybe . . . maybe Ember planted those studies. Yes, yes. That made sense.

On the reader, new sentences replaced the old. You need the Tome Society, and we want you. Think about what I've said. We'll speak again soon.

The screen blanked without any prompting from me. Heart thumping, I slid the device under my pillow and rolled to my side. For an eternity, I lay there, trying to cobble together a plan for my next steps, feeling as if I was stumbling around in the dark, trying to snatch answers from a field of questions. I should demand to speak with Cyrus now and confess what happened. Or do it later. Or not at all.

If I kept quiet, at least for a little while, I could snoop around Theirland.

Ugh. Had I really just contemplated sneaking around a military base and spying on my government, simply to answer queries posed by my enemy? Surely I wasn't so foolish.

But maybe?

Armed with information, I could conquer every doubt Ember had fueled.

If I got caught, I'd lose everything. *Mom* could lose everything.

But shouldn't a search for the truth be rewarded?

Acid seared my throat. This was a no-win situation. I should leave Fort Bala. Just grab my stuff and go home. I'd find another way to pay Mom's back taxes. Maybe work two jobs. Three even. There'd be no more messages from the Tome Society. No more confus_on.

Only the regret of not knowing.

Damned either way.

Run! The chain on my wrist pulled taut as I jolted upright. Trapped! I jerked at the cuff to no avail. Bit by bit, my lungs shrank, choking me from the inside. I couldn't breathe. I needed to breathe. Clutching at my throat, I collapsed against the mattress.

"This isn't resting and recovering, Bubble Gum." A rough, gruff voice drifted through my ears, startling me enough to capture my thoughts, allowing speculations to flood in.

"Cyrus?" He was here? I darted my gaze but saw no sign of him in the cell. The door remained closed, Mykal still sleeping. Was I having an auditory hallucination . . . like the maddened?

Just like that, the panic resurged. I pulled at my clothes. Too tight!

"Arden," Cyrus snapped. "Listen to me. We're both wearing transmitters. Your heart rate hit a certain threshold and activated both sets. Now we can hear each other. Tell me your mantra."

Transmitters, not infection. My motions slowed and my breathing followed. In, out. "Leave, fear. I'm brave," I breathed out.

"Yes, you are brave. You comprehend fear is the monster at your back with a knife at your throat. And what do we do to monsters?"

"This isn't a teaching moment," I shriek-whispered between pants. In. Out. At least Cyrus and Ember agreed on one thing. Fear was the worst. "I want to go home. I can't do this."

"We do not say *can't*, soldier."

"Fine." I sniffled, and there was no stopping the humiliating action. "I'm currently unable to can."

He had the audacity to laugh. "What do we do when fear attacks us, Roosa?"

"Fight back," I muttered.

"That's right. And you are growing into an excellent fighter, focusing on the correct opponent."

His compliment filled my head, and I calmed a bit more. With his voice a caress in my ears, I almost felt as if he were stretched out at my side, his arms wrapped around me. A true comfort. "How? How do I fight back?"

"Tell me your battle cry again. Punch the air with your words."

"Leave, fear. I'm brave." A soft thump sounded as I also punched the bed. "I'm brave." Another punch of the mattress. "I'm brave. I'm brave, I'm brave." Hey! Those battle cries had some heft to them. Maybe I *was* kind of a little brave. I mean, look at all I'd experienced and pushed through.

"Again. Louder."

"I'm brave." I smashed my fists through the air, one after the other. "I'm brave!" Knockout!

"Okay, we get it. You're the bravest. Can I sleep now?" Lark grumbled from her cell.

Other soldiers issued complaints too. Mykal rolled over and shoved a pillow over her head to smother her giggles.

I sank into my mattress, my cheeks heating.

"Get out," Cyrus grated with obvious annoyance.

Excuse me? "I'm chained to the wall and barred in. There's no way I can leave my cell."

He gave a little chuckle. "I wasn't speaking to you, Pink."

"To whom were you speaking? And what happened to *purple*?"

"The woman who entered my hallway. And I realized I prefer the classics."

"You own a whole hallway?" I asked because I didn't know what else to say. I wouldn't be surprised if the woman was Dr. Korey. He did seem to enjoy ordering her to leave.

"I'm confident we both recognize the fact that I own every hallway I enter." Amusement tinged his words. "I exited a meeting between instructors and team leaders as soon as the transmitters activated."

Shame pricked me. "My apologies, sir, for interrupting."

"I've attended hundreds of those meetings," he told me with a dry tone. "I can afford to miss one."

I wished I could see his face. Judge his expression. Decipher the truth about his mood. Why was he being so nice to me, and why did the answer matter so much? Wait. "What time is it?"

"A few minutes after four."

"In the morning?" I gasped out. I had stirred my cauldron of worries all night long, missing my only opportunity to sleep in semipeace. Now, in little more than an hour, I would be stepping into a whole new world for the very first time. "I'm brave," I squeaked.

"Yes. You are." Static crackled over our connection, as if he were on the move. "Prepare for travel and meet me at Transport One in ten minutes. And Arden? Do not remove the transmitters."

Had he forgotten I was chained? "What are we going to do?"

No response. I tapped the disks behind my ears. "Hello? Cyrus?"

Still nothing. A second later, the padded shackle around my wrist fell off and the door to my cell opened. I blinked rapidly. Wow. Okay. He'd been serious.

"What even is my life right now?" I muttered, pounding my fist into my mattress.

"Judging by the one-sided conversation I just overheard," Mykal said, snickering, "I'm guessing you're in a hurry to see the HP. Excuse me. *Cyrus.* Promise me you'll spill everything when you return, or I'll revolt."

"I promise. Maybe," I grumbled, earning more giggles from her. "I better go." Time was ticking.

My blood turned to fuel as I scrambled from the bed and zoomed to the locker room, where I cleaned up and dressed at warp speed. Both the hallway and the facilities were empty, most soldiers sleeping in their cells.

As I anchored my hair in a ponytail, an elevator carried me to the twelfth floor. A level I'd never ventured to. Perspiration dampened my palms. The cart stopped and opened. I spotted Cyrus immediately. He stood in front of a pair of guarded double doors, his hands in his pockets. He'd showered, shaved, and changed since I'd last seen him, his hair wet and his military fatigues crisply pressed. His wound looked better.

I approached him tentatively, my heart racing. "Hi. Sir."

A wry smile lit his rough features. "You're excited to see me."

"What? No." Embarrassment scorched my cheeks. "Why would you ever think—"

He tapped a transmitter behind his ear, and my shoulders rolled in. Right.

"Just so you know, it's not excitement," I grumbled. Probably. "You make me nervous."

"Ah. Nervous," he echoed, growing serious. "Brighten up, Pink. You're about to receive a treat few others have enjoyed. A private tour led by the king's son. I'll show you the rifts between worlds."

Rifts. Our mode of transport into Theirland. "Yes, please!"

The guards pushed open the doors, and Cyrus waved me inside the room.

I took a step, then hesitated, suspicions brewing. "This feels like a bribe. As if you're going to expect information about Shiloh." Or Ember.

He rolled his eyes. "I'm not foolish enough to bribe you for information you said you don't have. Take the tour or not. Always your choice."

Well. In that case. I strode past the door, entering a huge, mostly empty space with a glass-encased room in back labeled TRIAGE. The rifts occupied the center of the room, and wow. "They're like enormous claw marks. Air wounds." It looked like a massive beast had raked its nails through the air and cut into an abyss. Thick shadows slithered inside each.

Cautious, I edged around the rifts. They appeared the same no matter my angle. "Are there many of these throughout our world?"

At my side, Cyrus nodded. "Many. But these particular rifts lead to a CURED-protected building in Theirland. One by one, lords- and ladies-in-training will step into the darkness. You'll experience a moment of excruciating pain, then you'll be in Theirland." A muscle jumped in his jaw. A reaction I didn't understand. Unless he didn't like the other world. "The facility has a walled perimeter, armed guards, and cameras. There are few places you can go that someone isn't watching."

I heard the warning tucked inside the complimentary tidbit, and it didn't bode well for my goal. If he already suspected my plan to poke around, I was as good as caught.

He misunderstood my concern and promised, "I'll help you get through this however I can."

"Thank you. This helped," I whispered. I believed he meant his words. Yes, we'd had a rough start, but every day since, he'd aided me. I should take a risk and tell him about the Tome Society. He wouldn't blame me, and he might erase my confusion. My only shot at a win-win.

I braced. "Please test me for Madness. Use the most reliable method of testing available." My blood.

He frowned but didn't move away from me. "Do you have symptoms?"

"No, but I'm going to tell you something that could make you think otherwise."

The frown deepened. After a prolonged hesitation, he motioned to triage. "There's a kit in there."

He led me into the glass room. I sat on a gurney while he gathered supplies. Gloves, alcohol swabs, a bandage, and a press-and-release needle with a built-in test strip. After cleaning my right index finger, he slid the tester in place. The container covered the digit from tip to base. With the push of a button, three needle pricks sent a spike of pain up my arm, and I hissed.

The device clamped tight, tighter, squeezing blood from the wounds. Then the pressure eased, and he freed me, bandaged my finger, and stared down at the result pad, awaiting the verdict.

I'd be negative, no doubt about it. I must be.

But what if I wasn't?

"Negative," he said before I could work up another panic.

Thank goodness.

He tossed the kit into a biohazard bin, leaned against the gurney, and crossed his arms over his chest. "Start talking."

I'm brave. "I was issued an invitation to the Tome Society," I admitted before I convinced myself to keep quiet. There. It was done. The truth was out, and there was no erasing it.

"I see." His expression gave nothing away. "Who issued the invite?"

"A woman I met in the city." I refused to name her. No matter what. I wouldn't put Shiloh through that.

"I see," Cyrus repeated with a hint of resolve. Thankfully, he didn't ask me for her identity. "What do you know of the Tome Society?"

"Only that it's a secret society of Soalians, which I now understand to be glowers, and they claim the Rock is a doorway to a library filled with books written about the future."

"Allow me to fill in some gaps. Tome Society members believe the marks carved into the Rock are keys to opening doorways within the library, which is the lone entrance into a third realm. A utopia free of Madness known as Shaddai, ruled by the god Soal. The books you mentioned were written by Soal, and they include the past and present as well as the future, telling the stories of every individual ever born. One set reveals the life we're supposed to live and the other shows the life we choose."

So much to unpack. A third realm. A utopia, no less. Two possible futures for every person. I chewed on my bottom lip. "Do you believe the Soalians?" The way he'd spoken suggested he'd shared facts, not fiction.

"Do you?" he asked.

A nonanswer. I ejected from the bed, landing on my feet. "Is Soal real at least?" We'd start there. "Yes or no."

"Yes," he replied, astounding me.

Wait. "Are you serious?" Even Archduke Heta denied the possibility.

"I've had . . . dealings." Cyrus said no more about that, leaving me floundering. "How did you respond to the invitation?"

I disregarded his question, too busy floundering. "But I was taught . . . CURED says . . . Do others believe?"

"Those with clearance, yes."

I fluttered a hand to my throat, where my pulse thumped. An actual god, real and not imaginary. Hidden from the masses for reasons I couldn't fathom. "I'm a lowly lady-in-training. I have no clearance."

"You aren't a lowly anything, but you do have clearance, considering I just gave it."

But. A god. "What kind of dealings did you have? What's he like? What constitutes a god? Why keep him secret? Is there really a library with books about us?" As I spoke, anger and betrayal frothed deep, deep inside me. All my life, I'd defended a lie. Unless I'd misunderstood what Cyrus meant by "dealings." A total possibility. For all I knew, Soal was a computer. Or a tree. A talking worm. Something!

"He's kept secret because questions spur curiosity and curiosity spurs trouble. How did you respond to the invitation?" Cyrus repeated.

Frustration joined my internal party, clawing at my calm. I *needed* to know more about Soal. "Were you maddened? Is that how you met him?"

"The invitation, Arden."

The hardness of his tone told me I'd get no more answers. Fine. As I'd done thousands of times throughout my life, I dumped my emotions into the cauldron, sealed the lid, and forged ahead. "I declined, of course."

"But you can't stop thinking about what the Soalian said." Rather than chastise me, he nodded. "Sometimes the enemy can make sense. It's up to us to discern what's accurate and what isn't."

I waited for him to say more. He didn't.

"That's your only response to my bombshell?" I demanded.

"Yes. Wear the transmitters in Theirland," he said, changing the subject. "They'll remain in place until you pull them off."

"Won't you get tired of being linked to me?" Of knowing every time my heartbeat sped up?

"No." He offered the barest glimpse of his rare half smile. "I don't think I will."

Tendrils of something sharp but sweet tormented me oh, so good, and my heart rate sped up. He gave a rusty chuckle, proving he'd clocked it.

"I definitely won't," he said.

I didn't know what to say or do; he was just so adorable right now, and it was confusing. I decided to change the subject. "Tell me what I need to do to get my mother moved to Bala City. She's a hard worker, I promise. So dedicated! She loves children, and she'll be an asset to whoever hires her."

He shook his head. "Trust me when I say she's better off where she is."

"But—"

A door banged shut, and we went quiet. Archduke Heta and Duchess Mimidae entered the chamber with three soldiers trailing them. The guy who usually followed the archduke around, a young woman I'd seen in the halls, and Roman. The team leaders.

Roman noticed me with the HP and knit his brows together. I jumped away from Cyrus, as if I'd been caught doing something I shouldn't.

"You okay?" Roman mouthed.

I nodded, mouthing back, "All good." I'd reintroduce my mother's move another day.

The HP waved Roman over, and the soldier jogged between the rifts, totally unfazed. He entered the glass room and saluted his superior. Something I'd forgotten to do. I winced. Even though Cyrus hadn't complained about the lack, I gave a retroactive salute then and there.

The corners of his mouth inched up. "Things will be chaotic when we cross over. As the final two trainees in the welcome ring, I expect you both to go through first, recover quickly, and help the others as they arrive."

Roman nodded, confident. "You can count on me, sir."

"Yes. Me too." I mimicked the nod and the confidence.

Hiking his thumb at me, Roman teased, "I hear she's very brave."

Fire flamed in my entire face, amplifying when Cyrus rolled his lips under his teeth to prevent another smile.

"I've heard the same," he said. "Now go line up and wait for the others while I speak with the commanding officers."

Chapter Fourteen

If you do not ask for what you need, how can you
receive it?

—*The Book of Soal* 2.20.4.2

"Is something going on between you and High Prince Dolion?" Roman asked as the rest of our team flooded into the room, lining up behind the rifts. "Be honest. I won't be mad."

"What? Him? Me?" I sputtered. I'd meant what I'd told Cyrus. Argh! *The HP.* He made me nervous, and I didn't enjoy being nervous. My romantic interest centered around the very kind, very wonderful Shiloh. Who I hadn't kissed when I'd had the chance. An occurrence I still didn't comprehend. "He tested me for—" I gave Roman the look. *You know.*

"Ah. Yeah." He compressed his lips. "Because of Shiloh, I bet. Dude's been acting so weird lately. He was supposed to come with us today, but he's been confined to his room for observation."

Spending time confined to his room was a good thing. Maybe. Hopefully? CURED would see he was a smart, capable man going through a tough thing, forced to change his life plan for his health.

Marked for execution.

At the reminder of Ember's pronouncement, apprehension slithered through me. The glower might be a Soalian, and evil, but she wouldn't harm the brother she sought to recruit. Shiloh wasn't in any danger.

Unless he was.

I balled and relaxed my hands. "I wasn't tested because of Shiloh," I told Roman, unwilling to let the medic carry any blame. But explain the real reason? No.

Thankfully, Lark shouldered her way to us, claiming the team leader's attention. A myriad of other conversations started up around us, some charged with excitement, others dripping with nervousness.

I waited and watched for Mykal, but she never arrived.

Roman guessed my intent and stopped Lark midsentence to tell me, "Since our little kitten doesn't attend classes, she's not allowed to enter Theirland."

Made sense. Maybe Cyrus intended to ask me to assist him while there. I would absolutely without question refuse. Probably.

A horn blared, and the crowd grew silent. Everyone's attention whipped to triage, where Cyrus had been speaking with the archduke and duchess since my exit with Roman. Archduke Heta and the duchess exited as well.

From the doorway, Cyrus made a hand motion. Armed guards marched forward, posting themselves beside the rifts. Tremors invaded my limbs. In a matter of minutes—seconds—I would leave the only world I'd ever known and enter my nightmare. The realm responsible for the Rock and the Madness, where perpetual night ruled. Although. Hmm. The Rock led to the mysterious third realm, where it must originate. Which meant the Madness originated there, too, and not Theirland. But Cyrus claimed Shaddai was a utopia without illness.

More puzzle pieces I couldn't fit together. My heart rate spiked. How was I ever to make sense of anything?

The transmitters activated, and a husky voice whispered inside my ears despite the distance between us. "Remember, this is a simple training expedition. Travel will hurt, but it's fleeting."

I jerked my gaze to Cyrus. Looking right at me, he spoke again, his expression almost tender. "I'll be waiting for you on the other side of the rift. Just come to me."

His voice tickled my ears, and his words enveloped me like a warm hug. Calm washed over me. Yes. I could walk to Cyrus. I could walk to Cyrus, no problem.

He crossed the room, stepped into the darkness, and vanished from view. Gasps and murmurs sounded.

A grinning Roman kissed Lark on the mouth in front of everyone. "Take the spot at the end of the line and stop any runners."

"Yes, sir. See you on the other side." She gave him a return peck before hustling to the back. Guess they were officially a couple now, all games done.

"First walkers," the guards at the seams called.

Roman advanced with eagerness, disappearing inside the shadows.

Inhale. Exhale. Mere moments until departure.

"Next walker."

Knees knocking, I plodded forward, bracing for my first realm walk. Was I truly about to do this? I paused at the edge. Inhale, exhale. Last chance to stay. Inching backward . . .

"Go," Lark shouted.

Yes. Go to Cyrus. Fear wouldn't stop me. Fortifying my resolve, I took the final step forward. Shadows swallowed me. The foundation at my feet vanished, and I fell into an endless void. Head thrown back, spine arched, I screamed in anguish. Too much, too much!

Blink. The foundation returned, and the agony fled. I collapsed, my legs unable to hold my weight. But strong arms wrapped around me, catching me before I hit.

"I've got you." Cyrus's voice came from outside my head, not inside. "You're all right. You're here. It's over."

Panting, I clung to him, desperate for some kind of human connection. Anything to anchor me to this present sense of safety and security.

He righted me and didn't protest when I poured myself over him. He might have even petted my hair. "You good?"

"Yes, thank you. Sir." I forced myself to straighten and release him, but I secretly rejoiced when he maintained our connection.

"Good. Look up."

I did, and my jaw dropped. The ceiling was transparent. For the first time in my entire life, I peered up at a night sky, and the beauty stole my breath. Pinpricks of light glittered in a bed of black velvet. Stars I'd only ever read about in books or seen in pictures, unable to glimpse from my tiny bedroom window while pritis lights glowed from buildings around the city. The photos had failed to accurately portray the miracle of the in-person sight.

"It's glorious," I breathed.

"Yes."

"*This* is a utopia."

"Yes. Until you see past the veneer."

My brow furrowed. What did that mean?

Commotion around us drew my attention to the rest of the room. Rounded walls covered in iridescent crystals. A dazzling golden floor. Pure luxury. "Walkers" recovering from travel.

Behind us, Juniper appeared from thin air, dropping to her knees. A fully recovered Roman rushed over to pull her up, and Cyrus released me at last. He said nothing else before stalking off to join a contingent of uniformed officers.

Titus arrived, appearing shell shocked, and I bounded over to assist him. He clung to me, as I'd clung to Cyrus.

I patted his back and offered the same words of comfort I'd been given. "You're all right. You're here. It's over."

He drew in a ragged breath, his tremors fading. "Thank you."

"No problem."

As more and more soldiers showed up, free space shrank. On-site medics hurried to examine those who vomited, passed out, or screamed.

When Lark emerged, the last member of our team, Roman ordered us to huddle together.

"Welcome to the Annex. As the HP explained, we'll be safe inside a heavily guarded facility as we do our ride-along with ground patrol today and tomorrow. I'd love to tell you we get to take a beat and regroup before we start, but one day we'll be sent through a rift and straight into combat. This is how we prepare. For that reason, our shift kicks off in ten. We're heading to dock 3, where we'll be linked to a preassigned partner. Don't speak again until you're secured in a POD or in an off-duty sector."

I didn't understand the need for silence, but I chose to obey the rule.

Roman guided us through a building as massive as Fort Bala. Opulence abounded. Windowed walls revealed a sea of shadows with hints of flashing lights in the distance. Veins of gold ran through a polished white floor. High ceilings accommodated an array of statues featuring the same male, with the top half of a human and the bottom half of some sort of dinosaur. He was unlike any statue in Ourland. A hood covered his face, and a long tail curled in a counterclockwise circle. Precious gems glittered from top to bottom.

Did anyone offer historical tours?

We entered a large room filled with hundreds of soundproof cubicles. Each possessed a side table and a central dais with a fat metal bar protruding from its back end. In some of the cubicles, a soldier, appearing to mime, stood atop the pedestal, banded in place.

An older woman stood behind a counter. Roman approached her first, and she motioned to an ID pad. He pressed his palm flat. She typed something, swiped up a small metal card and a small box, and passed both to him. Off he went. When my turn arrived, she and I followed the same process.

I dragged my feet to an unoccupied POD. To whom was I to be linked?

Having memorized the steps I was to take, I entered, inserted the card into the proper slot on the console, and donned the required attire:

a two-piece bodysuit meant to go over my clothing, plus a headband and gloves, all of which waited on the side table. The box contained a pair of contacts.

I secured everything, then took my place on the pedestal. A whirling sound preceded the emergence of rounded bars from the pole. Those bars circled my waist. Multicolored lights flashed over the glass walls, a picture forming. A spacious bedroom with a massive bed, buttery-soft-looking sheets, and a nightstand with a decanter of amber liquid.

"What the—" My body moved of its own accord, directed by the bodysuit. It felt as if someone pulled my puppet strings. I couldn't stop and soon realized I was acting out the motions of putting a gun together.

"Hello, Pink." The familiar voice brimmed with amusement, spilling through the room from speakers instead of the disks behind my ears. "You're early."

"Cyrus?" *Oh no I did not.* I walked in place, a tread rolling beneath my feet. "I obviously meant *High Prince Dolion*," I said as I mimicked turning a knob. On the screen, a door opened. Because of the contacts, I saw the whole thing as if I were right there with him.

"Obviously." He didn't comment about my slip of the tongue any other way. Not giving me permission to use his name again but not issuing a rebuke, either, and I wasn't sure what to think.

He paused at a full-length mirror, giving me a glimpse of his reflection. *Oh my.* He wore all black, with tactical gear anchored in place. A vest loaded with weapons and a belt heavy with even more. Two swords crisscrossed on his back, the handles rising over his broad shoulders.

"Unlike the other soldiers," he said, "I'm not guarding pritis mines or fighting feeders. I'm on a special mission. There's a plant growing in a field that occasionally produces a bundle of red berries. Most maddened ignore the fruit, but a rare few flock to it. On three separate occasions, a feeder has eaten them and recovered from the Madness within seconds."

Talk about a major game changer. I must see this plant! "What happened to them after they healed?"

A prolonged silence only added fuel to my curiosity. Finally he said, "One made it through a nearby rift but two were killed by feeders." He refocused the conversation. "We've never managed to obtain the berries for testing, but we hope to change that tonight. There's a cluster in bloom, and I'm tasked with retrieval."

And I got to accompany him. Me. Wow. Excitement quickened my heartbeat. "Are you planning to bring back a soil sample, too, and if so, may I log a formal request to smell it?"

His husky chuckle thrilled me in ways it shouldn't. The images on the glass changed rapidly, gliding from the bedroom to a hallway to an elevator. Cyrus was on the move. "Be honest. You wish you'd accepted the job as my assistant."

Here and now? "Not even a little." I walked with him. "An assistant wouldn't be linked up for a special plant-and-soil mission, in the running for top lady." Surely a special assignment meant extra points.

Another chuckle sent waves of pleasure through my veins. "Where's your concern for my welfare?"

"Concern is fear's ugly cousin, sir. As someone surprisingly brilliant has taught me, I resist fear; I don't encourage it. Let's do this!"

He snickered. "When you go all in, you go all in. I like it."

The elevator doors opened, and we—he—entered a heavily guarded arena. Recalling my own mission, I took in as many details as possible. Searching, searching for something, anything, that might demolish Ember's suppositions. But everything I saw just looked like more of the same.

Barons, the rank above knights, and viscounts, the rank above barons, approached Cyrus, seeking instructions. He barked out orders, staying on the go.

"We'll be in a vehicle as long as possible," he explained, entering an empty room with built-in cannons protruding from small wall cubbies. Another door loomed ahead. There, he paused with his hand on the knob. "This is the entry to a garage, where a team is waiting for us."

He engaged his lens, covering his eyes and therefore my own. "Do you remember the sensations caused by RVM?"

"I do." And I still wasn't a fan.

"My lens will activate when I step beyond this final checkpoint, correcting everything. You'll experience what I experience."

"Thank you for the warning."

"Ready?"

A seed of worry sprouted. While I was tucked safely inside, he would be out there, risking his life. "Be safe."

"Always." Amusement returned to his tone. "Take notes."

"I'm drafting my report as we speak," I quipped.

He snorted. "Forget the paper. I intend to give you an oral exam."

My cheeks blazed at the sudden, unexpected, and completely inappropriate thought that followed his words. He had *not* meant to sound so sexual. The man was on a mission, and it wasn't to get into my pants. So. Moving on. "I'll ace it, guaranteed."

"I suspect you're right." His low, husky tone kept the illusion of carnality alive, but I ignored it. Then he was pushing into the garage.

As predicted, my world instantly flipped upside down. The abrupt switch played havoc with my equilibrium, and I teetered. The bars prevented a fall. Then the lens did its job, and the floor became the floor again, rather than the ceiling. I wasn't the biggest fan of feeling as if I peered into a virtual reality, or the promised ache in my temples, but it hardly mattered. We were berry hunting!

Cyrus stalked into a wide-open space brimming with all manner of armored vehicles. I could almost smell the scent of fuel. Six viscounts worked together, loading boxes into a truck bed rimmed by metal bars and pritis clusters. Nothing out of the ordinary here either.

Noticing Cyrus, one of the men stopped and saluted. "High Prince Dolion. It's an honor to join you in the field again, sir." The others performed the same actions the moment they spotted their superior.

"Thank you for the escort." He withdrew his swords from their sheaths, climbed into the back of the truck, and sat with his spine pressed against the cab. Meanwhile, I performed the same motions, even that of sitting. Thankfully, a seat unfolded from the pole, holding me steady. "I have a trainee with me. I'll be speaking to her throughout the expedition."

"Yes, sir."

The truck shook as four soldiers joined us and two more settled in up front. Was Cyrus nervous at all? As the vehicle jostled forward, an exit in the garage opened, revealing a road illuminated by pritis. No feeders approached until we cleared the compound.

Any outside light vanished—there one second, gone the next. The only illumination came from the vehicle and armor worn by the soldiers, providing shadowy glimpses of crazed eyes. Wild snarls competed with the sound of the revving engine.

I tilted as the truck executed a turn, abandoning the paved road to speed along dirt and gravel. We dodged any battlegrounds, swerving as necessary to avoid the knights and barons who engaged with feeder hordes. The two groups clashed with such violence in a field illuminated by pritis light, I longed to look away.

"No questions for me?" Cyrus asked.

A moment passed before I realized he spoke to me. "Tons." But few involved the mission. "I'm trying to absorb everything without distracting you."

"We're five minutes out," the driver called.

A body slammed into the windshield, shaking the entire vehicle. I gasped as I bounced with Cyrus. Feeders swarmed from every direction, as if the soldiers had driven into a trap.

The driver floored the gas, mowing down anything in his path.

"There are too many feeders. He won't be able to stop," Cyrus told me. "If he does, feeders will glom the vehicle, and we'll get stuck. I'm going to jump and roll, which means you're going to slam against your bars. My apologies."

"Don't worry about me." How could he survive hurling himself into a horde of the infected? "Do what you've got to do."

He did, following two of the four guards out the tail of the vehicle.

Cyrus rolled across a rocky tundra, and as predicted, I thrashed back and forth against the pole. Dizziness crested as he popped to his feet and swung, his glowing swords arcing through the air. I had no control of my body as he sliced and diced his way forward, with the soldiers doing the same at his sides.

Light flicked with their every movement, revealing details I would have missed otherwise. The skill Cyrus displayed awed me even as the sights inspired only horror. Heads flew without bodies, and blood sprayed in arcs. Severed limbs plopped to the ground. Hisses, grunts, and panting breaths packed my ears.

If the "true" purpose of the Annex was to keep these feeders from Ourland, I would be forever grateful to CURED.

"Go, go," Cyrus commanded, and he sprinted off.

As he jumped and dodged the maddened, I jumped and dodged. As he climbed pieces of fallen carnival rides, I climbed, pushing my stamina to the brink. Muscles burned and shook. No wonder we were forced to run obstacle courses.

He utilized weapons I'd handled in class and, when necessary, wedged himself in a safe cubby to give himself time to observe and think. Visibility increased as rays of stark white light beamed from a castle in the distance, surrounded by a large body of water. A structure I didn't recall seeing in videos or textbooks.

Cyrus veered right. "Glowers," he shouted to the other soldiers as he decapitated a feeder. He switched his attention to the next challenger. And the next. "They're protecting the berries."

I scanned the darkness, finally spotting an attractive fortysomething man casually plucking weeds near a lush green plant. At his side was a woman—I gasped, astonished to my core. Ember. Ember was here, in Theirland. Had she followed me?

Both Soalians looked like they'd swallowed pritis stones. Gold light speckled with red emanated from the circles etched into their flesh. How unbothered they were, taking no account of the battle that raged around them. In fact, they displayed the very peace I'd craved during my entire existence.

Yearning squeezed me. Oh, to have a little of what they had, without having to join team evil.

The unknown male extended his arm, palm up, offering the still-fighting Cyrus a small red fruit from a hand missing a thumb. "We have something for you and the girl. Come. Take."

In that moment, I registered his identity. John Victors. Leader of the glowers.

The realization triggered an emotional defense. A wrecking ball to my already-fragile calm, obliterating any sense of tranquility.

"Arden, listen to me—our comms—okay?" Cyrus slayed two more feeders as static overshadowed the bulk of his words. "The glowers—so don't—"

Our connection cut.

CHAPTER FIFTEEN

Follow the light and find life.

—The Book of Soal 2.4.8.12

I waited on the pedestal for my connection to Cyrus to reactivate, tension mounting.

Waiting.

Too agitated to remain immobile, I disengaged the metal bars and paced in the POD.

Still waiting.

Hours passed. One after the other, soldiers completed their shifts and abandoned their cubbies, either shell shocked or jubilant. Foreboding stabbed me. Where was Cyrus?

Roman, Titus, Lark, and Jericho remained behind, engaged in major conflicts by the looks of it. Still I waited, not letting myself shout for help or demand answers. I needed to know Cyrus was okay.

Again and again my heart rate bypassed the threshold necessary to awaken his transmitter, but nothing happened. In desperation, I jogged in place. I wasn't sure what to do, what to think.

Cheers resounded from the other PODs. I didn't hear them, but I noticed the expressions and actions of the remaining lords- and ladies-in-training. When Roman stripped out of his bodysuit, removed his accessories, and withdrew his card, I rushed to do the same. We exited our PODs in unison, and I burst out, "Tell me what happened. Please."

Roman grinned. "We mowed down the infected and captured eight glowers, that's what!"

A confusing mix of relief and remorse assailed me. I wondered if Ember was among the prisoners. "Did you see Cy—the HP in your feed?"

"I caught a glimpse of him fighting John Victors one on one, but I didn't witness the end result." Roman threw his arms around me, lifted me off my feet, and swung me in a circle. "We just made history, baby! The most glowers captured during an inaugural training mission." He set me down, ruffled my hair, and jogged to Lark, pretending to gobble up her neck while she laughed. "We're going to celebrate so hard."

"Those dead maddened were once human beings, and now they'll never get a chance to recover," Titus spat as he stalked past us.

That must be the reason for my remorse. If not for treatment, my own mother could've been among the masses too sick to realize her bloodlust came from an otherworldly disease.

"They were beyond treatment," Roman called to the other lord-in-training's back. "You'd do better sympathizing with the people those things enjoy killing."

Titus raised a hand, flipping him off without looking back, and marched on. Roman huffed, and Lark whispered something in his ear, making him laugh again.

Though I wished to search for Cyrus, I knew it wasn't my right. Not knowing what else to do, I trailed the lovey-dovey couple to the counter, where we turned in our cards. I was a total third wheel on the walk to a colossal common space, where a party already raged. Members of my team mingled with knights and more-decorated barons, snacking, dancing, playing games, and discussing today's adventures. The words *High Prince Dolion* came up a lot, but only references to his fight with Mr. Victors. A few lords and ladies fell asleep against the walls.

As I maneuvered through the crowd, wanting to be anywhere else, my stomach rumbled. What I wouldn't give for more apple-and-fig tartlets. Or a doughnut. I hadn't eaten all day.

Of course, the only food left on the tables was meal bars. Though disappointed, I snatched one. Better something than nothing.

Fatigue caught up to me after I swallowed the last bite, and I yawned. My eyelids were beginning to feel like sandpaper when I blinked. Though I searched, I didn't find a safe, private spot to rest. No way I'd ever sleep out in the open.

Noticing Juniper standing alone in front of a statue, I closed the distance. "Hey."

"Hey, Princess Panic." She nodded, keeping her focus on the dinosaur man. The bubbly greeting conveyed only affection.

"Ooh la la. A title upgrade. I've really come up in the world. In school, I was merely referred to as Panic Girl."

She snorted. "Please tell me you know something about these statues."

"I was hoping you did."

"I do, and I don't. I skipped ahead in the archduke's class, but details were vague at best. From what I gather, this statue represents a former king."

Okay, that caught my attention. "Tell me more."

Pointing to the base, where strange symbols were carved, she said, "I excel with languages, but this one is tricky. Some kind of mix between ancient Greek, Egyptian, and Norse. And yet, different." She chewed on her bottom lip. "If something as fierce as this creature stood no chance against the Madness, how are we supposed to win?"

"That's a fair question to which I have no answer, only more questions," I muttered, earning a second snort. I wondered what Ember might know about the guy.

"You're the brave one." Grinning, Juniper bumped my shoulder with her own. "You're supposed to comfort me. Assure me we've got this."

"We've got this?" I asked, and she grinned. "Honestly, before this conversation I thought we *were* winning."

"Especially if the HP got John Victors off the streets."

"Yes." That would be a great thing. Wonderful. So why wasn't I thrilled by the idea?

Find out the true purpose of Theirland.

My tension returned full force. So far, I'd seen nothing to suggest Soalians were the good guys and little to suggest CURED was evil. And yet, I remained unsettled.

"Juniper," Jericho called behind us. "We celebrating or not?"

She glanced over her shoulder, waved, then gave me a half smile. "Gotta go. See you later, Ardie." Off she raced before I could warn her about the sometimes-appealing, always-rotten Jericho Jones.

On my own, I shuffled around a corner and discovered a bench that overlooked a large window. No one gathered nearby. Guess this was as private as I could get. Easing down, I peered outside, on the lookout for flickers of light, wondering how many glowers were out there and what other purpose this world could possibly serve, other than containing the infected and mining pritis. CURED didn't mine the crystals, metals, or precious gems as well, so they weren't after the treasure. Unless there was another kind of treasure here. Something more valuable than diamonds and gold.

I sat up straighter. That wasn't a terrible idea.

"Well? What did you learn tonight?"

My gaze snapped up, my mind blanked, and my breath caught. Cyrus! He was alive. Relief propelled me to my feet. He towered before me, his arms crossed over his chest. Blood, dirt, and other things were splattered on him, and gashes marred his face and arms, but he wasn't dead or hospitalized.

"Are you okay?" A bloodstained bandage covered his branded cheek.

"I told you there'd be an oral exam. What did you learn?" he asked again.

My pulse accelerated. "I learned you are incredibly skilled with a sword. And your fists. And guns, whips, and daggers."

He rolled his eyes, drawing my attention to his long, long lashes. He motioned to the bench. We sat side by side, not touching but close, as if we were dating. Or at least building a friendship, what he'd claimed.

"Let's hear what will help in your coming battles," he said.

"For starters, you were right."

"That admission was inevitable, but please, do continue. Tell me which of my wisdoms you found most accurate tonight."

Easy. "Unless I get stronger, faster, and wiser, I'll be a danger to myself and others. I need more practice, study, and practice. And yes, I mentioned practice twice, because it's doubly important."

A beat of silence lasted for an eternity. "Congratulations, Miss Roosa. Recognizing your weaknesses is necessary to overcoming them. Never take on a giant until you've defeated a bear."

"I have no interest in taking on either, but I understand your metaphor. My weaknesses are the bear, and the maddened are the giant."

"That works. For now."

Hmm. What else could he have meant? "From this moment on, I will pour myself into improving." I required lots and lots of seasoning. "You have my word."

"Good. I'll help you. You'll spend your free time in special classes with me."

"Yes, sir. Thank you, sir," I said, meaning it with every fiber of my being. "And congratulations to you too. You survived a battle with the world's most wanted criminal."

He shrugged, as if the feat of the century were no big deal. "I captured him."

Captured. Wow. "There was a girl in the garden with him." Wait. "Please tell me you made it back with a berry." The most important issue.

"Ember escaped," he replied, and I ignored the little flicker of relief. "I didn't arrive with a berry in hand. But I did lose my transmitters during the fight."

Well, then. I had no use for mine. I removed both disks. He accepted them, and that was that. The last of our whispered conversations. And that was a good thing. Of course it was good. No longer would he clock every time he made my heart race. Which was far too often!

"I'm happy to say I held on to this." He fished a small vial filled with soil from his pocket and passed it my way.

"For me?" I squealed, popping the cork and sniffing the earthy goodness. Pleasure unfurled. No sourness or metallic twang. Healthy. Excellent quality. Now *this* was a treasure worth guarding! I could grow something in it, no problem. "You sack of sugar! This is one of the most incredible gifts I've ever received." Maybe the HP and I were *already* friends.

He almost smiled. "Sack of sugar. Yes. That's me." His attention returned to the window, and it wasn't long before strain overtook him all over again. Lines of tension branched from his eyes, and his lips pressed in a thin line. He looked as if he carried the weight of the world on his shoulders and he could no longer hide it. I didn't have to wonder if something extra bad had occurred during his fight with John Victors.

An ache ignited within me. Had Cyrus been anyone else, I would've taken his hand and—oh, screw it. He'd given me soil. I could risk my pride to offer comfort. I clasped his hand and squeezed, surprised when he laced his fingers through mine, not just accepting my gesture but welcoming it.

New flutters curled through my abdomen. This wasn't just comfort. This was something more. I should pull away. For Shiloh's sake, if not my own. But I didn't pull away; like a fool, I held on tighter.

"Any questions for me?" Cyrus asked.

Countless. I settled for a statement. "I'm intrigued by the castle with lights."

He flinched, clearly surprised by my chosen topic. "I can tell you someone lives in it, but you don't have clearance to learn more, and this time I can't give it."

Well. Curiosity engaged. I might have just discovered the answer to Ember's challenge.

"Look," Cyrus said, pointing.

I followed the direction of his finger with my gaze. A massive light exploded on the horizon, casting gold, lavender, and azure streaks across the midnight sky. From our vantage point, we had a view of the entire city as feeders raced to escape the light now illuminating buildings decorated with glittering mosaics.

I spotted a well-documented relic from Earth and marveled. If the memory from my elementary school days was correct, the statue was known as Lady Liberty. Hmm. A dark, jagged outline shadowed every statue, even ours, as if they'd been painted with a shaky hand.

Massive trees stretched barren, gnarled limbs through multiple structures. Some grew from inside the buildings, while others sprouted along the outside. Bodies and body parts were strewn along gold-brick streets. Judging by the clothing worn by the victims, those parts came from knights, barons, and maddened alike. Pools of blood in the process of congealing resembled tar pits.

Grimacing, I focused on the light. "I'm not sure what I'm seeing," I admitted. Not a sunrise, but not the stark white I'd seen coming from the castle either. The rays possessed a lovely golden tinge, but they were already fading.

"Whenever a glower is taken out of commission, others rise in the ranks." A pause. "Theirland is a beautiful and horrid place, isn't it?" The light died completely, pitch black returning to cloak the land. Cyrus released me and stood. "Yes, I'm on my way."

I blinked up at him, confused and already missing his warmth. Not a good sign.

He tapped a new transmitter behind his ear. "Duty calls."

Ah. He was in contact with someone else now. I wasn't jealous. Nope. Not me.

"Get some rest, Lady Roosa. When we return, we'll pick up our conversation about the medic."

I pressed my tongue to the roof of my mouth. "I don't need to rest." With the threat of our upcoming discussion, I doubted I could. A yawn belied my words. "I don't feel safe enough to try."

Another pause. Then, "That will change once you've had more training." His boots thumped against the floor as he stalked off.

With a sigh, I stood and aimed in the opposite direction, tucking the vial into my pocket. I wandered—well, I wasn't sure where. I just—I needed to flee my thoughts for a bit. Maybe I'd rent a private cell and avoid the crowds. An hour of extra work for every hour inside wouldn't be too bad. I was doing extra work with Cyrus, anyway. Maybe that counted as payment.

Along the way, however, I ran into Juniper and Titus, and they provided a much-needed distraction.

"Jericho ditched me," she said with a pout, "so we're going to the library. Want to come?"

A chance to snoop without rousing suspicion. Yes! But I looked to Titus. He might not welcome me tagging along.

"Please join us," he said with a nod.

What a change in him. "I will, thank you." I accompanied the pair along winding hallways and through doors we needed our IDs to open. On the journey, I got blunt. "I'm guessing you no longer dislike me, but I'm confused about why you did before."

He sighed. "Until tonight, when I saw your face after POD time, I thought you were Roman's minion. I know his type. Never considers the means, only the end."

We ascended a flight of stairs. "He's not perfect, but he's not a bad guy."

Titus shrugged, clearly unconvinced. "I hear you've joined our ragtag team getting special lessons from High Prince Dolion."

Oooh. I wouldn't be receiving one-on-one tutoring as I'd assumed. Well. That was wonderful. Not disappointing at all. The other trainees needed help as much as I did. "I am, yes. And his kindness is much appreciated."

"Oh, he's not doing it out of the goodness of his heart," Juniper piped up. "The instructor who produces the top soldier wins some kind of prize, plus a bonus if their team is ranked first. Roman says there's a scoreboard in a private conference room."

Wires in my brain connected, welcoming a free flow of hurt. Cyrus and I weren't friends, and there was no connection between us. He merely contended for a prize. Ouch. I shoved my hands into my pocket, my fingers bumping into the vial. Motivation for the hopeless kid, no doubt.

"Something wrong?" Titus asked.

I pasted a smile on my face. "Why do you require extra credit? You're strong and fearless. Leadership material."

"Apparently isolating myself is"—lips pursed, he performed air quotes—"'unacceptable.'"

"Ah." We entered an underwhelming room with square tables and cushionless chairs. Shelves lined the walls, each scattered with printed textbooks I'd read in school. Manuals that listed CURED's accomplishments, the symptoms of the Madness, the atrocities committed by Soalians, and the slaughters instigated by feeders. Nothing about valuable resources here on Theirland. No history of the people or the world itself or descriptions of their war with the maddened. There was nothing about Soal either. There wasn't even an article about Theirland foliage.

I scrubbed a palm over my face, once again homesick for my plants and my mother. While my companions dove into an edition about the most decorated warriors in CURED history, I wandered down the hall and came upon a gym, where I used a treadmill to clear my head, running and running and running, shedding uncertainty and disappointment I wasn't ready to face.

Afterward, I visited the locker room and lingered in a private shower stall. Yawns came more rapidly, and the sandpaper sensation in my eyes returned and intensified. I nearly dozed off while standing, leaning against the wall, warmish water raining over me. Once dressed in clean fatigues I found folded in a small square cubby, I searched for a spot to hide. Alas. Every room, shadowed corner, and alcove was occupied. I paced the rest of the night.

Before POD patrol the next morning, I grabbed a meal bar and ate it on the go. Dread eclipsed every other emotion as I sealed myself inside a POD and suited up. What would I say to Cy—the HP when we linked up? He was an instructor, nothing more, nothing less.

Except, I wasn't paired with the HP but a soldier who did nothing but stand guard at the entrance of a pritis mine. Hours passed without action, covered mine carts self-wheeling along a track located within a metal building. And that was fine. Great actually. From the beginning, this was the kind of job I'd hoped to score.

Only problem was, my fatigue continued to demand its due, and once again I nearly fell asleep on my feet. Once my shift ended, I shed the equipment, determined. If I didn't find a spot to rest, I might collapse.

Exiting my POD, I found an unfamiliar soldier waiting for me. She confiscated my key card and motioned for me to follow her. I gulped. Maybe one of the captured glowers had mentioned my name. I could be on my way to an interrogation.

Dread resurged, but follow her I did. We wound through the building, eventually entering a hallway with multiple metal doors. She stopped, waving me into a small closet-size room with a bed, nightstand, mirror, and toilet.

A private cell? A prison? Frowning, I stepped inside for a better look. Maybe there was a note?

Without a word, she closed the door, sealing me inside.

"Wait!" I lunged and pulled on the handle. The entrance remained locked. *Don't panic. No big deal.*

A digital note flashed over the mirror. Get some sleep. My son tells me you need it. You're safe, you have my word, and the time is my treat. King Tagin Dolion.

A thousand different thoughts swirled, but I had no idea which ones to boot. Not that this was the time to think. Moaning, I threw myself across the bed. The mattress was firm, but I didn't care. My heavy eyelids drifted shut.

I dreamed of Cyrus.

CHAPTER SIXTEEN

Our enemy has a sole purpose: to steal what's
ours, kill us, and destroy those we love, but I have
restored all.

—The Book of Soal 2.4.10.10

I didn't see High Prince Dolion in Theirland again, not even when we lined up to return home. And I was glad. I had yet to shed residual images of him from my dreams. Images of him smiling and laughing, utterly carefree and looking at me in ways I shouldn't like. I'd made a big mistake, letting myself get too comfortable with him. Had opened up a little too much and revealed vulnerabilities best left hidden.

Mistaking someone's personal goal as friendship was a rookie's blunder I wouldn't make again. The HP's concern centered on his own personal victory, not my well-being. And that was fine. His prerogative. But still it hurt. Now, at least, I knew my place. From here on out, I'd be all academy all the time, as promised. Well, except for my investigation into CURED, Theirland, Soalians, and the Tome Society. I'd also be a better friend to Shiloh. How was he?

"Next walkers," a guard announced.

My turn. Conversations faded from my awareness, my entire world revolving around the tear in the atmosphere. Ignoring Technicolor memories of pain and helplessness, I entered the shadows.

Agony consumed me, just as before, cells exploding, bones cracking. Or seeming to. My knees buckled. I crashed to the floor, air bursting from my lungs.

Titus swooped over to help me stand. "You all right?"

"Yeah. Thank you." I turned to aid the realm walker who exited after me. The ever-silent Cash appeared, ashen and quaking. I caught him when he fell, but his heavy weight dragged me down with him.

New goal to add to my list: build muscle.

Jericho appeared after him. He grimaced but didn't miss a beat. In fact, he bent to heft Cash and me to our feet.

"Thanks," I muttered and jetted off. No breaks on return days. Warm-up kicked off in fourteen minutes.

"Hey, Arden. Hold up." Jericho swooped to my side. "Look. I know you've got something going with the HP."

I sputtered with indignation. "That's the most ridiculous thing I've ever heard. And that's quite a feat, considering you once told me you'd already bagged me in your mind, and out of the goodness of your heart you were willing to show me what I did wrong in your fantasy so reality would be better for you."

Jericho puffed up his chest, his version of *you're welcome*. "Save your denials about a romance. During my first patrol, I was paired with a guard in the HP's truck. You made the coldest guy I've ever met smile. And I get it. You've got this whole understated beauty thing going on with your big eyes and pouty red lips. What I don't know is whether I saw the HP eat a Theirland berry and vanish." He lowered his voice. "No one else seemed to notice or care. Am I losing my mind?"

No need to ponder it. "Yes, you are." I wasn't the HP's biggest fan, but I didn't have to wonder if he'd eaten the fruit CURED wished to test. No, he hadn't. He wouldn't risk his life or his victory. Granted, he hadn't returned with a berry, but that meant nothing. Less than nothing. No doubt the strobe effect of light and dark had played tricks on Jericho's mind. "Another possibility is—and please excuse my reliance on logic—the HP seemed to disappear in the darkness."

Jericho narrowed his eyes. "Except I saw it. He was there, then he wasn't. So? What did *you* see?"

"My feed got cut before the big battle," I admitted, and he huffed.

As others in a hurry to get to class crowded behind us, he rubbed the back of his neck. "Do me a favor and talk to him about it and let me know what he says. Okay?" Jericho branched to the right.

Not okay. Not okay at all. What's more, I didn't appreciate his sudden nice-guy act. An obvious attempt to manipulate me to his will. Whatever. He wasn't worth another thought.

I shoved my hand into my pocket, where my vial of soil rested. Deep breath in. If the HP acquired a berry seed, I bet I could grow one . . . which might be a contender for the true purpose of Theirland. Maybe? But no. Whatever the treasure was, it would paint CURED in a bad light to Ember's way of thinking. There was no other reason she would tell me to search out such information.

In the commons, I grabbed a meal bar.

"Shouldn't we get a break after the return trip?" Juniper mumbled, at my side as we headed to class.

"I doubt a murderous feeder will take your need for a nap into account," Lark quipped from in front of us.

We entered the gym, other trainees arriving seconds later. The starting bell sounded, and we scrambled into a semblance of a formation.

Mykal swept in and called, "The HP is otherwise engaged and will miss this morning's warm-up. You'll keep Sunday's schedule today and run laps while evaluating your own performance in Theirland. Be sure to list areas you need to improve. There will be a test during your actual evaluation, and those who fail it will disqualify themselves from the title of top soldier." After blowing us a kiss, she skipped from the room, disregarding the discordant chorus of groans, complaints, and cheers.

A twinge of bitterness tempted me to anger. Something big must've happened to prevent the HP from being here. He needed to improve his chance of winning his precious contest, after all.

He could've, say, gotten in trouble for eating the berry.

No, no. Silly supposition. I bet he was in medical, getting his injured cheek repaired. Or celebrating his success with the powers that be.

"You heard her. Run laps and contemplate your failures," a knight commanded.

I did exactly that, intending to present the HP with a more detailed evaluation than the one I'd given him in Theirland.

During the second half of class, we practiced fighting a hologram. I gained fresh bruises and cuts on my left hand. They were small and had already stopped bleeding, but I should probably get them looked at . . .

After the bell rang, I made my way to medical, a pep in my step. A smile spread when I spotted Shiloh. He was alone, reclining on a gurney, typing into a digital file. He looked so good. Like his normal self. Relaxed and happy.

"Hey," I called, leaning into the lobby counter. No sign of the HP, thank goodness.

Shiloh glanced up, a return smile lifting the corners of his mouth. "Hey." He jumped to his feet, set the file aside, and crossed to me. "How was your first realm walk?"

"Better and worse than expected. How are *you*?"

"Great. I continue to test negative, and I've figured out my future."

"Shiloh, that's wonderful."

He smiled again, his eyes sparkling at their brightest setting. "If you go on a date with me Thursday, I'll tell you all about it."

"Deal." I beamed at him, pleased with the outcome. "Before I go, can I snag a couple bandages? For my hand." I showed him the "damage," winning a third smile, this one teasing.

"I should wrap you up to ensure infection doesn't set in. You'll be late to class, but I'll send a note to the HP excusing your tardiness. He'll understand. This is practically an emergency."

"Lifesaving medical care." I hightailed it around the counter, thrilled to steal this moment with him.

I eased onto the gurney he'd abandoned and watched him gather supplies. While relocating the file he'd left behind, I caught the name and frowned. *Lady Lemon Ade.*

"Did a new recruit arrive?" Someone who just happened to be named after our code word?

"No." He offered nothing more on the topic. After cleaning my cuts, he rolled a bandage around my knuckles. "I've learned an irrefutable truth."

Curiosity engaged. "About . . . ?"

"CURED." He paused to sign into my unbandaged palm, "Evil."

My blood flash froze. "Did something happen?" Because he wasn't—couldn't be—inferring what I thought he might be inferring.

He didn't explain. Instead, he released me and put up the supplies. "We'll talk on our date."

"But—"

Dr. Korey opened a door and stuck out her head, her gaze zeroing in on me as if she'd known I was here. "Don't you have somewhere to be, Lady Roosa?"

"My hand. Cuts." I showed her the bandage. A bell sounded, signaling the start of my evaluation. "But yes, you're right, I do have somewhere to be." I glanced at Shiloh.

"I won't forget to send the HP a note about your tardiness," he assured me, as if all were normal.

"Thank you." I zipped off, unsure how to feel about our interaction. He'd called CURED evil. Something only Soalians did.

"—practice the art of the attack," the HP was telling the class when I slipped into the room. His cheek was no longer covered by a bandage. A large scab marred the center of his brand. "I will make the rounds and ask questions about your performance in Theirland. You will answer."

He offered no rebuke, just motioned me over, where an unoccupied punching bag hung in a row of twenty.

He positioned himself behind me, quietly asking, "What did you do to your hand?"

"Cuts. You'll get a note from—"

"I know how the system works," he interjected. "You're good?"

I almost believed he cared. Yes, almost. "I am, thank you." Resentment dripped from the words, and I couldn't hide it. "What would you like to know about Theirland?"

"We've already discussed it." His voice hardened as he commanded, "Work on your technique. When you go on the offensive, strike first and strike hard."

"Sir, yes, sir." I executed a punch.

He readjusted my position and helped me execute several dirty jabs, the warmth of his palms a shock. "If there's something you'd like to tell me, Pink, do it. Speak."

What a loaded command. Uttered in his low, husky tone, no less. I opened and closed my mouth, but only little noises escaped. I wanted to say a thousand things, but none of them were wise.

"Never mind. If you aren't brave enough to admit it, I don't want to hear it." Cyrus strode off, leaving me baffled. And frustrated. My cauldron threatened to boil over.

The rest of class passed in a blur, my head filling up with a thousand different possibilities about what he'd meant. When the bell rang, he announced, "Tutoring won't begin until tomorrow." Then he left. Which was fine. Whatever.

I directed my attention elsewhere, rolling thoughts about Theirland through my mind as I ate lunch, completed Madness Basics, and took my first driving class. The realm was dangerous and shrouded in mystery. Someone lived in a well-lit castle. There was no evidence of the Rock, yet the streets were overrun with feeders in far worse condition than anyone in Ourland. Sometimes, berries grew on the ground, rather than the top of the Rock.

Maybe there was a piece of the Rock hidden in Theirland. I mean, the maddened loved the Rock. Surely the maddened in Theirland weren't content to live without it.

I pondered the disparity while I pretended to read about vehicle safety features. Also while barons escorted us inside to run drills. My thoughts only switched gears when I realized Jericho was nowhere to be found. In fact, Mykal was MIA too.

Rather than hang out with my team during free time, I holed up in my cell to think. But honestly, after only a few minutes, I gave up. I'd used up the last of my daily allotment of intelligence, my brain tired.

Stretched out on my bed, I traced different phrases carved into the wall.

Let the **CURED** rule
The Kingdom is **OURS**
Born of Champions
Your Tomorrow Depends on Your Today
Welcome the Wisdom that Comes
We are the **CURE** and **CURED**
They Will Fall, We Will Rise

I should leave a mark of my own, but I didn't even have the mental fortitude to come up with something. Although. Hmm. My gaze caught on the word *The*. Huh. The artist had placed a small bracket under the *T*, creating a downward-arrow effect.

Out of curiosity, I followed the arrow and found another bracket underneath a different word. That one led to another and another. Each bracketed word was spaced out, seemingly unrelated to the others, but when considered together they formed a circle, the emblem for the Tome Society—and a complete sentence.

The Kingdom of Tomorrow Comes and CURED Will Fall

Excitement dimmed, turning into irritation. Obviously, a Soalian once bunked here.

Needing calm, I freed my vial of dirt from beneath my pillow, where I'd stored it, and popped the lid. Ah. The good stuff. The scent of life itself.

"I'm here, I'm here," Mykal cried, sailing inside the room.

Relieved to see her, I corked the vial, returned it to its hiding spot, and launched to my feet to hug her tight. "We've got to talk."

"I know! I want to hear all about your travels, Theirland, everything."

The bell rang. A second later, our door closed and locked. I returned to the bed to strap myself in, saying, "Travel hurt, Theirland sucked, but I'm hangin' in there." With barely a pause, I asked, "Did the HP mention me today?"

"No." Her brow wrinkled. "Why?"

"Don't know. He asked me if there was anything I wished to confess." If he'd alluded to my dealings with Ember and the Tome Society, I was in big trouble. But no. He wasn't the type to hint about that kind of thing.

"He had a busy day. Attended meeting after meeting after meeting and had an explosive argument with his dad. The walls were soundproof, but they opened the door once and *oh sweet heavens.* The fury! The shouting! I'm surprised they weren't swinging. Then the HP stormed out, handed me a list of people to contact, and took off on the train, only to return a few hours later."

Cyrus had just captured the most wanted criminal on two worlds. His father should be praising him. Unless . . . the berry. "I wonder why they argued."

"From what little I overheard, I think the king pushed for the public execution of the new prisoner and the HP fought for time to gather more information."

There'd been no announcement, so maybe he'd won the argument.

Fast, pounding footsteps sounded from the still-bright hallway, and we both froze. A visitor at this hour?

A large shadow reached our doorway before a man stopped and gripped the bars, peering in at us.

"Shiloh?" I jolted upright, but the chain kept me from standing. He looked terrible. Dirt streaked his wrinkled clothes. His hair stuck out in blood-crusted spikes. A raw gash bisected his brow. "What happened?"

"What's wrong?" Mykal demanded. "Who did this to you?"

His attention whipped to her, and his eyes narrowed. A cold, cruel grin cracked his lips.

My stomach curdled. No, no, no. Please no.

Never looking anywhere but his friend, he pressed his hand against the ID pad outside our cell. The door slid open. "Listen to Soal. Love Soal."

Mykal and I cried out in unison, scrambling to make ourselves smaller targets.

Shiloh had broken, just as Amelia had, all those years ago. This was my greatest nightmare on steroids.

"Help us!" Mykal screamed, pressing herself into the corner. "Help!"

Chains rattled beyond our cell, soldiers shouting questions and pleas.

"Love Soal." Shiloh stomped over and swung. His fist connected with her jaw, and her entire body whipped to the mattress. Though dazed, she attempted to kick him off. Laughing, he swung again. Contact. Blood sprayed from her mouth, painting the walls. "Love Soal, love Soal."

"No!" I screamed, hot tears spilling down my cheeks. She hadn't trained, was helpless. "Shiloh! Shiloh! Look at me. I'm right here." The chain stretched as I extended my leg to prod him. The infection was so new; he must be in there somewhere. "This isn't you. You're good and kind. We make lemonade together. Remember?"

He craned his neck, meeting my gaze with a crimson-stained fist raised in midair. The cruel smile reappeared.

"Please don't do this," I begged.

From there, everything happened so fast. "Listen. Love." He zoomed over and swung, but I kicked him in the chest, sending him stumbling backward. Not that it bought any time.

Roaring, he lunged with renewed force. I launched a second kick, my bare heel slamming into his chin. Again he stumbled backward. Again he lunged at me immediately afterward. Left with no other choice, I tried again. Expecting my defense this time, he caught my ankle and yanked my lower body off the bed. I yelped when the chain snapped tight, nearly wrenching my shoulder from its socket.

The sound of my anguish must have penetrated his killer instinct. He paused and shook his head. Banged his fists into his temples.

"Shiloh, please. We're friends." I hung from the edge of the mattress, as still as a statue, doing my best not to startle him. "We're going on our second date in a matter of days."

"Love Soal." With a growl, he struck my stomach. Air exploded from my lungs. He struck again, his knuckles connecting with my cheek. My brain rattled against my skull, and blood flooded my tongue. Searing pain. Instant nausea.

When he drew back his elbow, intending to unleash another blow, I used my pillow to block, then maneuvered to my stomach, patting the bed, searching for the vial. There! He punched the back of my head, and I flopped over the mattress. But I didn't drop my best weapon. Stunned but not out for the count, I knew. He wouldn't stop unless I made him.

With tears in my eyes, I slammed the vial against the wall. Grains flew when the glass burst. A jagged shard remained in my grip.

He latched onto my ankle and gave another yank. The chain pulled taut, my abused shoulder screaming in protest. Choking on grief but no less determined, I twisted and swung. The tip of the shard sliced into his eye. Blood poured over his face, and he howled, instinctively reaching for the injury. I had a split second to attack or retreat.

Strike first and strike hard.

Snarling, Shiloh dove onto me. Instinct took over, and I did as I'd been trained, hammering the shard into his throat again and again.

Boom, boom, boom. My heart thundered in time to each stab of the glass. The blows cut deep, leaving gaping wounds. He tripped backward, smacking into the floor, where he gasped for a breath he couldn't catch.

Horror infiltrated every inch of my being as his motions slowed. As he stilled. As his head lolled to the side, his chest barely rising. He was dying because I'd hurt him. Just as I'd hurt Amelia.

No! No! I fought the chain with all my might. If I could just get free, I could stanch the flow of blood. He could get treatment. I refused to let him die. Wouldn't steal him from his family. "You—you'll recover and get medical care," I stammered. "We'll make more lemonade. This isn't the end."

His gaze held mine as blood gurgled from the corners of his mouth.

"Help us," I screamed. Bile burned my esophagus. I looked to Mykal. She was curled into a fetal ball, weeping. "Please!"

The sound of racing footsteps arose. A helper? Or another infected? I pinned my focus to the crimson-soaked glass clutched in my quaking hand. Shiloh's flesh hung from the tip. Crying out, I dropped the shard, my only weapon, as if it were laced with poison. I just, I couldn't harm anyone else.

Cyrus halted in our open doorway, a gun and dagger at the ready. Fury and fear dominated his features. He scanned the cell, seeming to take in everything at once.

His expression shuttered, erasing any emotion. He sheathed the weapons and reached for me, but I shook my head.

"Fix him," I commanded. "Tell me you'll fix him!"

Cyrus crouched beside Shiloh to administer aid. He worked on the medic for minutes that lasted hours before hanging his head and inhaling deep. He flipped his gaze to mine. No. No! A hoarse, broken whimper seeped from me. Blood rushed from my head, igniting a high-pitched ring in my ears. Numbness flowed from limb to limb, inside and out.

Time slowed to a crawl as medics rushed in. Cyrus directed them to Mykal, then unfastened my binds. Despite my newfound freedom, I couldn't force my body to move.

He examined my face and checked my vitals. Though his mouth moved, I heard nothing but that ring. I watched the happenings around me, feeling as if I were trapped in a dream.

A medic carried Mykal from the cell. Cyrus gently collected me and clutched my limp body to his chest. Aches and pains registered, but they weren't strong enough to shatter my haze of shock.

"—orry, sorry," Cyrus was saying as the ringing faded. He rushed me into the hall. Trainees shouted from their cells, demanding answers and freedom. "I've got you, Arden. I won't let go." But he did let go when we reached our destination, easing me onto a gurney.

I said nothing as medics took over, busying themselves with my care, cutting off my tank and shorts. The blue set I'd worn on my first date with Shiloh. Who was now dead.

My chin quivered. I looked away from Cyrus, the medics, everyone and everything. I didn't want to be here. Didn't want to be anywhere. I'd killed Shiloh. Me. I'd ended his life and erased his future. Because that's what I did. I drove people to the edge, then pushed them over.

The night Amelia died, we fought. She was older than me. She'd tried to sneak out of our bedroom, but I'd stopped her. She begged me to relent, promised to return in a few hours, but I hadn't wanted her outside the safety of our bedroom walls, vulnerable to attack. She told me I was the worst sister ever born.

I proved her right only hours later when she broke. What if I'd let her leave? What would've happened? What if I'd shared with Cyrus everything about my interaction with Ember, hiding nothing? What if I'd aimed lower when I'd struck Shiloh? What if Cyrus had arrived sooner?

A soft caress against my cheek lured me from my haze of thoughts. I almost leaned into the contact, desperate for comfort, but I didn't. I deserved to feel every emotion now plaguing me.

At my bedside, Cyrus tenderly traced his fingertips on the unbruised side of my face. "You tested negative. Arden, do you hear me?"

So I'd tested negative. So what? So had Shiloh. But I didn't care anymore. I'd reached my limit. The cauldron of frustration had iced over, the fire beneath it snuffed out. I was too tired to bother.

"Go away," I mumbled and closed my eyes. For once, I didn't fight sleep. I let it whisk me into its deepest depths.

CHAPTER SEVENTEEN

Guard your heart, for it steers your life.

—*The Book of Soal* 1.20.4.23

I awoke with a start, bolting upright. The swift movement ignited discomfort in every inch of my body and unbridled a tsunami of memories. Shiloh. The Madness. Pain. Blood.

Death.

A groan rumbled in my throat, trapped. The shock of what had happened was wearing off, taking my precious numbness with it. Shiloh was dead. Because of me.

White-hot tears welled, searing my corneas. I sat atop a plush bed rather than the gurney I'd fallen asleep on. The room I now occupied was twice the size of my cell, with iridescent crystals growing over the walls and medical equipment throughout. An open doorway revealed a bathroom with a private toilet and shower stall. A small planting pot and a reader sat atop a wheelable table.

I was alone with a barrage of tormenting questions. When did Shiloh become infected? He'd tested negative only hours before. What infected him? Not the Rock. There wasn't a section nearby. Or if there was, I didn't know about it. Shiloh could have found one. He'd probably been on the hunt, desperate to investigate his theories about the cure. Though why not use the non-Rock Rock Mykal used for study?

Fatigue bubbled from a never-ending well. I curled into a ball, barely resisting the urge to pull the covers over my head. Had Ember learned of her brother's death? If she didn't know, she needed to learn. Maybe I could find a way to message her.

I patted for the reader and pulled it to my face. As soon as the device switched on, the glower consumed my screen, her eyes red rimmed.

"Hello, Arden."

She knew. Every muscle in my body tensed. Live feed. I flopped to my back, breathing out, "I'm so sorry."

"I warned you, but you refused to believe." Ember's lids fluttered shut for a moment. A tear rolled down her cheek. "They killed him."

My calm frayed, denying my tears no longer an option. She must not have the full story. "I was the one who wielded the weapon, not CURED. Me."

Anger flashed over her features. Her irises blazed. "You were the weapon, not the wielder."

That . . . no. It made no sense.

"He joined us, you know." She leveled me with a brutal stare. "While you were in Theirland, he accepted an invitation into the Tome Society."

I absorbed her confession and reeled. "He told me he'd figured out his future." To learn he'd signed on with the Soalians, to recall how he'd exhibited the same peace as the glowers—puzzle pieces clicked into place.

"You infected him," I snarled. The worst of the worst? Yes! I should have spilled everything to Cyrus. He'd given me plenty of opportunities.

"I freed him," Ember snarled back.

"You condemned him."

"You are a fool!" she screeched. "You know nothing about anything and act as if you know everything."

Silence stretched, both of us panting. She calmed first, her expression smoothing into polite serenity.

"I gave him his first instruction," she said. "Told him to leave the base. He wasn't supposed to be there. But he refused to leave. He decided to remain in his invisible chains *for you*." Her eyes closed for a moment, and she drew in a shuddering breath. "I'm responsible for overseeing his last request. Your freedom." Staring at me with swirling irises, she commanded, "Look. See."

A massive three-story room replaced her, dominating the screen. And my reality. I felt as if I stood among leather-bound books meticulously stacked upon freshly polished shelves.

I didn't have to wonder what I was seeing. The infamous library of Soal.

"This isn't real," I rasped. But I did gawk and marvel. Genuine or not, the sights stunned.

Wooden tables with elaborate carvings displayed treasures from the ages. Musical instruments, vases, and breathtakingly sparkly jewelry. Cushioned couches and chairs were positioned under trees that grew from the floor. Flower-heavy branches extended in every direction.

People glided here and there, moving in sync with soft music waltzing across the airwaves. Plush chairs offered cozy spots to read. I cast my gaze from face to face, searching for anyone I might recognize. A woman and a man sat together on a bench, talking, and I was almost certain I'd seen them in the halls of Fort Bala.

A soft feminine voice overshadowed the music, inviting people to listen to *Meg on the Reg* in an hour.

This is realer than anything you've ever seen before. Ember's voice filled my head. *Come. See more.*

My view swept forward with dizzying speed, stopping inside a small empty room. A single book waited on a table. The intricately decorated cover read *The Book of Arden*.

One half of my being shouted, *Run! Leave this place.* The other whispered, *Open. Read.* What was written inside it?

I reached out . . . and the screen blanked.

"Bring it back," I commanded with a huff.

Ember's image returned, determination fierce. "Only members of the Tome Society are able to open their books. Soal is eager for you to begin your story."

She wanted to make this a recruiting moment? Fine. I only cared about information. "Now I know you're delusional. A god wouldn't desire someone like me on his team."

"Come talk to him. Ask him why." She cleared her throat and raised her face. "Arden Roosa, this is your second invitation. Will you join the Tome Society?"

"No." Nothing more needed to be said on my part.

"Very well." She sighed. "I'll ask you once more, then never again. Until next time." The screen went blank.

Teeth grinding, I threw the reader against the wall. Glass shattered and tinkled over the floor, but I felt no satisfaction. I rolled into a fetal position and closed my eyes, empty inside.

A light thump of footsteps registered. Defenses activated, and I bolted upright, ready to punch.

"Easy." Cyrus approached me slowly, palms out in a gesture of innocence. He sat at my side. The bed dipped, and he gently patted my arm. "You're safe with me."

Exhaustion had aged him at least a decade. "Safe." I almost laughed. No one was ever truly safe in either world. "Where am I?"

"A recovery room."

As if I could *ever* recover from this.

He stroked my hair, but I flinched from the touch. No, thank you. I hadn't deserved comfort before, and I didn't deserve it now.

Hurt flashed over his features, there and gone. Drawing his hand away, he softly asked, "How are you?"

I'd been irrevocably changed by what had occurred, as if someone had reached inside my chest, cut out my heart, and transplanted a new one. From fragile porcelain to steel wrapped with barbed wire. I merely said, "I'm fine."

"Are you thirsty? Hungry?"

"Just curious."

He frowned with concern. "You slept nineteen hours. You should be starved."

Nineteen hours. Wow. I'd lost an entire day.

His gaze slid to the broken reader on the floor. He tilted his head. "Read something you didn't like?"

Instead of explaining my mistreatment of the device, I asked, "Where's Mykal? How is *she*?"

"Shaken and bruised but improved. At her request, she was transported to a treatment facility in Bala City, where she'll remain until she's ready to return. That option is available to you as well."

Part of me wanted to take time to heal and accept. The rest of me insisted I train. Forget top lady. I wished only to become too strong to defeat.

"I'm ready for class," I stated. "Or I will be after a shower." I kicked my legs over the mattress.

"You can go to class if you wish, but we'll finish our conversation first." His tone firmed at the end, leaving no doubt he'd issued a command.

I stood anyway. "If you want me to stay in the bed, you'll have to chain me."

He didn't protest as I padded into the bathroom, shut the door, and turned the lock. Let him punish me for it later. Better yet, let him leave. A set of folded fatigues waited at the edge of the sink. Brand new toiletries filled a basket.

With the twist of a knob, water sprayed from the upper spout of the stall and heated rapidly. I stripped, trying not to notice the bruises, cuts, and smears of dried blood marring my skin. How much was mine, and how much was Shiloh's?

I pressed my tongue to the roof of my mouth. As scalding water rained, I soaped up, rinsed off, and thought of my medic. He'd been such a wonderful person. So kind and supportive. Protective and dependable. And funny. His smile had lit the room.

Why hadn't I kissed him while I'd had the chance? Now he was gone, and I'd never get to see him again. I hadn't even told him about lemonade.

Maybe my heart wasn't steel after all. Fresh tears trickled down my cheeks. I swiped at the droplets with rigid fingers. How dare Ember suggest CURED used me to kill the medic? She merely attempted to shift blame from herself. The infection had come from her, no doubt about it.

Although, she *had* warned me of a coming execution.

I flattened my hands against the stall wall and ducked my head under the water. Why warn me of her own plan? Unless she had planned to kill him and had issued the warning in order to say *Told you so.* But why oversee his death at all? The outcome didn't benefit her or the Soalians in any way. Did it?

Appendages beginning to prune, I switched off the water, dried, and dressed. A glance at my reflection in the steam-proof mirror above the sink revealed a bruised, ashen girl with red-rimmed eyes. A lady-in-training on her own, with zero allies. *Trust no one. Get strong.*

Nose in the air, I exited the bathroom. Cyrus sat at the foot of the bed, his elbows resting on his knees, his head bowed.

He flipped up his gaze and demanded, "Tell me everything, Arden."

"There's nothing to tell." Currently, he was the one with answers, not me. "Shiloh gained access to my cell, where I was chained and vulnerable. You saw the results."

Shame pulsed from Cyrus. "Medics are given unrestricted entry in case of emergencies."

"A practice that endangers the people who rely on your protection." Boiling cauldron. My nails cut into my palms. I pressed on. "I'm late for drills."

He stiffened. "You'll stay here until you are dismissed. I've been lenient with you and allowed certain liberties, and that was a mistake. You've forgotten that I outrank you. Today, you will remember protocol and act accordingly."

"Sir, yes, sir," I grated with a salute. I didn't push to know why he'd allowed those "certain liberties." I didn't care. I just wanted to go.

A muscle jumped within his brand, a sure sign he neared the end of his patience. "Did Shiloh mention anything odd before he died? Or give you something?"

"No, sir."

"Did he tell you what he meant by *irrefutable truth*?"

My breath caught. Cyrus had listened to a recording of my final conversation with the medic, and he wasn't trying to hide it. "No, sir. But I can tell you an irrefutable truth of my own. Shiloh was happiness. He was a good guy. I really liked him. He patched my wounds, and I caused his." My chin quivered, and hot tears welled again. I spun before my companion noticed. "The scale is forever unbalanced."

Cyrus crossed the distance between us and settled his hands on my shoulders, his touch light. The heat of his body enveloped me, bringing with it his heady scent. "What happened isn't your fault." Even his voice proved a comfort, as soft as velvet.

In that moment, a part of me hated him. "I didn't say it was, but either way, I'm not interested in your opinion. I'd like to go. Sir."

He sighed and severed contact. "While Mykal is away, you'll serve as my assistant."

Oh, I would, would I? The threat of tears ended, and I whirled around. "You said you'd always give me a choice. Did you lie?"

"I did not. But I know you're hurting and furious and counting on your training to help you set things right."

"Things can never be set right."

"Let me finish." He stared me down, resolute. "I intend to train you myself, after hours. You'll learn more with me on a one-to-one basis, in less time."

I waited, silent, fuming.

"Speak," he demanded.

"I'd rather learn with the rest of my team, sir." The words burst from me.

He gave a clipped shake of his head. "You're making decisions from a place of hurt and ignorance. You don't yet fully comprehend the enemy you're fighting, the war you're waging, or the weapons being used against you, so how can you accurately judge what helps or harms your situation?"

His words were an echo of Ember. "Enlighten me then, sir. That *is* your job. Or perhaps you're too busy winning your contest with the other instructors to aid your students."

A line formed between his furrowed brows. He stepped into my personal space, leaving little distance between us. I stepped back. Undeterred, he followed me. This time, I remained in place. If he tried to comfort me again, he would regret it. The thick veneer of docility I'd worn for so long was beginning to crack, liberating an aggression I hadn't known I possessed.

"I've been where you are." He didn't touch me in any way, but his heat got a firmer grip on me, attempting to lure me closer of my own volition. "I've experienced the horror of wielding lethal force against a loved one. I understand the surge of guilt, hatred, and rage."

Maybe, but he knew nothing of helplessness, vulnerability, and uncertainty. He was a Dolion. Powerful beyond imagining.

I pointed a finger of accusation in his face and opened my mouth to hiss and scream and curse him. Only sputtering noises escaped.

He gave me a soft look, as if daring me to unleash. Or begging me to.

The ridiculous thought acted as a twenty-pound bag of common sense, slamming into me. As if the emperor's grandson would beg for anything. "I want to train with the others, not share my feelings, or fetch and carry for you. I *need* to train with the others. Don't take that away from me."

He worked his jaw. "Very well." His motions clipped, he waved to the pot I'd noticed earlier. "The soil is yours. I planted a seed. Something I thought you might enjoy. Put it in your room and go to class. But you *will* spend your free time with me. Even your days off."

A gift? I looked at it, then looked at him. It. Him. I'd defied him, and he rewarded me? Knocked off kilter, I swiped up the pot and admitted, "I don't understand, sir."

"Stop calling me *sir*," he snapped, then scrubbed a hand over his face. He drew in a deep breath. "There was a pre-Fall custom of sending flowers to someone who lost a loved one. I thought . . . it doesn't matter. Just water the seed once a day. Go."

I said nothing else, just raced from the room.

⤜⤏⤚

I threw myself into my education, improving by leaps and bounds with every combat simulation and obstacle course. But no matter what I did, Shiloh remained a fixture in the forefront of my mind.

Again and again I replayed his death. Our conversations. Certain facts became an itch I couldn't scratch.

On our date, Shiloh had spoken of scientific findings suggesting the Rock cured the infected when they ate bits of stone and drank the internal liquid, whatever it was. I knew he was wrong, but a denial, even logical, was no longer good enough. I craved proof. Nothing else would silence the questions whispering on repeat in the back of my mind. What if Shiloh could've been saved? What if I'd killed the wonderful man destined to bring the cure for Madness to the worlds?

Other questions followed, tormenting me. What if the Rock did, in fact, heal the Madness? Why had Jericho left the base?

More than a week ago, the day after the attack, Cyrus had announced the lord-in-training's departure, but he hadn't cited a reason.

Jericho believed the HP ate a Theirland berry, and he had intended to get answers. Then, suddenly, he opted to desert his post? *Make it make sense.* He might have discovered something truly frightening and run because he'd felt unsafe. Perhaps he'd met an untimely end.

Had Cyrus eaten a berry given to him by his enemy? Surely not. There was no reason good enough to take such a risk. Unless he was a

Soalian desperate to keep CURED from acquiring it. A secret worth killing for.

A humorless laugh barked from me as I turned a corner, headed to the medical sector to speak with Shiloh's coworker. If Cyrus was a Soalian, I would eat my shoes.

A baron walked past me and nodded a greeting. I nodded in return, then performed a double take and frowned, certain I'd seen him inside Soal's library, on a bench with a woman.

Propelled by a force I couldn't quash, I turned and chased him down. Or tried to. He'd rounded the corner I'd just vacated and vanished. But. There were no doors. No windows.

My heart thudded as I backtracked. I must have gotten lost in my thoughts for longer than I realized and missed his full departure.

I trudged to the medical sector. Empty. Dang it! Although . . .

Hello, opportunity. I skirted the counter and peeked at shelves, inside cabinets and drawers. Where had Shiloh stored the Lemon Ade file?

Voices penetrated my awareness, and I darted from the sector, heading for my cell, where I found Mykal. She sat at the edge of her bed, staring down at the floor.

"You're back," I said, rushing over to hug her.

She cringed away from contact, saying nothing.

Dismay congealed in my chest. "I'm on break between classes. Cyrus had canceled our day off and demanded we train today. I came to strap on my armor and water my pot." I still had no idea what kind of flower/herb/shrub Cyrus believed I would enjoy. No sprout had broken the soil yet.

The soil itself reminded me of what my mother had procured on the black market, but it felt richer. Silky, even. Smelled much sweeter too. Wherever he'd obtained it in Theirland, he'd selected the best of the best, with no hint of cross-world contamination.

Mykal remained silent. Didn't even glance up as I put action to my words.

"I'll see you after class," I said, gentling my tone.

Still nothing.

Worried about her state of mind, afraid she blamed me and unsure how I could ever make amends for ending the life of our friend, I sprinted outside to the specified obstacle course. I arrived with only minutes to spare and took my place in line.

Cyrus stood on a metal platform, drenched in sunlight. As usual, he looked good. Better than usual, even. Chin high, shoulders back. From the rigidity of his posture to the firmness of his muscular frame, he conveyed strength. He'd stopped shaving again, thick scruff accentuating his stubborn jaw.

At the sight of him, something foreign and unnamable stirred inside me for the first time. It was hot and bubbly, yet weighty, and it saturated every cell.

He scanned us after the bell sounded. His demeanor projected absolute confidence, daring anyone to get too close. Until his attention landed on me. He jolted, as if hit by something, and the usual charge between us sharpened.

Suddenly, he projected a different message. *Come closer.*

Awareness consumed me, an electric current that zinged dead parts of me back to life. Desires surged and crested. To wrap my arms around him. To feel his arms wrap around me. To pour my body over his and forget the rest of the world.

Okay. So. This was new.

He'd been so good to me, giving me space, and I appreciated it. Here, now, I missed our talks. Missed *him.*

Cyrus wrenched his attention from me and called, "Tomorrow, we go on our next outing to Theirland. You'll be taking your first trip outside of a fortified building. Show me you're ready. Split off in three groups of four and one group of five, selected by Roman, Titus, Lark, and Arden. Choose one soldier at a time, in that order. Go."

Me? A leader? When my turn arrived, I requested Juniper, who brightened. By the time we finished, I had added Miller and Cash to my roster.

"Same order, starting sixty seconds apart." Cyrus stalked across the platform. "If one member fails, all members fail, and you start over. Go."

Roman and his team jumped into action, a mix of exhilaration and dread thickening the air. At the proper time, my group took off. We crawled through mud and evaded holograms.

"Good pace, Miller, but keep your eyes up," Cyrus called.

"Yes, sir."

"Be faster, Arden." He no longer referred to me as *Pink*, *Purple*, or *Bubble Gum*. Not *Miss Roosa* or *Lady* either. "You're lagging. Hustle or get left behind."

"Yes, sir." I shoved the words through clenched teeth. I barely trailed Miller. But I also pumped my arms at a faster clip, increasing my speed. Didn't take long for my muscles to burn and my limbs to shake inside my heavy body armor. This was my fourth hardcore workout of the day.

Juniper tripped behind me, and I slowed to help her stand.

"Thanks," she muttered.

"Anytime."

"I thought I told you to hustle, Arden," Cyrus barked.

Together, Juniper and I approached a brick wall, where Miller pulled himself over the top. Using handholds, Juniper scaled up, up, up, and I remained close behind her. She threw her upper body over the edge, but she miscalculated the weight of her armor and tipped. Then she was falling. On instinct, I reached out to catch her by the collar. But I misjudged her weight, too, and followed her down.

She slammed into Miller, and the pair smacked into the ground. I crashed into them. Juniper screamed upon impact; Miller bellowed. My brain rattled against my skull, and my lungs flattened, stealing my breath. My wrist throbbed.

Though dizzy, I attempted to climb to my feet. The movement hurt Juniper and Miller further, so I stilled.

Soldiers zoomed over, surrounding us. Cyrus shouldered his way through, the medics behind him. Grim faced, he checked me over while the professionals dealt with the other two.

"Are you hurt?" he demanded, testing my wrist's range of motion.

I winced with a particular movement but tried to hide it. "I'm good to go." Mostly. My dizziness faded with every breath, at least.

"X-ray her wrist." He snapped his fingers at someone, then helped me to my feet.

A third medic arrived. Cyrus handed me off, and the guy escorted me to the medical sector. All rooms were empty. An idea dawned, and I hustled past my assistant to enter exam room two, where I settled atop the gurney.

The medic got to work, stripping me of the upper armor and palpating the bones in my wrist.

When he exited to fetch the proper equipment, I knelt beside the gurney and patted the ground just in case Shiloh had—Yes! A chip. He'd left me a message.

Heart racing, I shoved the gift into my pocket and resituated myself on the gurney. Perfect timing.

Cyrus strode past the curtain, asking, "How are you really?" He stopped and gripped the railing at the foot of the bed.

Easy. Don't act suspicious. "I'm good." Better than good now that I had a message from Shiloh in my possession. But, um, why did Cyrus have to look even more noteworthy close up? He projected a shocking amount of tenderness. And I liked it. "I'm ready for tomorrow's trip, sir."

A muscle jumped beneath his eye. Bye, bye, tenderness. "You are lying to me, Arden."

"I'm really not."

The medic entered with the machinery, and Cyrus stepped aside, allowing him to perform his task.

"There's no damage to her bone, sir," the medic pronounced.

"Excellent. Leave us."

We were alone in seconds. "Always so rude," I muttered.

"I prefer to paint a clear picture so that no one is confused about my wishes." Cyrus anchored his arms behind his back, assuming a formal position. "Juniper sprained her ankle and Miller cracked two ribs."

Nothing too terrible. "Hopefully this won't damage your chances of being crowned instructor of the year."

"It won't. I only make champions." He canted his head to the side, studying me. "The contest irritates you. Why?"

Why not be honest, even if it got me in trouble? He valued truth, after all. "Some people might misconstrue the motive of your interest."

"I wasn't aware I'd given anyone else a reason to believe I harbored interest."

He did not just imply he harbored special interest in—no. Impossible. I'd misunderstood.

Unless I hadn't.

I gulped and dangled my legs over the side of the bed. "All I'm saying is motive matters."

"Agreed. But you don't know why I do the things I do, Arden." A simple statement without heat. "You don't know me."

"You're right. I don't." I scrubbed my hands over my face. "I apologize."

Silence reigned until the soft pad of his footsteps filled my ears. In front of me, he clasped my fingers with his, surprising me. He maintained his hold as he lowered my arm, keeping us linked. We stared at each other, searching.

"You don't know me," he repeated softly. "But would you like to?"

I blinked, unsure I'd heard what I thought I'd heard.

"I see the questions in your eyes. About me. CURED. The Soalians and their Tome Society. I'd appreciate an opportunity to respond. When you're ready, tell me. We'll have dinner, just the two of us, and you can ask me anything. I'll answer."

"Why would you do this?" I breathed out, my world rocked. There was no good reason to offer such a priceless prize.

"That is one of the questions I'll be happy to answer over dinner." He winked at me. "Settle in for the day and let your wrist heal." Order given, he released me and strode from the room, leaving me floundering.

CHAPTER EIGHTEEN

Abhor lies, for they will always return to devour the
one who birthed them.

—*The Book of Soal* 1.20.13.5

I shelved the HP's bombshell offer of . . . friendship? A romantic relationship? And holed up in my room, as ordered. Mykal was gone. Alone, I hurried through my usual evening routine. Test the moisture level of my soil. Check. Adjust the lamp rigged over the pot. Check. Gather everything I would need in the morning. Check, check, check.

Practically foaming at the mouth with eagerness, I jumped onto my bed, looked around for any prying eyes or hidden cameras, and exchanged the chip in my new reader.

Waiting for the first page to load proved difficult, but I did it. When the words *Lady Lemon Ade* appeared on the screen, I squealed with delight. He'd given the file to me! Abuzz with curiosity, I swiped to the next page and read.

Hmm. Medical records of former barons and knights. Certain sections were highlighted, including dates of both negative and positive Madness tests, notes from the attending physician listing various reasons for requiring said tests, and the astronomical cost of "damages." Only, the specifics of those damages weren't mentioned. In multiple reports, that physician—always Dr. Korey—recommended a dose of "seil" or "aidem 2" before the individual broke.

Shiloh had typed notes of his own in the margins. *Weaponizing the Madness for profit?*

There were photos of the soldiers in question. One of them resembled the maddened who'd broken the day I met Shiloh. I'd never forgotten his face. According to his chart, he'd received doses of both seil and aidem 2 three days before the incident.

Cold invaded my fingers and toes. Hadn't I received aidem on my first day here?

Evil. The last word Shiloh had signed to me echoed inside my head.

His supposition about weaponization couldn't be right. Odds were greater Ember had planted fake case studies for her brother to find. What better way to convince him to join her and her fellow Soalians?

I almost turned off the reader, but I had to learn what else waited in the file. Had to know what Shiloh had died believing on the off chance I discovered a nugget of truth.

Bile singed my throat when I came upon pictures of corpses with their chests split open and hollowed out. Beside the first, Shiloh had written, *Known Soalians.*

Another case study followed, comparing the two different strains of Madness. The one responsible for feeders and the one responsible for glowers. All results were redacted.

Frustration simmered. Next came reports filed by lords and ladies who had defied orders for one reason or another and entered a pritis mine. A death certificate accompanied each complaint. Each offender had died in a treatment facility or broke on the streets soon after their breach in protocol.

Trembling, I flipped the page, and discovered a personal note from Shiloh, dated the day of his death. Tears instantly welled, blurring the words. Amid a series of sniffles, I wiped my eyes and read.

Dear Arden,

So much has happened, I might as well dive straight into the deep end. Two days ago, I was stretched out on my bed, unsure what to do, when I blinked and found myself inside a library. *The* library. Well, I was there, but I was also in my room at the base. I know. That's impossible, but it's true. I wasn't imagining it. I was there. I saw the books and met Soal.

He's real, Arden. I can't even begin to describe what being in his presence is like. He spoke to me, two words that have forever changed me. I can't go back to who I was. My purpose is so clear. Dangerous, yes, but I don't care. People deserve the truth. They've lived with lies for too long.

The Rock eradicates the Madness. CURED produces and spreads it. That's why they keep us afraid and indebted. From what I gather, they need us. I think it has something to do with the sleeping gods hidden in Theirland. When they wake, the real war begins.

I 100% get that I seem maddened right now. I know I've scared you. Give me a chance to prove I'm right. Be leery of the HP and his father. They get their orders from someone named Astan, who makes the Dolions look like children with toys. If I break with Madness any time soon, it means CURED suspects I've defected, and they took measures to discredit me. But you know what? I wouldn't change anything. I'm finally on the right path.

Okay, I'll stop now. I've thrown a lot of seeds at you. (See what I did there?) If you turn me in, I won't hold it against you. I'll understand, I promise. I've turned in others for much less. Either way, I still want to date you.

Yours,

Shiloh

P.S. Ember sent me the following exchange.

Horror collided with sorrow. Despite testing negative when he'd written this, Shiloh had been sick. Clearly. He had all the signs. Considered CURED evil. Believed in sleeping gods and Soal. This was the Madness, full throttle. The ravings of an individual on the cusp of a break. And yet, even Cyrus touted Soal as real, and he wasn't ill. A small part of me whispered, *Something doesn't add up.*

I mopped up my tears and flipped to the last series of pages in the document. Emails from the king and Archduke Heta discussing messages between two Soalians known as Sparrow and Unicorn. Shiloh had highlighted certain sections, and after reading everything, I focused on those.

Sparrow: You're ready for your first mission. Agreed?

Unicorn: Considering I submitted a formal request eight months ago, yes. Agreed.

Sparrow: You weren't ready then. You're barely ready now.

Unicorn: Have you even read my file? I'm the best of the best.

Sparrow: We'll find out soon enough. You will recruit Arden Roosa.

Unicorn: Seriously, read my file. The best of the best—in battle. Recruiting isn't my thing.

Sparrow: Recruiting is every Soalian's thing. But don't worry, I'll take care of introductions.

The next highlight came from the second message.

To: Baracas Heta

From: Tagin Dolion

Subject: re: A potential problem
This is a job for the High Prince. My son lacks
charm, but he never fails.

Realization dawned, as horrifying as Shiloh's letter. This explained so much. Ember's—or rather, Unicorn's—interest in me. I even understood why she incriminated herself by sharing her communications with Shiloh. There was no better way to incriminate Cyrus.

I pressed a hand to my mouth. No wonder he and his father had a personal stake in my training.

The betrayal I'd felt about the contest for top soldier paled in comparison to what consumed me now. In an effort to catch Ember, the HP had feigned interest in me. Lavished me with attention and special gifts. Offered me a prize beyond imagining: personal information, secrets, and intimacy. What a fool I'd been. He'd only hoped to use me as bait and catch the Soalians attempting to recruit me.

A shuffle of footsteps jerked me out of my whirling emotions. Mykal entered the cell. She didn't glance my way, just kicked off her boots and muttered, "Dr. Korey interviewed me today."

I jolted upright, instantly snared. "Why?"

"She asked about Shiloh." My roommate climbed into bed. "And you. What you've said, what you do during downtime, that kind of thing."

I gripped my blanket, nearly ripping the fabric. "Did she give a reason for her curiosity?"

"As if the medical czar has to explain herself." Mykal rolled to the side, facing the wall. "I'm going to break up with my boyfriend. He's Shiloh's older brother, Erik. Every time I think about him, I remember what happened and—never mind. Good night."

"Oh, Mykal," I whispered, hurting for her. "Please don't—"

She shook her head and smashed her face into her pillow. Translation: Conversation over.

Very well. Air seeped from between my teeth as I lay back down. I stared up at the concrete ceiling, minutes passing in silence. Eventually, my thoughts returned to Cyrus, and my sense of betrayal magnified. He claimed to value the truth above life, yet he had lied to me again and again. His father had lied to me too. Like the king's wife had even heard my name, much less read my essay. What else had my illustrious superiors lied about?

I balled my covers in my fists. To my knowledge, Shiloh had never lied to me. Even in his letter, he'd shared what he perceived as reality, despite the potential cost to his life. If I were a good friend, I would investigate his claims. Settle the incongruities he and his sister had raised, once and for all.

Determination forged my bones into steel. I would do it. Investigate Theirland, the Rock, Soal, other gods, and even CURED. From this moment on, I sought the truth, my holy grail. I would dig and dig and dig until I found the treasure. Forget Cyrus and his dinner invitation. Unless . . . Hmm.

All night, I considered my options, never sleeping. Wondering how to handle Cyrus. Considering the castle in Theirland and how to sneak there. A place so-called gods might be inclined to rest. A plan began to align.

Mykal didn't sleep either. We both tossed and turned. When Friday morning arrived, I was all but foaming at the mouth, ready to get started.

Mykal smiled at me, trying to act like her old self, but her eyes lacked their usual sparkle. "You going to Theirland today?"

"I am." I would seize any opportunity to speak with Cyrus, then come back and wring information from Dr. Korey. On Thursday, I would return to Bala City. Check out the Rock. A dangerous path to walk with possible life-altering consequences. But allow fear to stop me? Not ever again. "You gonna be okay?"

"For sure. I get to rest and relax while the HP is gone. I'll water your dirt."

"Thank you." Though I wanted to hug her, I wouldn't rush her progress. "I love you, Mykal."

"Love you too." She rolled to her side, saying nothing else.

I cleaned up and hustled to the rift room, where I watched Cyrus enter the darkness and vanish. He'd once told me to utilize every weapon in my arsenal. Well, his invitation to question him was a bright, shiny new weapon loaded with special ammunition.

I didn't care that he hoped to use me to learn more about Unicorn. As long as I guarded my tongue, taking in more info than I gave up, I'd come out ahead.

A light shove from behind snapped me into the present. My turn. I strode into the rift. Pain racked me, an instant, all-consuming filleting from the inside out. I merely cringed. Perhaps I'd gotten used to the sensation. Or my determination had hardened me to difficulty.

Either way, I remained steady on my feet upon entering the Theirland landing dock. The spacious chamber contained fewer people than usual, and the lack of bodies highlighted the prisonlike quality of the gray walls and scuffed floor. The transparent ceiling still dazzled, displaying those pinpricks of light in a bed of black velvet.

Cyrus stepped into my personal space. "You good, Pink?"

His use of the nickname after such a long absence disconcerted me, and I narrowed my eyes. Nice play. An obvious attempt to keep me off kilter. "I am," I said, forcing a smile. "Thank you for asking."

Let the games begin.

I expected him to move on, but he remained close. "You can return to Fort Bala if this is too much for you. It's not too late."

"I said I'm good. Also, I'd like to speak with you after patrol. In private. I accept your offer. I have questions."

He blinked, as though astonished, then nodded. "I'll arrange it. Your only goal today is to remain unharmed. Understand?" His gaze dropped to my lips before he strode to another trainee, then another, checking on everyone to mask his supposed interest in me.

I stood rooted in place, furious. The way he'd just looked at me . . . as if I were the center of his entire world. His most telling lie of all. But oh, he was good at this. So good I almost believed I'd mistaken his intentions, despite what I'd read. Almost. I had a strategy, and I was sticking with it.

Resolved, I followed my team into a massive room where knights and barons manned booth-lined walls. In single file, we visited the various compartment, each of us obtaining an official uniform, shoes, armor, two netters, and extra clips of ammo. From there, we entered a third chamber. A locker room with benches, where we suited up and prepared for patrol.

As soldiers exited beyond us, opening the far doors, an automated voice spilled from overhead speakers. "You are entering a loading zone." The last protected area before we reached the outside world.

My nerve endings crackled with a burst of wild energy. Yes, I had a personal mission to undertake, but this was real life. In a matter of minutes, I would venture into the night for the first time in my life. I'd be fighting to survive, practice though it would be. Was I ready?

"I've been dreading this day since joining the academy," Juniper admitted from the bench across from mine as we secured our combat boots. "We need bullets. And whips. And axes. Why only give us netters?"

I glanced up, meeting her fear-filled gaze. Empathy welled. If not for my personal mission, I'd probably be in a similar condition. I couldn't even assure her we'd recover from this. "Probably for our protection, so we don't kill each other. But it's okay. We're well trained."

"Some of us are better trained than others, eh," Lark chortled, striding past us to join Roman near the exit. For once, he didn't welcome her with open arms. He was too busy flirting with a pretty knight.

Lark hung close, ignored by the pair and growing irritated.

"Clearly he prefers the conquest more than the prize," Juniper told me softly. She stood and offered me a helping hand.

I accepted the aid, straightening as Titus joined us. He slung an arm around each of us, saying, "We're together, we've worked hard, and we'll be with the HP. We've got this."

Basically what I'd said, yet tension gradually faded from her. "You're right." She batted her lashes at him, obviously smitten. "We've definitely got this."

We crossed to the doors as a unit, stopping behind Lark and Miller. Roman's new romantic target gave a flirty wave and sauntered off.

Lark got in his face, demanding to know what was going on. He shrugged at her, all *What'd I do?* then called out, "Line up in the order I call your names. Arden, Titus, Juniper, Cash."

The four extra-credit kids. Those of us who trained with Cyrus after hours.

Juniper and I hustled into place as Roman shouted other names. He took the spot at the tail end. Wait. I was number one going into Theirland? That couldn't be correct.

"Here's how this is going to go." Dressed as we were but loaded down with all kinds of weapons, Cyrus exited a side door and strode to the front of the line. We jumped to attention, and I admit, my heart did the usual blip at the sight of him. "We will walk a preselected path and let you get used to the sights, sounds, and sensations. The area is contained, only twenty feeders on the loose. They will attack. Use your netters and fight with everything you've got. Your goal isn't to survive but to thrive. I'm here to intervene if things go bad."

"Yes, sir," we called. Deep breath in. Out. Twenty feeders. One for each of us, with a couple extras thrown into the mix.

His gaze slid to me and lingered before he turned on his heel. "Lenses in place."

Suddenly I didn't have to wonder why I'd scored such an "honored" spot. He'd put me directly behind him. A way to protect his target. Another move in our game.

Waggling my jaw, I secured and activated my eyewear. Encrusted with pritis, they projected rays of light around me, ensuring I'd have a five-foot radius of visibility, no matter which way I looked.

"Remember," Cyrus called. "These feeders are not holograms. They are very real. Any injuries you receive will be very real as well." He rolled his shoulders and shook his head while jumping up and down, as if psyching himself up. "If you want to be top soldier, prove you can protect yourself without harming your teammates."

I'd thought I had dismissed the notion of winning the title, but interest sparked anew. The winner might gain access to previously restricted areas and meetings with royalty.

"Let's do this." The HP beat his fist into a lever on the wall, and the double doors slid open, revealing a void of darkness.

My world turned upside down, as expected, RVM at play. When everything righted, thanks to my lens, I unsheathed my netter.

"You better come out of this intact, Pink," Cyrus muttered low enough for my ears alone, tapping buttons on a wall panel.

"Nothing will stop me." A warning wrapped in agreement.

Pritis stones lit up before us, highlighting a long, winding path. He marched forward. I forgot everything else. With my heart in my throat, I set my finger on the trigger of my netter and followed him.

Chapter Nineteen

The bloodiest battlefield is your mind.

—*The Book of Soal* 2.8.10.5

With my first step outside, a thick blanket of heat and darkness swallowed me whole. Old fears stirred, shooting icy spikes onto my spine. Nausea churned, growing more insistent. But I didn't freak out and run. No, I plowed ahead. This was life and death, in more ways than one. A test of my mettle, a chance to prove I'd grown stronger, and an opportunity to see more of Theirland. I wouldn't fail myself or my mission.

While my lens corrected the RVM, it made me feel as though I walked inside a dream. A sensation I hadn't encountered during practice sessions. The light stands that dictated the direction we traveled didn't help the illusion. Nor did the sounds of gunfire in the distance, proving other battles were taking place.

From what I could see of our periphery, a wire fence created a domed tunnel, protecting a concrete path that led us into the practice arena. Thanks to the slight glow cast by his armor, I could see beyond Cyrus. No feeders waited within sight, but they were definitely nearby.

My ears twitched as varying noises registered. Grunts, pounding footsteps, and the clang of metal. Hot wind infused with a fetid stench ruined every breath. How was I supposed to clock an enemy's approach with the stink of rot clinging to my nostrils? Sweat trickled over my brow and beaded above my upper lip.

"Once we pass the checkpoint, the procession of light ends," Cyrus called. "Prepare for total darkness."

Made sense. Glowers, I'd learned, often broke into restricted areas, and stole pritis stones.

We reached the end of the fenced walkway. The checkpoint. A buzz sounded, and the door opened, allowing passage. We continued without a hitch in our steps.

"If you spot a feeder," Cyrus added, "don't hesitate to take it down. Chances are good you're the only one who can see it."

We traversed a street with buildings on either side. I couldn't tell their shape or size, but I sensed them, as if the walls themselves beckoned me closer. It was weird. Though I looked for the well-lit castle, I spotted no evidence of it.

Cyrus halted abruptly and shouted, "Incoming from all sides!"

Already? I stopped behind him and braced.

Suddenly, a shrieking feeder lurched from the gloom, breaching my five-foot perimeter. I didn't take time to think. As I'd been taught, I aimed and fired the netter, launching the expandable metal trap. The impact drove the maddened to the ground. Upon its crash landing, the seams of the filigree adhered to the concrete, locking him in place.

More and more worm-infested feeders arrived. Battle sounds crested. A blend of grunts and groans, curses and yelps mixed with the whiz of nets. I lost track of everyone as I ducked and dodged, working to immobilize my next target.

Sweat trickled over my skin. Maybe blood. Aches and pains registered, only to get lost in spikes of adrenaline. Another feeder joined the fray, making it two against one. I aimed and squeezed. My netter clicked. Empty. Before I remembered to reload with extra ammo, I dropped the weapon and palmed my backup.

Something sharp cut a vulnerable part of my arm, and I stumbled back, tripping over a slain feeder. I dropped the weapon on impact. A heavy weight smacked into my chest, pinning me down. The scent of rot filled my nose, and I knew. A feeder had fallen on me. Since it wasn't moving, I assumed it was dead.

Desperate for freedom, I scrambled out from under the bulk. As I leaped to my feet, lights flashed all around, granting glimpses of the other trainees. They remained in a constant flow of motion, continuing to shoot and reload, netting feeder after feeder, and, oh, their ferociousness wowed.

I patted the ground for my netter, resolute. Help or die trying. Big mistake. A feeder appeared in my line of sight, whipping through the air, aimed straight for me, his mouth open and teeth bared.

Boom! The maddened jerked to the side and crashed into the dirt, never making contact with me. Cyrus was at my side a second later, pressing a new netter into my hand before moving off to help others.

I fired. Again. And again. More adrenaline surged, becoming a fire in my veins. Intermittently I caught sight of Roman, who fought with his fists. He was smiling.

Between one blink and the next, ten spears of light split the dark sky. No. Wrong. *Glowers* split the darkness. They wore red robes and hurled closer as if they had wings.

"Glowers," someone screeched.

The feeders released awful high-pitched noises. I raced for Juniper—who'd gone statue still—intending to stand guard.

A glower crashed into me, throwing me to the ground. Instinct kicked in, overriding any fear. I fought, not to defend myself but to hobble my foe, but I needn't have bothered. The beautiful Ember hovered over my fallen form, peering down with eyes as bright as stars and as deep as an ocean. Shock immobilized me as a shimmering force field formed a bubble around us. Her light filled it, pushing out all darkness. The rest of the world faded from existence.

"So far you've been nothing but trouble," she snapped, holding two feeders by their throats. The worms hissed while the infected men screamed in pain. Contact with her flesh seared them, tendrils of smoke curling from their skin. Unbothered, she added, "Another victim is slated for the chopping block. If you wish to know more, come to Soal. But do it quickly. Time runs out."

"Ha!" Hurry. Limited time. Almost too late. The same tactic CURED had used to lure me here. I intended to advance my investigation into Soal and his Soalians, yes, but this wasn't the way. "Let me guess. That victim is me."

"Come to Soal," she repeated. "You won't like what happens if you don't." With superhuman strength, she slammed the feeders together and tossed them aside. The bubble vanished, taking Ember and her light with it.

"Where'd the glowers go?" Roman shouted.

"Get in formation," Cyrus commanded. "Now!"

"Someone netted me," Juniper called, and it was clear she was near tears.

"You probably shouldn't have moved into the line of fire then," Lark snarled.

My ears twitched in time with rustling sounds as I climbed to my feet.

"Thank you," Juniper cried, and I figured Cyrus had freed her.

I raced to position myself shoulder to shoulder with my fellow trainees. Panting, I darted my gaze, on the lookout for a threat and wondering who had noticed my private moment with Ember. Seconds blurred into an eternity, but I detected no new flashes of light. No feeders either. Most surprising, no one launched accusations of fraternizing with the enemy my way. Maybe the bubble had hidden us.

"Everyone all right?" Cyrus called. "Sound off in order."

"Arden, alive and well," I rasped.

"Titus, scratched up but good."

On and on we went—only a few soldiers with minor injuries. I didn't expel a sigh of relief until everyone was accounted for.

"We'll finish our trek," Cyrus informed us. "Don't drop your guard. We don't know how many feeders are lingering in the shadows." He started forward, a gun and bloodstained axe in hand, and I followed.

Our team made it to the base without incident, entering a well-lit room. We immediately relocated to a second area for group decontamination. Ragged, I ripped off my headpiece and scanned my teammates. They looked as shell shocked as I felt, with wild eyes and crimson-splattered armor.

Cyrus was just as battered, his features etched with anger I didn't understand. His brand pulled taut as he scanned me from top to bottom. When he met my gaze, he arched a brow, silently asking *Are you truly okay?*

Physically? Yeah. Mentally and emotionally? I wobbled my hand back and forth. Probably not.

Turning on his heel, he escorted us to a row of private stalls. After sealing myself inside the one assigned to me, I stripped, showered, bandaged my wounds with the provided supplies, and dressed in the waiting T-shirt and fatigues.

I emerged from a second door into a sterile hallway, where Cyrus stood alone, freshly showered and changed. His fatigues molded to his strength.

Warmth danced over my skin, my nervous system awakening. Not because of the HP, his sizzling hotness or his insidious intentions, but because of the plan. Only the plan. My objective came with risks.

"Would you like to visit a medic?" he asked, his easy tone doing nothing to settle me.

"No, thanks. I have a few bumps, bruises, and gashes, but I'm in pretty good condition, all things considered."

"Good." All smolder, he asked, "Would you like to interrogate me over dinner, Arden? Just the two of us."

Blood at the boiling point raced in my veins, and flutters tickled my belly. *Careful.* He might have taken things up a notch, but the man who claimed to hate lies was still only playing a part.

But so was I. "Yes, thank you."

He extended his arm in my direction, as sturdy as steel. I hesitated only a beat before twining my fingers with his. *Ignore his warmth. Ignore the sweetness of his hold.* "This isn't very professional of us." Someone should say it.

"We bypassed professional on day one." He shepherded me to an elevator, where he flattened his free palm on an ID pad. "Will I be forced to bargain with you so you'll eat?"

"No, sir." I wasn't too nervous to ditch my meal bars. "I'll consume my portion and probably half of yours."

Chuckling, he traced his thumb over my knuckles, sending the most delicious tingles up my arm. "Then I'll be sure to add dessert. And please call me Cyrus."

Do not be charmed. "You are very good at flirting," I told him, matter of fact. Well, *kind of* matter of fact.

"No, I'm good at bantering. There's a difference."

The perfect opening. He'd told me I could ask him anything. So, I kicked us off with something personal. "Do you usually banter with the soldiers under your command?"

He didn't take offense. "I've only ever bantered with one other."

The compartment stopped, the doors sliding open, preventing me from asking a follow-up. He led me into a fairy tale, and my eyes widened. In the foyer, pritis stones dangled from a glass ceiling, making the lights appear to fall from the sky itself. Polished wood walls displayed paintings of past royals and their families. Crystals grew from a corner in three tiers, each edged in gold.

Average citizens rarely glimpsed such luxury. A realization I found disturbing on multiple levels.

He released my hand and pressed his palm against my lower back, guiding me deeper inside. An intimate hold I liked far more than I should. We cut through a tricked-out living room and stopped in a breakfast nook neighboring the kitchen. A round table with a smooth, diamond-esque top displayed covered platters, from which wafted the most succulent scents.

Moisture flooded my mouth. Each piece of dishware looked as if it had been made from a single pearl. Glittering sapphire wings extended from the backs of four cushioned chairs.

"You expected me to say yes," I muttered.

"I hoped you would." Cyrus offered me a seat, his eyes alive with amusement. "Just so we're clear, there are no rules with us. You can say anything without consequences."

Another lie. There were always consequences with the Dolions. "You're being kind, and it's weird."

"You're being enchanting, so I'm good with that." He was smiling as he sank into the seat beside mine. So close I could scent *him*. All that fairy dust and ambrosia fanned the flames of temptation.

"I am never enchanting." Ready to get us back on track, I settled my napkin in my lap. "Tell me about the other woman you bantered with."

"I was a lord at the time. She was a lady." He lifted the tops off the platters, revealing the widest array of roasted vegetables, meats, and pasta I'd ever seen outside of videos. "We didn't last. Because of our connection, she became a target of the Soalians, but I wasn't yet in a high enough position to protect her as I saw fit."

Smart answer. It painted him in a chivalrous light and invited me to spill about my own targeting. I'd bet part of it was even true. I sipped from the half-filled cup near my plate instead. A sweet citrus flavor exploded on my tongue, momentarily superseding every thought in my head, and I gasped. "Oh! This tastes like happiness." I wished with all my being Mykal were here to sample it.

"Then I chose well," Cyrus said, low and quiet with hooded eyelids. "And yes, Arden, you are enchanting. Always."

Warm flutters erupted in my belly. I gripped my knees, feeling as if I'd jumped into shark-infested waters with no idea how to swim. He was a pro at this, while I was a novice.

"Don't tell me I still make you nervous." He scooped a hearty sampling of each dish onto my plate, his biceps flexing. The visual delights surprised the culinary ones. A true feat, considering the creamy sauces and buttery vegetables. But. His muscles. *Delicious.*

"You do." No reason to deny it. "But not in the same way." Moving on. "Be honest. Have you ever tasted a meal bar?" I entertained a smidgen of guilt that my compatriots were subsisting on meal bars even now.

"I have. The extravagant foods are a recent indulgence."

Ah. They were a means to an end—meant to aid my charming. "Don't stop there. I'm curious about what changed." Or what he would cop to. I speared a piece of carrot and nibbled on the end, my eyes nearly rolling back in my head. "This is incredible."

"Mmm." The low noise contained a thousand caresses, and I shivered. "What changed is this," he said. "I met a beautiful grower who lights up when she sees produce." He speared a carrot of his own.

So. Danged. Smooth. Unable to lessen my blush, I glued my attention to my potatoes and forked a bite. Even better than the carrot! I shoveled in two more mouthfuls, giving my wits an opportunity to overshadow my emotions. Any hint of elegance flew out the window.

Best to be blunt and strike to the heart of the matter. "You'll have to excuse me if I'm baffled by your fascination with me."

He leaned against his seat back, slow and deliberate, watching me. The old me would have squirmed under such scrutiny. Today's me betrayed nothing. Probably nothing. Very little, anyway.

With his elbow supported on the arm of his chair, he reached up to rub two fingers over his lips. "I have a confession I've hoped to make for a while. Until yesterday, you weren't ready. I'm not sure what carried you over the mental finish line, but I'm glad for it."

"Don't be so sure I'm ready now." I had no idea where he was headed with this, but it couldn't be good for me.

"I know you well. Before you arrived at Fort Bala, I was tasked with digging deep into your history. That isn't something I'm normally assigned, but I did it. I dug. I meant it when I told you I'd read everything about your life."

Okay, why would he admit this? "That doesn't endear you to me."

"There was a reason. Viscounts intercepted a message between two Soalians. In it, they discussed recruiting you. CURED wished to discover why."

Shock punched me. He'd just, like, admitted it, verifying a portion of the Lemon Ade file. My head spun. There was no good reason for Cyrus to cop to this. It gave him no advantage that I could see.

"I see the wheels turning in your head," he said with a half grin. "You think I plan to win you over and convince you to name names."

"Do you?" A bitter twinge seeped into my voice.

"That's merely a bonus. I admit, I've been intrigued by you from the start."

Lie! "On day one, you disdained me."

"You've mistaken interest and a lifetime of distrust for dislike. The moment I saw you, I realized I comprehended everything and nothing. Then you proved to be so much more than I expected. Brave. Kind. Resilient."

Do not melt. Stay strong! "I wasn't brave or resilient then." I wasn't even sure I qualified for either description now. Though, yes, I had improved by leaps and bounds.

"No matter how many times you fall, you rise. That takes an incredible amount of bravery and resilience." He sipped from his glass, casual as could be as he battered my defenses. "I admire you."

That couldn't be true. It was a ploy, only a ploy. A way to do exactly as intended and win me over. "I don't know what to say," I admitted. Had no idea how to advance my own ploy in the face of his.

His gaze intensified, cranking up an invisible dial. Nearly breaking out in a sweat, I shifted in my seat. I'd agreed to share a meal with him to gain information, assuming I could control the tone of the interaction. A mistake. I'd never dealt with this Cyrus before. The seductive suitor.

"Since Shiloh's death, I've come to accept three vital facts." Voice as thick and smooth as honey, he said, "You don't trust CURED, and you don't trust me. But I want you anyway."

CHAPTER TWENTY

Do you not understand the power you wield?

—*The Book of Soal* 1.1.1.26

I shifted in my seat. Fiddled with my fork. Shook my head. Nothing changed the trumpet blast inside my head. *I want you anyway.*

I almost believed him. I *yearned* to believe him. But I wasn't the same gullible girl anymore.

I was a woman determined . . . who still didn't know how to play this. I could pretend to share his interest. Or pretend to pretend. No, wrong move. The situation was already complex. Adding in other intimacies might lead to my downfall. If I'd learned anything from him, it was to know my strengths and weaknesses and work accordingly.

"Let's be clear. You're saying you want to date me," I managed to croak, buying time.

"Yes." He set his glass aside. "For most of my life, I've been focused on preparation to rule CURED, a position I was born for. I know it with every fiber of my being. Then you came along and distracted me."

"But that's ridiculous." This *must* be some kind of bold new strategy to upend my entire world before he pounced. "I'm no one special."

His frown contained a gentle rebuke. "Your response is an insult to us both."

I cringed and tried another route. "You're seeing Countess Soti's daughter."

"I'm not. I dated her casually last year. Now our parents throw us together whenever possible." Lowering his chin toward his sternum, he reminded me of a predator locking on its prey. "You don't need to give me excuses or an answer. In fact, I'd like to provide you with a peek behind the curtain first. Grant you access to places necessary to gain the answers you seek. Consider it pre-dating that will lead to real dating."

He had no idea what answers I truly sought. But dang him, he'd presented me with something I desperately needed. Now, at least, I understood how eager Cyrus was to capture Ember and do whatever else he had planned. There was no other reason to offer me something so valuable.

"You want something in return for this special access, I'm sure," I stated, tracing a fingertip around the rim of my glass.

"Only your trust."

I snorted. "My trust doesn't come easily." With him, it wouldn't come at all.

"Believe me, I'm aware," he replied wryly.

A million thoughts burst through my mind at once, all centered on a "should I / shouldn't I do this" debate. I mean, yes, I'd planned to use him this way. But now that he'd gift wrapped it with a pretty bow of his own free will, I wasn't so sure. "Explain how it will work."

He got more comfortable. "You'll be tasked with a unique assignment I'll explain after you accept my proposal. It will ensure you have a reason to remain by my side even outside of the base. I can introduce you to anyone you wish to meet and share classified documents. At the same time, you'll get to know me."

Great for my mission, bad for me personally. I searched his eyes. "You, the emperor's grandson, are implying you're willing to help me spy on CURED, the government body he rules. The government body you intend to rule. This is obviously a test. And entrapment!"

He heaved a sigh. "It's not a test or entrapment. Not for you. You very obviously lack confidence in CURED but have hope for Soal, which means you're expendable. The special assignment facilitates an open door to information. And because I'm so confident in the one I serve, I'm willing to risk my position and future to allay your doubts."

A lie. No one jeopardized their future for a romantic relationship or even sex.

Okay, so, some people did risk everything for relationships and sex. But not the indomitable Cyrus Dolion. "Explain what *you'll* be doing while I'm busy allaying." Besides taking notes, setting traps, and ensuring I discovered only bits of info he approved.

Resignation and amusement dominated his features. "I suspect I'll be busy cleaning up your messes and keeping you safe."

Oooh. Great response. Honest and blunt yet also somehow romantic and swoony. "You mentioned my lack of trust, and you're right. I don't trust anyone anymore."

"Let me assure of you one thing, Bubble Gum." Voice lowering to a rumble, he said, "I crave you. All I require is a chance to prove it."

My breath caught. He—oh! I wasn't buying this. I wasn't! Maybe he was attracted to me. It was possible to desire a target. But I was still just a target to him.

I slid my gaze over his body, as if I inspected him with his proposition in mind. My heart rate picked up. "There's a chance I'm not—and won't be—interested in you romantically." I mean, there was always a chance of anything. If I was going to say yes to his shocking proposal, and I might, I should set boundaries and expectations right at the start.

Cyrus's lids hooded his eyes, as if his lashes were suddenly too heavy to hold up. His smile turned indulgent and softened the puckered scar tissue webbing one-half of his face. "You're good at many things, Pink, but hiding what you feel isn't one of them.

Something changed for you yesterday. I clocked the moment it happened. You're interested."

I hated that he read me so well. I also knew the exact moment he referenced. When our gazes met while he stood upon that metal platform and a shock of electricity hit me.

"Give me a chance," he said, using that husky tone I was beginning to loathe.

I drew in a breath. "I might learn the people you love are doing bad things."

He didn't hesitate. "If that's the case, I'll help you bring them down."

Another good answer. Too good. "I'm not saying yes, but I'm not saying no. Tell me about the special assignment first."

A long while passed in silence before he agreed. "Very well. Do you recall the Theirland berry I sought?"

"As if I will ever forget it." Or Jericho's claim.

"I ate it. Now CURED is studying my blood."

Wait. He just admitted it? Just like that? I spiraled once again. "You told me—"

"That I didn't make it back with a berry in hand, and I didn't. As I'm sure you've gleaned, information is doled out on a need-to-know basis here."

"But. You ate it. And it seems like *mis*information is what's doled."

"My mission was to return with a berry, and I did. The eating of it was a choice I made in the field. Had I declined to do it, I would have lost the berry entirely. As the highest ranked soldier at the compound, I was the only one with the security clearance to handle it. I decided to take the chance. For the record, I've tested negative for Madness every morning since, I feel fine, and I've suffered no ill effects. You'll be tasked with monitoring me outside of class."

You've got to be kidding me. "The assignment is babysitting."

He hiked his shoulders. "Use whatever label you prefer."

So reasonable. Let's see how he did with accusations. "Did you or CURED threaten or kill Jericho because he witnessed your actions?"

My companion didn't bat an eye. "I was told he interrogated soldiers about my actions, so I called him to my office and demanded he stop. He was alive when he left the compound soon after."

The lord-in-training must have concluded something damning to send him fleeing.

In the distance, a door opened and shut, and I jolted. Cyrus worked his jaw. Heavy footsteps preceded the arrival of the king. He rounded a corner, saying, "Give me a full report about the glowers."

Expression blanking, Cyrus stood. "Now isn't a good time."

The king halted when he spotted me. He arched a brow at his son, all *mystery solved.*

I wiped my mouth with my napkin, attempting to mask my discomfort. This man had used my essay as an excuse to have me watched.

"Hello, Arden," he said, as smooth as his son. "Lovely to see you. My apologies for intruding upon a private dinner. I wasn't aware Cyrus decided to host a guest this evening."

"Hello, King Dolion." Should I salute? "We were just flirting. I mean talking," I corrected in a rush. My cheeks burned. I would shut up now.

"I gave express orders that I wasn't to be disturbed," Cyrus stated.

"My apologies." The king offered me a quick smile before focusing on his son. "No one was brave enough to inform me. Since I went to the trouble of realm walking, I'm sure you can guess I come with a matter of importance. Let's chat before I go." He strode off, making it clear he'd delivered an order.

Cyrus tossed his napkin onto the table. "Stay here."

I batted my lashes at him. "I'm happy to act as your assistant. Consider it a sampling of this special access you've been trying so hard to sell me."

"Nice try." He gently chucked my chin, his eyes glittering. "All samplings will wait until we've negotiated our terms." A tower of strength, he strode off.

Hearing a door shut, I popped to my feet. Cyrus had basically put his stamp of approval on all snooping. As quietly as possible, I snuck around the room, opened drawers, searched under every piece of furniture, and inspected for secret safes. I discovered absolutely nothing. But then, he'd known I would do this, so he'd probably taken precautions. Smart HP.

Before the Dolions returned, I returned to my seat. Might as well eat. I mean, the food shouldn't go to waste.

I cleaned my plate, then Cyrus's, then I finished off our juices. Eventually, he returned without his father. He reclaimed the spot beside me, his good humor gone. He radiated fury, triggering a dozen defenses rigged to blow inside my mind. And yet, nothing detonated. I didn't flee as I would've done in the past. An odd sense of calm glued me in place.

"You got in trouble for fraternizing with a Soalian's target, I'm guessing," I said.

"I consider you an asset. But no, that wasn't it."

Ooh la la. Lady Arden Roosa, an asset. "So. Tell this asset about your conversation with your dad."

"I can tell you many things, but not that," he said, dancing his gaze over the table, taking in the results of my feast. A corner of his mouth quirked. "You ate my food."

"I told you I would." I ignored the flutter in my stomach. "You mentioned a negotiation."

He fixed his attention on me and crossed his arms over his chest, flexing well-defined biceps. A definite power play. "Each night, you'll turn in a report listing any oddities in my behavior. There will be none, of course. While we're in Theirland, you'll stay in these quarters with me. You are welcome to sleep in my room, without chains. That's my preference. There's a second room if you'd rather be alone. When we return to Ourland, you'll fulfill your training duties but spend all free time with me. That includes meals."

"Will I spend the night with you there too?"

"Only rarely. I live off base. I'll wear a monitor."

Okay, so, that did sound kind of wonderful. Free weekend room and board, zero chains. But. "You can wear a monitor all the time. You don't need me."

"I don't want to wear a monitor *ever*. No one wants others to know where they are and what they are doing at all times."

Yeah, that tracked. "The whole idea is thready at best. You yourself have admitted I don't know you that well. I'm not qualified to recognize an oddity in your behavior."

"You might not know me well, yet, but you do know plants."

Seriously, he had an answer for everything. "You're setting me up for jealousy and trouble with the other trainees. No one will be comfortable around High Prince Dolion's babysitter."

"You aren't wrong, but there's no other way to do this. No other reason to key you into certain locations you can't and shouldn't access otherwise."

To be honest, I could endure any amount of animosity for answers. "Since this is supposed to be practice for real dating, I should probably call you *bunny baby boo*. Or *sugar bear. Honey buns*."

"I'll let you render the final verdict, but I'm partial to *sugar bear*."

He actually uttered those words with a straight face.

"Don't tempt me, Cyrus. I might do it."

"Tempting you is the whole point of this, Arden." He reached out, slow but steady, giving me plenty of time to protest. My breath hitched as he smoothed a lock of hair behind my ear. "After tomorrow's patrol, I'd like you to speak with John Victors. He asked to see you."

That . . . no. It made no sense. "Why me?"

"A question you can pose to him. And no, I'm not offering you this assignment to wring intelligence from him. I think you should meet him. To judge him worthy or unworthy of your allegiance."

Me, interrogate John Victors. A glower. Leader of the most violent gang of Soalians, who requested my presence and hoped to recruit me. "Okay, I'll speak to him with or without our bargain."

"Speaking of," Cyrus said, "you won't mention what we're doing to anyone, and you'll only talk of it with me when we're alone in my private quarters."

"As if I would ever tattle." Which meant what? I'd accepted his offer, and we were officially roomies this weekend?

Dazed, I looked here, there, imagining myself puttering around. Enjoying a bedroom rather than a cell. Hanging potted plants, even growing a whole garden and experimenting with the different soils and seeds. Leaving a pair of socks on the floor. Getting to know the enigmatic, hauntingly beautiful Cyrus better. Fulfilling my obligation to Shiloh. Perhaps winning top soldier for completing a special mission.

My heart lurched. "I listened to your terms, now hear mine. Move my mother to Bala City."

He huffed with frustration. "That isn't something you want me to do. She won't be safe there."

He'd claimed something similar before. "Tell me why."

"There are fewer breaks of Madness, but there's far more crime."

"I witnessed no crime while there," I pointed out.

"Doesn't mean it wasn't taking place."

Now I was the one to huff. But I would let this issue rest. For now. "I want Shiloh's files, nothing redacted. Medical, disciplinary reports, research papers. Everything." Maybe he received shots like the other soldiers who'd broken. Maybe the documents would be altered in some way, maybe not. There was only one way to find out.

"Done. Next."

Under the table, I twisted my fingers into the napkin. "You can't go easy on me during class." My determination to improve had only amplified.

The look he gave me said *baby, please.* "Pink, slacking off will never be on the table. I'll train you harder than I've ever trained anyone. Next."

Was I truly bargaining with Cyrus Dolion in order to spy on CURED? "Once a week, you gotta give sandwiches to the entire team, including Mykal." My way of apologizing for unbalancing the scales.

"Done. Next."

"I want to know who lives in the castle and hear about your experiences with Soal."

The satisfaction glinted anew. "When I trust you, I'll share."

"Fair enough," I grumbled.

"Anything else?"

Though I racked my brain, I came up empty. "Not currently."

"Then the deal is set." He extended his hand in my direction.

Yes. No. Yes. I nibbled on my bottom lip.

His hand remained steady. "If you can trust nothing else, trust that I have your best interests at heart."

That wasn't possible. But for better or worse, I reached out and slid my palm against his to shake. For Shiloh, my mom, Mykal, and everyone who deserved the truth. "The deal is set."

⬧

While Cyrus made calls from an immaculate office, I searched the rest of the apartment. Shiloh's claim that CURED lied about Theirland remained a whisper in my ear. But what, exactly, was the supposed falsehood? What CURED did here? Kept here? The origins? What!

Unfortunately, I found no personal items, papers, files, or hidden chips. No classified history books.

In the smaller of the two bedrooms, I came upon a full suite of golden body armor. Every accessory imaginable was scattered over a pair of nightstands, a dresser, and a bed. Weapons, audible and visual transmitters, and a plethora of small gadgets I couldn't identify.

The kitchen was stocked with fresh fruit juices and an array of goodies. Such variety. Sweet desserts and savory sandwiches. Clotted creams and rich jams. Like any good babysitter, I deposited a beverage and a snack on Cyrus's desk whenever I took a break and prepared something for myself. Which happened often, allowing me to unabashedly listen to his calls. Not that I learned much there either. Well, other than that calls could be made between Ourland and Theirland.

Cyrus paused each time I supplied him with sustenance, giving me an odd look, as if stupefied by the gesture.

He was arguing with someone when I set a plate of cookies at the edge of his desk. I paused to listen, going still for the first time since forever, it seemed, and fatigue got the better of me.

"I'm asking you to move her to a safer area and put her in a safer apartment," he snapped. "Not construct a new building in a day."

I stood in the doorway of his office, my chest constricting. He was working to protect my mother. Probably a means of indebting me to him but also the kindest thing anyone had ever done for me.

Catching his eye, I smiled softly and mouthed, "Good night, sugar bear."

"Hang on." He pressed a button and set the phone aside. "You have everything you need?"

"I do."

"Good. By the way, I like the nickname even more than expected."

"Way to ruin it for me," I muttered with mock affront. As I marched off, his laughter followed, enchanting me. Dang it!

I locked myself in the bigger room after confiscating a netter from his, then set the personal alarm via a keypad on the wall. Maybe I'd get some rest tonight. Maybe Mykal would, too, considering she had the cell to herself and wouldn't need a chain. Hopefully she hadn't forgotten to water my seed.

Sighing, I cocooned myself in what must be the largest, softest bed in the world . . . where I tossed and turned, my mind unwilling to settle. The rules of my investigation had changed. I now had Cyrus to contend with, and he may or may not be setting me up, so I needed a new game plan.

Arden Dawn Roosa.

The soft, whispered voice registered, and I blinked, frowned. "Cyrus?" I jerked upright to look around and found no sign of his presence. He hadn't bypassed my locked door.

Heart thumping against my ribs, I rasped, "Hello?"

Arden Dawn Roosa.

Realization. The voice hadn't wafted into my ears but had sprung up inside my head. Exactly what had happened the first time I'd met Ember.

I swiped up the netter, jumped to my feet—and found myself standing in front of the Rock. But this . . . I . . . I stood in my new room, seemingly in two places at once. Exactly what Shiloh had said he'd experienced.

Palms sweating, I looked left, right. This couldn't be real. Must be imagined. A dream. This section of the Rock wasn't located in an area I recognized. A lovely desert oasis teemed with lush trees and foliage, beautiful flowers, and colorful fruit. Birds perched on the branches. Butterflies and bees, insects I'd only dreamed of seeing in real life, flew from petal to petal.

Awed, I reached out and traced my fingertips over a cluster of ripe purple berries. Cool to the touch. Soft.

Along the Rock, the lines inside the circles drew together, repositioning. I glided forward without thought, my feet moving of their own accord. Upon perfect alignment, the circles eased into a slow rotation. Spinning. Faster and faster with each completion until flames sparked with the seven colors of the rainbow. Smoke rose, blurring the stone until the wall appeared to be as insubstantial as mist.

The bearded man in the red robe materialized. He wasn't glaring this time, but he wasn't smiling, either, as he motioned me inside.

No, thank you. I backed up a step, but invisible hands caught my waist and pulled me forward. I dug in my heels, but I couldn't halt my momentum. When I stopped, the urge to fight drained completely.

I stood in the library, taking everything in. *My goodness.* Far better than the vision Ember had provided. There were no people present, and I was glad. Nothing distracted me from the decor. Vibrant sunlight streamed through stained glass windows bearing the same markers as the Rock, beaming multicolored lights upon sparkly vases, hand-carved ornaments, and polished shelves. My eyes closed for a moment, breathing in the smell of cleaner, worn leather, sweet peaches, and creamy coconut. What bliss!

The bearded man stepped from thin air to stand at my side. I set my finger on the trigger of my weapon—or tried to. I no longer held the netter.

"I'm Domino Crane." His deep voice fit his ancient eyes. And yet, he was probably only a few years older than me. He was the kind of rough, rugged handsome that must draw scores of women into his orbit. "A member of the High Guard. You might know me as a *librarian*."

"Are you kidding me?" A librarian? Seriously?

He didn't appear offended or explain further. "Permission was granted. Look around. Touch."

Though confused, I refused to waste this opportunity to advance my investigation, forced though it was, and eased forward, aiming for a towering bookshelf. The book covers faced outward, each rimmed by crushed gemstones. I extended my arm, intending to handle the tome on my left. Such lovely rubies. A split second before contact, my hand shot to the right. I curled my fingers around a leather-bound beauty and lifted. A nice weight, with small, golden swirls decorating the page ends. Flowers bloomed before my eyes, forming letters, revealing the title. *The Book of Arden*, volume 20, *Daily Updates*.

A smile bloomed and fell. My book. The story of my life. Supposedly past, present, and future.

With great trepidation, I turned to the first page. Hmm. Written in an unfamiliar language. Flip, flip, flip. Lots of words and symbols I couldn't read. Oh! I came to a portion of text I comprehended and gobbled up the sentences.

> I rush down the hall as fast as my feet will carry me,
> determined to get my hands on Cyrus's transmitter.
> All I must do is adhere the camera to a mine cart,
> and I can watch the feed to see what's being mined.

Uh . . . That was the only tidbit I got? I didn't even know what it meant!

"Show me the rest," I demanded, my voice echoing off fading walls. No, no, no. I clutched the tome to my chest. I wasn't ready to leave. "Don't send me away." But the book was fading too. Then the library and Domino vanished completely, and my bedroom reformed.

I sank to the mattress. Frustrated and unsure, I glanced at the digital clock displayed above the dresser, then performed a double take. I'd lost hours. Had spent most of the night inside that library, though it had felt like only minutes. Now, morning was here.

I rolled my lip under my teeth. According to CURED, what I'd experienced was the first sign of the Madness. But I didn't feel sick. I felt normal. So what was I? In between, as Shiloh had been?

A choking sound left me as I sprang to my feet. I padded to a private bathroom, where I showered and worked to center myself. Once I convinced myself I wasn't teetering on a break, I realized I'd forgotten to send a report about Cyrus. Not that I knew where to send it.

First day on the job, and I was already failing.

I'd do better. I dressed in clean fatigues stacked in the walk-in closet. Oh, wow. The clothes were softer than usual and in my exact size. Cyrus had anticipated my acceptance, proving his claim: he knew me well.

A hard rap pierced the air. I sheathed a dagger in my boot as my host called, "Let's go."

Showtime. I exited the room and followed his ambrosial scent to the kitchen, where he waited, freshly showered and at ease. He looked good. Very good.

"You need to test me for Madness," I stated. For the good of all.

"There's no need. If you were infected, an alarm would go off."

I blinked. "Tests are airborne now?"

"Only in Theirland, inside CURED buildings." He poured a red concoction into two glasses and thrust a beverage at me. "I ordered you to rest, Pink. Drink every drop and tell me why you appear exhausted."

I accepted, relieved and disturbed, saying, "I've had trouble sleeping my entire life." Truth without sharing the whole story.

"Guess I'll have to play hardball to help you," he replied with a pleasant smile before draining his glass.

I would've asked what he meant, but a sip of the juice awakened atrophied taste buds, and my mind hopped on a new track. *Must have more.* Down the hatch! Mmm. More than delicious, the liquid invigorated me from the inside out. Cells came alive, and muscles plumped with strength.

"What is this stuff?" I asked, practically slurring my words.

"Bait." He winked and offered his hand, sending my heartbeat into overdrive.

I licked my lips, reached out, and reluctantly twined our fingers. *Ignore the warmth of his skin. The calluses on his palm.* Impossible. "Hand-holding doesn't fall under the category of babysitter," I said, embarrassed by my breathlessness.

"Ah. But it does fall under the category of pre-dating."

Well. "We should talk about the best way to introduce my new position to the team."

"No need. I'll make the announcement, and that will be that." He led me from the apartment and into a private elevator, where he released me. *Don't protest.* "You'll be pleased to know I should receive the requested documents when we return to the base."

"I am, thank you."

Tone dry, he told me, "Do us both a favor and remember this feeling of gratitude."

Um. "That's kind of ominous."

"I know."

The elevator doors dinged and opened, revealing a hallway. Cyrus hit me with a mind-melting smile, then shuffled me and my liquid brain along a winding path. At the first security point, he logged in my ID chip, ensuring I received all access. I noted a second glance from some of the soldiers, their curiosity palpable.

Cyrus explained nothing and his harsh demeanor discouraged questions. I did my best to appear nonchalant, as if I babysat decorated officers daily.

Now, to face my teammates. We reached a gym filled with mats and exercise equipment. The team had beaten us there, and every gaze zoomed our way as we entered. Conversations ceased midsentence, everyone rushing to stand at attention. Thankfully, I didn't receive any loaded looks.

"Lady Roosa is working on a special project," Cyrus announced. "You are not to ask her about it or mention it to others. Details are classified." He motioned for me to join the others. "Hustle."

"Yes, Sir Sugar Bear," I muttered and jogged over.

"Today is reckoning day," Cyrus called. "Archduke Heta's trainees did a better job than mine, and my disappointment cannot be measured. You will practice until you improve."

That is exactly what we did. Practice. There wasn't time for personal matters. Cyrus pushed us to the brink, me most of all. No joke, he ordered me to do extra everything. Yes, I loved exercise, but I didn't enjoy the buckets of sweat pouring from me. My muscles quivered and burned.

"Lark, you disabled five holograms that round. Not bad. Roosa, you also disabled five. Do better," he snapped. "And run six laps. One for every hologram you should have felled."

"Yes, sir," I snapped back.

When the clock timed out a short while later, I dropped to the floor, wheezing. Lark winced with sympathy as she passed me.

"Everyone but Roosa out," he commanded. "You didn't do terrible, so you may enjoy yourselves while you can. There are free sandwiches in a private commons. Follow Baron Thomas."

Cheering, the class poured from the gym. Several other soldiers cast me looks of commiseration along the way. A frowning Roman held my gaze until he disappeared beyond the door, and I couldn't decipher the emotion he projected. I couldn't force my legs to work either.

Cyrus strode over and crouched beside me. "What do you have to say for yourself?"

"You are an awful person," I grumbled.

He arched a brow, not the least bit apologetic. "Maybe now you'll sleep when you're told."

"Maybe now you'll sleep when you're told," I mocked, and the corners of his mouth twitched. "Do you even hear yourself?"

"I'll give you thirty minutes to clean up and recover." His other brow lifted. "Unless you'd rather skip the interview with Mr. Victors."

I snapped to attention. "I'll be ready."

CHAPTER TWENTY-ONE

Wisdom cries out to you; are you listening?

—*The Book of Soal* 1.20.1.20

Elevator doors closed, confining me inside a small space with two armed guards and Cyrus. I was mere minutes away from facing a glower. *The* glower. A Soalian I'd considered a terrorist my entire life, who now had answers I sought. The true purpose of Theirland. Why the Rock bloomed with flowers. The origin of pritis stones. Why Soal hated CURED. What else I might find in my book.

I rallied every defense, resisting the onset of fear, but the continued strenuous effort left me on edge.

Cyrus noticed and told me, "You'll be safe. Victors will be restrained on one side of a table, and I'll be with you on the other side, with guards posted outside the door."

"I've never interrogated someone," I muttered.

Ding. The doors opened, revealing a hall brimming with soldiers, who lined both walls and stood at the ready. Cyrus led me forward, no one daring to look in our direction. A perk I cherished.

We paused at a thick metal door, and he faced me, intent. "Don't react to anything Victors says or venture down any verbal mazes. We have only five minutes in there. Stick to your main topics of interest. I guarantee he'll stick to his."

No reaction or mazes. "Five minutes isn't long enough."

"The king wishes to limit your exposure to such a powerful glower. They can be—" He thought for a moment. "Persuasive."

In other words, dangerous. I squeaked, "I'm brave. I can do this."

"Yes, you can. Now shed your weapons. Anything you prefer not to be used against you." As he spoke, he handed a guard his personal arsenal.

My instincts screamed a negation, but I did the same, leaving myself with nothing but my wits. Not exactly 100 percent reliable anymore. "I'm sure you guys want me to ask him something."

Cyrus flashed a humorless smile. "CURED is more interested in what he asks you."

Well, they might change their mind if I got sloppy and posed the questions I didn't dare mention. "I'm ready."

Cyrus pressed his palm on the ID pad. The scanner read his chip, and the doors slid open. I followed him into a boxy, sterile room. Laser lights extended from small holes in the gray walls, each aimed at the prisoner shackled to a table.

I inwardly flinched. Here he was, John Victors. The villain of many nightmares. A metal collar circled his neck. He looked to be a few years older than my mother, with a sallow complexion and hollow cheeks. Bruises ringed his eyes. His lips were chapped and cracked.

His fragility shocked me. This wasn't the healthy, smiling foe I'd seen gardening. Either he'd failed to recover from his battle wounds, or CURED had attempted to persuade him to talk.

He wore a bright-white uniform, pressed and clean. Metal cuffs bound his wrists to the table and his ankles to the floor. He didn't glow, and I saw no symbols embossed in his skin, yet despite it all, he radiated the same peace he'd displayed while picking berries. The same peace Shiloh had displayed.

"Good evening, Victors," Cyrus said, pulling out a chair for me.

"Nice to see you again, High Prince Dolion." The leader of the Soalians studied me as I eased down. "I'm glad to see someone has manners. Hospitality has been in short supply here."

"Be sure to give me a detailed list of your complaints." Cyrus claimed the chair next to mine. Taking his own advice, he evinced zero emotion. "You told me you allowed yourself to be captured for a chance to speak with Miss Roosa. Here she is."

What! The opening bombshell landed like a hard punt to the gut. Not that I believed the Soalian had willingly surrendered, but being listed as the sole reason blew my mind.

"No, I allowed myself to be captured for a purpose," the prisoner corrected. "Speaking to her is a bonus."

Well okay then. I could breathe again. Barely.

"Did you tell her about the intercepted messages? You did, didn't you?" A slow smile spread as Mr. Victors leaned forward. He tapped his fingertips against the tabletop. "I knew you would." His gaze shifted to me. "Just as I know you spent time in the library, reading a portion of your book. Unless you just imagined it. In which case, you don't have a date with mine carts."

I jolted, expecting protests from those listening in. Rapid-fire queries. Something. Seconds ticked by in silence, no orders forthcoming.

"No need to worry, Miss Roosa," Mr. Victors said. "They can't understand my words. Not all of them, anyway."

I snorted. Yeah. Right. The Soalian had spoken in English. Although, yes, there had been a slight twang to some of his pronunciations. I hesitated only a moment before swinging my gaze to Cyrus to gauge his reaction. His blank mask remained firmly in place.

Leaning into him, I whispered, "Do you comprehend what he's saying?"

The HP turned his face to mine and searched my eyes. "Do you? He's alternating between English and an unknown language."

What! I jerked my focus to Mr. Victors. "How do I understand you when others can't?"

"How do you think?"

I didn't know! Tick tock. No mental mazes. "Did *you* read a portion of the book?" I asked, being careful of my phrasing.

Mr. Victors lifted his shoulders, giving the semblance of a shrug. "Not yours, but mine. Tomes intersect as lives do. But I prefer the tales depicting my past. That's how we learn." His head canted thoughtfully. "Do you like to learn, Miss Roosa?"

"I do. In fact, I'd love to learn why you requested to speak with me specifically."

"Who wouldn't want to speak with the much-desired wife of the high prince? Though I suppose you are merely his future much-desired wife at this point."

Excuse me? "I'm not . . . that isn't . . ." Heat scorched my face. He was lying. Obviously. Trying to get a rise out of me. And it was working!

Tension radiated from Cyrus, and I could only pray he hadn't understood those particular words.

"Explain what you think I bring to the table," I demanded of the prisoner. "Tell me why I deserve such a valuable resource when I'm not married to *anyone* and I have no plans to change that."

"Do you see no worth in yourself?" Mr. Victors reclined in his chair as much as the chains allowed. "Either way, the answer is simple. Soal asked, and we acted. And your darling HP isn't the reason."

I waggled my jaw.

"I read your paper, you know," Mr. Victors said. "The essay meant to win over your dream college. Such passion for your subject is an inspiration."

Oh, look. Someone else attempting to use my paper as a manipulation tool. I admit, though, I admired his confidence. His ability to steer a conversation. To intimidate while remaining unflappable. His peace hadn't wavered for a nanosecond.

"Does Soal require a gardener?" It was as good an explanation as any, I supposed. And yes, it was a temptation unlike any other. To get my hands on the flowers growing atop the Rock . . . No! *Focus.*

The glower grinned a little. "Sitting here, speaking with you, I'm reminded of a time I found a pritis stone. It was so dirty, I almost tossed it. Had I done so, I would've lost the key to my own rescue, simply because I didn't recognize its value."

I guess I was the dirt-crusted stone in this scenario. "I thought the maddened hated those stones."

"They do. Soalians hate that CURED misuses them. Of course, you have no idea what they are because you filter everything through their ocean of lies."

"Enlighten me, then. Correct my wrong assumptions. Help me understand your truth."

For the first time, he demonstrated a thread of anger. "It isn't my truth but *the* truth."

Anger blasted from Cyrus, too, but he said nothing.

"Enlighten me," I reiterated.

Mr. Victors drummed his fingers against the table. "Give me a second to remember my serious face, so I don't accidentally lighten the gravity of the moment." As he experimented with different facial expressions, I bit my tongue.

Are you kidding? Tick tock. I had a thousand more questions, and he was playing games.

Deciding on a stoic veneer, he continued in a heavy tone. "Soal is the answer to every problem. The old gods rise. The war heats. Pritis stones die but shouldn't. There's no such thing as coincidences. Judging by the sections of your book you've told me about, we both know you help us bring down CURED."

"I never told you—I won't ever—" I caught myself. No more mental mazes. "Please, go on."

He leaned in. "Do you wonder if Shiloh broke from EOS . . . or if CURED broke him without it?"

I clutched the edge of the table. Of course he'd brought up a topic sure to set me off. "People can't be made to break without the Madness."

"Can't they? Do you even know what *EOS* stands for? Let me answer for you: no. You know only what you've been told."

"Time is up." King Tagin's voice spilled from overhead speakers, dripping with anger.

Mr. Victors chuckled with delight. "I must say, his upset is intoxicating." He smirked at Cyrus. "Astan's defeat is assured, and all the Dolions know it."

Astan, a name Shiloh had mentioned as well. A detail I might've latched on to at any other time. Now, I worried more about people breaking without being infected. If they could be *made* to break . . .

Cyrus eased to his feet, helped me stand, and ushered me toward the door. Though I didn't want to leave, I didn't protest. I cast a probing glance over my shoulder.

Mr. Victors's innocent smile returned, shining with megawatt brightness. "The pleasure was mine, Arden. I look forward to our next interaction."

The door slid closed, ending our interaction but not my inner turmoil. I couldn't deny he'd made an impact.

"Brace yourself," Cyrus muttered. Frustration and concern percolated in his command. "*Your* interrogation begins in five. Four. Three."

My stomach lurched. Yeah, his father must have questions. Before I responded, I needed to decide what to admit and what to keep to myself. It all depended on what the listeners had understood and what remained a secret between the prisoner and me, but I wasn't sure how much they'd heard.

Tagin Dolion exited a room beside ours, and every soldier near us jerked to attention, saluting him. "Dismissed," he barked with none of his usual charm. The men and women marched off in a hurry. "Tell me what Victors said to you. Leave nothing out."

I met his probing stare head on. *Here goes.* "Mr. Victors gave me the usual Soalian spiel. Soal is the answer to every problem, old gods rise, and a war heats. He mentioned reading a portion of his book and said he'd once found a pritis stone but hadn't recognized its value until he washed it. He implied Shiloh Cruz broke without being infected with Madness, asked me if I knew what *EOS* stands for, and stated someone named Astan is defeated." No part of me wished to mention the marriage thing. "What does *EOS* stand for?"

The king scowled and jumped his gaze to his son. "When you get back, make sure she receives a dose of aidem."

"I'll take care of it personally," Cyrus replied with a firm nod.

Aidem. The same injection Dr. Korey wasn't positive she'd given me on my first day at the academy. One of the shots mentioned in the Lemon Ade file. "I don't need another." I wasn't even sure why I'd gotten the first or what aidem was.

"You need whatever I say you need." The king pinned me with a hard stare. "If I discover you've lied—"

"She falls under my jurisdiction." Cyrus stepped in front of me, acting as my shield. "I handle her."

My eyes widened as the two faced off.

"You fall under *my* jurisdiction," the king snapped.

"Do I?" Cyrus said nothing else. He tilted his head, all calm and assurance.

To my shock, the king backed down. "Just . . . see to it, or we'll have this conversation again, and it will end much differently."

Cyrus turned on his heel and strode off, expecting me to follow. Which I did. "Not another word until we're alone," he commanded at low volume.

As if I knew what to say.

We entered the elevator stall.

"You know what *EOS* stands for, I'm sure," I remarked as soon as the door had closed.

"You're due for guard duty at the pritis mines," he said, as if I hadn't spoken. "I'd rather you stay with me. Stay, and I'll share one of my interactions with Soal."

My heart fluttered at his husky tone, and oh, the temptation. But I couldn't shake a portion of Mr. Victors's speech. *Pritis stones die but shouldn't. There's no such thing as coincidences.*

"I won't neglect my duties." I hoped my easy tone masked my frothing determination to peek inside the mines. "And I won't stick my teammates with extra work because I fail to do my portion." Excellent reasons. Very true and totally buyable.

He inhaled sharply, then nodded stiffly and poked at a panel of lights. The elevator shuddered into motion. "Victors told you more than you admitted to my father," he stated, matter of fact.

Everything inside me seemed to stop. I looked straight ahead and admitted nothing.

"It's okay. Don't share the details with me until you're ready." He interwove our fingers, then brought my knuckles to his mouth for a kiss, leaving me breathless. "But maybe do me a favor and get ready in a hurry."

My defenses threatened to crack. *So soon?* "How did I understand his words when others couldn't?"

A muscle jumped in Cyrus's jaw. "You weren't given an aidem shot. If you had, Victors would've been forced to speak in a way we could all understand."

"My file says I received the shot." I remembered Dr. Korey and the medic discussing it. "I don't understand how the aidem prevents me from detecting the use of a foreign language." Or why CURED would ever desire to suppress such an ability.

Cyrus's gaze captured mine. With his free hand, he brushed a lock of hair from my cheek. Ambrosia scented my next inhalation, and I shivered inside. "Why don't I tell you what I'd say to you if we were a couple."

I licked my lips and clasped his wrist to push him away . . . or hold him close. He'd turned up the heat again, taking his pursuit of me a notch higher. I wasn't immune.

I held him close.

Maybe I'd misconstrued his reasons for doing this. Maybe it had nothing to do with capturing Ember and everything to do with his feelings for me. Or even keeping me tied to CURED. But no matter the reason, encouraging him was anything but wise.

"Yes, please," I rasped like the fool I was. "Tell me."

He cupped my cheek, branding my skin with his searing heat. "I would tell you I wasn't supposed to like you. Then you showed up wearing your pink running clothes, broadcasting all kinds of vulnerabilities. Afraid but determined. Unwaveringly loyal yet guarded. Serious while being exceptionally fun to tease. It wasn't long before staying away became the problem."

I wanted to look anywhere else. Needed to. But I couldn't. He'd trapped me in a web of yearning. It was okay, though, because right now we were only pretending.

"If I trusted you completely," I said with a wispy catch of breath, leaning deeper into his personal space. "I would press myself against you, like this. I might even play with your hair and tell you things I shouldn't."

"Show me. Give me examples," he commanded, nuzzling the tip of his nose against mine and releasing my hand.

Stomach fluttering, I glided my nails up his arm and caressed his jawline. His brand. I traced my thumb over the raised tissue, fascinated by the intricate webbing. As soon as I realized what I was doing, I tried to pull away, but he clasped my wrists and returned my hands to his face, then snaked his arms around my waist and locked me in place.

"Continue." Another command.

I melted into him. "I'd probably tell you I'm amazed by your strength," I rasped. "That I admire you." My hooded gaze dropped to his mouth. He might be harsh, but parts of him appeared so soft. "I'd definitely wonder if you would kiss me if I trusted you."

His eyes smoldered. "I would move mountains to kiss you." He gently pressed the pad of his thumb into the center of my lower lip and stroked, almost but not quite letting his finger slip inside my mouth.

My knees went weak. We stood like that, with his hand on my face and my hand on his, breathing each other in with ragged inhalations. Waiting. Hoping.

"But I won't let myself," he stated, and I nearly whimpered. "I'll wait. When you're ready, you'll take your kiss because you want it for no other reason than you want me."

The elevator stopped and dinged, shattering the moment. Common sense returned in a blaze, and I dropped my arms to my side and stepped away from him. I'd let myself be distracted. Traded the opportunity to learn more about the aidem injection for round two of bantering. A mistake. One I wouldn't make again.

The doors opened. Armed guards marched the hall outside our little hideaway.

"I will be exceedingly displeased if you endanger yourself during guard duty today," Cyrus stated.

Did he suspect my intentions? "I'll be safe," I intoned, going for businesslike but not sure I succeeded.

"Make sure you are, Pink." His expression softened. "Find me when you're done."

"Yes, sir." Gathering my resolve, I marched off as if I weren't planning to do something very, very bad.

CHAPTER TWENTY-TWO

I will help you; do not fear what they can do to you.

—The Book of Soal 2.19.13.6

Focus! I stuffed my riotous thoughts about Cyrus and our momentary indiscretion into a box, along with worries about a second aidem shot, and labeled it "Unpack and Dissect Later."

Let Operation Mine Peek begin.

I was living the development *The Book of Arden* had predicted. Though I hadn't memorized the passage I'd read, the words now filled the corridors of my mind.

I rush down the hall as fast as my feet will carry me, determined to get my hands on Cyrus's transmitter. All I must do is adhere the camera to a mine cart, and I can watch the feed to see what's being mined.

The perfect plan, there for the taking. I dashed for Cyrus's quarters. Well, "our" quarters. Perhaps he was headed there too. Perhaps not. I was banking on not. He probably had meetings or something. The passage I'd read hadn't mentioned him. But one way or another, I'd make this work. His transmitter was the only way to get inside a pritis mine without leaving my post.

I pumped my arms, fueling my feet, only slowing when I reached the security checkpoints. I did my best to breathe and not alert the guards to my mission by insisting they hurry. Just when I thought I might snap, I entered the suite. No sign of Cyrus. Good. He probably wanted me to do this. He'd all but begged me to speed up my snooping, after all.

I sailed into his bedroom. The armor and its various accessories hadn't been organized or relocated. Where were the camera and the transmitters? I scanned each piece on the bed. The right nightstand. The left. There! He'd never miss them in this mess. I put in the contacts, but I didn't activate them. I would watch a recording of the feed as soon as I was dismissed from duty.

Single minded, I shoved the small case into my pocket, raced out the door, and retraced my steps.

A clock kept time above the locker-room door. One minute and thirty-three seconds until the start of my shift. Doubts slithered in, as insidious as a feeder's worms. Mr. Victors or even Soal himself might be manipulating me, and I was playing right into their hands. According to CURED, that was standard maddened behavior. But I had to know more about the pritis stones. They kept coming up. Shiloh believed they were a secret worth killing to keep. Mr. Victors claimed the stones died, as if they had once lived. Ember challenged me to dig into their origins.

I wavered, going back and forth. Do this. Don't do this. My skin flashed hot and cold. Agreeing to pretend babysit Cyrus to gain access to forbidden places was one thing, but doing full-on spy work was another. A true betrayal of CURED. Treason.

If I intended to back out, I must do it now. Before I stepped over a line.

Head high, I flattened my palm against the door and pushed into the locker room. Truth was too important.

Conversations tapered to quiet, and every gaze found me. I discovered a mix of my teammates and knights. Saying nothing, I soared past them all, going straight to my locker.

"Congrats on your special assignment." Boots in hand, a grinning Juniper sidled up next to me. "Or maybe I say *condolences*."

I snorted. "Probably both."

"You're sleeping with him." Miller stood at the adjacent bay of lockers, a little huffy. "Admit it."

Titus elbowed him in the gut.

Rather than insult Miller in front of everyone, as he'd done to me, breaking my vow to protect my teammates, I said, "If it makes you feel better to think I was chosen because I'm sharing his bed, that's on you." I refused to let his accusation intimidate me. Granted, Cyrus's dating hopes had played a part in my selection, but it also had something to do with the Soalians and my expertise with plants.

"Wow, Mills, wow." Juniper tied her boot with extra force.

"What?" the soldier demanded, tossing up his arms. "I can't be the only one who noticed their steam."

"Making fun of me for sweating during a workout when I ran triple the laps you did. Not exactly a boss move." I tsk-tsked.

He scowled. Several of our teammates threw towels at him.

"Leave her alone." Lark tugged her hair into a ponytail. "You might also try thinking before you speak. Desire can be one-sided. The HP is royalty. Top tier. He has more kills and captures than anyone who's ever completed the program. There's no way he'd lower himself to consort with a lady-in-training."

Um. Thank you?

"More importantly, Arden's love life isn't our business," Titus announced.

"He's right." Roman approached and slung his arm over my shoulders, showing his support. "Say another word about her assignment, and you'll earn us all an extra hour at the mines."

Sign me up for that extra hour! But one by one, soldiers resumed what they'd been doing before my arrival.

"I'm worried about you," Roman admitted at low volume. He bent his head, ensuring no one overheard him. "I believe your assignment is legit, but that doesn't mean feelings won't change with proximity. Just . . . be mindful. The HP has a high body count off the battlefield too. From officers to our hot doctor."

I stiffened, even though I had no right to care. I'd heard about Miss Soti, and I'd suspected Dr. Korey, but not others. "I'm really not sleeping with him." And I wouldn't. I'd never trusted a guy enough to risk being so vulnerable. Most breaks occurred at home.

Who wouldn't want to speak with the much-desired wife of the high prince? Mr. Victors's pronouncement drifted through my head, and I bit my tongue. Still not happening.

Roman released me and shrugged. "I'm only relaying what I heard. Knights, barons, and viscounts love pillow talk."

Guess Cyrus wasn't the only one with a high body count. "I appreciate you looking out for me, but there's no need to worry."

"Okay then." Roman ruffled my hair, spurring a laugh from me. "Let's go do our duty."

"Yes, sir." I finished strapping on an array of weapons. "Let's."

Together, we made the trek to our designated mine. Lights illuminated the windowless stone-and-metal enclosure built on the side of a mountain. Huge boulders and braces bracketed the mine itself.

We joined the current guards, and Roman called, "Everyone shadows a knight. Every hour, they'll switch positions, and you'll move with yours."

I was one of two knights in front of the boulders nearest the cave's darkened entrance. Titus claimed the second space, beating Juniper and Lark, and we exchanged nods of acknowledgment.

The knights didn't speak to us, but noises spilled from the mine's wide opening. Muffled voices. Hammering tools. Thuds. Signs hung from the rock face.

NO SOLDIERS PAST THIS POINT.

STOP! AUTHORIZED PERSONNEL ONLY.

UNAUTHORIZED ENTRY RESULTS IN A FINE AND PRISON.

DO NOT SPEAK TO MINERS!

Cameras peppered the entrance, recording our every move. Thankfully, I didn't need to enter the mine; I just needed a trolley to exit. But the first hour passed to no avail.

At the position switch, I moved with my assigned knight, dragging my feet to the second boulder, taking Titus's place. *Come on, come on.*

"We shouldn't have to do this," Miller complained, standing beside the trolley door on the other side of the chamber, netter in hand. "This facility is protected from the outside. There's never any action in here. And it's not like feeders can touch the stones anyway."

"It's practice with minimal risk, so shut your mouth and do your job," Roman commanded from the center of the room. He and his knight acted as lookouts from a center dais. "Remember what the HP said. Everything is a test, and we will be quizzed."

"Bet Arden aces it," Miller quipped, and a handful of our teammates snickered.

"I bet I do too," I replied without heat. I'd picked this path, and I couldn't complain about it now. "Thank you for the vote of confidence."

He scowled at me.

"Focus up," Roman snapped.

I obeyed. He really was a good leader. Someone who took control of every situation and never cracked under pressure. But I might. As minutes ticked by, my final hour at the mine neared its end without the emergence of a cart.

I shifted from one foot to the other.

"Eager to see your sugar bear?" Juniper teased softly. She'd taken my previous spot.

My head fell forward, and I groaned. "You guys heard that?"

"Everyone on base heard, but only because none of us kept quiet about it."

"I was joking," I whined.

An intermittent, high-pitched squeal registered at last, and I stilled. A mine cart! I readjusted my stance, stealthily reaching into my pocket to free the transmitter from its case.

"Switch," Roman called. We'd reached the end of the hour.

My knight stalked to his next position. Another switch. No, no, no. I hung back.

Roman noticed and clapped his hands. "Put some hustle in your steps."

Juniper and her knight approached me. But the trolley wasn't close enough.

"Oops." I bent down and fiddled with the tie of my boot, keeping my concentration on the squeak. Almost . . . Now! I leaped to my feet and darted to the side, as if chasing my knight. Meanwhile, I moved right in the trolley's path. We collided, and I purposely fell, stopping the motion-sensitive hauler in its tracks. Good so far. Pretending to use the transporter to help myself stand, I covertly adhered the disk onto the cart's rim.

"Do not touch," an automated voice announced, spurring two knights to rush over to intervene.

"Apologies," I muttered, hightailing it to my next post. I tried not to trip as elation mixed with trepidation. I'd done it. I'd succeeded with step one.

I'd all but thrown myself into the fire now. There was no going back.

As the next hour passed, my trepidation reached new heights. If that transmitter was spotted, CURED would track it to Cyrus, then me. Had I destroyed both of our lives?

Odds were low the transmitter *wouldn't* be spotted. As low as the odds Victors hadn't set me up for a trap.

By the time I reached my fifth post, my knees were knocking. I began to wheeze my breaths. No, no, no. Not a panic attack. Not here, not now. I'd done so well. Had grown so brave. But, but . . . *What had I done?*

I needed to think, but I also needed to breathe, and breathing was becoming more and more difficult. In, out. In. Why couldn't I breathe in? Lowering into a crouch, I ducked my head.

"Take five, Arden." Roman's directive penetrated the panic.

Yes, yes. Five. This would probably cost me the top-soldier title, but I didn't care. I seized the chance to watch the camera feed. To see everything was fine. I would calm and come up with a plan to retrieve the camera.

Oh, dang! The camera. Retrieval. A step I hadn't considered.

I launched from the room, certain of only one thing. My life had been forever altered by my actions today.

In the locker room, I sealed myself inside a shower stall. Inhale, exhale. In. Out. Okay, I could breathe. In, out. In, out. Maybe there was a chance what I'd done wasn't such a big deal. I mean, if the pritis mines were on the up-and-up, no one should care that I'd seen inside one.

Fighting tremors, I adhered the tiny transmitters behind my ears. *Inhale. Exhale.* I pressed the correct button inside the case and started playback. Suddenly, the gray stall walls vanished, superseded by the camera feed. The building that housed the mine formed around me. Sweet goodness, it was as if I had become the mine cart, watching myself glide along the track.

I saw Roman marching on the dais with his gun at the ready. Spread out around him were other teammates in the process of assuming new positions. I continued moving, exiting the room through a tunnel door. The world blackened, all light snuffed out, and I pressed my hands over my mouth to silence a spontaneous protest. I could see *nothing*.

A high-pitch squeak sounded, and I jumped. But no big deal. It was just the cart's wheel. I increased the speed of the feed, swallowing a whimper of relief when the cart cleared the tunnel. Light flooded in. Too bright! I flinched, pressing into cool tile. The feed glided forward, an unnerving sensation made worse as I logged my new surroundings. A room with two workers. An oil-smeared mechanic and a tech girl.

"Check the front right wheel," she called.

"Got it," he said, hustling over with tools.

The closer he came to the camera, the stiffer I grew. Yes, the transparent disk was designed to be invisible, but come on. He worked on the wheel with his face directly in front of the camera lens.

I didn't expel my breath until he called "Good to go" and jogged off. Then the cart was rolling on. No one checked for pritis. The cover was never removed, a load never dumped before the cart returned the way it had come, going through the dark tunnel and into the mine.

Again I increased the speed. Finally, the cart reached the heart of the mine. Rocky walls supported by beams. No workers labored nearby, despite the soundtrack of clanking metal. The dimly lit, winding path led to a dead end.

Hmm. There wasn't even mining equipment. No tools of any kind. The place looked abandoned, as if it had dried out. But that presented a new mystery. There was no reason to pretend to mine pritis. No reason to guard the mines at all.

I was missing a lot of facts, the puzzle growing murkier, and I had no idea what to do next.

Chapter Twenty-Three

Those who refuse the truth will die with CURED.

—*The Book of Soal* 1.19.37.9

Guard duty ended in greater disappointment. The cart never reemerged, so I never retrieved the camera. But panic didn't get the better of me again. I carried too much anger. I wanted, needed straight answers about something, anything, but no one was willing to give them.

Dragging my feet, I made my way to the apartment I now shared with Cyrus. Maybe I'd tell him what I'd done and give him a chance to prove he intended to clean up my messes.

At the first security checkpoint, a viscount said, "You need to come with me, Lady Roosa."

I forgot how to breathe. "No, thank you."

"I wasn't asking," he repeated, holding my stare. Clearly, he'd mastered the art of intimidation.

My bravado cracked. CURED must have learned of the transmitter. "I'm due to meet High Prince Dolion for a secret project I'm not allowed to discuss."

"This has priority. *King* Dolion has requested a meeting."

"I see." Breathe! "Did he say why?"

The viscount simply blinked at me.

I'd take that as a no. "I'll just contact the HP and inform him of my tardiness. You know how Dolions can be when they're kept waiting. People lose their jobs." Cyrus might not be aware his father had summoned me.

"He'll be contacted on your behalf and informed of the delay. This way." The viscount marched down the hall.

I trudged after him. We navigated different hallways, took two elevators, and descended a flight of stairs, then entered an elaborate underground catacomb with walls comprising the same gemstones that decorated the statues aboveground. A set of towering arched doors blocked our entrance into, what was this place? The ragged ends of my nerves frayed further.

"He's inside," the viscount said, stepping aside.

Like a brave girl, I pushed inside a spacious chamber. The opulence caught me off guard. Murals covered a cathedral ceiling, depicting battles between men and beasts. Golden statues lined the walls, bracketed by ivory columns veined with crushed rubies. Each figure featured a colossal man with ram horns and wings encrusted with diamonds. A white marble floor gleamed. The air smelled of cloying, clashing perfumes, one too musky and the other too sweet.

King Dolion stood at the other side of the room, beneath the dais steps, peering up at the biggest statue. The horned, winged man towered behind a massive golden throne, gripping its top. His wings folded in at the sides, the tips brushing the arms of the royal seat.

My nerve endings buzzed with something I did not like. "This place is . . ." Awful.

"Glorious, I know. Welcome to the Temple of Astan." The king kept his attention on the throne. I detected no anger in his tone. No accusation or irritation. "My thinking spot."

I shuffled deeper inside. "Why am I here?" In a temple for the man Shiloh had claimed was leading CURED. Looked like the medic had gotten something else right.

Perhaps he'd nailed other facts too. The sleeping gods and heating war no longer struck me as such an outlandish idea.

"Two reasons," the king said. "We believe you can handle the truth, and you are important to my son. He's made that very clear. Therefore, I'd like a chance to get to know you better."

No, he hadn't discovered what I'd done with the transmitter. Otherwise, I'd be in chains right now. "I can handle anything but more lies." I forced myself to breeze past the admission about Cyrus.

The king waved to the throne. "Astan is a god and Soal's greatest enemy. As Victors mentioned, the two are at war."

Anger returned redoubled and wove between the fibers of my surprise. After all the deception and denials, the king had just admitted it. Just like that. As if I hadn't spent my entire life scoffing at anyone who voiced such preposterous ideas.

"Ordinary people are ostracized for making such an outrageous claim," I ground out.

"A necessary evil for the good of the world."

"There's no such thing as a necessary evil."

He frowned, as if disappointed in my inability to see beyond myself. "You speak of what you do not understand, Miss Roosa."

"Everyone is fond of saying that, but no one is willing to explain." I was just furious enough to push, even if it got me into trouble. "There are some who've claimed Soal is the cure to Madness."

He compressed his lips. "Ah, yes. I've heard the same. I assure you, they lie."

I wasn't so sure anymore. Didn't know what to believe.

Maybe he read my uncertainty. "The eating of the stone and the drinking of the sap is what births glowers."

I swallowed a humorless laugh. Well, well. Another fact Shiloh had gotten right. According to the reports he'd provided, glowers bore no trace of the Madness as we knew it. "To eat and drink of the Rock, they must crack into it. An impossibility, I thought."

"It is and it isn't. Only glowers can do it. We have yet to replicate their method." The king strode forward. "Once, Astan ruled Theirland with his wife, Briar. I'm sure you've noticed the statues sprinkled around the compound. They represent the most trusted members of their council before Soal decimated the entire realm, forcing them into hiding and hibernation. Astan says a time is coming when the old gods will awaken and the final battle will erupt. That's why Soal has inserted himself into our society. He hopes to build an army and slaughter the rest of us."

I balled my hands into fists. Yet another suspicion of Shiloh's confirmed. While I knew little about Soal, I now comprehended an appalling fact. From the beginning, his Soalians had spoken the truth about the gods and their war. And they were punished for it.

Needing a moment, I asked the first question to pop into my head. "What is that dinosaur hybrid thing?"

"That is Bala, Astan's beloved pet and the namesake of our military base." The king braced his arms behind his back. "The Madness comes from Soal. It is his favorite means of eradication. His way of weakening a world before striking. Astan has the antidote, and it has the capacity to immortalize even the most average of citizens. Currently that antidote is too powerful for humans and requires modifications we haven't yet mastered."

I wondered if Soal would tell a different story. Actually, no. I didn't wonder. He would. According to Shiloh, a confirmed Soalian, the Madness was spread by CURED. If he was right . . .

The king watched me, gauging every nuance of my expression. "You've met Soal, I take it."

"No." I hadn't, and that was the honest-to-goodness truth . . . but suddenly I wanted to. Needed to.

"You will. Soon. He's targeted you for a reason."

I flattened a hand over my fluttering stomach. "I don't know why."

"I have my suspicions," he muttered.

"Well, please enlighten the rest of the class."

But he didn't. "I've read firsthand accounts of the violent massacres Soal committed here, and they are chilling." He exhaled with gusto. "A great war is coming to Ourland, Arden, whether we're ready or not. A final showdown between Astan and Soal, and we will play a part. Our people must unite if we're to survive it."

A war between gods, with people as casualties. How *dare* CURED conceal such vital information.

The king wasn't done. "We don't understand the mechanics, but Soal's work in Ourland is limited to the Rock. He can only access us and our world through the stone, which is why he raises up glowers and mindless feeders. The two may be at odds, but each serves a purpose. We do whatever is necessary to ensure people pay Soal no heed. There's no being worse than Soal. We either help Astan defeat him and his armies, or we die in agony."

He believed what he was saying, his conviction undeniable. I wanted to believe him, too, but I also comprehended his certainty didn't make him right. Should I trust Soal, though?

Each side claimed the same about the other, and they couldn't both be correct.

"You shouldn't suppress this," I said. "People deserve the truth."

"The masses cannot handle stories of gods and an eternal war. How many will believe Soal's lies and flock to the Rock, risking infection? How many more will break? How many will die at their hands?" He heaved a sigh. "Consider all I've told you. My son and I don't always get along, but I love him, and I don't want you putting him at risk."

The king suspected I'd lost faith in CURED. He must. But he didn't press the issue.

"Stay here as long as you like, Miss Roosa. I'm sure my son will find you soon enough." He strode toward the door just as a stoic Cyrus stomped in. "I'm disappointed. I expected you sooner, son."

The HP wore a clean T-shirt and fatigues, but his hair was in disarray. His eyes were bright and alert, his jaw shadowed with stubble. He swept his gaze over me, relaxing slightly, then focused on his father.

What he didn't do was exhibit surprise. He knew all about Astan, this temple, and the alleged war.

"I must've missed my invitation to the party," he said without an emotional inflection.

"I admit, I seized an opportunity to learn more about the first woman you've ever keyed into your security detail." The king shrugged. "I'm not sorry."

Cyrus fisted his hands. "She's monitoring my health."

"Yes, that too."

The exchange occurred while they passed each other, neither missing step. My narrowed gaze remained fixed on my "patient."

"CURED is hiding a war that impacts the entire world," I stated as soon as the door closed behind the king.

"Yes." Cyrus met my gaze, unabashed.

"What else don't I know?" I demanded.

"Many things. What, specifically, would you like to learn?"

"Admit who lives in the castle." He'd refused before.

Cyrus sighed, reminding me of his father. "My grandfather is there, among others. He presides over Ourland from Theirland. He's a major target of glowers and safer here than in Ourland." He cupped my face and peered deep into my eyes. "I know you're in shock and angry."

"Yes." I should have pushed him away, but I nestled deeper into his touch. "I wish you'd prepared me."

"I told you what I could and offered hints I shouldn't." He traced his thumbs over the rise of my cheeks. "Now, at least, you're privy to CURED's secrets."

Yet I'd never been closer to siding with the Soalians.

The realization shattered the moment of camaraderie. I straightened, more confused than ever about CURED, Soal, and even about Cyrus's intentions toward me.

He shoved his hands into his pockets, his expression shuttering. Guilt flickered. More and more, his affection struck me as genuine. But look at all I'd misconstrued in the past.

Great! Now I was more frustrated than ever too. One day, my cauldron would overflow.

"Come on." With a tilt of his head, Cyrus motioned to the exit. "We'll talk, but not here. I can never get comfortable in the temples."

So there were more of these things.

He led me past the double doors and out of the catacombs. On our way up, an intermittent booming noise discharged, shaking the building with each new flare.

"What's happening?" I settled my hand on my netter, gazing around. Sounded like we were under attack.

"Ah, this is your first Theirland storm." Amusement tinged his voice. "There's nothing to fear. The storms are loud and animated, but the maddened hide from the deluge."

We passed an armored window lit by pritis. Fat water droplets poured from the midnight sky, hammering the glass and pavement. Lightning flashed, vibrant streaks of white splitting the darkness in half. The air electrified, raising the fine hairs on my nape. As the rain pounded the pavement, I almost leaned into Cyrus.

"Have a seat," he said once we were sealed inside our suite.

"I think I've done enough chatting today." So much had been thrown at me, I needed time to catch up.

"Very well." His tone hardened somewhat. "We'll jump to the interrogation portion of our evening." He got in my face and slowly, steadily backed me against a wall. My breath hitched. "You had a panic attack during guard duty. Explain why."

Careful. "As if I need a reason." His nearness did strange things to my insides. Flutters, tingles, and heat spread with the same intensity as the storm outside.

Thunder boomed, shaking the room. He flattened his palms near my temples, caging me in. His incredible scent fogged my head. "My optical transmitters are missing." He searched my gaze and repeated, "Explain why."

Dang him. He'd discovered the theft too quickly. "Your room is a mess." I shifted from boot to boot. "I'm happy to help you search for the transmitters."

He kicked my legs apart and inserted his knee between them, leaning closer. "I advise you to take a different path with me, Arden."

My heart skipped. I glanced at his lips. "But I prefer this one."

"I'll give you one more chance to come clean."

His casual timbre rankled. "You promised to let me spy and snoop. Unless you lied."

"My word is good. But I never said I wouldn't question your activities." He inched closer, erasing the gap between us. "Outline what you discovered in the mines."

Sweet goodness, he'd already surmised what I'd done. "How?" I squeaked out.

He understood the query. "You left a trail of breadcrumbs. Returning here. Invading my room. Taking equipment programmed to my file. Stopping a mine cart. The panic attack. Shall I go on?"

"No." I closed my eyes for a moment. "I'd rather hear where pritis is really mined. An explanation about what, exactly, pritis is would be good too."

His eyelids narrowed to slits. "That isn't something I can discuss with you yet."

More secrets. Oh, how that burned. "Then tell me if I'm going to spontaneously break now that I'm aware the mines are empty." I jutted my chin. "Tell me if I was used as a weapon to execute Shiloh. If someone made him break. If we can be *made* to break."

Cyrus set his hands on my waist. Heat radiated from his calloused palms. "You're not going to break. As for Shiloh, I'm unsure what happened to him. I've been unable to get my hands on certain documents."

"So foul play is possible, and you suspect it occurred." I gripped two handfuls of Cyrus's shirt, intending to shake the information out of him. To push him away. To kiss him. To anchor myself while the storm raged. I did nothing but cling.

He brushed the tip of his nose against mine. "I look into every crime involving a member of my team."

An answer that wasn't an answer. My cauldron of frustration bubbled, steam curling from the surface, clouding my mind. In that moment, I could think of nothing but the days and weeks and months and years I'd remained silent, pretending not to have an opinion. Always agreeing with anyone in authority, no matter how desperately I objected, too afraid of the consequences.

"Give me a straight yes or no, Cyrus. Please. I'm a wreck inside. Like a plant that's outgrown its pot, slowly being strangled by its roots. Tell me what you know about Shiloh's death."

His posture softened. "I've told you what I know."

Hardly. "You are royalty. You know more than anyone else in the world."

Irritation crossed his features. "You have a skewed perception of my life." Brighter lightning flashed, chasing away shadows, revealing hints of anger and sadness. "I'm kept in the dark, on a need-to-know basis, just like everyone else. About a year ago, I experienced a time of uncertainty, wondering who to trust and what to do. I launched my own investigation, but every door to understanding led to more questions. I was desperate for hope and starved for truth. Then something happened, revealing the heart of both Soal and CURED, and clarity came. I made my decision with absolute certainty that I was doing the right thing, and I've never regretted it." His fingers flexed on me. "One day I'll share the details with you."

One day. Just never today.

A choked noise burst from me. "I'm done with—you can't just— there's too much—" Argh! The words lodged in my throat, my cauldron boiling over at long last. With tears clouding my vision, I beat at his chest. "I hate this! I hate it, I hate it, I hate it!"

He caught my wrists. His expression conveyed understanding and affection. "Venting might feel better in the moment, but the aftermath makes everything worse."

"I can't feel worse!" I wrenched free of his clasp and beat his chest harder.

"Very well." Resolve infiltrated his tone. "Hit me and mean it or pull yourself together."

How calm he was. How confident. How infuriating! Hit him? With pleasure. I screeched and swung with all my strength. He caught my fist before contact, so I kicked him. Though he angled his body, he wasn't fast enough, and my knee clipped his thigh. Not good enough.

The fight was on.

I hit. I kicked.

"Harder," he instructed. "Faster."

My temper redlined. "Be quiet!" I swung.

"Make me." He blocked with ease. "If you can."

A banshee howl heralded my next punch. The ruthless warrior batted my fist away, as if it were a pesky fly. New howl, new strategy. I lunged at him. We grappled across the room, jumping on furniture, leaving a path of destruction in our wake. I utilized every skill I'd learned in his class, but no matter how many times or ways I struck, he never retaliated. He only ever blocked, which made me more furious.

"You're making me question my teaching skills, Arden. At least try."

Aaah! I attacked with fury, shouting things I'd yearned to say for minutes, hours, days, weeks, months, and years. "I refuse to take the aidem shot! I'm not getting it. I choose my path. Me! Not someone in a cubicle who knows nothing about my life. My money is my money. I should get to decide what to do with it. I have a right to know my test scores. They're mine! Meal bars are disgusting. Uniforms are ugly, stiff, and itchy. There should be pritis in pritis mines. You're only using me. I miss my mother and my plants." My voice broke at the end. That, too, only stoked the flames.

I feigned a punch to the left. When he dodged, I kicked his boots together. He fell on the couch, and I followed him down, intending to pin him. With masterful precision, he flipped me onto my back.

His weight settled over me, making me the pinned. Though I struggled with everything I had, I couldn't dislodge him. "Thank you for sharing with me," he calmly stated. "Are you ready to surrender now?"

"Never." Despite my claim, I sagged against the cushions. I glared at him, and he stared at me, and we panted in unison. "I'm not sure I will ever be able to trust you."

"Judge me by my fruit. An apple tree cannot produce oranges."

Dang him! I hated that he had learned my preferred language so proficiently.

"I'm not using you." He arched a brow, a bead of blood dripping from a cut under his eye, collecting in his brand. "You feel worse." A confident statement.

Yes! "I thought I told you to be quiet," I spat.

"And I told you to make me. Neither one of us succeeded."

Oh, I'd make him shut up, all right. My narrowed gaze dropped to his stupid mouth. Exactly where I'd hit him. I could . . . I would . . .

"Do it," he challenged.

"I will. Don't think I won't." But I didn't move. Just panted with more force. I couldn't tear my attention from his lips. They looked so soft.

He traced his tongue over the bottom. "Do it," he repeated, temptation itself. "I dare you."

I . . . did. With a hoarse groan, I clasped his cheeks and lifted my head. He lowered his. Our mouths met in a heated tangle, his tongue thrusting against mine. He kissed me as if he couldn't breathe without me. As if no other woman existed. As if he'd found a treasure he'd waited his entire life to obtain.

I kissed him back, every fiber of my being engaged in the act and entranced by the man. Not an ounce of frustration tainted the exchange, my cauldron amazingly empty. In my veins, blood burned like fuel, burning hotter and hotter. Thoughts fragmented and defenses cracked until the kiss grew frenzied. I mewled, ceding emotional ground to him. What I ceded, he conquered, and I only craved more and more and more. I clutched and kneaded at his back. Clung to him. Threaded my fingers through his hair.

My bones liquefied. Somehow I rallied the strength to wind my arms around his shoulders and gasp out "Cyrus."

He pinched my chin, angled my face in the direction he desired, and deepened the kiss, forcing us both to slow. Strength fizzed under the surface of his skin, yet his touch remained gentle, infinitely tender.

My aches and pangs amplified. I met each languid roll of his tongue with a roll of my own, relying on him for every breath. Desperate to be closer to him, I cupped his cheeks. He leaned into my touch as I traced my thumb over the puckered scar tissue. A precious badge of strength and survival.

Groaning, he grazed my bottom lip between his teeth and lifted his head. He still panted. I panted faster. Our gazes held. I couldn't look away. Didn't want to. His glittering irises reflected the night storm, electrifying me.

With another low groan, he pressed his forehead to mine. "What are you doing to me?"

"Hopefully the same thing you're doing to me." The huskiness of my words summoned a sizzling flush to my cheeks.

"Do you want more?"

"Yes," I admitted. More than anything.

"Good." He gifted me with a soft kiss, then lifted before I could demand another. He stood and offered me a helping hand. "To get your next kiss, you'll have to ask me nicely."

I sputtered. He wasn't going to . . . he expected me to—oh! I sat up and batted away his outstretched arm. "That is cruel and unusual punishment, sugar bear."

He caught my wrist, just as before, and hefted me to my feet. "No, it's the best play for my endgame. Now for the teaching moment. When you strike at someone, always mean it. Remember to hit hard and fast." He passed me a dagger and backed up. "And don't allow your emotions to lead you. They are fickle and prone to giving bad advice. Come at me again, but show no mercy."

"You are so irritating," I snapped, but I did obey. Another unsuccessful assault.

"You're wrong," he said, stopping me with ease. He spun me around and shoved me against the wall, locking my arm and the blade over my head. "I'm irresistible. There's a difference. By the way, a student usually improves with practice. Why haven't you?"

The taunt did its job. I bared my teeth. "Ask my instructor."

"I did. He says you didn't listen."

Further annoyed, I executed a countermove, breaking free of his hold. We grappled throughout the living room, rolling over the fallen coffee table, kicking at each other, punching and blocking. He still didn't land a blow, but it wasn't because he lacked opportunity.

In the end, I wound up right where I'd started: pinned. My spine pressed against the wall. One of his hands trapped my arm and the blade, while the other gripped my waist.

"Do you surrender?" he asked with a grin. He was barely winded.

"No. Consider this an extended time-out."

He chuckled, his warm breath fanning my face. "When we return to Fort Bala," he said, releasing me, "do whatever you feel is necessary to find what you're searching for, and I'll continue to clean up where I can. I just hope my babysitter does a better job of hiding her activities while attending upcoming functions with me."

Me too. I couldn't not spy on the powers that be in their natural habitat. But, as much as I desired to be at his side for every function, I couldn't waste an opportunity to bargain. "Hold up. Event attendance wasn't part of our original negotiation."

"It was, though I concede it wasn't mentioned specifically. Therefore, I'm willing to renegotiate." He crossed his arms over his chest. "Demand compensation, and I'll supply it."

No need to ponder. "Let me move into your place in Bala City." There was no faster route to reach the Rock. Tomorrow, I would speak with Soal, or die trying.

A half smile played at the corners of Cyrus's mouth. "You want to spend more time with me. You enjoy being with me. Admit it."

"I enjoy access to restricted areas," I hedged.

"Lady Pink, you enjoy both." He reached out to lightly bop the end of my nose. "I agree to your demand. Now go get some rest." The smile widened, making a spectacular debut. "Dream of me."

CHAPTER TWENTY-FOUR

The only power Astan can wield against you is the
power you give him.

—*The Book of Soal* 1.23.54.17

Despite another sleepless, dreamless night, I dressed and bounded to
the kitchen early with extra energy, determined to make breakfast for
Cyrus. But no, he'd beaten me there. He stood at the counter, gripping
the edge, with his head bowed.

The somberness of his posture struck me, and I skidded to a
halt. A terrible jumble of emotions created a force field around him.
I recognized the sting of guilt, the prick of shame, and the siren's call
of fear. But. This made no sense. He was the intractable, unflappable
Cyrus. A warrior as unbending as steel. Had the berry finally caught
up with him?

Sensing my presence, he stiffened and straightened but didn't face
me. In a heartbeat, the emotional cloud evaporated. Tone upbeat, he
said, "Good morning, Pink."

A staggering change. Had I not seen him seconds before, I would
have had no idea he was anything but eager. "Tell me what's wrong."

"I'm not looking forward to going back. Something I've never said
before," he added with a wry smile. "I despise Theirland. But I despise
the dangers to come more."

Not the full truth, I'd bet, but at least he hadn't attempted to deny a problem. I didn't like his reluctance to share, but I did understand it. Until I gave him my trust, he couldn't give me his.

Before I thought better of it, I strode over and hugged him from behind. An offer of comfort. A gesture of thanks for all the times he'd comforted me. A show of affection I couldn't contain. "I promise to be as careful as possible. Does that help?"

"It does." He spun, wrapping his arms around me too. "What's this for?" he asked, resting his chin atop my head.

"I don't know, so don't ruin it with questions."

"Yes, ma'am."

Snorting, I snuggled closer. We stayed like that a long while before I eased away. "We should go."

"We still have minutes, and I refuse to relinquish a single second alone with you." He passed me a glass brimming with his signature drink. "Once again, you didn't rest," he stated, his disappointment clear.

"I could've gotten an abundance of beauty z's," I stated with mock affront. But yes, I'd tossed and turned, but it was for an entirely different reason than usual. Thanks to our kiss, I *still* ached. I'd be smart to maintain my distance from him today. And yet, I didn't stop myself from leaning into him as I drained my breakfast. Mmm, that was good. The best yet.

"I thought we discussed the fact that your face hides nothing, Pink."

"Bad face," I pouted.

"Beautiful face," he corrected, kissing my brow.

Shivers cascaded over me in warm waves, freeing Mr. Victors's prediction from its mental prison. Future wife of Cyrus Dolion.

Nope, not going there today. "Are you planning to overwork me as hard as yesterday?"

"Probably harder." He took my glass, finished off what remained, and herded me through the suite. "There's something we need to discuss first."

"Agreed. Soal. Astan. The war of gods. Pritis. I'm ready when you are."

He tsked. "You think you've won my trust so easily?"

"Maybe I could win it if you finally shared your secrets, giving me a chance to prove myself trustworthy." We exited into the hallway.

He snorted. "That's an excellent manipulation tactic. So good I could've taught it to you myself."

"Thank you." I curtsied, earning the world's most endearing, rusty chuckle.

We approached the elevator, and the doors opened automatically. In the stall, he bumped my shoulder with his own. "What I intended to tell you is this. We're not leaving anything behind here." Peering down at me, he arched a brow. "Do you understand?"

I thought I did, and relief washed through me. He'd managed to retrieve the transmitter undetected. "Thank you."

"For you, anything."

Things inside me bloomed with his praise. A sudden curiosity directed me to a different track, topic-wise. "Dr. Korey doesn't seem like your type. Or even like someone you once admired."

"Pondering my love life, I see. Perhaps even a wee bit jealous." As I sputtered out a denial, he let a lock of my hair pass between his fingers. "Back then, I didn't even know my type."

"Let me rephrase. Dr. Korey doesn't seem like anyone's type. She's too . . ." What was a good word to describe her and not get written up for insubordination? "Haughty."

"She is. But she took care of me when I was injured. Or I thought she did." He rubbed his brand. "It was a confusing time. Thankfully, I wised up to her desire for power. The more she's given, the more she craves."

"Yeah, I've noticed." Whatever she'd done must have been bad, considering the way he treated her. "I'm guessing the relationship occurred after your first fight with John Victors."

"Correct." He made a distracted sound in the back of his throat. "I was trapped in the darkness without my gear, and a horde of feeders surrounded me. Victors showed up and helped me fight them. When we killed the last, we turned on each other."

I tensed at the thought of Cyrus in so much danger. How close he'd come to dying.

He said no more, and I didn't press. The elevator stopped, the doors opening. We strode into a private hall.

"This is where we part, Pink." Giving my chin a gentle chuck, he said, "Join your teammates, and I'll see you on the other side."

"Sir, yes, sir." I didn't know why, but I felt lighter on my feet than I had in years. No, not true. I did know why. The kiss. His embrace. He'd helped me drain a thousand pounds of boiling frustration. I smiled as I gave *his* chin a chuck. "Stop being cute. It's beneath you."

He barked out a laugh. I pivoted on my heel and sashayed through a door, satisfaction accompanying me inside the transport room. How I enjoyed making him happy.

Clusters of soldiers formed a line in front of the three rifts. I claimed the spot at the end of the far right, behind Juniper. We didn't speak as Cyrus marched in and a guard hightailed it to his side. They went through a rift first, one after the other, and the rest of us made our way forward. When my turn arrived, I approached without hesitation.

Pain hit the second I stepped inside the gloom, just as it always hit, but I noticed it less this go-round. Then I was standing in light, Cyrus directly in front of me.

"You good?" he asked, expectant.

"Yes. You?"

"I am, thank you." He flashed a warm smile before stalking off and calling, "Get to decontamination. We have a busy day ahead."

As a team, we headed for the decon stalls. Alone, I stripped and stood under the water spray, anticipation suddenly warring with foreboding. By the end of the day, I would be standing in front of the

Rock, hopefully speaking with Soal. If he wanted to recruit me so bad, he could take a few minutes to answer my questions.

I dressed in clean fatigues, blown away by the softer-than-usual material. Good gracious. It was like being engulfed by clouds. Hopefully, Mykal and the others received the same upgrade. Amazed and thankful, knowing Cyrus was responsible, I exited the stall.

Cyrus waited for me at the end of the hall, no one else around. No doubt he'd ensured the other stall doors remained locked from the outside.

His expression turned hot and languid as I closed the distance. "We'll keep our normal schedules," he said, leading me through a secluded corridor. "I'll get you keyed into my quarters after drills."

"Keying in can't be done remotely?" The longer we remained at the base, the less time I'd have at the Rock before night arrived and curfew activated.

"At such a high level, both remote and in person are required. Once that's taken care of, we'll deal with the aidem injection."

I gave a violent shake of my head, lengths of hair slapping my cheeks. "I meant what I said. No shot." I wouldn't surrender the ability to decipher glower-speak. Nor would I risk being poisoned, as Shiloh and others might have been. "Please don't try to force the issue." I'd leave the fort. Somehow.

He slipped his fingers through mine and traced his thumb over my knuckles. "Explain why you are so adamant about this."

Nope. No, thank you. I wouldn't be revealing details found in the Lemon Ade file.

"Do you trust me, Pink, even the slightest bit?"

I did. Maybe a little more than slightly. It was the only reason I'd agreed to any of this. "You, but no one else," I admitted.

"Good. Because I meant what I said when I told you I would never do anything to harm you. So let me administer the shot. I'll take care of the details, keeping everyone happy." He didn't say it out loud, but his tone suggested there was a way to fool the system.

This was a risk. A big one. It would mean his loyalty belonged to me, not CURED. That he was courting me, for lack of a better word, for the very reason he'd provided. That he wanted us to be together. A concept almost too good to be true.

I'd asked him to put me to the test. Now, I would do the same to him.

"All right," I said and nodded. "Yes. I'll get an injection as long as you're the one who administers it."

"Thank you. I'll see you at your evaluation." He gave me a little squeeze before releasing me. We turned a corner, and he picked up his pace, striding off.

I watched him until the last possible second, then hurried to my cell. No sign of Mykal, unfortunately, but my soil looked well hydrated. Still no sprout, dang it. With a sigh, I headed to class.

For the first time, I floated through the exercises, eager to get to my evaluation. When the bell rang, I sprinted out the door.

Dr. Korey waited for me in the hall. She stepped into my path, ensuring I couldn't bypass her. "Follow me," she commanded.

Not this again! "Is something wrong?"

"I'll be overseeing your aidem injection."

What! A tsunami of adrenaline crashed into my veins. "You need to speak with Cyrus. He insists on being the one to handle it."

"He's *High Prince Dolion* to you, and he's not a medical professional."

I called upon all the bravado I possessed. "Well, I'm his minder, and there's a chance my title outranks yours, so I decline the invitation to join you." Shoulders squared, I soared past her—or tried to.

Two armed barons made themselves known, stopping me. My stomach sank. She'd brought muscle.

"Follow me, or I'll have you escorted to our treatment facility," she informed me with a smirk. She didn't wait to hear my response, her heels clacking against the floor tiles.

A baron motioned me on. Focused on my breathing, I trudged after her. Where was Cyrus? I searched for his face every time I turned a corner. No sign of him. Somehow, I maintained my cool even when

I sat on a gurney in an exam room, with the barons posted at my sides. Their hands rested on the hilts of their netters.

"High Prince Dolion will be upset—furious!—if he's not with me for this," I told the doctor as she moved about, gathering what she required. "I'm working on a special project with him, and it places me under his exclusive jurisdiction."

"His father outranks him, and my orders come directly from the king." She met my gaze and canted her head. "For your sake, I hope you've realized you are nothing but a temporary amusement for Cyrus."

I almost snapped, "It takes one to know one," but I refused to sink to her level.

Usual scowl in place, she approached me. "Let's get this done. I'm needed elsewhere."

A cold sweat glazed my nape. If I protested, I could be painted as a traitor to CURED. If I didn't, I'd lose my ability to communicate in secret with Soalians. Maybe even Soal himself.

She cleaned my bicep and picked up the syringe. Protests tangled on my tongue as she uncapped the needle. Finally, one escaped.

"No." I jumped up, avoiding the barons, and shook my head. "No."

"Miss Roosa," she snapped. "You will sit back down, or I will—"

"Thank you, Dr. Korey, but you and the others are dismissed." Cyrus's command echoed in the room. He entered in his usual manner, as if he owned the place, then held out his hand and stared at her, expectant. "I'll take it from here."

Relief dulled the burn inside me as the guards left without a word. I remained silent, aware of being recorded.

Shock flashed over the doctor's features. "Your father requested I personally administer this dose."

"My apologies for not being clear." Cyrus spoke with firm patience and staunch purpose. "The dismissal wasn't a request."

"I'm under strict orders." Fury simmered under her skin. "I must bear witness."

"Very well. That, I'll allow." He waved his fingers, silently demanding the syringe.

She handed it over but misjudged the distance, and the serum fell to the floor.

"Dispose of that." He stepped over it. "I'll prepare a new one."

With his back to us, he did as promised. Dr. Korey observed him with narrowed eyes, while my attention jumped between them. I didn't panic when Cyrus marched over and stuck me with the needle. The sharp sting barely registered. A cold sensation spread through my arm.

"I'll inform the king what transpired," the doctor said, her tone flat.

"Please do. I will, as well."

She paused only a beat more before striding from the room.

He adhered a bandage to the injection site and murmured, "Thank you for trusting me."

"Thank you for showing up on time."

We exchanged smiles, and my world brightened.

"I have unscheduled meetings today," he said, "so evaluations are postponed. I won't see you again until drills." He winked and strolled away, calling, "Miss me, Pink. Because I'll be missing you."

❧

The day passed both at warp speed and with agonizing slowness. I didn't mean to, but I did miss Cyrus. The fact that I suffered no ill effects from the shot—so far—helped convince me of his sincerity. I thought I might be able to trust him with my suspicions and plans. Talk about a game changer. No longer would I be forced to undertake my investigation alone. I'd have a partner.

I really, really wanted a partner.

When we reunited for drills, I wanted only to snuggle up to him and talk. Somehow, I quashed the urge. Then he gave his first order, and I wished only to kick him. Cyrus pushed the entire team to the max. Me especially. I don't think anyone in history had ever exercised so much.

He pitted me against Roman, Lark, Miller, and Titus in practice rounds and ensured multiple holograms glommed me at once.

When class ended, the team poured out of the gym, eager to enjoy their free time. Panting and sweating, I crawled to a bench. I had to muster the strength to accept a jug of water Cyrus extended my way.

"I quit as your babysitter," I wheezed after draining the contents.

"Do you want my kisses—I mean *access*—or not?" he asked with a teasing tone.

"Fine. I just tore up my mental resignation letter." Shivers rushed through me at the soft, husky undercurrent in his chuckle. "Since we're such solid business partners, maybe you'll tell me what's going on?" He'd spent all of drills divided between running me ragged and speaking privately with Roman, as well as various viscounts who'd stormed in and out.

Cyrus's amusement vaporized. "There's a possibility for a . . . situation."

Oookay. "I require more information."

The door opened, and a knight rushed inside, carrying my pot.

"Where's Mykal?" I asked, frowning. She should be the only one handling my stuff.

Cyrus couldn't hide a flinch. "That's something I wanted to talk to you about tonight. She quit the program and left the base."

What! "That can't be right." She'd seemed to be getting better.

He accepted the pot from the newcomer. "I'll take the documents too."

The knight shook his head. "My apologies, sir. Dr. Korey couldn't find them."

No reason to wonder what documents they were discussing. Shiloh's records. I gave Cyrus a look as I claimed the pot, my message clear. The doctor was lying.

"I'll get them," Cyrus vowed before refocusing on the soldier. "Has the train arrived?"

The man checked the tiny screen on his wristband. "Yes, sir. Your guards are securing the area now."

"Since when do you need guards?" I asked.

A muscle jumped in his jaw. He dismissed the soldier before focusing on me. "They activate with heightened threats."

"Okay, I demand more information."

"There's been a sudden spike of breaks in Lucrea."

Worry gripped me by the throat. "My mom." She was so weak. No way she could withstand an attack.

Cyrus clasped my hand. "You're the emperor's grandson's babysitter. The position comes with benefits. I've assigned a knight to your mother. He's with her now, and they haven't encountered any problems."

Tears of relief welled, my surroundings blurring. "Thank you, Cyrus. You really are a sugar bear."

He snorted. With his warm palm on my lower back, he steered me to the door. Officers and knights hurried through the bustling hallways. Strain electrified the air and infused every conversation, but I remained surprisingly steady, if distracted.

What had caused multiple, sudden breaks?

The deeper we traveled through the base, the fewer people we encountered, yet the strain remained. I resisted its familiar allure, doing my best to capture every worried thought, imagining tossing it out of my ears, then replacing it with facts. Mom was protected. I would soon face the Rock and might even meet Soal. I wasn't alone. I had Cyrus.

We descended the stairs, the area shockingly empty of potential passengers. Within minutes, we were situated within a private cart, with an entire contingent of soldiers at the ready around us. An intimidating sight to be sure.

Cyrus guided me to the farthest bench. I sat, and he situated himself at my side, his intoxicating scent enveloping me. His usual mask slipped, revealing raw sadness and the heavy weight of responsibility. No doubt he'd gotten used to being inside this train alone and finally unwinding.

I reached over and pressed my palm against his. He curved an arm around my waist, clinging to me. Let rumors about us keep spreading. I didn't care anymore.

"I'm almost ready to tell you my secrets," I admitted quietly. "What I've learned, what I suspect. What I plan."

His fingers flexed on me as he searched my gaze. "I'll help you, whatever it is."

And I'd probably fall deeper in like with him.

He smiled, as if he'd heard my thoughts. "Now might be a good time to tell you I have three cats."

I sputtered for a moment. "Excuse me, but did you say three *hats*? Or *tats*?" Oooh. I rubbed against him and pretended to paw at his chest. "Do you have tattoos, Cyrus?"

His smile brightened. "I do, and I'm eager to discuss this tattoo fetish of yours," he replied, brimming with amusement. "But I did say *cats*."

Who? What? Me? "I don't have a fetish."

"You can hardly contain yourself, Roosa."

Maybe. "But three cats?" Due to the price of food and care, I'd never allowed myself to entertain the possibility of having a solo pet, much less an entire trio.

"I rescued a pregnant feral, and she gave birth to two little girls."

How was he getting more interesting and beautiful by the second? "What are their names?"

"Iris, Daisy, and Poppy," he admitted, ducking his head.

I laughed and snickered in equal measure. "You have a bouquet of cats. This might be my new favorite thing about you."

"Just wait until you see the tats."

I admit, I shivered.

Wheels squealed as the train slowed, reminding me of our audience. I eased from him, and we both stood. No one watched us overtly, I realized, but the level of interest was palpable.

The cart stopped, and the doors slid open. An older, decorated baron-elite stepped forward and saluted Cyrus. "New orders came in during transport, sir."

He stiffened. "Arden, this is Baron-Elite Rita Harper. BE Harper, Lady Roosa. Tell me," he commanded, his mask firmly in place. "What are we dealing with?"

I collected my pot, all ears.

Tone brusque, the BE explained, "Reports came in. Breaks have begun happening within each surrounding province. It's only a matter of time before Bala City experiences the same. Your father demands we take no chances. We are to escort you and your companion to the Lux as quickly as possible. Citizens have been commanded to return home, and the roadways are clogged. We'll have to walk."

It wasn't fear that hit me but determination. I held out my free hand. "I need two daggers, a netter, and extra clips of ammunition."

The BE darted her gaze to Cyrus.

He narrowed his eyes. "You heard her."

She nodded and waved to different barons. They handed over the required weapons. Seconds later, we strode from the train, ready for anything.

CHAPTER TWENTY-FIVE

In times of trouble, find safety and help in the Rock.

—*The Book of Soal* 1.19.27.5

Apprehension tainted a stifling breeze as the sun descended on the horizon. A lovely sight, to be sure, the sky ablaze in colors. From the palest of blues to the most vibrant of pinks, with swirls of glittering gold. An exquisite canvas that elicited nothing but terror in the people of Bala City. As soon as the light vanished, feeders would come out of hiding.

This wasn't a drill, a practice, or an exercise in a contained area. This was real life, with real consequences. There were no medics waiting nearby to administer aid.

Only one hour of light remained. The crowd poised at a razor's edge of aggression. Vehicles jammed the roads, horns blasting. Traffic remained at a standstill. The sidewalks weren't much better, people in a mad rush to escape the throng and lock themselves inside a safe space.

If the buildings here were anything like those in Lucrea, the doors locked automatically at sundown. Not even the chip embedded in a resident's palm allowed entrance. Entire families could be stuck outside all night.

If we didn't pick up our pace, *we* might get stuck. A prospect that would've terrified me in the past. And yet, as we made the grueling trek to Cyrus's apartment, fear remained at bay. I was armed, and I had a strong, experienced warrior I trusted at my side. Together, we could overcome any obstacle in our path.

Along the way, we helped those in need. I clocked every pritis stand, just in case I needed to lead people to safety. Whatever the stones were, wherever they came from, feeders still despised them.

"There aren't enough knights assisting citizens," Cyrus told the BE, having to shout to overcome the sheer volume of noises around us.

"All off-duty knights have been activated, and the newest crop of gentry won't be ready for weeks yet."

I took no offense. She wasn't wrong.

"Are the Havens open?" he asked. To me, he explained, "Facilities filled with hundreds of small individual quarters. New builds scattered throughout the city, meant to be used like the cubbies in Theirland."

How wonderful.

"I'll find out, sir." The BE used a transmitter to speak with whoever monitored the other end. "Yes, sir. The Havens are open, and many individuals and families have entered, but few are staying put, citing the expense is too great."

Anger pulsed from Cyrus. "This is a state of emergency. The chambers should be free. If that's too much to ask, I'll pay. Just get it done."

My admiration for him skyrocketed. "Why don't we send the guards to escort any kids or elderly to the shelters? We can take care of ourselves."

"You are sure?"

Had he kept them around for my peace of mind? A sweet but unnecessary gesture. "I've got you. I'm good."

He clasped my bicep, gluing to his side, calling, "Disperse, and lead the most vulnerable to the Havens."

BE Harper glanced over her shoulder. "I have orders from your father. Don't let you out of my sight."

"Then you don't let me out of your sight. The others leave now."

She scowled but bellowed, "Happy, you're with me. The rest of you, go, go, go."

The others scattered, weaving into a crowd that quickly closed in on us. Our foursome picked up speed, pushing forward, navigating the surge, with the BE in front and Baron Happy at our rear—after he claimed possession of my pot, stuffing the entire container into a pack he then hefted over his shoulders.

"Thank you." Hands free, I palmed a dagger and a netter.

"We're halfway there," Cyrus told me. "In case we're separated, you need to know some things."

I groaned. "Now we're for sure getting separated."

"I live in the Lux," he continued, heart attack serious. "From here you'll take three lefts and two rights, in that order. Repeat my instructions."

"Three lefts and two rights." The problem was, I couldn't get into the building without him. I hadn't yet been keyed into the system.

A high-pitched scream rang out, followed by shouts of panic. My heart and the rest of the world paused. Someone had just broken.

Cyrus tightened his hold on me as the masses erupted in hysteria. The sound of thumping footsteps blended with squealing tires and colliding metals. We quickened our pace, dodging runners. I had no trouble keeping up. Breath sawed between my lips, adrenaline breaking free of its dam, pumping through me and searing my veins.

Another high-pitched scream rose above the commotion. Pops of gunfire joined the symphony. Around us, the terror level spiked. More and more people bumped into each other, including us. Cyrus took the first left to the Lux, pulling me with him.

A vehicle veered off the road, hopped the curb, and crashed into a building. Thick slabs of stone flew in every direction, dust clouding the air. The driver emerged with a shout of "Love Soal!"

Cries blended into a discordant song. The mob swallowed us, ripping me from Cyrus and shoving me backward. Pushed through the ranks, I stumbled for purchase. With great effort, I maintained my grip on my weapons, even when a sharp pain slashed over my eyebrow. Warm liquid dripped into my eyes, blurring my vision.

"Arden!" Cyrus bellowed. I heard him, but I cculdn't see him through the haze.

"I'm here!" I bellowed back, wiping at my face. Where was he? Where were the maddened?

The dust thinned, the world crystalizing. A sea of unfamiliar, frenzied people hemmed me in. Drawing on sheer grit, I fought my way to a building and pressed against the bricks to avoid being trodden down.

"Cyrus?" I yelled, scanning my surroundings. The gunfire ebbed and flowed, rising in short, erratic bursts. "Cyrus," I yelled louder. No response. He must be nearby.

How long did I dare to wait? On my own, I wasn't ready for this. But I was less prepared to spend the night outside. And I wasn't without skill or weaponry. Besides, we'd agreed to a plan, and I should stick to it.

I dragged in a deep breath and shoved my way into the crowd. Though I flowed against traffic, I started jogging. Running. Sprinting. Dodging. New screams added to the soundtrack, raising the fine hairs on my nape as it reached a terrible crescendo. Eerie laughter came next. My finger twitched on the netter's trigger.

Taking the second left, according to Cyrus's instructions, I spotted a maddened in the process of tossing a teenager to the ground. *Here goes everything.* I charged forward, taking aim.

When the attacker raised his fist, I shouted, "Look at me."

He whipped his attention in my direction, as hoped, then sniffed and licked his lips, as if he scented something especially tasty. A grin appeared, and he dropped his victim. The perfect opening. He stepped toward me; I fired. The bullet whistled through the air, growing as it opened. Yes! Upon impact, he hurled to the concrete. Fine metal latticework secured itself around his body, pinning him in place. Satisfaction bloomed, buoying my confidence. Oh, yeah. I could do this.

I quickened my steps, netting any maddened I came upon as I got closer to my destination. Five shots remained in the chamber of my last clip. My heartbeat kept rhythm with my pounding footfalls. Faster. Faster. Nothing slowed me.

The crowd thinned as I approached the final corner. Faster.

Heavy treads erupted behind me. I cast a glance over my shoulder and huffed. Two feeders gave chase, swiftly gaining on me.

Rounding the corner, I expected to see the Lux. Shocked, I drew up short. Not an apartment building, but the Rock. But how, why, when—no, it didn't matter. I was here. It was there. Currently, four people were clawing at the surface, as if desperate to get inside. No sign of Domino Crane, the librarian.

Deal with the imminent threat; figure out the rest. I turned and fired on one of the maddened chasing me. Yes! Another dove my way. Evading, I squeezed the trigger. Two down. Three shots left. No chance to pause and plan. The other four pegged my arrival and converged in unison. Definitely infected. I netted two, but the weapon jammed, leaving me with one less net than anticipated and two opponents to go. Like a pro, I exchanged the gun for my second dagger, prepared to engage in up-close combat.

Suddenly a net I hadn't released whizzed through the air, caging a challenger. I jolted with satisfaction when Cyrus zoomed into view, a weapon in each hand. He incapacitated the remaining infected with expert skill.

"You good?" he demanded, tossing me a new netter.

I caught it with ease. "Very." He sported bruises, gashes, and ripped clothing, but he was alive and well. "You?"

"Been better." His focus jumped over my shoulder, and he scowled. "Three incoming. The biggest is carrying a severed arm."

I geared up to help him save the day, but. The Rock. My gaze landed on it. A powerful connection gripped me and refused to let go.

I couldn't look away. Didn't want to. Everything else faded away, utterly insignificant.

A pulse vibrated over the maze of veins that branched through the iridescent, mirrorlike stone. Crimson flowed straight into the outer rim of the circles. The inner lines shifted and clicked together, forcing a connected crisscross, sending the symbols into a spinning rotation. Vibrant flames sparked within each loop. *Mesmerizing.*

Just as I'd seen in my vision, dream, or whatever it had been, the wall vanished in the smoke. An image appeared in the rock face, shaking me to my core. A man sat upon a throne made of sapphire. He appeared as human as anyone else. Or would have, if a crown of light hadn't radiated from his head, obscuring his face, and flames of the purest blue hadn't bathed his lower half. A flawless metal breastplate shining and golden covered his torso.

Noises garbled in my throat. My knees knocked, threatening to buckle. I knew his identity without being told.

"Arden, Arden," he breathed out. "Troubled by so many things."

His voice nearly buckled my knees. The sound carried the weight of many rushing waters, sending ripples over my entire being. "You are Soal."

"I am. You desired an audience."

Heaviness settled over me, but it wasn't confining. More like a velvet-soft winter coat, warm and comforting. "You aren't what I expected."

He chuckled a little. "What did you expect, hmm?"

Good question. "To be honest, I'm not sure." I released the first query in the ammo clip of my mind. "Did you cause these breaks? The maddened are killing in your name."

"What do I have to gain from such deaths?" he asked.

"Depriving CURED of its citizens." To start.

"They do that job well enough on their own."

I waited, but Soal provided no more. No real defense or evidence. Frustrated, I took a step closer. "My friend Shiloh told me you're the solution to every problem. From my vantage point, you don't seem to be doing much."

"That's because your vantage point is too low. Read my Rock. Unless you prefer to continue dealing with Astan."

I wouldn't read the Rock, risking Madness, possibly playing right into his hands, until someone convinced me of its safety. "I've had no dealings with Astan."

"You have. Often."

I sputtered. No way I'd met a god with huge ram horns and wings and not realized it. Just no way. Since we were getting nowhere, I shifted gears. "I'm told you hope to recruit me."

"I seek to recruit everyone. Only some are ready to hear."

"Well, you made a mistake, thinking I'm ready."

"Then let's get you there." His image began to fade.

"No!" I surged forward the rest of the way. I had some many more questions, but the image of a book took his place. My book. Tremors rocked me in my boots.

The familiar tome opened of its own accord, flipping through pages to reach a specific point. Text rose from the page, drawing together to form an image. Amelia! My beautiful sister twirled across the pages, straight from the vaults of my memory, and I pressed a hand to my fluttering pulse. Her laughter filled the air, and I couldn't help but laugh, too, even as tears spilled down my cheeks. I remembered this day. We'd celebrated her acceptance into a gifted program for the best and brightest.

"If I get to pick my field of study, I'm choosing pritis," she said. "They release a frequency I swear I feel in my bones. It's like music. Soft and lyrical."

Hmm. I'd forgotten she'd said that.

All too soon, the pages flipped, erasing her. "Go back," I croaked. "Please."

It didn't. It stopped on a new chapter, and once again text rose, this time revealing my mother. "Oh," I breathed out. I remembered this too. Health and vitality radiated from Mom's pores. She beamed at an eleven-year-old Arden, who had just propagated her first weed.

"You are going to grow a paradise, baby," Mom proclaimed with a hug.

In the present, I felt her arms around me. More tears dripped down my cheeks.

"What's a paradise?" young Arden asked.

"A garden of delights filled with everything we could ever need or want."

This was the day I'd decided my path. Agriculture or nothing.

Once again, the pages flipped and stopped, and suddenly Shiloh was making funny faces at me, turning a bad day into a cherished memory. I giggled and cried in unison, so happy to see him but also torn to shreds inside. A beautiful life cut short. Why show me these things? *Why!*

The book flipped to another page, revealing text without an image. The code is 80630941507. As soon as my gaze grazed the final number, the book closed, the library faded, the stone returned, and the symbols ceased spinning.

"Give me more!" Except for the code thing, each of those moments had marked me. They were slices of peace and joy within a chaotic world. Was that what the Tome Society—Soal?—offered me? "Just one mo—"

Cyrus appeared in my line of vision, blocking the Rock. Nooo! I attempted to slide past him, but he moved with me. With a viselike grip on my arms, he forced my attention onto his face. His mouth was moving, but no sound emerged. Wait. I frowned. Blood dotted him, sweat soaked his hair, and raw concern dominated his harsh expression.

Snap. The world returned to normal, noise bombarding my ears. Alarms, sirens, footsteps, shouts, bangs. Dead bodies scattered the ground.

"—need to run before doors are locked. Arden? Do you hear me?"

I blinked rapidly, confused and horrified. "Y-yes," I responded. "Run."

Cyrus slung an arm around my waist and tugged me along the street, away from Soal.

What. Just. Happened?

CHAPTER TWENTY-SIX

Though the storm blusters and the fire rages, I will
bring you through unscathed.

—The Book of Soal 1.23.43.2

We reached the Lux six minutes before lock-in, but it wasn't relief I felt.
I longed to return to the Rock. Felt as though I'd left pieces of myself
behind and I would not be complete until I retrieved them. Or offered
to give more of me.

Yes, yes, I should go back. So I'd be trapped in the darkness with
feeders. So what.

According to CURED, this was maddened behavior, but I wasn't
sick. I wasn't! I just needed more information.

Cyrus might have sensed my intentions. He maintained a firm grip
on my hand and a swift pace.

A pair of armed barons guarded the entrance to the towering
building. They let us inside. We didn't slow. A concierge rushed through
the lobby to open elevator doors for us. No other patrons congregated
in the area, giving me a full view of the opulence. Crystal walls, flawless
furnishings, and a gold-veined floor proved this structure came from
Theirland.

Cyrus and I entered the lift, leaving everyone behind. Tension
hummed between us as the doors closed us in.

"Are you—" I began.

"We'll talk about it when we're alone," he interjected, cutting me off sharply.

I pressed my lips together, noticed the blood soaking the side of his shirt, and whimpered. "Cyrus, you're—"

"When we're alone," he repeated.

Maybe we were being recorded. Otherwise, he'd be asking a ton of questions. I had a few for him, too, considering I'd received a code I had no idea how to use, viewed more of my book, and conversed with Soal. The god intrigued me.

I'd told myself I wouldn't focus on the Rock, but I'd done just that. Now, I was emboldened. And curious. What if the structure *didn't* cause the Madness?

"Is your security detail okay?" Surely we could discuss that. Ugh. He was still bleeding all over the tiled floor. I whipped off my shirt and pressed the material into his wound. Cool air kissed my exposed skin.

"They are fine. Happy arrived before you did, and I went looking for you."

"Thank you." Had he not been there, well, I shuddered to think of what might have happened. "If it's okay, I'd like to ask your contact about my mother."

"Already planned on it." He gritted the words.

"I hope you sent someone to watch Mykal too."

"I tried, but I'm not sure where she is."

Dang. Maybe she was holed up somewhere safe. "Hopefully people are filling the Havens."

"They are. But those who don't make it into a room won't be left unguarded. Archduke Heta is leading multiple units to Bala City. They'll patrol the night and set up temporary pritis stands."

Ding. The doors opened to a suite with a comfy couch, two cozy chairs, and a solid-wood coffee table with legs balanced on the backs of golden turtles. My pot rested on the edge. On the walls, holographic images moved within gilt frames, showcasing a beautiful young woman who resembled Cyrus in many ways. Maybe a sister or his mother.

With a wince, Cyrus led me forward. Three cats sprang from different parts of the living room, prowling toward us. A gray tabby, a black beauty with sprinklings of white, and an orange cutie. I twittered at their preciousness. Must pet and cuddle and kiss!

The felines noticed me and froze before scattering in every direction.

"I'll win you over," I called. We passed a pair of glass double doors that led to a balcony overlooking half the city. Even from here, several pieces of the Rock were visible. My longing crested, reaching new heights.

"I know Dr. Korey has taught you how to repair organ damage on a battlefield," Cyrus said, quickening his pace.

Oh, no, no, no. My heart galloped. "She shared only the basics." He couldn't expect me to patch him up. "There's no way I—"

"The basics are enough. You can patch me up." He herded me into the kitchen.

A groan escaped. "There must be a medical professional who lives in the building." One had lived in mine, though the title "professional" was being generous.

"There are several. I'm sure they're barricading like the rest of us. Besides, we don't want anyone else locked within our walls."

"You're right, but—"

"Stay here." Off he went, leaving droplets of blood in his wake.

I immediately set to work, opening the light-blue drawers and the cabinets trimmed in gold, rummaging for cloths to soak up blood. The gleaming ivory countertops appeared spotless, so hopefully we wouldn't have to worry about infection. Small potted plants in varying stages of growth were strategically placed. Nothing I could use as medicine, though.

Cyrus returned with a field MD kit, set it on the counter, and gripped the neckline of his shirt to tug the material over his broad shoulders. My jaw nearly unhinged.

"Look at you." All that cut strength and that masterpiece of a tattoo. A tree spanned from the base of his spine up his back and over his shoulders, to his collarbone and different parts of his chest, the branches blooming with different things. Flowers and fruits, yes, but also keys, weapons, and coins. Without thought, I reached out and traced my fingertips over a rose.

"As much as I'm enjoying your admiration," he told me with a wry tone as he bent over the counter, "I'm bleeding out."

Oh goodness gracious, he was! A gaping wound in his side seeped fresh crimson. I scrambled to the kit, hands trembling as I collected the items I required. "I've never done this in real life," I warned. Never done anything for anyone while shirtless. "I'll probably make mistakes."

"I promise to grade you on a curve. And if I survive, you automatically pass."

"That's not funny." I licked my lips and claimed the first tool. "I'm guessing you'd prefer to forgo the painkiller so you can remain clearheaded in case I break."

"*Murder* the pain," he commanded, and I almost laughed. Almost.

"What happened?" With quaking fingers, I administered the first injection, numbing the wound. From there, I cleaned the raw flesh with the proper chemicals and tried not to think or feel.

"A pack of feeders ambushed me."

This occurred while Soal distracted me, no doubt. I just didn't know if he'd done it on purpose or inadvertently. Either way, guilt flared, and I bit my cheek. "We should talk about what went down out there."

Cyrus stiffened and shook his head. "We should, but not until tomorrow, after the drugs wear off."

Were his words already slurring? "What if I break?" A very real possibility, considering my new obsession.

"I'm not worried, Arden."

Not good enough. "You can't be sure. Better safe than sorry."

"Why are you so pretty?" he asked.

Oh, yeah, his words were definitely slurred. I tried not to smile as I secured the C2U—critical care unit—to speed up healing, then wrapped a bandage around him. And I did a danged good job, if I did say so myself. By morning, he should be much improved. Not fully healed, but on the path.

"Tell me what you like most about my prettiness."

"Your kindness."

No stopping my smile this time. "Let's get you to bed. You can make that phone call before you pass out." I moved to his side to act as his crutch.

"Help me to the couch and stay with me awhile," he said, letting his weight rest against me.

"I'll join you after I clean up our mess."

He actually pouted, and it was adorable. "We'll tidy up later." Pause. "You have the most amazing smile," he added with a drunken grin.

"Thank you." I kissed his brand. "Come on, lover boy." Though I strained under the burden of his weight, I got him to our destination without toppling.

He plopped onto a cushion and pulled me down with him, ensuring I stayed put. As he stretched out and rolled to his side, he pinned me between a soft throw pillow and his hard body. Skin to skin. Warmth to warmth. Strength to softness. A sense of connection instantly bloomed, deeper than any I'd previously experienced.

"Finally got you where I want you," he murmured, smoothing the hair from my face.

"I could get away if I wanted," I murmured back, while melting into him. No better way to make sure he didn't start bleeding again than to stay right where I was.

As he made the call to inquire about my mother, he kept me tucked close. When he hung up, he filled me in. "She got scared and ran from him, but he tracked her chip and brought her back to her apartment building. She's now safe and sound."

Relief crested, only to crash and burn. Tracked. By her chip. Just like the one embedded in my palm. Just like those embedded in everyone else's palms.

How easy citizens of the provinces were to find. CURED could log every instance we neared the Rock or lingered a little too long. They could lock us out of any and every building or apartment, as they'd done to Mr. Garfield, the day before I'd left for the academy.

Unease prickled my skin. This was a complication I needed to consider. "Fair warning. I will be taking advantage of your temporary openness to pry into your secrets." I flattened my palm over his pectoral to gauge the strength of his heartbeat. Fast but steady. Good.

"I expected that, kitten, and I'm prepared. Even drugged, I'll resist temptation. Me warrior. No crack." He pounded a fist against the pec not covered by my hand, reminding me of a big, strong gorilla. Then he winced, wringing a snicker from me.

"I'm *kitten* now?"

"Mmm hmm. Part of my bouquet. Maybe I should call you *buttercup*." He nuzzled my cheek. "I was teasing before, you know. I'll tell you anything as long as you're holding me just like this."

Adorable man. "I was teasing before too. I won't take advantage of you." Even for answers.

"I'll tell you a secret." His expression turned wistful. "A year ago, a part of my book played on the surface of the Rock. My own personal movie. It showed me an event to come. You were in it, though we hadn't even met."

What! "You can't stop there. Tell me more."

Cyrus yawned and settled his face into the hollow of my neck. "You always smell so good."

"Thank you," I repeated, all but bursting from my skin. "Pretty please with extra please, elaborate."

"Well, there are notes of roses, lemons—"

"Not my scent," I interjected with an involuntary chuckle. "Describe the movie you watched on the Rock."

"Your laughter makes me happy."

Warmth spread over the surface of my skin. "Cyrus. Your book. Movie. Me."

A sigh slipped from him. "You looked at me with such love and trust, and I wanted it to be real so badly. When finally I met you, I wasn't sure what to think or do."

Every part of me liquefied. "I think Soal is trying to bring us together. Victors may have mentioned—and this isn't an admission—that we might, maybe, eventually . . . get married."

"Let's serve apples and figs at the reception."

I snorted. So not the reaction I'd expected. All right, interrogation over. I traced my fingertips over his brand. "Get some rest. You lost a lot of blood."

"That's okay." He nuzzled into my hand. "There's extra in the fridge."

What! "You keep bags of blood in your refrigerator?"

"You don't?" Mirth glittered in his sleepy eyes. "The blood is my own, used for infusions after combat. We'll begin harvesting yours."

"I know a plot to clone me when I hear it," I teased, rearranging our positions to more comfortably rest my head on his shoulder. "Does this hurt?"

"No. It's good. Everything I imagined and more."

Mmm. His radiating heat wrapped us in a protective bubble, where a sense of connection simmered, sweetened with *his* scent. The trials of the past two years faded into mist, easing strain's vise grip on my muscles and bones.

"Don't go spying tonight," he muttered. "The building holds three active counts and countesses, plus the former count of medical, and my father. Cameras are everywhere."

Interesting. I'd like to meet the former head of medical. And the other aristocracy. They oversaw every aspect of our lives. "We should host a party soon. Invite the neighbors." I had questions. Somebody knew something about this latest outbreak. What caused it. Who gained.

"Party," Cyrus echoed, toying with the ends of my hair.

I wasn't sure I'd ever enjoyed anything more. Other than his kiss. "Don't stop." Oh! Two felines peeked out from beneath a chair, only to hide after our gazes collided. I grinned. New side mission: win them over so I could nuzzle those precious faces.

"You did amazing out there," he said, sounding more awake.

"Your wound is calling you a liar."

"I understood what was happening with the Rock. I'm talking about before. You didn't crack."

Well. "I did do amazing, didn't I?" Fear had never overwhelmed me. I hadn't let it. "You did amazing too. You kept us both safe."

"As a reward, I'd like to hear about your book. What you saw. Don't want to wait, after all."

As if I could keep secrets while he continued playing with my hair. "I saw memories plucked from my history. The happiest day of my sister's life, when I was in awe of her determination to achieve her goals. I was reminded of her desire to study pritis and her belief that they sing to her. Then I relived the time my mother encouraged my agricultural dream followed by the moment I met Shiloh." I saved the code for tomorrow, when he had a clearer head. Maybe it was a key to help me decipher the marks on the Rock.

"You miss him," my companion said with a soft undertone I didn't quite understand.

"Yes. Shiloh made me smile and helped me feel safe."

Cyrus brushed locks from my temple and focused his ministrations on my nape. "What do I do to you?"

Make me crave. "That's a confession for another day."

"Fair enough." He closed his eyes and rested the back of his head against the highest part of the couch. The petting gradually ceased. A long while passed, and I suspected he'd fallen asleep. Understandable. The more time that ticked by, the heavier my eyelids became.

Even with the perils of our situation; the sudden, unexplained breakings; and my encounter with the Rock, I couldn't imagine Cyrus attacking me. Especially shocking, considering my vulnerable state. Maybe I was riding too high on the waves of confidence. Perhaps I was drunk on the joy and peace Soal had showered upon me. Or maybe a part of me trusted Cyrus more than I'd realized. Whatever the reason, I stayed put.

He rewarded me, murmuring, "I'm going to tell you another secret."

Not asleep, after all. My heart thumped. "Yes. Please do."

He grazed my cheek with his thumb. "When I was a little boy, I witnessed a feeder beat my mother to death."

Horror delivered a one-two punch, waking me hard and fast. "Cyrus, that's awful."

"It was. He beat me first and left us both to die. I crawled to her as soon as he fled and stretched out beside her as she breathed her last. Afterward, I couldn't bring myself to let go. I kept replaying words she'd said earlier that day. *Never ignore a possibility.*"

Tears stung my eyes. I had a store of them at the ready today. I ached for the child he'd been and the childhood he'd lost. "She sounds very wise."

"She was." A sad smile lifted the corners of his mouth as he grazed the pad of his thumb beneath each of my eyes, collecting the moisture. "Do you know what I think about every time I look at you, Lady Arden Dawn Pink Bubble Gum Kitten Buttercup Roosa?"

"Please, tell me," I said, frantic to learn.

"Possibilities," he replied, drifting to sleep at last, his breaths evening out.

Dazed, I lay still, quiet, and utterly tormented. He saw possibilities in me. I might see a future with him. I liked him. A lot. He encouraged me, helped me, built me up, and always told the truth. Kissing him again was a must. And for the first time in my life, I wasn't afraid of the future. Despite my uncertainty, the investigation, and my latest dealings with Soal, I carried hope.

"Mine," Cyrus muttered, tightening his hold on me.

My eyes drifted shut. I snuggled closer, reveling in the headiness and joy of being his. It wasn't long before a sweet cloud settled over my entire being and carried me away.

⁓

"Wake up, sleeping beauty."

The amused voice tugged me from a deep slumber. I blinked open my eyes, realization dawning. I stretched out upon a sun-drenched couch. Cyrus leaned over me, one hand braced on an armrest. He'd showered and dressed in a crisp white T-shirt and well-worn jeans. Combat boots adorned his feet. He was casual and beautiful, and I thrilled at the sight of him.

"How do you feel?" I asked, stretching sore muscles.

"Like I've been chewed up and spit out." A wide smile bloomed. "Someone slept draped across me."

"Oops," I muttered.

"I liked it."

I ignored the instant fluttering in my stomach. And the fact that I still had no shirt, only my bra. Did he recall what he'd said last night?

Wait. "I slept out in the open," I stated, astonished. "With you."

"You did. Guess that means you trust me."

Did I detect a note of smug satisfaction in his words?

"Now it's time to rise and shine." Merciless, he ripped off my blanket and tugged me to my feet.

"Okay, okay. Hint taken. I'll tend to your wound."

"No need. I cleaned and rebandaged it after I showered." He wrapped his arms around me.

"So what's the hurry?" I grumbled, toying with the ends of his hair.

"We'll get to that. First, you'll be glad to know there are a surprisingly low number of casualties last night, with no new outbreaks this morning. CURED has ordered a two-day lock-in."

Two days. Stuck inside with Cyrus and numerous higher-ups of CURED. An opportunity rife with possibilities. "Has CURED stated an official cause for the breaks?"

A muscle jumped beneath his eye. "Word is, Ember's teams freed the infected from treatment clinics and loosed them upon the public. That's why CURED ordered the lock-in. They're still hunting five of the patients."

Wow. Ember, leading Soalians now. Loosing the infected on innocent people didn't strike me as her style. So I had to wonder if CURED had issued another lie for the good of the public.

The thought lit me up with anger. Enough was enough. No more secrets. No more mysteries. No more deceptions. We deserved the truth, and I was going to get it, one way or another.

"Whatever you're thinking, keep doing it," Cyrus commanded. "I like the fire. You're going to need it. We're attending the party you requested. I convinced my father to host it tonight."

Excitement stirred. Interrogations, here I come! "Thank you, thank you, thank you." Except. "Why isn't your dad at the base, overseeing restoration efforts?"

"For the same reason I'm here. In times of crisis, the children and grandchildren of Emperor Dolion are forced to work remotely. It's for the best. Both men need to retire. My father doesn't show it to outsiders, but his health is declining. His obsession with Astan doesn't help."

I caressed his brand. "You care for him."

"We've locked horns my entire life. He's stubborn, suspicious, and exacting and often expects too much while giving too little, but yes, I do care for him." He nuzzled into my touch. "I also honor his position. Without him, I wouldn't be here. And without his leadership, thousands—perhaps millions—would be dead." Smoothing his hands across my lower back, he asked, "What about you? Tell me about the man who helped bring the indomitable Arden Roosa into this world."

"Aren't we in a rush?"

"Now that you're in my arms? No."

I smiled, though it didn't last long. "My father abandoned me and my mom after my sister died. I hated him until my mom told me a bedtime story called 'The Tale of the Cursed Dagger.' Ever heard of it?"

"No. But I'm about to. Tell me. Please."

His usual air of intensity sharpened to a razor point, as if he were 100 percent invested in what I had to say. No wonder I was falling for him. He couldn't be any sexier.

I rested my head on his chest, letting his heart beat against my cheek. "Long ago, a fierce warrior found a dagger able to cause irreparable wounds. He told himself he would only use the weapon for good. Bad guys beware." I wrinkled my nose and lifted my head. "Are you sure you're interested in this?"

"I want every detail." Cyrus nipped my bottom lip before easing my cheek back to his pec. "I will have them."

Yes, apparently, he *could* be sexier. "One day, the warrior came upon a masked thief in the process of fleeing the scene of a crime. They fought, and the warrior nicked the bandit before he got away. But our fearsome warrior wasn't concerned. That small cut promised to do his job for him, since the wound could never heal, only worsen. The would-be thief was set to suffer for the rest of his too-short days. The perfect punishment for his crime."

"This is a bedtime story for a little girl?"

My chuckle possessed a delighted tinge. "Don't worry, it gets better. The warrior went home to discover the wounded thief was none other than his treasured son. In that moment, the warrior realized he himself now suffered a far worse fate than his child, for he was doomed to live long with the consequences of what he'd done."

"Aaah. She was telling you that your father hurt himself far more than he hurt you."

"Exactly." My shoulders rolled in as I sighed. "I admit, there were times I took comfort from the thought of his torment. Other times, I pitied him. Now, I rarely even think of him."

Using the gentlest of tones, Cyrus told me, "His inability to see your worth speaks of his faults, not yours."

I was beginning to believe it. Lifting my head, I smiled at him. "Your father cares for you too. He even questioned me about my intentions toward you."

Cyrus's eyes brightened. "Did he now? And how did you respond?"

Grinning, I eased from his embrace. "I'll have to tell you later. We have a party to prepare for. I assume all the counts and countesses in the building are attending."

"All," he confirmed. "No one turns down my father."

Perfect. I rubbed my hands together. "Fair warning. You're going to see Arden Unleashed tonight. I no longer care who I offend or what rules I break. I won't stop pushing for answers."

"I thought you'd say that." He backed up, putting distance between us. "Get ready and join me in the office. I'm going to teach you how to break into locked drawers without leaving a trace."

CHAPTER TWENTY-SEVEN

Don't you know you are a gateway into the eternal?

—*The Book of Soal* 1.19.24.7

I rode inside an elevator with Cyrus, headed for his father's penthouse apartment. My steps were confident, and not just because I wore the prettiest, frilliest, pinkest garment I'd ever seen, with a scooped bodice and a tiered hem that reached midthigh. A seamstress who lived in the building had measured me, made alterations, and added embellishments with each new cycle of on, off. Soft slippers adorned my feet, anchored in place by ribbons that crisscrossed up my calves. I also wore a pair of thin pink gloves.

A stylist tamed my hair into a sleek bun, to make me "the epitome of sexy sophistication." Flawless, barely there makeup gave me a delightful, dewy freshness. I even wore special pieces of jewelry that doubled as weapons. Things Cyrus just happened to have on hand for reasons he'd refused to explain. The only trinket that didn't double as an armament was a silver bracelet he insisted I wear for reasons he refused to explain.

"By the way. You can speak freely." He traced a fingertip along the chain around my neck. "You're wearing a device that prevents voice recordings."

Nice! "Well, I meant what I said earlier. I am Arden Unleashed." I'd floundered around for answers long enough. Tonight, I would bypass boundaries. Make waves. Speak up. Put myself in danger, if necessary. "I may not get another opportunity like this, and I intend to make the most of it," I vowed. Not just for my loved ones but for the world. This wasn't a game between gods but life and death, and it was time I treated it that way. Time to go all in, whatever the consequences.

"I'm ready for anything," he replied, confident. "Do what you must."

His unwavering support meant everything.

I chewed on my lower lip and glanced at him. Mistake! The sight of him set my heart into a pounding race. "For starters, I'm going to stop looking at you. The sight of you fries circuits in my brain." He wore black slacks and a white dress shirt with the sleeves partially rolled, revealing the world's hottest forearms. Multiple rings adorned his fingers.

"Now you go too far," Cyrus replied with pretend outrage.

The elevator stopped, and I drew in a deep breath. We were about to enter the lion's den and converse with some of the world's most influential people. Those running CURED. Maybe Astan himself would make an appearance. Did a god walk among us, or did he sleep? Had I actually met him?

Before the doors slid open, Cyrus jammed his finger into a button and gave me a slow once-over. His eyes heated. Burned. I felt the warmth in every cell of my body, any defenses against his appeal torched in the flames. "Have I told you how beautiful you are?"

"Only twice, so not nearly enough."

He snickered, and I chuckled. Somewhere along the way, this man had become synonymous with security, laughter, and desire. I was falling in love with him. Yearned for a future with him. Beginning tonight.

I nibbled on my bottom lip. Perhaps we should ditch the party and—

"See!" I burst out. "I'm thinking about cuddling you instead of unearthing deadly secrets."

He pressed the sweetest kiss onto my lips. "Do what you must tonight," he repeated, "but know I'll do the same."

In the beginning of our relationship, I would've taken those words as a threat. Today, I understood him better. "You're going to treat me like a girlfriend." A statement, not a question. His way of providing an added layer of protection. "You want everyone to think we're dating."

He arched a brow. "Aren't we?"

"Yes, dang it. You won me over. I'm not sure how it will change things on base, but I'm with you, okay," I grumbled. "Happy now?"

"Very. We can hammer out the semantics after the party." He released the button, and the elevator doors slid open.

Cyrus wrapped his arm around my waist and led me forward. We entered a foyer with a handful of other partygoers and armed viscounts checking names in front of an open door. People glanced our way and performed double takes.

He maintained a blank expression. "Good evening," he said as we bypassed the line.

The main soldier bobbed his head as we approached and granted us immediate access into the apartment. I took in the large space, momentarily awestruck. A breathtakingly high dome broke the room into two levels, one overlooking the other. Floor-to-ceiling-windows revealed an empty, sun-drenched city. Waitstaff carried silver trays, offering an array of foods and drinks.

Groups of varying sizes congregated here, there, everywhere. Most faces were unfamiliar to me, but some I recognized. King Tagin Dolion, of course, and a smattering of others I'd seen on newsfeeds. The head of education and the woman who managed our water supply. Where was Count Van Folley, the former head of all things medical?

My heart skipped a beat when I spotted Countess Jade Dills, head of agriculture. At forty-seven, she was the youngest aristocrat in office and someone I'd admired for years.

"Oh, that you gazed at me the way you're gazing at Countess Dills," Cyrus muttered with wry amusement.

"Well, I mean, she increased CURED's produce yield by six percent her first year in office, which is double any of her predecessors." I forced myself to look away and studied the remaining guests. Hmm. Everyone but me wore black and white.

I curbed the urge to squirm. "This is the last time I let you pick my outfit," I huffed, smoothing the pink fabric. "I don't exactly blend in."

"Trust me on this. I know what I'm doing." He led me forward. "Who would you like to speak with first?"

"Count Folley, please." Might as well kick off my mission with a bang. "Though I don't see him."

"I do." He led me through the crowd, ignoring everyone who attempted to solicit his attention with a wave. "Try to introduce your questions as smoothly as possible."

"Smooth. Got it." Laughter rang out nearby. The fact that no one seemed bothered by what happened last night, well, bothered me.

Finally I spotted my first target, and I had no idea how I'd missed him. Even at seventysomething years old, he presented a powerful picture in a slick black tux. He held court in front of a smiling multitude, relaying what must be an amusing story.

"Hello, Van," Cyrus greeted when he paused for breath.

"Cyrus." He shook the HP's hand. "I hate that it took such awful circumstances to bring us together, but I must admit I'm happy to see you."

"Awful circumstances indeed." He leaned into me. "I'd like you to meet Arden Roosa, my girlfriend."

Count Folley's attention shifted to me, his eyes widening. "Girlfriend, hmm? You must be the lady-in-training everyone is whispering about."

Whether it was a barb or a simple observation of fact, I gave no reaction. "I, too, hate these awful circumstances. Cyrus mentioned Soalians caused this outbreak, which made me wonder what caused mass breakouts in the past."

He blinked at me, his good humor fading slightly. "The Rock . . . altered frequencies . . . a complicated subject to explain." He pressed his lips together, going quiet.

Frequencies. Something my sister had highlighted as well. "How do these frequencies cause an individual to break, then?" So much for smooth. "Surely that's a little easier to explain."

Those around us either stiffened or gasped, as if I'd entered taboo territory. I hadn't. Not yet.

"That is something you should have learned in school," the count said. "We should fire your teachers."

"Oh, they taught me. But you're the expert of experts. I'd like to hear it from you."

When Count Folley glanced at Cyrus, he nodded, encouraging the other man to go on. Stiff, the medical czar said, "Well, the Rock releases different sound waves. Certain frequencies activate only when an individual focuses on the stone. If that person has prolonged contact, EOS is birthed inside their mind."

An echo of nearly every other explanation I'd heard. "Interesting. What does *EOS* stand for?"

The count laughed without humor. "This isn't a topic fit for a party."

Obstructed again. I pivoted the conversation. "The cure is a welcome topic for any occasion. Tell us about recent advances in its development."

"We're closer than ever." He signaled for a drink. "I hear you're doing well at the academy, Cyrus. Training a new batch to excel."

"Yes," my companion—boyfriend—responded, not helping with the subject change.

I kept going. "I've always wondered how we're able to study the Rock and get any answers at all without scientists breaking left and right."

"We take precautions." Count Folley flashed a brittle smile. "I'd be careful if I were you, Lady Roosa. Curiosity is not your friend. Excuse me."

As he walked away, the others made excuses, leaving as if I'd begun leaking toxic waste.

"Learn anything?" Cyrus asked, casually sipping his champagne.

"Yes. Innocent questions are considered dangerous, and discussions are shut down out of fear, not logic." I wasn't sure what Count Folley feared, however. The disease he'd spent decades studying or CURED. "For the next cross-examination, I'll give that *smooth* thing you mentioned a try."

"Come on," he said, his eyes glittering as he led me to another group. "Hello, Jade. I'd like you to meet Arden Roosa, my girlfriend."

I floundered for words. Jade Dills!

"Cy. How wonderful to see you again." Countess Dills hugged him and acknowledged me by looking me up and down. "You're the trainee helping our beloved high prince." She gave an airy chuckle. "Sorry. 'The Lady.'" She even used air quotes. "And now you're dating. What a surprise no one saw coming."

It took a moment for my brain to function properly. The head of agriculture was speaking to me. Looking at me. Most likely insulting me, considering those air quotes. She was also frowning as she waited for me to respond. Eek! "Yes," I rushed out, "that's me. The trainee. Though gardening is my passion."

"A worthy pastime," she said, returning her attention to Cyrus. "What's this special assignment I keep hearing about, hmm? Rumors suggest it has something to do with your latest capture. Congratulations, by the way. The world is a much safer place with John Victors off the streets."

He flashed a humorless smile. "I think yesterday's death toll suggests otherwise."

"Such a tragedy." Countess Dills pressed a hand over her heart as her companions twittered their agreement. "I'll never understand Soalians and their reverence for the source of the Madness."

Here goes. "Speaking of the Rock, I've always wondered how it grows flowers without soil." Not even Countess Dills was safe from my probing.

Like Count Folley, she blinked at me. "That isn't something we've figured out yet." A slight inflection of strain infiltrated her voice. "As you probably know, testing is limited for the safety of all mankind."

"I'm sure you've considered propagating the buds in a contained area."

"Yes, but it's an impossible endeavor, considering the buds die as soon as they're plucked," she said, stumbling over her words. Not used to being grilled about her job after hours? "If you'll excuse me, I see Cloward Bosworth." Off she went, leaving me stewing in a fresh cauldron of frustration.

"Perfect timing," Cyrus muttered. "I've been summoned." He navigated the throng, bringing us to his father, who stood beside a stunning thirtysomething woman with a killer smile. "Arden, you know my father, Tagin. This is Madison, his wife."

The woman who'd supposedly read my paper. "Hello. So wonderful to meet you," I said.

"Wonderful to meet you, as well," she replied with a welcoming grin.

"I'm told we have something in common," I began, gearing up to grill her about soil and seeds.

"Oh?" Her brows furrowed together, a line forming between them.

"Madison wishes to know how you rate Cyrus as an instructor," the king—Tagin—interjected with ease.

Talk about smooth. "He's harsh but fair. Kind of dreamy." The words slipped out before I could stop them, and I winced. "But. I mean. He is." We were officially dating now, and I didn't really care what anyone thought about the matter.

Madison laughed, while Tagin maintained a neutral expression.

"It pleased me to hear Cyrus assigned a guard to your mother," Tagin stated with his usual politeness. "I've been in touch, and he assures me she's doing well."

I went cold inside, certain I'd detected a threat hidden within his words. That if I persisted with my investigation, CURED would use my mother to punish me. But. No way he'd suggested such a thing.

But what if he had?

No, no. Cyrus hadn't reacted in the slightest, and he would've reacted. Unless his love for his father clouded his judgment and he'd missed the warning.

I gulped.

The questions I'd planned to ask Madison died a swift death. In the name of damage control, I rested my palm against Cyrus's heart and offered a sickly-sweet smile. "Hopefully the guard is as diligent with my mother as I am with your son." A threat of my own. Not that I would ever harm Cyrus, but a point had to be made. *Touch what's mine, and I'll take what's yours.*

Cyrus tightened his hold on my waist. "Heads will roll if any harm comes to your mother."

Oooh. Maybe he had detected the threat. Because he'd just issued one of his own.

"Your concern is unnecessary," Tagin said, giving nothing away. "Stop by in the morning, Arden. I have a proposition for you. Something that will thrill you." He shifted his gaze to his son. "You are invited, too, of course."

Clear commands, not requests. Cyrus nodded.

I flashed an unconvincing smile and muttered, "How exciting." What kind of proposition?

All girlfriend-like, I clasped Cyrus's hand and signed the word *go*. Surely he understood.

He lifted our joined hands to his cheek and nuzzled. "I could use some fresh air."

"Me too." Excellent. He'd understood his assignment. That alone did wonders for my disposition.

The king blinked at us. "You let her touch your brand."

"Did I?" Cyrus responded and led me away. "I'll take you to my father's office for fresh air. There's a balcony."

Ideas percolated, generating new excitement. "I'm suddenly very glad you shared the dirty tricks of the B and E trade."

"You're about to be gladder. While you were sleeping, I met with him in there, and he stored a chip I'd like to read."

Well, well. Getting my hands on that chip shot to the top of my to-do list.

"Cyrus."

The soft entreaty slowed our pace, allowing a beautiful woman to step in front of us.

"Nova," he replied with zero inflection.

Ah. Nova Soti. The ex. She wore a slinky white dress that molded to her hourglass figure.

"I'm glad you're here." She kissed his unscarred cheek, near the corner of his mouth. "I've missed you."

"Arden, this is Countess Soti's daughter," he said, drawing me closer. "Nova, this is my girlfriend, Arden."

Just as he'd understood my request for help, I understood his. Petting his chest, I rested my head on his shoulder. "Nice to meet you. I wish we had time to chat, but my Cyrus is taking me for some air. Shall we, sugar bear?"

"Yes, kitten, we shall."

Her mouth formed a small O as we maneuvered around her.

"I did good," I said, giving myself an evaluation.

His answering half grin suggested I'd earned extra credit. He steered me into a hallway guarded by two armed soldiers. They allowed us passage, and we sailed by without incident.

We stopped at a locked entrance that required a palm scan to enter. He pushed open the door, revealing a spacious office with a shockingly plain desk. Supplies were organized in rows of three on the surface. The only decoration was a portrait of Tagin Dolion himself, decked out in his uniform. No files were out and about, ready for a quick glance. Bet the computer dock activated only with his chip.

The scent of cigar smoke and whiskey thickened when we reached the sitting area in back, where a worn sofa and coffee table waited. A highly frequented area, no doubt.

Towering double doors led to a balcony, as promised. Interesting. The king had a perfect view of the Rock.

"The office is available to me and my guest only." Cyrus opened the balcony doors, allowing cool fresh air to wisp inside. "There are no voice recorders here, but there are multiple cameras hidden throughout, and they are being monitored by several viscounts."

Well, of course there were hidden cameras. "We'll find a way." Because we must.

"Not *we. You.* Now is probably a good time to tell you that your dress renders you invisible to cameras."

I squealed a little and threw my arms around his shoulders to hug him. Although. "Won't my invisibility rouse suspicions?"

"Not necessarily. The people my father deals with wear the same material all the time."

So, the higher-ups. Those who might have something to hide. "You always think of everything."

"I'm going to sit on the couch and pretend you're sitting with me." He kissed my brow, awakening a deeper ache in me, then strode to the couch, as if he still led me about, and sat. He fiddled with the band around his wrist, then pretended to wind his arm around my shoulders. "You have five minutes. Look anywhere. I won't stop you."

"But you watched him store the chip."

"Yes, and telling you where it is violates a vow I made."

"But covering for me while I search doesn't?" Wait. Cyrus had taught me to break into the guy's drawers. Therefore, it stood to reason it occupied a drawer. Duh! Except. "The camera feed will show drawers opening on their own. Someone will understand what's happening."

The look he gave me. *Lady, please.* "Do I always think of everything or not?"

In other words, keep trusting him. I sighed, and leaped into action, using different pieces of my special jewelry to open locks without leaving a smidge of evidence.

"Three minutes," Cyrus piped up.

I riffled through the contents of a drawer at a swifter clip. A digital reader without a chip. A loaded handgun. A box of ammo. A tin of candies only the upper class could afford. Guess the king had a sweet tooth.

"You could help, you know," I grumbled.

"Very well. Look harder. Faster. You can do it, Arden. I believe in you," he deadpanned.

I rolled my eyes. "You are so irritating sometimes."

"Only sometimes is a vast improvement from always. Is someone falling for me, perhaps?"

Yes! "There's obviously a safe in here, and you must know where it is," I hedged. "I get that you aren't comfortable betraying your dad and everything, but could you give me a hint?"

"Of course. Ready? Here goes. There's only so many places a safe can be hidden."

"*So* irritating," I reiterated.

"Because I like you, I'll give you a second tip free of charge. Not everything is what it seems."

"That's the story of my life," I muttered. *Think!* Chips required minimal space for storing. They were tiny. Could be taped to anything. Or hidden within.

"Two minutes."

Gah! I opened the ammo box, searched the bullets. Studied the candy tin, on the hunt for—jackpot! A small panel on the bottom, used for reading a fingerprint. More specifically, the king's personal fingertip. It must be the key to opening the tin.

"Thanks to the gloves, your prints will register as his," Cyrus informed me. "The greatest difficulty will be the code." Trusting him once again, I pressed my index finger within the allotted lines.

Numbers lit up, awaiting said code.

"How am I supposed to know—" I sucked air between my teeth. The code. Which I might have. Because Soal had given it to me.

Could it be?

Pressing my tongue against the back of my teeth, I typed in the numbers now flashing inside my head. 80630941507.

My breath caught as I waited. Then, I heard it. A click sounded as the lock disengaged.

CHAPTER TWENTY-EIGHT

In the end, all will reap a harvest of what
they've sown.

—*The Book of Soal* 2.6.2.6

Cyrus straightened with a snap. "You knew the code." Incredulity drowned out his previous amusement.

Had he not expected me to get this far? No, no. He'd said he wanted to read the chip, and I believed him. "Soal gave it to me," I admitted, opening the little flap to reveal a lone chip.

"I thought I'd have to walk you through decoding," he insisted.

See. A perfectly reasonable explanation.

Heart beating like a war drum against my ribs, I freed the tiny device from its prison. *Closer than ever to answers.* Even still, indecision beat against my brain. Stealing secrets from the king meant prison for life, if not outright death. If he discovered the chip's absence before tomorrow's meeting, he'd know who took it, no matter what the camera feed showed. If he didn't need it before then, I could return it. No harm, no foul. But the risk didn't swing in my favor.

Cyrus pretended to stroke invisible Arden's hair. "There's a replacement chip in your bracelet. When it's inserted into a reader, it shows all files are corrupted and secretly opens a back door." He checked his timer. "One minute remains."

"I love having you in my corner." Relieved, I fiddled with the bracelet until I found and removed the fake chip. As I'd donned the other pieces, I'd learned one of my new rings acted as a single-shot netter, while the other hid a powdery sedative strong enough to put a hulk to sleep. The hairpin sheathed a small dagger laced with a paralyzing toxin. One of the necklaces could be used as wrist cuffs.

"Any other secrets I'm wearing?" I inquired.

"Many."

A nonanswer answer. I didn't push for a list as I switched one chip with the other. "Thank you, Cyrus. For everything." He'd prepared me for war while doing everything in his power to protect me, exactly as he'd promised.

He gave me a sheepish smile. "My intentions aren't entirely altruistic. I like having you around."

I only hoped he'd say the same if the files implicated CURED of wrongdoing.

Sickness stirred in my stomach. I returned the candy tin to its proper place and locked the drawers. Cyrus stood, and as he mimed helping me to my feet, I closed the distance and gave him my hand for real. He led me from the office, my heart thudding harder with every step away from the scene of our crime. Part of me expected someone to leap out from the shadows and inform the whole party of what I'd done.

I pasted on a smile, attempting to control my too-expressive face, and we rejoined the throng.

Cyrus kissed a corner of my mouth and stated softly, "I'm ready to go home. You?"

Home. The word echoed in my mind. "Yes, please." I rasped. I'd gotten what I'd come for and then some.

We maintained our silence as we walked the hall, rode the elevator, and entered the—*our* apartment. He wasted no time, removing a reader from a drawer and ushering me to the couch. After unbuttoning his jacket, he sat in a corner and tugged me onto his lap. I didn't protest. I liked where I was.

He held up the reader. "We'll go over the documents, whatever they are, and talk afterward."

"Okay." My preference as well. With trembling fingers, I removed the chip from the bracelet and inserted it into the reader. The stirring in my stomach graduated to churning as the blank screen lit up and a blurry video appeared.

With a tap of the screen, the image crystalized and played, revealing a room I recognized. Cyrus's office at Fort Bala. He perched behind his desk, Jericho across from him.

In real life, he stiffened behind me. "I've changed my mind. Let's talk before we watch."

The churning worsened, and I shook my head. "No." We watched now.

He paused the video anyway, grating, "Let me think. I don't understand why my father would want you to view this. To hate me."

"Hate you?" I twisted to examine him, ready to vomit. "What did you do?"

He scrubbed a hand over his shell-shocked features. Still speaking to himself, he muttered, "He had to know this would send you straight to Soal, something he's hoped to avoid from the beginning. What Soal wants, Astan wants too. Therefore, my father is determined to win you. So why would he do this?"

What would send me straight to Soal? "Cyrus," I croaked, clutching the lapels of his jacket. "I'm hearing you say your father purposely put this chip in his safe, hoping I'd steal it and watch."

"Yes. He must have." His head canted to the side. "He must believe you'll join Soal and recruit me, succeeding where others have failed. This is his countermove. Give you up to keep me." He closed his eyes for a moment and braced, as if preparing for a blow. "Do it then. Watch. But give me an opportunity to explain afterward."

I almost couldn't bring myself to press Play, but in the end, I did it. Because I had to know.

The video resumed. "You were overheard speaking with Arden today." Video Cyrus tapped his fingers against his light board, working on his computer. "You told her you saw me eat a berry given to me by John Victors."

My grip tightened on the reader. He'd spied on me.

"So did you?" digital Jericho demanded.

"I won't be answering any of your questions, and you won't be mentioning this again. You will pack your bags, leave the base, and keep your mouth closed. That's an order."

"I won't let this go," Jericho spat. "Are you a Soalian?"

On the screen, Cyrus flipped up his gaze and went still. "That's a serious accusation." He stared at Jericho so long and so hard, the lord squirmed in his seat.

"But is it true?"

Determination hardened the HP's features, and I stiffened. I knew that look. Consequences were about to be dished out.

Casually reaching inside his desk drawer, he said, "You are rude and self-centered. Ready to hurt anyone you deem weaker to prove your so-called strength. Character is something that can only be taught to a willing participant, and as of yet, you don't qualify. Your disobedience will cost you dearly."

"I had a purpose for doing what I did," real Cyrus said, pressing his forehead between my shoulder blades and tightening his hold on me.

Bile seared my throat.

Video Cyrus lifted a gun and squeezed the trigger twice. *Pft. Pft.* Jericho jerked and grunted. Bright crimson spread over his shirt. He gasped for breath he couldn't catch while sliding out of his chair.

I jolted with both shots. With a ragged groan, I dropped the reader and wrenched from Cyrus, bounding from his lap. He jumped to his feet, and we faced off.

"You killed him," I gasped out, hit by an avalanche of horror. "You murdered him to hide what you'd done."

"His inquiries made him a target. He was going to break, as Shiloh did."

I flinched. "How do you know that?"

"This isn't the time to—"

"Enough! You told me Jericho left Fort Bala and didn't return. You lied," I accused, desperate for a reasonable explanation. "Unless this is a doctored video. Tell me it's doctored, and I might believe you."

A moment passed in terse silence. "I can't tell you it's doctored," he said, his voice raw. "But I didn't lie. Jericho was still alive when he was carried from the base."

Cyrus might not have lied, but he'd misdirected. Again. Anger heated into fury, boiling in my blood. I couldn't stay here. Couldn't stay with him. Not in this building. And I didn't have to.

"Did you or someone else force Shiloh to break?" I demanded.

"I didn't."

"But someone else did. Or could have." More misdirection. "I'm going," I stated flatly, backing away. How did I ever fall for this monster? "Don't try to stop me. You won't like what happens if you do."

His posture turned rigid in an instant. "You're staying here, Arden. Darkness comes in a matter of hours."

I didn't care. Because I was going to do it. I was going to sign on with Team Soal. Full stop. Nothing held back. Decision made. CURED and its associates only ever dished out betrayal.

"I can be in front of the Rock in a matter of minutes," I boasted. "Consider me your enemy. I'm accepting the invitation to the Tome Society. Until my dying breath, I will fight to dismantle CURED." Soal wanted my loyalty. Very well, I'd give it. But he would have to help free my mother. "You and your family have done enough damage to the world. It's time someone ended the deceit, thefts, and destruction."

A muscle ticced beneath his eye. "I'll escort you to the Rock in the morning, when I can do it without alerting CURED."

"As if I will ever trust you again." I pivoted on my heel and marched toward the door. "I'll come back for my plant. If you or your father bring any harm to my mom—don't harm my mom, Cyrus."

Pounding footsteps sounded behind me, fast and sure, and I knew he'd overtake me any second if I didn't stop him. So, I shifted, aimed, and fired my netter ring. He flew backward and hit the floor, pinned by a metal cage he couldn't remove.

"Arden," he snarled. "Do not leave this apartment. I mean it."

"Goodbye, sugar bear. In case it's not clear, we're over." I turned the knob, opened the door, and sailed into the hall, then the elevator. I removed a glove, pressed my palm onto the ID pad, and selected the first floor.

Down I went, determination hardening into unshakable resolve. Though my heart pounded with increasing heaviness, I exited as if I hadn't a care, my steps unhurried. Chin up, shoulders back. Happy smile for all to see, even those watching the camera feed. But inside I boiled hotter and hotter.

Shiloh had tried to tell me. Ember had warned me. The more time it took to make my decision, the more tragedy I would be forced to face. Because of my hesitance, two men were dead. I wasn't waiting a minute longer than necessary to join the Soalians.

I scanned the building's lobby. An armed baron guarded the door.

"Please help me." In my pink finery, I must look the part of a silly, lost little woman. I approached him, and he let me. All the while, I fiddled with the proper ring. "A tenant immobilized High Prince Dolion with a netter."

Concern instantly seized the man. He palmed the gun holstered at his side and stepped my way, meeting me in the middle. "Do you know who did it?"

"Yes. Me." I wasted no time in blowing half the powder into his face.

His eyes widened, and he jerked just before his knees buckled. He hit the floor hard. I stepped over him and approached the final ID pad. Thanks to Cyrus giving me royal access, the door unlocked.

Deep breath in. Out.

Ready for anything, I left the safety of the building and entered the warmth of the day.

CHAPTER TWENTY-NINE

The command was spoken, and the light came.

—*The Book of Soal* 1.1.1.3

I hurried down the abandoned street, my new mini dagger in hand. I expected a horde of feeders to attack, but a lone glower dressed in a hooded bloodred robe stepped forward.

Removing the hood, revealing a crown of rubies and skin aglow with symbols, he bowed his head in deference to me. The bearded guy—Domino—followed me in the flesh rather than from inside the Rock.

Trepidation proved a formidable foe, but I pushed on, even when second, third, and fourth glowers glided into my field of vision. None of the other faces looked familiar, but they wore the same hooded bloodred robes and ruby crowns. They also repeated the same actions as Domino, treating this as some kind of ritual. Soon I had an entire convoy of glowers behind me. They even lined the road, and it was an intimidating sight.

My trepidation magnified, but so did my determination. Every step increased the distance between me and Cyrus, the man who had betrayed my trust. If I intended to join the Tome Society, and I did, these glowers were my allies. I had nothing to fear.

I neared the Rock. My shadows stopped behind me, utterly silent. Ember stood before what had once been the bane of my existence but now acted as my only beacon of hope. She wore a robe, too, though it possessed golden trim studded with jewels. Hello, mistress of ceremonies. Her hood was already down, her ruby crown double the size of the others.

I paused several feet away and gulped. This wouldn't be a casual thing. These Soalians meant business. Took this seriously. I must as well.

"Thank you for the welcome," I said, perspiration dotting my palms. The sun set in the sky, light gradually fading, but it didn't matter. Thanks to the glowers, the area remained well lit. "I'm ready to accept my invitation into the Tome Society."

"Kneel or fall," Ember stated, clear and concise. "Your choice."

Prostrate myself, as if she were my queen and I was some kind of helpless servant? I opened my mouth to protest, only to snap my teeth together. Right now, the Soalians were my only weapon and defense against CURED. Because yes, I intended to dedicate my life to dismantling their power over innocent families. I would avenge Shiloh and Jericho too.

While I was ignorant about this process and the significance of Ember's request, I refused to do anything to disqualify myself. I willingly, happily sank to my knees.

Satisfaction flickered in her irises. She stretched out an arm and rolled open her fingers, revealing a pebble. Or a crumb from the Rock. "Eat."

I trembled as I claimed it. The moment of truth. Once I did it, there'd be no going back. But then, I didn't wish to go back.

With confidence, I placed the piece on the tip of my tongue. No need to chew. The bit dissolved in seconds.

My eyes went wide. And I thought I'd tasted sweetness before. Warmth sparked in the center of my chest, spinning and growing, growing and spinning, washing over every inch of me, reminding me of a cozy blanket in front of a fire.

The mistress of ceremonies performed the same act with her other arm—stretching it out, rolling open her fingers, and presenting me with a corked vial of crimson liquid. "Drink."

This time, I wasn't trembling as I obeyed. I emptied the container. More incredible sweetness filled my mouth. Like the warmth, strength spun within me and grew, saturating my being.

Ember wasn't done. She performed the act again, extending both arms, and a huge sword appeared in each hand. Blue flames danced from the tips to the elaborate hilts. When she slammed the two weapons together, they joined, creating a double-edged blade, shooting sparks in every direction.

Alarm and awe fought for dominance. Was I soon to possess abilities like hers?

"Arden Dawn Roosa," Ember announced. "We vow to protect you with our lives, give you aid when needed, and come when you call. To be accepted into the Tome Society, you must vow to do the same for us."

Without hesitation, I rolled back my shoulders and braced. "I do. I vow it."

"Say the words."

"I will protect you with my life, aid when needed, and come when you call."

A bright smile spread over her face, and she stalked closer to me. Trepidation flared anew as she planted the tip of the sword just above my heart. Though the flames flickered, heat spreading over my body, I didn't burn.

"May you find the peace you seek, gain the wisdom of the ancient of days, and grow into the garden you were created to be." With that, she shoved the blade deep.

I gasped, jolted inside and out. Except, the blade didn't pierce me. Not physically, at least. It disappeared into my torso, becoming a part of me. The heat cranked up, flaring in my veins, becoming a roaring inferno. Okay, now I burned. Too much!

"You're good. You're all right." Ember's voice wafted into my awareness. "The fire kills the Madness and dissolves the poisons CURED injected into you. Let it happen."

A scream parted my lips, and if I'd been on my feet, I would've toppled. Dizziness struck, but I panted through it. My world went dark, my thoughts disintegrating. Then light came. My pain vanished as if it had never been, and suddenly I felt lighter, as if I'd shed a thousand pounds of uncertainty. A thick, gloomy fog I'd never truly shed cleared from my mind, leaving no trace. No place for fear to hide. Thoughts snapped into focus, crisp and sure, and I laughed.

"She's free!" Ember called, helping me to my feet.

Other glowers cheered and crowded around me, giving hugs. Again and again, they called, "Fight one, fight all!"

More laughter bubbled from my core. Even the world looked different. The Rock dazzled. I'd considered it beautiful before, but I hadn't glimpsed a tenth of its glory. I could detect every individual grain of dirt that composed the stone; they glittered in a self-contained light. The symbols were as bright as precious gems.

Bala City did not possess the same radiance. An oozing, shadowy film covered the buildings, and I cringed, repulsed. That was when realization struck. I'd really done it. I'd severed my connection to CURED, making me officially an enemy.

Zero regrets.

"Come with me," Ember said. The crowd parted, giving me a front-row view as she marched into the Rock.

My awe doubled. Tripled. Legs trembling, I walked forward—and smacked into a solid surface, rattling my brain against my skull.

A grinning Ember poked out her head. "Guess you need instructions. Focus on the seal, let it reveal its wisdom, and command it to open," she said, and then she was gone again.

I drew in another deep breath and shifted my gaze to a symbol carved in the Rock. "Open?"

Sound waves rippled across the stone. The lines inside the symbol moved, aligning, and the circle spun. Crimson rushed along the veins that branched throughout the stone, and a small section turned to mist right before my eyes.

Steady feet carried me forward. The mist proved cool, an unexpected caress against my skin. In the blink of an eye, however, I was standing beside Ember, breathing in the most exquisite floral fragrance.

"Welcome to the Door of Shaddai." She spread her arms.

Shaddai. The utopia free of the Madness, filled with everything we could ever need or want. I perused the vast room live and in person for the first time, marveling. Flowers grew over the walls and beneath a transparent floor, several buds blooming only when I stepped toward them. Freshly polished tables gleamed, made from the purest gold. Books were shelved covers forward. Whenever I focused on one, the title lit up. Just as before, men and women, young and old, congregated here and there. Many ceased what they were doing to smile and wave at me.

Oh! I recognized her from school. And he'd lived in my former building, down the hall from Mom and me. There were a handful of knights, barons, and viscounts I'd seen at the base. I marveled anew.

"Everything you see," Ember said, walking slowly, allowing me to gawk as I kept pace, "came from Shaddai."

"It's breathtaking." Mom was going to love it here.

My mother. I bit my tongue. I needed to speak with her. Tell her she'd had it right and I'd been wrong.

Ember continued. "You'll find in-depth world histories, memoirs, biographies of triumphs and failures, languages, word studies, parables, and detailed outlines of what's to come. Anything you seek to learn is available. Though some books are open to everyone, others must be unlocked to be read."

"So unlock them."

"If only it were that easy. The symbols on the Rock contain the wisdom of the ages, and that wisdom acts as keys. When you understand

and act on what you learn, those keys work, exposing more wisdom. Similar to the one you used to open a door into this realm."

Um. "To enter, I just stared at a symbol and spoke. I didn't learn anything new."

"Not in your mind. Not yet. But our hearts pick up things on a deeper level without our intellects realizing it. Recognition will eventually come, but the speed it happens depends on various factors. Most of the other symbols will require a more concentrated and conscious effort. But don't worry. You'll be trained, learning as you go. It's the same for all of us."

I gazed about, trying to take in everything at once. A huge fountain made of jasper in the shape of a lion showered anyone nearby, but the droplets didn't wet them or their books. A row of cherry blossoms—unpotted, living trees—grew inside the building, offering quiet spots to rest.

"I have so many questions," I said, amazed.

"You always do. Right now, I'll answer three. Go."

My gaze caught on Domino, who stood off to the side, observing me with unabashed interest. His intensity blazed off the charts. "What's the purpose of a librarian who's part of the High Guard?"

"First, don't mind Domino. He read something in his book that confused him. Anyway. Librarians are the best of the best and the highest members of *our* royalty, bound by a specific set of laws. They live in the library and help Soalians on and off the field."

Hmm. "If they're so good at their jobs, why are so many Soalians beaten and arrested?"

"Failure to read the book. The breaking of our laws. Fear. Pick a reason. But you'll see how good librarians are when you're in the field," she replied, and I grunted. I hadn't meant to ask my second question. "Let's hear your final query."

Fine. I'd traveled this road. I might as well take it to its end. "When can I strike at CURED?"

"After you've trained. Now then. In this part of the library," she said as if we'd never deviated from the tour, "time passes the same as in Ourland."

Okay, so, there were places where time *did* pass differently. Good to know.

"The more you visit, read, train, and study, the more missions you complete, the faster and brighter you'll be able to glow. One of many ways to recognize other Soalians. Don't worry," she repeated, "non-Soalians won't notice. Their infection prevents them from seeing our slightest radiance."

"I noticed the glow before becoming a Soalian. So have others."

"No, you saw a beacon we intentionally released. That, we can control, and the infection can't mask it. Mostly. There are rules to everything. You'll need to learn them."

Assorted layers in the symbols. Unique keys and different luminosities. My brain threatened to short-circuit from everything I had to learn. Data overload paired with emotional uncertainty, a toxic combination. In less than a blink, my entire life had changed. Who I trusted, who I didn't. What I believed, what I didn't. "I want to help you bring down CURED. That's why I'm here."

"Don't get ahead of yourself. You should learn to slay a bear before you take on a giant."

My chest constricted hard. Cyrus had once advised the same thing.

"You'll return to the Lux in the morning," she said, "and we'll contact you with an assignment when we feel you're ready."

She must be kidding. "I can't go back." No way. "I attacked Cyrus Dolion and a guard to get here!"

She snorted, halting my coming speech. "Cyrus will forgive you. He must. He joined us a year ago." A smile lifted the corners of her mouth. "John won him over when I failed. Cyrus is Unicorn. I'm Sparrow."

"What!" I shouted, my voice echoing from the walls. I halted as shock rocked me. "But, but, Cyrus captured John, killed a lord named Jericho, and might have caused Shiloh to break."

"He did not. I'm prohibited from sharing all the details, but I can tell you that John ordered Cyrus to take him in so that he could deliver information Cyrus and the other Soalians couldn't. Most of Cyrus's conversations are recorded, each move monitored and dissected by CURED. He has to guard every word he utters, so he needed to appear to recruit you for CURED. Let's face it, there was always the chance you'd ruin the Unicorn's cover, and we need him positioned where he is."

A barbed lump grew in my throat.

"Any secret message we sent you was intercepted. You were surveilled more heavily than Cyrus. John took steps to get the mission on track. As for the boys," she continued, as if she hadn't already rocked my world. "Cyrus saved Jericho. The boy had been marked for elimination even before the berry incident. Cyrus injured him enough to pass for dead, without striking vital organs, and got him out of the facility in a body bag. He also saved Shiloh. Not even I knew it at first." She unveiled a sheepish smile. "You really did a number on his face and throat, but the HP patched him up, keeping him alive and getting him to John just in time."

Blood rushed from my head. Everything I'd assumed, everything I'd done . . . all wrong.

I closed my eyes and breathed. That's the only thing I could do as facts solidified. Shiloh was alive. Jericho hadn't been murdered. Cyrus was Unicorn. The one meant to charm me, who might have fallen for me in the process. Unless I'd been a mission, after all.

No, I couldn't have been. He'd shared as much as he could without blowing his cover. And yet, I'd hurt him. He'd been nothing but good to me, and I'd netted him, leaving him helpless in a den of lions. He'd risked his life to save others, and I'd punished him for it.

Guilt and shame churned within me. I owed him a thousand apologies, but they wouldn't be enough. "I need to see him," I rushed out, referring to all three men. Cyrus, Shiloh, and Jericho.

"This way." She led me to a closed door. A door she then blocked with her body. "Before we go in, you should know neither Shiloh nor Jericho are allowed to leave the library. They would endanger Cyrus, so here they stay for now. No weaving plans to take them with you."

"Fine," I said, eager to enter.

She stepped aside, and I raced inside. A conference room, with a long narrow table and a multitude of chairs. Shiloh and Jericho sat on opposite sides. The medic spotted me first, leaped to his feet, and rushed over.

A groan of relief and joy burst from me as we embraced. "You're alive." He had healed super fast. Though, yes, he wore an eye patch and possessed jagged scars on his throat.

"I can never apologize enough, Arden. Dr. Korey fed me some kind of drug. The things I did to you, to Mykal." He pulled away and peered down at me. Tears streamed over his cheeks. "When I woke up, the memories came rushing back. I can't describe the horror I experienced. If I could time travel—"

"You're forgiven," I interjected, cupping his cheeks to ensure he knew I meant business. His patch and scars were a permanent reminder of my actions. "I stabbed you, Shiloh. Many times. If *I* could time travel—"

"There's nothing for me to forgive," he interrupted. "You defended yourself from a madman. I could never be angry with you for it."

We smiled watery smiles and released each other. Friends. But. Seeing him and Jericho made my mistakes with Cyrus so much clearer. I pressed a trembling hand to my lips. He'd tried to tell me the truth. To the best of his ability, he'd tried, and I had betrayed him. Me. I was the disloyal one.

Guess I needed to eat my shoes.

Guilt and shame churned with more force. I'd lost him and for what? Failing to take a beat and listen.

"Do I get a hug too?" Jericho asked with his usual snark.

"No," Shiloh and I answered in unison.

"Then we're agreed." Impatient, Jericho shifted his gaze to Ember. "Can I go now?"

"No." The harsh male voice filled the room, and I spun to face the newest arrival, my heart thudding.

Cyrus stood in the open doorway, a tower of strength despite a dozen cuts and gashes littering his face and hands. His expression remained blank, his eyes as cold and hard as steel.

He didn't glance my way as he strode inside. "I broke from the unit searching for Arden, so my time is short. Let's get this done."

CHAPTER THIRTY

You must see your victory inside before you can see
your victory outside.

—*The Book of Soal* 2.19.11.1

I remained in place, heart thumping, a thousand words tap-dancing across my mind. Only two mattered. *Cyrus. Here.*

Ember swept past me to claim the head of the conference table. "Sit. Please."

As I made my way over, my weight nearly proved too much for my legs. Everyone took a seat, with Cyrus situated at Ember's right. From my spot in the middle, I watched, agonized, as he placed two books in front of him. Shiloh sank into the chair next to me while Jericho plopped beside Cyrus.

He must hate me. After showing me only kindness and consideration, he'd asked me only for the slightest bit of trust I'd told him I'd given him. Clearly, I'd lied. Something he despised. I'd also incapacitated him, leaving him helpless against his enemy.

"Are you all right?" I rasped.

"I'm fine." An all-too-brief statement that gave nothing away. Still he didn't glance in my direction.

I wetted my lips with a nervous swipe of my tongue. "Cyrus, I can't apologize enough. I—"

"There's time for that later," Ember interjected. "Besides, he isn't injured because of you but himself. I told him not to venture out with a search party. But nooo, he just had to go and disobey. Be advised now. Nothing good ever comes from that. Unlike you, he had to battle numerous feeders to get here."

Guilt seared me. Despite her reassurance, I laid the blame at my door.

"Hey, Arden," Jericho said with a toothy grin. "How does it feel to know you've dated every guy in this room?"

Unfazed, I merely arched a brow. "Two of the three were gold star and I highly recommend. Care to guess my opinion of the third?"

"Sure. You can't get over your secret crush on him, so you continue to lash out and pretend you hate him," he quipped, far from chastised.

Cyrus slammed his hand upon the table. Everyone but Ember jumped. "Begin the meeting," he demanded. "Please."

"I did begin. You all interrupted." She leaned back and crossed her arms over her chest. "Obviously, Arden and Cyrus will return to the Lux and continue with business as usual."

Yes, but would I continue to live with Cyrus, the girlfriend monitoring his welfare for that "special" project, or go back to being a regular lady?

"You'll keep your upcoming meeting with the king," she continued. "But first, check your book. Judging by snippets read in the books of others, you'll be met with great opposition. The more you know, the safer you'll be. Also, you'll probably learn how we rescue your mother."

Blink. "My mother requires rescuing?"

"Oh. Right. I forgot to mention that part. Yes," Ember said with a nod. "She's in danger. But you have nothing to fear. I've been assured—"

I leaped to my feet, demanding, "Take me to her."

Shiloh clasped my hand, drawing my attention. "Let my sister finish," he offered gently. "As *I've* learned, you can't win without her."

I didn't sit, but I did return my focus to the frowning Ember and nodded, a silent command to proceed.

"We'll save her," she said. "I haven't discovered how yet, but I did read a passage about a victory party."

Not good enough. "You actually saw her name with your own two eyes and came upon a sentence that mentioned her status?"

"Not precisely. But I spotted *your* name. The brief reference revealed you were laughing, so. Tada! Proof that all ends well."

No. No, that wasn't proof.

"The best way to help your mother is to pore over your book." No nonsense, Cyrus slid one of the tomes he'd brought toward me. "You can uncover your enemy's plans and proceed accordingly."

I sank into my seat when I spied the title. *Arden Dawn Roosa*, volume 20, *Daily Updates*. The same book I'd read before. Embossed on the upper right edge were the words *Book of Soal*. Desperate, I worked to crack the spine. But the cover remained glued to the pages, refusing to budge.

Was staying here to mess with a book truly worth it?

Ember cleared her throat. "When we rush in without taking time to consult the books, we lose without exception. CURED has books too, courtesy of Astan, and they predict the different paths we can take. But they are unable to see the path provided by Soal. Therefore, it is our only path to triumph."

New bombshell. Each side had a set of books.

"Know the future, take the steps, stop the enemy," Cyrus muttered.

Very well. "I'll stay. I'll read."

"Do it from your heart, not your mind," Ember instructed.

The seal branded in the center of the cover caught my notice. A circle with seven broken lines. The key. Though I peered at it for a long while, the lines never moved. I tried to open the tome the way I was to read it, from the heart—whatever that meant. Nothing happened. Tried willing it open. Still nothing.

My stomach churned, the first spark of panic stirring. If I failed to succeed, my mother might die.

There had to be something I could do. I waved the book. Slammed it against the table. Boom, boom, boom. I pulled and strained and screamed, all to no avail.

Shiloh rested his hand on mine, offering comfort, but I experienced none. Then my gaze collided with Cyrus's.

"Remember what I taught you about fear," he stated flatly.

I gave him a clipped nod, wishing so many things. "Leave, fear."

"Shiloh and Jericho"—Ember waved to the door—"give Arden some breathing room. Return to your studies."

Jericho's mood instantly soured. He jumped to his feet, his chair skidding away from the table, and exclaimed, "I'm tired of studying. Give me a day off at least."

"No. And now you'll write two reports today."

He kicked a table leg. "I've cracked a single volume, and it's a tale I didn't want to read. But nooo. I can't burn it. I've got to"—his voice took on a mocking tinge—"'learn myself before I can grow myself.' You're the one who needs to grow up, Em." He marched out the door.

Ignore him. I returned my attention to the book, fighting fear and concentrating on the symbol.

"I'd like to stay, sis," Shiloh said.

Tune him out.

"Shiloh Cruz, we've talked about this," Ember exclaimed. "In official meetings, I'm your boss."

"Please," he said.

She gave a little laugh. "Arden?"

"He's fine," I responded, staring at the book with all my might, refusing to blink. Still nothing, dang it. *Come on, come on!*

Shiloh murmured encouragements.

Frustration boiled within me, melting the lock on my anger. My fingers tightened on the book until my knuckles ached. I ground my molars. Why wasn't this working? And was the room shrinking? The air was definitely thickening. And heating. I tugged at the scooped neckline of my dress. I was going to fail. My mother was going to die because I failed.

"You have reverted to old ways," Cyrus said with his hard, intractable instructor voice. "You will defeat the fear, Lady Roosa, because I say you will. So do it."

My lids flipped up, and my breath caught. His irises smoldered at me. "You think I'm not trying?"

"I didn't say *try*. I said *do*." He stood and marched around the table, approaching my side. My heart went haywire.

"Give her a break," Shiloh snapped. "She's doing the best she can."

"A break isn't what her mother needs." Cyrus kept his gaze glued on me as he crouched beside my chair, becoming my anchor in the storm. "Am I a liar? Do I spew falsehoods, even to spare myself trouble?"

"No, you never lie." His nearness erased the rest of the world from my awareness. Calm, quiet strength radiated from him, enveloping me. I drank in his decadent scent. A calming fragrance I now knew originated here in Soal. "You tell the truth, dishing as many clues as you can without endangering yourself or others. It isn't your fault when someone reacts wrongly, which they regret with every fiber of their being." The confession left me in a rush.

"Correct." He blinked with surprise but recovered quickly, readapting his stern demeanor as he cupped my cheeks. "Are you brave? Did you face down the emperor's grandson to do what you perceived was right because of the damning evidence offered to you?"

I almost believed he might possibly be saying he'd already forgiven me. Almost. "Yes. I'm brave," I boasted, gripping his wrists to hold him close to me. Uh-oh. Shiloh wilted. I tried to release Cyrus out of respect, I did; but I failed in that too. "Is there a secret to success? A hot new tip? A tried-and-true process? Am I doing something wrong?"

"Anytime you open a new book, your readiness is tested. You must be willing to do what it says, even if it seems foolish. Sometimes it's easy to pass, sometimes it's difficult."

I swallowed a whimper. "But I suck at tests."

"You've been acing mine." Cyrus flashed the world's fastest grin. "Forget everything else and simply study the seal. Let it unveil itself to you. It wants to." He released me, forcing me to release him too. He straightened partway and gripped the edge of the table and an arm of my chair, then pivoted to tap the cover of the book. "Whatever you see or hear or feel, do not draw back in fear. Press on, and the book will open."

Forget. Study. Press on. "Got it." I nodded for emphasis.

Breathing deep, I homed in on certain details. The leather and its three nicks. The circle. The seven broken lines inside it, each embossed in gold.

Mom is in danger.

I squirmed in my seat.

She might die.

Gah!

"Look deeper," Cyrus said.

My eyelids narrowed, and my gaze zeroed in on the lines. Wait. There were lines inside the lines. Something about them prodded the back of my mind. What, what?

Was that—I frowned, focusing on the tip of the center line. Yes! Another line was growing, as if a seed had been planted inside it and a sprout had just broken through the surface.

Excitement bloomed, and I snatched the book for a closer look. Suddenly, blocking out the rest of the world wasn't difficult. The more intently I watched it, the faster the sprout grew, until it split in two and flowed over both sides of the line. Still growing. Curling around the other lines. Drawing them closer. Closer. None stopped until all were side by side, with no gaps between them. The seal spun, and whatever force had earlier prevented me from lifting the cover vanished. Giddy, I cracked open the spine.

"That's my girl," Cyrus said, clasping my nape. But the touch didn't last long. He stiffened and pulled away, asking, "Does it reveal something about your past, present, or future?"

"Let's find out." I flipped through the first group of pages. A disclaimer. The title. "Why did you bring me this particular book?"

"When John asked me to turn him in to CURED, he also instructed me to pull two specific books the day you joined the Tome Society. This one is for you, and the second is for me."

Finally I reached the meat of the story. I read the first couple of paragraphs, my brows drawing in. I frowned. "It's—hmm. A scene from my past. The day I agreed to attend the academy. I returned home to find my mother left work early to celebrate my acceptance into the Center or console me for my rejection." I paused, frowned. "I'm not sure how this helps me."

"Most likely the key to save her is in that moment of your life, so you need to read it over and over until clarity comes," Ember explained, standing. "I have a feeling this will be a long night, so I'm going to gather snacks. Be back soon."

The door closed behind her. Suddenly I was alone with Cyrus and Shiloh. I shifted, uncomfortable.

Cyrus wasted no time redonning his emotionless mask. He strode around the table and swiped up his book. "I'll have a better chance of opening mine if I'm alone. I'll learn what I can and return." Without glancing my way, he followed Ember's path, exiting the room.

As the door shut behind him, dejection hit.

Shiloh leaned toward me, and I cast him a small smile. He appeared south of grim. "I get that you're under pressure and time is limited, but I also don't want to be a burden for you tonight. So, let me resolve any possible conflict within you and remove this worry from your plate. You like him."

My shoulders rolled in. "Yes," I admitted softly. Cyrus was mine. I chose him. If he decided I wasn't the one for him, so be it. But I refused to fear something so right.

Shiloh released a heavy breath. "I can't even blame you. He's pretty dreamy."

"That's what I said!"

My companion sighed. "He had to perform expert tricks to lose his guard and visit me here. Told me you were mourning and hardening to challenge and that when you and I next came together, you wouldn't be the same. He also said I wouldn't be the same, either, and we'd both realize we weren't suited for each other. Now, here we are. A guy I really wish I could hate but can only admire nailed it."

Tears burned my eyes as I wrapped my arms around his shoulders and hugged him. "You're pretty dreamy, too, you know."

"Even with the patch?" He gently stroked the pads of his fingers over the material.

"Especially with the patch."

As I pulled away smiling, he said, "Don't beat yourself up about my poor battered heart. I'll recover, I promise. And honestly, there's no reason to worry about the HP's feelings for you. My guess is he's trying to give you space to process my return."

I truly hoped that was the crux of it. "In your letter to me, you mentioned two words that Soal spoke to you. How they changed the trajectory of your entire life." At long last, I asked, "What were the two words?"

"I'll tell you when the time is right." Shiloh waved to my book. "Right now, I want to help you keep your mother safe. You've got me for another half hour, so use me."

I didn't push because I had no right to do so. "Give me a minute to scan this." He nodded, and I dove into the "story," letting the text remind me of the details. And it was odd reliving my past self in written form, as if it was authored by someone else. I logged the facts, then dove deeper, searching for a key. Any key. "Help," I squeaked. "How am I supposed to know what's important and what's not?"

Shiloh didn't miss a beat. "Explain what happened."

Okay. "I walked in the door. Mom blew a horn and tossed confetti. I confessed my acceptance into Fort Bala Royal Academy. She offered to complain to CURED, but I declined. I claimed it was a good thing, that I would now have a chance to obliterate my nightmares. She blamed herself for my predicament, professed fear for my life, and suggested we go on the run. Oh! Maybe I'm supposed to get her and go on the run. Although, my boast. *Nothing gets in the way of my dream, not even death.* What if I'm *not* supposed to flee? What if she dies if I don't?"

"Ember tells us to never venture into a rabbit hole. The foxes lie in wait."

In other words, calm down. Easier said than done. I jumped to my feet and began to pace parallel to the table. "I *must* figure out if I'm supposed to run or stay. Unless escaping isn't even the question."

Cyrus burst into the room, his expression grave. He no longer held his book but a necklace with a small metal star hanging from the center.

I froze, my heart racing. "You learned something."

He gave a clipped nod and fit the necklace around his neck. "I know how to remove your mother from CURED crosshairs."

No need to think about it. "I'm ready," I said, closing my book and jumping to my feet. "Let's go."

CHAPTER THIRTY-ONE

A fool's mouth will usher in his destruction. his
words an unavoidable snare.

—*The Book of Soal* 1.20.18.7

I worked to control my breathing as Cyrus led me through a maze of hallways, reading nooks, storage rooms, and exhibits. We still sported our party clothes, unwilling to stop and change. Not that our appearance garnered much interest. Few Soalians noticed us. They were busy rushing in the other direction, assembling weapons on the go, as if they were headed to a different battle.

"Tell me what you read," I pleaded.

"I first opened the book six months ago, but I've only deciphered a few passages. The newest snippet featured a heavily redacted scene from the future." Tone flat, he told me, "My father has done something terrible to certain trainees and knights to ensure they obey the worst of his commands. At some point, he leads this group into your mother's building. Unless we get there first."

"Hurry!" I pumped my arms faster, increasing my speed.

We entered a narrow hallway. "The guard I sent to protect your mom is working for my father," Cyrus continued. "He has orders to incapacitate you if you show up. I'm not expected."

My heartbeat quickened. "So the plan is, we take out the guard and move my mom into the library."

"She can't access the library, which is the sole doorway. Even if she manages to bypass the stone, the librarians will stop her."

"She'll become Soalian. She wants to." Guilt threatened to weigh me down. Twice I'd convinced her not to travel the very path she'd needed. "Maybe she and I can share a room."

"Even if she's allowed to stay, you can't. You have orders to return to Fort Bala."

"People will learn what I am—what *we* are—when we snatch my mom from the guard."

"We'll think of something. I won't allow harm to come to either of you."

But what about to himself? He planned to destroy his future over this; I knew it. And I couldn't let him. Maybe I was supposed to face my deepest nightmare alone. For too long, I'd allowed terror to hobble me. Again and again, I'd crumbled under the pressure of what-if. But here, in the battlefield of my mind, with the lives of Cyrus and my mother at stake, I accepted a forever fact. For their safety, I would risk everything.

With the decision, peace bloomed, offering me the fruit of tranquility. For the people I adored, I could face my fear head on. Nothing would stop me from doing everything in my power to win this.

"Get me to the building, and I'll do the rest," I told Cyrus. "I'm still decked out in my wonderful new jewelry. I'll be fine." I'd only used half the ring's powder on the doorman. Plus, the mini dagger hairpin hadn't lost its sharpness.

If I could snag my mom without detection, I'd tell her about Soal on our way to the Rock. She'd join the club, and I'd return to the base with Cyrus and run missions for Soal. But I knew. I couldn't avoid detection.

My powerful companion shouldered his way through huge arching double doors into another exhibit. A display of ancient rockets used to fly into space. Pinpricks of light scattered over the walls and ceiling, resembling the star-studded sky I'd only seen on my trips to Theirland. *Breathtaking.*

The sweetest peace filled this place, an invisible lace woven through the air, and I knew. The night was never supposed to be a time of fear but beauty, rest, and renewal.

"You are surprisingly calm," Cyrus said, helping me into what looked to be a liquid chrome cart. But it wasn't liquid. We sat on a solid bench, side by side, and the cart shot into action, zooming us through other hallways.

Wind whipped through my hair. I clasped his hand, squeezed. "When you know the end from the beginning, there's no reason to fret over the rest."

He almost grinned, I was sure of it. "Who even are you?"

"Yours," I wanted to say. But I didn't. Not yet. "You once told me you were born to rule CURED. Is that still the case?"

"Yes. But I intend to do it with Soal, not Astan."

Would I be at his side? "Shiloh and I admitted we weren't right for each other." And my friend was correct. Best to get the extra stuff out of the way while we had the opportunity. "I told him how much I care for you."

Cyrus didn't respond for a moment. "You care for me?"

"Very much. You are strong and amazing and wonderful, and if you give me a second chance, I promise I will trust you from now on." The words erupted from me, my confession spewing all over him. At the same time, thoughts bubbled up. I couldn't let this man destroy his future for me. And that's what he would do, because it was what he did. Risk everything for those in his care. But this time, I was looking out for *him*. In the process, I'd show him how much I trusted him. Prove how much I adored him. Ensure he reaped a harvest from the seeds of protection he'd planted.

If I used the sleeping powder as soon as we reached the final entryway, he wouldn't lose his position in CURED and become forever labeled an outlaw. Only I would.

"Please give me a second chance," I repeated. And forgive me for what was to come.

Another pause, this one almost more than I could bear. "Will you give me time to explain myself, if ever you doubt me again?"

"I'll never doubt you again," I vowed in a rush.

"You will. Many times."

"Then I'll give you as much time as you need."

His gaze burned into mine. "Yes, I'll give you a second and a third and a fourth chance."

Joy burst from the chambers of my heart. "I do want it noted that I was the brave one who mentioned feelings first."

"So noted." He kissed my lips, a swift pressing of his mouth to mine, and—no joke—multicolored lights exploded overhead. "And hint taken. I care for you, too, Arden. We're in this together."

I ran my hands up his chest, pausing at his racing heart, where my fingers got tangled in the new necklace. "What's this for?" Another weapon, no doubt.

"A last resort," he muttered, grim.

That didn't sound good.

The cart stopped, ending the reprieve, and we climbed out. We continued motoring forward on foot, hand in hand, crossing a few more halls and rooms before we stopped in front of a plain, ordinary door with an extraordinary glass handle. The inside swirled with more of those glittering stars.

"This section of the Rock is the closest one to the apartment building where she now lives," Cyrus said. "It's known as the Fork because it has four sections and it's one street over."

"Yeah, I know it." For years I'd walked miles longer than necessary to see the building. One of the most secure in the province. "Thank you," I rasped, overwhelmed by his kindness.

He squeezed my fingers. "It's still dark, so the doors are locked, but you'll be able to key in. I gave you my security clearance in the provinces as well as the base, which means you can override lockdown protocols if we get separated. But we won't get separated."

Oh, we were going to get separated all right. "The last time you said something like this, we were separated minutes later," I reminded him. My way of preparing him for what was to come.

"Trust me." He kissed my lips and smiled. "You're ready." A statement, not a question.

"I'm not. Not yet," I told him, preparing my ring. Wasting no time, I struck.

He caught my wrist, his smile widening. "I read the future, remember?"

"Yeah, but only some of it," I grumbled. I'd had to take a chance.

"I'm doing this, whatever the consequences. You are a priority to me, and I will never again give you a reason to doubt it." With that, he reached for the door.

"Wait!" I tugged, stopping him. "It's pitch black out there. We need a source of light."

He craned his neck to wink at me over his shoulder. "We are the light."

Opening the door, he rendered any objection from me obsolete. Determined, I followed him into the unknown. Goose bumps spread over my limbs as screams and howls sounded in the distance. Still we continued forward.

The second the thick cloak of darkness fully encompassed us, a shocking heat sparked deep in my chest. Fronds of warmth radiated from me, seemingly pulled out by my companion. He produced a soft golden light as peaceful and calming as the library itself.

"I want to glow like that," I said, awed.

"You already are," he said, and I gasped.

A bright light flickered over my skin. "We're like pritis," I breathed out.

"That's because we produce pritis. But that's a story for another day. Incoming."

What did he mean, *we produce pritis*? Movement snagged my attention. I stiffened as a group of maddened approached, snarling and swiping at us but always stopping just short of contact.

Fear attempted a surprise attack, swooping in, but I resisted. Cyrus wasn't afraid, and he knew more about the situation than I did, so why should I let panic rule my thoughts? "This is awesome. Did you not light up to reach the Rock after I netted you?"

"I couldn't. I was with the king's men. They wouldn't have seen the light, but they would have noticed how the feeders avoided touching me. My father doesn't know I'm Soalian. Just assumes I've lost my mind for you. A truth I can't deny."

I smiled inside.

We made it to the Fork without incident, entering the lobby. A much ritzier place than Mom had ever lived. A knight patrolled the area.

"High Prince Dolion," the guy said, saluting.

Ring time. Except, Cyrus unsheathed a gun and shot him. The guy collapsed, unmoving.

"Pegged him with a sedative," Cyrus told me. "He'll wake up in a few hours."

As we rode the elevator to the proper floor, I told him, "I'm assuming we're shooting my mother's guard, too, then collecting her and racing to the Rock. Unless you've got a better idea."

"Just follow my lead, and we'll get to where we need to be, when we need to be there."

The cart stopped, and the doors opened. I halfway expected Tagin to have soldiers waiting for us, but no. The hall was empty. We keyed into the designated apartment, and Cyrus entered first. We checked every inch, but Mom and her "protector" were nowhere to be found. Fear tried again to invade.

"Let's try the commons," he said, and I agreed. Many people chose to gather together inside their buildings, even at times of great risk. Something I'd never understood. "From what I read, at least one other person was with her."

"All right." It wasn't a place my mother usually visited, but maybe she'd taken my advice and made friends during my absence.

We took the elevator to a higher floor. I exited first, with Cyrus directly behind me. Around fifty adults congregated in the area. Some were eating, others shopping, while most occupied the bar section, playing an array of games. I scanned . . . there! Mom sat in the food court with two other women.

At the sight of her, my chest clenched. Tension etched her face, and she'd lost weight she couldn't afford to lose, no doubt due to worry for my safety.

Oh, how I'd missed her. The guard was . . . hmmm. Frowning, I expanded my search. Finally I spotted him in the shadows behind her. A big burly man with enough muscles to bench-press an entire city and a scowl that proclaimed *I kill for fun.*

People noticed Cyrus, and conversations tapered to silence. Eyes zoomed in his direction. Murmurs arose, many containing his title.

My mom spotted me and shrieked. "Arden!" On her feet, she hurried over and threw her arms around my shoulders.

"You shouldn't be here." The knight closed the distance, his concentration centered on Cyrus. "The system automatically alerted your father when you entered the building."

Cyrus shot him without hesitation. The knight banged into a table as he fell.

Other people reacted, scrambling out of the way.

"Everything is fine," I announced. "We're leaving. Please, for your own good, don't try to stop us."

My mother's excitement vanished, and the color in her cheeks drained. "What's going on?"

"Come with us." I hurried her to the elevator, Cyrus a watchman behind us, daring anyone to make a move. "Should we leave through the front or back?" I asked him as the doors closed around us.

"Arden," my mom repeated, her voice frayed and almost as shaky as her grip. She eyed Cyrus.

"You were right. Mr. Garfield was right," I told her. "There's an invisible library and so much more. I'll explain when we're safe. Okay?"

A tear tracked down her cheek, but she nodded.

"Let's go through the front," Cyrus said. "Ember should have a car waiting for us. But that's the last detail I gleaned. The remaining details were sparse."

The elevator came to a stop. I tensed, and Cyrus readied his gun. The doors slid open and we headed for the exit.

"We can't go out in the dark," my mother screeched, digging in her heels.

"Mom. Mom, Mom." I faced her and cupped her jaw. "As long as you stay near us, you're safer outside than inside. Trust me, please."

"You're wrong." She shook her head from my clasp, locks of hair slapping my wrists. "We can't go out there. We can't. We can't!" Hysteria layered her voice.

I cast my gaze to Cyrus while readying my ring. "Do me a huge favor and catch."

"What are you—" she began, attempting to back away.

I blew the powder in her face. Her eyelids slid shut and her knees buckled. Cyrus caught her as requested, then hefted her into his arms. Ignoring a tide of guilt, I sailed forward, opening the door and entering the night. Battle sounds grabbed my attention. Grunts, groans, and the clink of metal against metal. The darkness hid a raging war.

Before the heat sparked in my chest, igniting the glow and allowing me to see, pritis lights were uncovered all around, spotlighting us. I drew up short, Cyrus stopping behind me.

"Hello Arden." Tagin Dolion's calm baritone hit my ears, and I stiffened. "Cyrus, thank you for doing as promised and delivering the infected ladies to me. Let's get them to treatment."

CHAPTER THIRTY-TWO

Tell the others.

—*The Book of Soal* 2.2.16.15

We were frisked, our weapons taken—though not Cyrus's necklace, I noticed. A guard gave me a little push toward a fancy limousine, earning him a much stronger push from Cyrus. I climbed inside the vehicle. Cyrus entered after me and eased my sleeping mother into the spot on his other side. His father claimed the seat across from us and poured himself a glass of iced amber liquid as the guard closed the door.

Despite the man's words, or maybe because of them, I clutched Cyrus's hand and signed, *I trust you.* And I did. As if I would ever again believe a known liar over the one who'd constantly guarded my back.

He kept his attention on our adversary, but much of his tension drained.

A dark partition divided us from the driver and guard up front. We sat quietly until the sun rose on the horizon, casting muted rays of light over the landscape. The maddened who'd wandered the streets, on the prowl for helpless victims, rushed to shadowy hideaways.

Our little trio didn't speak until we bumped along the roads, making our way . . . somewhere.

"You have questions, I'm sure," Tagin said.

"And comments," Cyrus quipped. "I never promised you a thing."

"What else was I supposed to say to convince the guards you aren't a traitor of the highest order?" Tagin snapped. "This woman you refuse to discard is now a Soalian. She partners with glowers, and you are helping her."

"You planned to break her mother, just as you did her friend," Cyrus snapped back, and I stiffened.

Was he guessing, fishing, or had he found evidence?

"Something else you should be thanking me for." Fury danced in the older man's eyes. "You wanted her, so I gave her to you. I took out the medic digging around where he shouldn't, undermining years of work, research, and planning. Finally, I stood at the ledge of success, and he attempted to sow dissent while his sister was doing everything in her power to recruit the person who has an unnatural hold on you. Not on my watch."

Well, here it was. Proof of guilt. A full-on confession. With my free hand, I gripped my knee, my nails digging into my skin.

"You were supposed to win her over," Tagin snarled, "yet she pulled you further and further away from our cause. Astan isn't happy with you." His narrowed gaze slid to me. "If you had stuck around after watching the video of my son killing the lord, whatever his name was, I intended to offer you a job with Jade at the Center for Agriculture. But we're past that now."

"I desire nothing from you," I said, fighting for calm. "What's your new plan? Take me in for treatment I don't need? Because we both know I'm free for the first time in my life."

A muscle jumped beneath his eye. "Like all glowers, you will be strapped to a table, cut open time and time again, and used as a pritis factory until you die."

Choking sounds left me. Pritis really were cut out of Soalians.

Ice clinked as Tagin drained his glass. "Son, I'm sorry to say you must be reeducated."

"I'm past reeducation." Cyrus smiled at the man responsible for his conception. "I'm a glower myself."

Tagin blinked twice. With a roar, he tossed his glass at me. Cyrus dove in front of me, letting the missile slap into his chest. Ice cubes went flying. Cold liquid dots splashed my face. Tagin leveled his fiery gaze on me as his son straightened. "I will kill you with my own hands."

"You can try," I said simply.

"She didn't recruit me," Cyrus announced, shocking me further. "I recruited her. I'm Unicorn, and I arranged for you to read the messages about Arden, knowing you would recruit me for the job. I read the strategy in my book."

Denial roared from Tagin. But as he glanced between us, hatred contorted his face. His nostrils flared with every labored breath. Suddenly he exploded, pounding a fist on the partition and shouting, "Stop the car."

The vehicle halted with a screech.

Tagin withdrew a gun from a holster at his ankle. "Get out," he commanded.

I looked to Cyrus, who nodded. My legs shook as we exited. When Tagin followed us out, leaving my mother in her seat, I exhaled with relief.

A field of weeds and sand surrounded us. There were no trees or buildings. But there were two SUVs parked in front of the limo and two parked behind it, each filled with guards.

Those guards emerged, three familiar faces among them. Titus, Lark, and Juniper. I groaned. The trio was very clearly infected, worms already slithering from their scalps, ruffling what remained of their hair.

Sorrow and dread collided. They didn't appear to be mindless, on the hunt for pain and violence, like the maddened in Theirland. Rather, they seemed as blank as a fresh canvas. Metal collars were cinched to their necks.

"The glowers may have taken out half my forces this morning, but I still have my pride and joy," Tagin said. "They are proof we have created a Madness of our own."

He truly believed Soal created the first Madness. Didn't connect the dots and see his god lied to him as much as he lied to people. "No longer pretending to care about the greater good, I see."

"We're past appearances and pretenses, Miss Roosa. But what we've crafted isn't a disease but a privilege. These soldiers are . . . enhanced." Tagin motioned to the group, and they quickly formed a circle around us. "I command, and they obey. That makes them a treasure. But I'm willing to part with them to teach you a lesson. Titus," he called, glaring at me. "Shoot Juniper Henrick in the head."

I shouted, "No!"

My denial didn't matter. Titus lifted his gun, aimed, and squeezed the trigger, putting a bullet in her brain.

Acid filled my stomach when she toppled. As if he'd done nothing wrong, Titus returned to his ready stance.

"Enough," Cyrus bellowed.

"I could've made you a god," Tagin shouted at his son, "and this is how you repay me?"

"Your question highlights the biggest difference between us." Sadness drenched his tone. "I'm in control of my own life. I don't need to control others to feel powerful."

Tagin popped his jaw. "Titus, shoot Lark Foster in the head."

"No," I gasped out, but it was too late. Titus aimed and pulled the trigger, and Lark fell, blood gushing from a hole in her temple. The unmaddened guards watched, letting it happen, doing nothing when they could have changed everything.

Tears welled, and I couldn't stop them.

"This is my son," Tagin announced. "A traitor to CURED. He chose a Soalian and joined the enemy. They hope to destroy us from the inside out."

Fury pulsed from our audience. Everyone but the maddened; they remained blank, and my heart ached for them. This could have been me.

Tagin pointed a finger at Cyrus. "Strangle Arden before these witnesses and renounce all ties to Soal, and you'll be pardoned." He cocked his gun. "Refuse, and I'll kill her myself. Then her mother. Then I'll bury you deep in the mines with their corpses. You'll have the girl with you, just as you wanted, but you'll never experience happiness. You'll know only suffering and sorrow."

Cyrus stepped in front of me and rolled his shoulders back. "Astan is destroying your life, filling you with his thirst for power. But you can be freed."

"You will kill her, or you will die. Decide!" Tagin shouted, spittle flying from the corners of his mouth. "Put your hands around her throat and squeeze. It's not hard. Doesn't take long."

"I'm begging you to let us go. End this now, before I'm forced to do something that will haunt me for the rest of my life." The two stared at each other, neither rendering the final blow.

Had he foreseen more than he'd admitted? The pain Cyrus projected threatened to undo me.

"I'll give you one last chance, son." Tagin clearly loved his child. And I hadn't forgotten Cyrus's profession of love for his father. I couldn't let him hurt the man to save me. And that's what he planned, judging by his reaction and his words.

With the realization, I found my key. A ray of light beamed from deep within me, penetrating my mind. Any apprehension over my path burned to ash. I knew what to do without a shadow of a doubt.

I'd vowed to face my nightmare and stop running, and now I must keep my promise. Today, I had the opportunity to do it. And I would.

A panting Tagin aimed at Cyrus. His nostrils flared. I prepared to act. But, in a blaze of motion, he swung the gun to a guard and squeezed the trigger. He aimed and squeezed again and again and again, eliminating each soldier with a single shot. One by one they crashed to the ground, even Titus.

"They'll be no witnesses to our dealings," he announced when he finished.

I peered at Juniper's, Titus's, and Lark's fallen forms, feeling raw inside. "It's okay, Cyrus. Do what he told you. Put your hands around my neck."

"See! She wants you to do it," Tagin demanded, aiming at Cyrus once again. "No one will know you were once a Soalian. You'll be reeducated but then we can go on as if this episode never happened."

Cyrus didn't hesitate. "I will not."

Tagin's breathing grew more ragged. "Don't make me do this, son."

"He's not making you do anything," I said, drawing his aim my way as hoped. "This is your choice, Tagin, and yours alone." I wouldn't let Cyrus die or kill for me. My play was simple. Ensure he lived his best life, even if I had to die in the process. I wasn't afraid of pain. Not anymore. I wasn't even afraid of death. I'd do what needed doing, no matter the consequences.

"Shut up," the older man commanded. "You're going to die one way or the other. What happens to Cyrus afterward is up to him."

"Do it," I told the high prince. "But kiss me first."

He drew in a deep breath, held . . . held . . . then nodded, as if he'd reached a grave decision. "Let me say goodbye," he croaked. He waited for his father's stiff approval before turning to face me.

A thousand regrets, sorrows, and joys glimmered in his eyes. He cupped my cheeks as a tear streamed down one of his. "I wish there'd been another way."

I knew he had no plans to kill me, just as I knew what he needed me to do. "I hate that it came to this," I rasped to him. He might hate me for what I did next, but that was okay. He would live without regret.

"Me too. But it's okay. It's all going to be okay." Slowly he bent his head and kissed me, pressing his lips to mine and tangling his fingers in my hair.

I wrapped my arms around his shoulders and kissed him back, telling him everything I hadn't yet said as I stealthily worked at the clasp of his necklace. The last resort. When we parted, I tightened my fist around the little star. The sharp edges sliced into my palm, blood welling.

Resolve glazed his eyes as they searched mine. "Aim true," he commanded, and I nodded.

"Kill her or move," Tagin demanded.

Cyrus extracted himself from my hold, faced his father, and braced, as if preparing to launch forward. "I choose Soal. Goodbye, Dad."

I didn't let myself think. I acted immediately, throwing the star as I'd learned in class.

Time stood still as the metal whooshed through the air. The tiny blades expanded and sliced into Tagin's eye. His brain. He bellowed as crimson poured down his face and fell.

Cyrus rushed forward, kicking the weapon from his father's grip and crouching at the wheezing man's side. "There's a piece of the Rock inside the star. You can be saved, but you must not fight its effects. It won't work if you do. Please. Don't fight it."

I flinched at his pain and desperation, but I wasn't sorry I'd acted.

Tagin Dolion thrashed. White foam oozed from the corners of his mouth. He clutched at Cyrus, panic glittering in his eyes, and gasped his last breath.

Head bent, Cyrus sagged into the sand, and my heart shattered for him. I forced myself into action, hoping against hope someone had survived. But no, everyone was dead, not a single victim still breathing.

Those shattered pieces of my heart broke into smaller pieces. I examined the field as a whole. So many lives lost. And for what? Someone's quest for power. Mom, thankfully, had slept through it all.

I focused on Cyrus, who hadn't budged. Hmm. Dark mist was rising from his father's body, a body seeming to form. Then it opened eyes of the brightest red. Heart in my throat, I rushed over and yanked Cyrus from the entity. It stared at us with the same hatred I'd seen in Tagin before it whisked off, vanishing.

"What was that?" I gasped out.

"One of Astan's minions. Or as you know it, the Madness."

Okay, so, I had a lot more to learn about the world around me.

Cyrus stood and tugged me close, burying his face in the hollow of my neck. I clung to him. "Thank you for doing what I couldn't."

"I wish . . ."

"I know."

We stood in the sunlight, reality settling in. The immediate threat had been eliminated, but others remained. CURED had a way to control the worst of the maddened now, and the amount of damage they could do was incalculable.

John was still locked up or worse, on a table or buried in a mine being used as a pritis factory.

Mykal, Roman, and others I admired were currently puppets on strings, doing whatever CURED commanded. They aided our enemy, they just didn't know it.

"What will happen now?" I asked.

"There are seven high princes. We'll be tested and a new king chosen among us. What remains of my team will probably be split in half and doled out to the other instructors."

A bright red sports car screeched to a halt, and we braced for another fight. But Ember and Domino flew out. They were smeared with blood and littered with wounds, but still they'd come to help us.

Being able to trust and count on other people was new and wonderful and terrifying.

Cyrus described what happened and kissed my temple. "No one knows what we are. The witnesses are dead."

"All the witnesses here, yes. But I powdered a guard to sleep at the Lux," I admitted. "Not to mention the guards Cyrus sedated at my mom's apartment and the people in the commons."

"Most have already forgotten what they saw. There are ways." Ember pinched the bridge of her nose. "Enemy troops aren't far behind us, so we can't stay. Tell them your father broke, because he did. Go on with life as usual and await your next assignment."

"What about my mother?" I chewed on my bottom lip. She couldn't enter the Rock without embracing Soal, but she couldn't return to her home and job either.

"We'll put her in a shelter with others we protect," Ember vowed. "When she's ready, we'll bring her inside the library."

"Thank you." I couldn't ask for anything more.

"Arden?"

Mom! She'd awoken. She lumbered from the car and stumbled toward us. Confusion and fear pulled her skin taut.

I rushed over to prevent her from seeing the worst of the carnage, then ushered her near Ember's vehicle. "I need you to go with my friends, okay? They'll take good care of you. You can trust them."

"Baby, baby." She faced me and gripped my shoulders. "Are you sick?"

"I'm fine," I assured her, giving her hand a reassuring pat. "For my sake, forget everything CURED has ever told you about the Madness. It's all lies. Join Soal—like me."

"There's no time for this," Ember called, striding over to herd my mother to the vehicle.

Mom resisted for only a moment, floundering, her mouth opening and closing. In the end, she allowed the pair of Soalians to drive her away. My chest clenched. In the distance, I spotted military trucks barreling our way.

Cyrus pulled me into his arms once again.

"Does a part of you resent me?" I asked. It was a risk I'd been willing to take.

"You're alive and well, kitten. I'm grateful." He pressed his brow to mine. "Have you discovered what's growing in your pot yet?"

"No!" I gripped the lapels of his jacket. "Tell me."

He smiled a mysterious smile. "Give it time."

"You fiend." But I returned the smile and rested my head on his shoulder. We stood together as the "rescue" squad arrived. We were examined and questioned, then loaded into a van and driven back to Cyrus's apartment.

I sat as close to him as possible and signed into his hand, *Together.*

Together, he signed back.

We would do everything in our power to destroy CURED at the root, and salt the earth. There was no going back for me now. I'd chosen my path, and I would see this through to the end.

No matter what.

THE GREAT AND TERRIBLE

No Monsters Like Hers

When twenty-year-old college dropout Moriah Shaker runs into an empty chapel to escape an unexpected storm, she's catapulted into another world *Wizard of Oz* style. Unfortunately, she winds up in the treacherous realm of Hakeldama, a fantastical but brutal land where justice is twisted and innocents pay for crimes committed by the elites—and she's now marked for death.

On the run and determined to get home, Moriah heads for the City of Lux, where a rumored portal between worlds exists. At her side are the most unlikely of companions. A scrappy hustler, a cranky ex-mayor, and a growing beast-dog. But the one who fascinates her most is Jasher, a heartless executioner who hides a terrible secret. Together, they'll battle bounty hunters, lethal poppies, and winged monsters. Though Moriah doesn't yet know it, there's nothing more dangerous than their forbidden attraction.

ABOUT THE AUTHOR

© 2024 Sara's Photo Creations

Gena Showalter is the *New York Times* and *USA Today* bestselling author of nearly one hundred novels. While most of her work falls under the genre of romance—from paranormal, fantasy, contemporary, to young adult—she's also coauthored a quirky cozy mystery series and a nonfiction guide teaching how to write a book in one year. A dedicated mother, grandmother, and fur-mom, she's currently writing her next novel and already in love with the hero.

Printed in Dunstable, United Kingdom